JOHN
KING

THE
LIBERAL
POLITICS
OF ADOLF HITLER

LONDON BOOKS BRITISH FICTION

LONDON BOOKS
39 Lavender Gardens
London SW11 1DJ
www.london-books.co.uk

Copyright © John King 2016

A catalogue record for this book
is available from the British Library

ISBN 978-0-9568155-8-3

Printed and bound in Great Britain by
CPI Antony Rowe

Typeset by Octavo Smith Publishing Services
www.octavosmith.com

THIS NOVEL IS DEDICATED TO MY MOTHER

EDDY KING

For her love, faith, humour and courage across the years,
and for believing in 'the India book'

'Europe's nations should be guided towards the superstate without their people understanding what is happening. This can be accomplished by successive steps, each disguised as having an economic purpose, but which will eventually and irreversibly lead to federation.'

Jean Monnet – founding father of the European Union

ONE

RUPERT RONSBERGER WAVED a finger and waited for Himmler to scan the file. The latest smash from Roman teen sensations Abba played as the software rolled. Despite the frowning red face attached to this new investigation he would treat it with an open mind. As a dedicated Crat – Bureau (B+) – anything less than total fairness was unacceptable. Rupert was a professional. Checks and balances had been built into the system, with every case carefully considered before the only possible conclusion was reached. Positive, dedicated, oozing empathy – he was a credit to the United State of Europe. He was making history, bringing truth, justice and an exciting brand of democracy to one of the USE's most backward areas.

The zone in which Rupert found himself working had long been an irritant. Even today, after so much investment and education, dangerous levels of both Englishness and Britishness remained. This had to be addressed, and so yet more idealistic Crats were dispatched by Brussels. Rupert was one of this cheerful band, a loyalist who was able to empty his mind and totally focus for extended periods. These stretches were longer than those achieved by most Crats and his ability had already seen him tagged. He absorbed information easily, but more importantly *believed*. This skill had also been noted and, following his graduation from the Bech Institute, he had been invited to extend his studies at the prestigious Hallstein Centre in Luxembourg. Here he was one of the lucky students chosen to attend a series of lectures by the legendary thinker Horace Starski.

Controller Horace was a visionary. In those dark, pre-State days he had been honest enough to insist that true democracy meant conformity rather than debate, that the rough edges of Europe's cultures had to be smoothed and society fully homogenised. There could be no more wasteful disputes. What was the point in questioning laws that had been painstakingly created by honest Technos? There had to be a level of trust if the USE was going to progress. A new order had since been established, but it needed honing if it was going to achieve its full potential. While a young Rupert readily accepted the logic, hearing it repeated first-hand by such a respected figure filled him with relief. Life could be this easy? Tears had filled his eyes. Such was his love for this Controller that he had wondered if he might one day come close to matching his guru's achievements. He was the best role model a young Crat could have. And Rupert was nothing if not ambitious.

By nature an optimist, he knew that every Good European was inherently decent, but since arriving in London it had become clear that too many of the common people were polluted by incorrect thought. Helping them all to see sense was a monumental task. There were plenty of natives embedded in the system – and he respected their passion for Europeanisation, which was so often married to a disgust for all things British – but at the commons level there was a rejection of progressive politics. The workers lacked the intelligence to see that Brussels knew best, that it was working hard for Berlin and the good of everyone.

As the USE existed for the benefit of its citizens, it was vital that trade was free and easy and strictly managed, thereby allowing business to make the wealth that fed the masses. Profit drove society forward and prosperity created trust. Corporate leadership provided the checks and balances needed. It was an exchange of skills built on mutual respect. Love flowed when credit was available and profits increased. He remembered Controller Horace paying tribute to the efforts of the Crat legions who had gone before. Earlier generations of Bureaus and higher-level Technos had made today's affluence possible. He had placed a responsibility on the students to continue the crusade. Those who spread discontent had to be monitored. Rupert had a vital role to play.

The new case flickered on his terminal as he listened to the chorus of the Abba hit. A disco queen popped from the graphic and bopped, while Himmler drilled at the core of the file. As the security officer worked his magic, Rupert recalled how Controller

Horace had paused, sighed and removed a star-spangled kerchief from his jacket to wipe the sweat of a creased brow, going on to explain that the most dangerous threats to the USE could come in the smallest, most innocent-looking forms. Terrorists were waiting for tiny lapses of concentration. They were ready to strike. There could be no complacency, and Rupert nodded now, forever wary of the infections that could slip into society and cause chaos. It was essential to confront every possible threat. Emotion had to be cooled. There was no place for slackness when New Democracy itself was at stake. Contagion must be avoided. Rupert felt his fists tighten. He was decisive, strong and important.

Forward-thinking had long been the foundation of the State's success. Long-term planning had replaced that older idealistic, yet failed, blitzkrieg approach. Slowly-slowly was more sustainable, with successive generations introduced to correct ways of thinking. Time eased the effects of attachment. Change was good. Change meant progress. And yet despite the USE's kind efforts and the billions of eurodollars spent on development, prejudice remained. False history festered in this retarded zone. Racists questioned the centralisation of power and the corporations ensuring fair government. The more vocal of these bigots had the ability to stir up anger among the commons, and it was Rupert's job to evaluate such glitches. Once the correct decision had been reached he advised Cool. He would then move to the next case and never look back. It was an open process, based on equality, fairness and a deep-rooted love of the people.

Rupert was in a fine mood. His career was moving faster than even he had hoped. He was already a B+ and approaching A-, and then, surely, full A and finally A+ status. Not yet thirty years old, life was good. He was brilliant when it came to implementing belief structures, while the smallest of policy changes was instantly logged for recall. These abilities and the rewards he received meant that he was continually experiencing great highs, huge surges of pride and joy, with no real lows or dips in form. He slept soundly at night and woke with a need to shower and dress and hurry to the office. He hated to think it, but the wider population could be slow-witted, accepting suggestions through apathy and habit, but his colleagues were different and he was exceptional. Good Euros really did reach for the stars, wrapping themselves tight in the blue and gold flag of the State.

The scan ended. Abba faded and Himmler strutted. The file started to reload and Rupert raised his head slightly as the national anthem played. He was the only Bureau still at his desk and felt good about this, floating along with Beethoven's 9th, repeating the lyrics of 'Ode To Joy', proud he was actively honouring the sacrifices of previous generations as urged by Controller Horace. The features of Konrad Adenauer and Joseph Bech floated from his fixed screen... Alcide De Gasperi and Altiero Spinelli followed... And other unifiers emerged to hover in the background, creating a collage effect. Caesar and Charlemagne... Napoleon Bonaparte... Joseph Stalin and Adolf Hitler... Jean-Claude Juncker and Angela Merkel. They hung in the air for a few seconds before fading as Rupert was drawn to the file and the shock of a strange face.

The intensity of the eyes made him move back in his chair, but he refused to be intimidated. His poise recovered, he checked the name – Hannah Adams – and hurried to her details. These were suspiciously vague. He was stirred by such a lack of depth, the prospect of a chase honing his interest. Facts craved discovery. Truth, justice, transparency... Hannah was forty-two years old, yet looked a lot younger, her blonde hair pulled back and fastened tight around the skull, revealing the bones of her ancestry. She was described as a care worker in a hospice and a part-time musician. His professional instincts told him that something was amiss. He checked further, found that she was a *folk* musician. It didn't say what *sort* of folk. This was a concern. His suspicions increased. Fine detail... This was a trail he needed to follow.

Rupert motioned fingers, using his wands to whistle Hound Dog. There was a flash and he closed his eyes. Shook his head. He hadn't checked all the Adams data yet, which would have been the norm, had a strong urge to locate her early, to know exactly where she was at this precise second. Usually he left this part of the puzzle until later, preferring to assess a customer outside of their physical location, to isolate and apply a spotlight. But for some reason he broke with protocol. This was thrilling in itself, as while he had been trained in procedure, flickers of genius were also a part of the Crat's armoury. The cheerful face of Hound Dog appeared, panting softly, orange tongue lolling from a half-open mouth. The digital canine was eager to serve his master.

Rupert paused to admire his creation. The structural options were supplied by the manufacturer, but the fine-tuning was his own work. He added Hannah's code. She lived beyond the Reading Line in what the locals there liked to call a Free English town, even though its continued existence relied on the generosity of the USE. If the Controllers had wanted to crush the commons and impose their will then they could have done it years before, but consent was essential and they were in no great rush. The State would persuade them in the end. It always did.

Cheerful barking sounded. A purple heart thumped deep inside grey concrete. Using a zoom, Rupert dropped into the streets from his aerial view, immediately feeling the threat posed by those who chose to live outside the system. The heart pulsed, filling and emptying of blood, and he was racing towards a window. His virtual eyesight was ultra-sharp and Rupert was able to watch Hannah as she sat at her kitchen table, eating a bowl of cereal. Aggressive music played on a turntable, a small disc spinning in sick-making circles. Digitisation had clearly been flouted, which was reason enough to ask Cool to pay her a visit, although it would be impossible in this particular location. It could well be the brand of folk the woman pedalled. Maybe it was *punk*. He wasn't sure. Listening to this noise was bad enough, but if she was performing it live then she had made a further mistake. These errors were now on her record. Her time would come.

He had to admit that she was a good-looking woman, her expression more relaxed in the flesh, but Rupert wasn't the sort of Crat who could be fooled by flattery. Hannah Adams might try to appease him, without even knowing that he was on her trail, but he would remain professional. He couldn't rest until he had every answer, and he was willing to wait for hours and days and weeks and months and, if necessary, years. He never gave up, but maybe he should return to his usual protocol. And yet he was transfixed. Something was wrong.

He noticed a figure standing in the shadows behind Hannah and jolted. A man was watching her from the hall, further into the house. Husband, lover, friend? He stepped forward and dropped a wire noose over her head and pulled it into the neck. A sexer hired for gameplay? The steel was tightened. This seemed real and Rupert froze. Hannah gasped, eyes bulging as blood lined the noose, fingers raised to her throat. The pressure was increased, big hands turning the knot, black-leather gloves creasing, Rupert looking from Hannah to the face of the killer, which was hidden behind a Captain Euro mask. He felt sick. Blood gushed as the wire cut into the neck and then the jugular was opened and it pumped across the table. Hannah was panicking and kicking her legs, eyes seeming as if they were about to burst. She was turning blue. Rupert could hardly breathe. He tried to stand, but his legs failed him. He didn't know what to do.

There was a pop and Hannah was gone. Abba resumed their performance. Despite himself, Rupert tapped a finger in time to the tune. To be interrupted during such sensitive work was shocking, but he was more concerned about the attack. He had broken with routine and stumbled across a terrible crime. He had seen into the darkness of those who considered themselves rebels. It was clear that Hannah Adams deserved to be under surveillance. What sort of folk did she play? Why was she eating alone? How had she driven the stranger to violence? Why had she not digitised? What was that song actually saying? It didn't make sense. He searched for the file but it had vanished. Himmler had been involved. How could this happen?

Rupert felt a friendly pressure on his right shoulder, turned to see the smiling face of his Super. Kat Romero was a jolly sort, forever concerned and interested in the lives of those in her charge. She ran her section in an orderly, disciplined manner, but wasn't averse to the cracking of jokes – just as long as current correctness was upheld. For some, this could be difficult, as the weight of individual words was constantly changing. Experts scanned the European language; studied and dissected, searching for prejudice, dishonesty, subliminal hatreds that might lurk in the corners of polite society. It wasn't enough to be superficially correct. A Crat had to remain pure on a much deeper level. Supers such as Kat were always active on the ground, watching and listening, studying directives and staying on top of the evolutionary process. Cool was called in to discuss matters with any Crat who showed deviance from the ever-changing norm, but Rupert was a master when it came to correct behaviour. He moved with the times.

Rupert started to open his mouth, was about to tell Super Kat about the intensity of Hannah Adams, her maniacal eyes and cruel, tied-back hair, how he had turned to Hound Dog, whistled for his faithful friend, inspected the town from above before dipping into the colourless streets and finding himself in an alien landscape where the people were ungrateful, clearly a violent place where a Crat could never stroll. It would be hard to take education to such a locale. It made him think of those endless dollars pumped into schemes decided by the finest minds in Brussels. He was about to tell Kat Romero about the suspect Adams, how she was sitting at a table eating, that he had been wondering exactly what *sort* of folk music she played, how he feared it was *primitive* in its nature, *English* perhaps, *Irish* even, involving banjos and mandolins, banned analogues, non-digitals, but then he had spotted a turntable and vinyl, finally seen a figure standing in the darkness of the hall, and that it was a man who had stepped into the light, slipping a noose around Adams' throat, pulling it tighter and tighter like a trained assassin, a professional killer, so those cold eyes began to bulge and weep and just as they seemed as if they were going to explode an artery had broken and blood blasted and splattered, a beating love-heart lost in the flood, and yet the murderer couldn't have been trained, it had to come naturally, because Cool wouldn't do such a thing, and neither would Hardcore, and so it had to be typical commons behaviour. But Hound Dog had run off. The images were lost. He could hardly believe what he had seen. Their technology never failed. He was confused. Didn't understand. He was going to say all of this but didn't, as the pressure on his shoulder increased and he remembered that he had broken his pattern, questioned the process laid down in training, showed impatience as he whistled for his customised tracker.

– Everything okay, Rupert?

– Great, he replied, raising his head. Fabulous...

– That last file...

– Hannah Adams?

– I will be dealing with her case myself. There is an element of fiction to the matter, a fixation on role play that has been worrying neighbours. The reality is harmless, but there is a dangerous edge to her choice of scenes. Poor Hannah feels she should be in the movies. There's nothing to worry about, Rupert. For an amateur, it was a fine performance. Very realistic. Creative even. You are sure you are feeling great, now?

– Definitely.

He smiled broadly.

– I feel fantastic.

The firm hand and wise words were a relief. He didn't like to see anyone suffer. It was logical that a confused woman living in a commons-only town in one of the more reactionary zones of the USE should want to escape to Hollywood. The regions of these islands became more desolate the further they sat from the major European cities of London, Cardiff, Dublin, Belfast, Birmingham, Sheffield, Manchester, Newcastle, Glasgow and Edinburgh, so this sort of escapism was inevitable. In such centres of excellence, Heartland culture had become embedded.

Rupert accepted that the racists who despised unification were as close to evil as humans could stray, that the physicals he had seen in the movie were no innocent props. Hard copies of songs, books and films were traded semi-openly in Hannah Adams' world. It was unacceptable, but he knew Kat Romero would do her duty. Such formats could never be edited or remixed or removed from circulation for the protection of the public. There was no safety control. Deletion became impossible, while the flow of funds from leasing halted. It made no sense.

The Adams incident was in the past, as were his questions, wands waving and a new file appearing. The sweet sound of Abba returned as he asked Himmler to start a scan. Like all Crats he had been trained to look to the future. There was no profit in the past and Super Kat was already halfway to the door. He turned his head to watch her departure, the confidence clear in the swing of arms and legs. He admired this Techno's management skills. She was a cheerful, efficient Crat, and yet he knew that he would step past her on the career path. It was true that he was younger and had less experience, but he was mentally stronger. Pulling his chair tight to the desk, Rupert couldn't wait to get started on his next case.

TWO

HORACE STARSKI FELT the love flowing as he looked out across the Brussels skyline. The metropolis was a showcase for New Democracy, the place where the dreams of the European elite came true. The view from his Monnet Tower pad was one of the best, and at night it was truly magnificent. The illuminations were cutting-edge spectacular and carried memories. Special glass coated the walls of the scrapers, and these were saturated in light, resident mixers subtly altering hues to match and counter moods. The sight of billions of scales pulsating as if still attached to their fishy hosts was a natural wonder. Brussels was more than a centre of politics and business – it was also one of the most cultured cities on the planet.

The tower nearest to Controller Horace was topped by a Tenderburger logo, the latest movie from this corporate benefactor playing on a range of street-level screens, scenes looped and repeating in silence, the bulls involved mimicking Euro hero Ted Munch's masterpiece 'The Scream'. The other big CBs were present with their own brilliant advertising, showing in both motion and stills. This area of Brussels was a catwalk of light, colour and form, the fun factor a tribute to the inventiveness of the greatest multi-nationals. Controller Horace never tired of these shows. Sitting in a panda-skin recliner, he routinely spent a hour or more gazing here and there, revelling in the nuances involved. As the owner of the Monnet penthouse and eleven rented premises below, pride of income added to the thrill of living at the throbbing heart of the USE.

If perfection existed, then his home was an example. Covering the entire top floor of the tower, there were five bedrooms, six bathrooms, a large reception, two offices, a huge free-plan living area with an open kitchen, three further relaxation rooms and a storage unit. The lounge linked to a terrace cut from the best Acropolis-sourced marble, part of a friendship deal struck with one of his Controller pals in Athens. It had taken the regions formerly known as Greece decades to recover from the foolishness of its people. Troika loans and a shifting of assets from outdated national to private control had saved the commons from themselves. Controllers, Crats and Cool had been hurt by the ungratefulness of the locals, so the later arrival of such beautiful marble was seen as a deserved reward. In the summer he spent many hours outside, dipping in and out of the pool, enjoying the vitamins of dome-filtered sunlight. Despite his amazing achievements, he was still a humble man, the sort of person who...

A polite cough crashed his reflections.

He sighed, frowned, turned, headed towards the elevator. It was a terrible shame to have to leave like this, but he had duties to perform, his trademark positivity returning once he entered his private cube. He loved the sensation of floating in space, the rush of air on his feet as he began his descent, energy flowing into his legs as the speed increased, excitement lancing stomach, chest, brain. Evens and odds flashed fast on one of four horse-bone walls, and although he was descending through the centre of the tower, real-time images of Brussels played on the remaining surfaces. He would rather have stayed at the summit, close to the stars, but it was important to stay in tune with the masses, to hear and see and smell and touch street-life graphics. There was so much work to be done.

On either side of Controller Horace stood his loyal buddies Bob Terks and Baby. Former USA agent Terks had come to Brussels after twenty years in the CIA, the peak of his service the Los Angeles slum clearances that saw a successful release of Compton real-estate urgently needed for condo development. It had turned into a bloody conflict and Terks was decorated for his valour, the award aiding his transfer to a position of trust within the USE. A hit movie had captured the essence of the LA riots, the contest played out between misguided locals and those upholding the right of entrepreneurs to generate profit and create community.

Gentrification had defeated self-interest. The USE and USA had long been bonded through free trade, currency and business law, and with a loose federation already in existence, the sharing of secret-service personnel was encouraged.

Baby, meanwhile, was a Good Euro, a career-racer ripping the superhighway to stardom. From the start her Côte d'Azur heritage had impressed the Technos, who adored the area's holiday facilities. The daughter of rustic hoteliers and part-time wine producers, she had set her heart on serving the USE from the age of eleven, having become infatuated with the original *Eurogendfor Wins* series. Starring Nice sensation Liz Bergman, the storytelling was based around Paris and Rome, all the Hardcore action taking place in fringe regions along the Med. Plots followed rewrites of historical battles between this early version of the State's elite commando unit and the racist groups opposing unification. Baby loved her Controller dearly. He had fought ignorance and prejudice and deserved his place in the stars. She, along with Bob Terks, would happily sacrifice her life for this man.

The elevator came to a halt. The door opened and Baby pushed into the foyer, moving nimbly, built-in sensors noting Monnet employees and long-term residents, searching for strangers. There was nobody suspicious present, which was to be expected. Horace Starski was safe here, and secure in the majority of cities, but his visit to London made her nervous. Every buddy knew about British terrorism. The Welsh, Scottish and Irish rebels were bad enough, but the English surpassed even those degenerates for incorrect thought and a love of ultraviolence. But she couldn't be sidetracked, had to stay in the moment, as an accident could happen anywhere. It was also important to be *seen* to be alert. Controller Horace was a stickler for concentration, the standards he himself had achieved expected of those who wanted to help. It was only right. Bob Terks, like Baby, was ambitious. He was also worried about the trip to London.

Bobby followed Baby, shielding the Controller, right hand at an angle, Palm scanners pulsing, adding another layer to Baby's preventions, wary of false friends and foul language. Rumours had reached Central that rudeness was imminent, and this added to their usual concerns. The suspects were believed to be English, but the details were faint. Bob Terks and Baby didn't want to lose Controller Horace to a partisan mishap. A failure to protect him was unthinkable. They feared the loss of their mentor as a human being, their relationship having evolved to the point that he was a father figure to them both. They may have been needlessly cautious in Brussels, but their training taught them that every single possibility had to be considered. No detail was ever too small. This was a core value. From Bureaus and Technos to Agents and Controllers – success and failure rested on the minutiae.

Horace Starski was the last to leave the transporter. He moved casually and was clearly relaxed, displaying his usual charisma, facial expressions studied and intelligent. He was a broad-shouldered man, tall and strong, decisive in his motions, and would have been impressive even if he was a commons, but add his political responsibilities and business interests, and he was a stand-out. Age made him stronger, as his relevance increased with every passing year. He was loved by those who worked and played inside the great domes of the USE, largely unknown to those on the outside. This was how it should be. Great leaders were rarely seen by the masses.

– How are you today? he asked Francis Doyle, a Dublin-born concierge who had been employed in the Monnet since it opened.

Francis felt as if he was in the beam of a spotlight, dazzled on an InterZone platform, his throat tightening as heads turned in anticipation of a worthy response. Within seconds a Crat cluster had formed. Recording was blocked here, which was frustrating, but an exchange seemed imminent. The concierge steadied his Palm and expanded an image of a shaven-headed thug. Behind him rose the East London Mosque. Famed as a symbol of the cross-cultural love promoted by the USE in the days of organised religion, Preventative Care Orders had been needed when it was attacked by local racists. Safe passage to Middle-Eastern lands had been instantly arranged for the worshippers, the building transferred to technology giant Mango Services. The area was quickly upgraded to prevent further violence, then absorbed into the East Side Gates development. Francis meant the gesture as a recognition of the task Controller Horace faced on the other side of the Channel. At last he was able to speak.

– Couldn't be better. Thank you for asking.

Francis Doyle adored Horace Starski. He was always prepared to back up his opinions with action, had taken the Dubliner under his wing following an unfortunate incident off one of the boulevards thirteen years before. Cool had moved Francis into safe-keeping and were about to send him to a location where his health could be improved, but the Controller learned of his trouble and offered him promotion at the Monnet and the chance to remain in Brussels. Francis was living a clean life, with modern rooms, excellent wages and a range of benefits. His loyalty was total. Everyone deserved a second chance. Without Horace Starski's help he might even be dead.

– Glad to hear it, Francis. I think it will rain soon. Like it does in your region.

Francis floated a finger across his hand, saw the smiling face of Pam Andersen, the weather forecast constantly updated. He smiled and nodded.

– You are correct...

But Controller Horace was on the move, sweeping across the foyer, his famed determination clear in the swing of arms and pump of legs. It was inspiring that such a successful man of seventy-two years still possessed a lust for life. He certainly kept himself fit, on numerous occasions reminding Bob Terks and Baby that mind and body should not be separated, that clear thinking was impossible if muscles turned tired and endorphins stopped streaming. Stimulants were fine, but core strength was better. His pals recognised this truth, as both were toned above the level required for service. Bobby was also a decorated fitness trainer from early days, and part of his brief was to keep his Controller in the best possible shape. Baby was educated in massage and the ancient European art of acupuncture. Together, the three companions made a fine team.

– See... it is starting to drizzle.

Horace Starski had reached the Monnet entrance, stopped and stood for a moment, sheltered by the whale arch linking in and out. Waves of salty warm air were being released by panels that had been arranged to ease the transition. Two Cool officers were stationed on either side, filters noting every pulse and eye-movement. The drive leading to Monnet Tower was accessed via a marble gateway – part of the Athens deal – and staffed by one Cool and numerous Gendarmerie. Solitude had to be maintained if the mind of the man keeping the people healthy was going to operate at its optimum level. It was a routine arrangement, shared by every Controller. It would help nobody if the elite were interrupted in their hard graft. Noise pollution was a negative.

It was a fact of life that fanatics tried to meet Controllers. Sadly, they had to be persuaded to leave them in peace, with a smile and reassuring pat on the shoulder. Coffee and muffins were generally served. Two months earlier a rogue Bureau had returned after a chat with Gendarmerie, scaled one of the walls warming the tropicals in the gardens of the Monnet, using a shooter to aid the breach. Cool sensed him and had been forced to zap the man before he inflicted damage. It was an unfortunate incident and had zero to do with the mythical Belgian Resistance.

Logic dictated that there was a chance the devotee would arrive at the tower entrance when Cool was rushing to help a fallen resident, and with the foyer clear he might have reached the elevator just as a cleaner was leaving and having their load shared by its guardian, thereby gaining access and heading to the penthouse, emerging at the very moment Bob Terks and Baby were brewing coffee and heating croissants in the kitchen, the uninvited fanatic strolling over to greet Horace Starski personally. Accidents could so easily happen. The man would naturally be overcome by his love for this brilliant Controller, tears of joy bursting as he rushed to his hero with the innocent intention of kissing both cheeks and thanking Herr Starski for his contributions to society. There was, however, the possibility that these tears could blur his vision, leading the fanatic to slip and instinctively reach out, grabbing and pulling Horace

Starski down so he banged his head hard on the edge of a table, thereby killing one of the State's greatest assets. This would be a tragedy. The death of the fan was regrettable, but only the Cool officer involved, Controller Horace and his buddies Bob Terks and Baby knew exactly what had occurred.

– Good evening, sir, said a Gendarme, who happened to be approaching as the Controller's party emerged.

Forever upbeat, these free-market Gendarmes were carefully vetted by Cool. The life of a Cool was far more demanding, but required the same ability to remain cheerful in the most trying of circumstances. In return they were highly paid, exempt from tax, and received plenty of vacation time.

– How are you? Controller Horace asked, turning to study the Gendarme.

– Excellent, sir... Excellent. Thank you.

Horace Starski smiled and nodded, head tilting slightly, eyes straying as a slow-motion ripple ran across the side of his tower, blue light flowing through scales as if a massive shoal of fish was swimming inside the glass. The scraper became a living ocean, and yet the experience was far more sophisticated, manufactured and loaded with mimicry, the ideals of plagiarism and nature-control merging. It had a strange effect on him, stiffening arms and legs, so for a moment he thought he was suffering a stroke. But he knew better. His memory had been focused by the illuminations. He was a young man standing on the promenade of a seaside town. In an England he had helped to destroy. Dismissed images returned. He felt an incredible sadness, a pain where his heart sat, and he wished he could return to his apartment and look out over Brussels for the rest of his days. He didn't want to travel to London. He hated that crude island where the monkeys drank and sang.

He realised an awkward silence had settled, returned to the eyes of the expectant Gendarme.

– See how the light from the show reflects on Jean Monnet's features.

The man narrowed his gaze and studied the statue outside the entrance. Recognition spread across his face.

– I can see it, Controller Horace. It is almost as if Controller Jean is weeping.

It was an interesting interpretation, one that Horace Starski hadn't considered.

– You have excellent visuals. Very good indeed.

The Controller respected every Good Euro, had nothing but love for this Gendarme, but his secret faves were the younger Crats coming through the ranks, the students who had become Bureaus and were aiming to turn Techno. He admired their ambition, had himself started at the bottom, attending university and studying the unedited history of Europe before the curriculum changed. He had accepted the long-term plan to create a superstate, overjoyed when he was tagged a Crat, making the leap from Bureau to Techno fast, that ability to believe accelerating his progress. He made Controller at the age of thirty-six, which remained a record, and he hadn't rested either, as there were levels, further elevations linked to location and spheres of influence.

– The Mustang is ready, Baby remarked.

– Thank you, Controller Horace replied, hurrying into the car.

– Good evening, sir, Chauffeur Christian said.

Controller Horace raised a hand and sat back in the tanned-mustang seat, adjusting his position so that he was fully comfortable. Baby was by his side, Bob Terks across from them to the right where he could watch the pavements. The door pinged and the temperature adjusted, the A-Team barely feeling the machine's movement as it turned away from Monnet Tower and glided down the driveway, passing the statues that decorated the fibre lawn, the perfect bamboo and exotics. A more comfortable silence fell and everyone present knew not to interrupt these precious moments.

Controllers were forever innovating. The tightening and easing of laws and directives was a task that could never be allowed to slow. Great states did not depend on armies and weaponry, but rather administrators. Bureaucrats had succeeded where storm-troopers had failed. The fine-tuning of existing regulations must never cease, while new suggestions drove society on. Committees discussed and debated, Controllers decided, Crats produced drafts and corrections and documents, went on to implement and monitor. More and more idealists needed work, and it suited the State to keep them busy. At the same time the commons could never be left to their own devices. Change was important, but so was the speed at which it occurred. The difficult alterations took place over decades, the smaller shifts in days. Flux could be good. Flux could be bad. Controller Horace closed his eyes. His mind was moving elsewhere. He could smell beer and frying chips, hear a woman singing.

Once they were out of the compound, the Mustang was joined by a Cool escort. One transporter in front, another behind. Breakdowns and collisions had to be avoided, so they would be taking a State lane once they were outside Central. As they picked up speed, more towers rose on either side, their grooving scales an extravaganza of fashion and ethical practice. Ten minutes later and they were moving through the outer rings of the city, the housing drab and rundown in comparison to the core, but the Controller saw none of this, his concerns with the next generation of Crats, those with the same zeal that had driven him when he was a young man, and he had been forced to compromise, to make hard decisions. Didn't the ends justify the means? Truth was a process. It changed, mutated, emerged in refreshed forms. Horace Starski would never forget this revelation. He carried it with him to this day and would rely on it when he reached London. Of that he was sure.

THREE

WHEN HE WAS off-duty and ready to rock, Rupert Ronsberger morphed into Rocket Ron – a free-spending, fun-loving charmer. He worked hard and he *played* hard. The long office hours and tunnel vision required of a go-ahead Crat led to an incredible sense of belonging, but it was also important to reap the benefits offered. Honest pleasures led to spiritual cleansing, which in turn resulted in sharpened focus, increased productivity, a renewed longing for routine and minutiae. The USE's official face was complemented by the full Euroland experience. Special access to the best R&R.

Internal Crat memoranda regularly highlighted the case of Jacques, a promising Bureau (B), who had grafted too hard and refused to come out to play, ending up a very dull boy whose concentration failed. Mistakes occurred. Depression set in. Today he was cleaning toilets at a sports stadium in Marseilles. It was a sad story, but promoted as a well-intentioned health warning.

Tonight Rupert was meeting Polestar, who had been recommended by his colleague Gio. The past week had been tough, with several complicated cases to unwind, today's incident in Yeovil or Swindon or wherever it was, the final stress. He needed to cut loose, sample the joys of Euroland. Polestar was the best sort of date – ethical, forward-thinking, sustainable – and as he waited for Himmler to process his terminal closure he couldn't help wanding his Palm and opening a screen, checking the clips pinged by the Crat from Milan. Gio had recorded Polestar on their second and last meet, Rupert appreciating the nakedness of her oiled body and portable dancing stick, the gangsta soundtrack pounding in time to her moves. Gio was soon working his magic, the woman's face contorting in ecstasy for the lens. The usual shot concluded their coupling. There was more in his Palm, but Himmler had secured shutdown. Rocket was on the move.

Their rendezvous had been arranged via Chums, one of the top dating agencies. He had suggested they dine at Ribs, but it turned out that Polestar was a Kangowrap nut – succulent joey-cuts covered in breadcrumbs, tucked inside a tortilla with jalapeno peppers and hen-flavoured mayo – and these were a Tenderburger trademark. The corp's secret recipe was buried deep inside the meats, and it was this that drove the Kango community wild. Ever the gentleman, Rocket agreed to the venue, seeing this flexibility as a shrewd investment.

He stood and stretched, left his office and proceeded along the corridor leading to the elevator, waving to those Crats who looked up while working in adjacent spaces. He stopped when he came to the floor's chill-out room, went inside, continued through to the grooming unit where he showered and perfumed and donned casual clothes kept in his locker – Saviles trainers, Rebel slacks, pink Lacoste, a trusted Friends jacket. He inspected himself in the nearest full-length mirror and had to admit that he looked fantastic. Remembering his cap, he slipped it into a pocket.

It was a short walk to the Overground, reached via a vanilla-scented lane and, once he had taken the escalator to his platform, he was confident he would reach Tenderburger on time. State employees rarely used the Underground, which was dark and dingy and packed with commons, knowing that they had to remain unflustered in order to focus fully on their graft. It was for the good of the travellers they avoided. The Overground was reserved for Crats and other Good Euros, the new Rubettes smash 'Sugar Baby Love' rocking the concourse. He had been so moved by the tune that he had invested in the same headwear worn by several of the band. He reached inside his jacket and removed the white cap, slightly conscious of it being different to the norm, placing it at a jaunty angle on his head. Rocket felt great – stylish, modern and a little daring. He noticed a female Crat glancing over, and when their eyes met she nodded to show her approval.

The platform was enclosed in plastic, the temperature perfect, in contrast to the cold city beyond the domes. London was dirty and loud, and while Rocket was root-free and so never felt homesick, he did know that if it wasn't for his work here and the positive effect it was having on his career, he would be living in a Heartland location. Even Athens would be better than London. Like every other Crat he craved a move to Brussels. The capital was where ambitions were fulfilled. Great men and women went there to raise their credit. They shaped laws and increased profits and indulged their needs. He was sure he would make it there one day. Reach the highest of heights.

Looking out from his vantage point, he saw how the Crats below crisscrossed Parliament Plaza in unintentional formation. The dome protecting them from the weather meant most were in shirt sleeves, at least half sporting Rocker Ts and slogans such as *Just Do It* and *Live On The Edge*. Outside of Central and the Gates it was wet and cold, inside it was always dry and warm. The space was dominated by a twenty-metre statue of Joan of Arc, food outlets and seating arranged along the north and south sides. Parliament itself had been converted into offices, the European Central Bank investing in a much-needed modernisation. Big Ben flashed the time as the gold stars of the USE flag rolled from left to right. The former abbey had been gutted and converted into Crat offices. This was where Rupert worked.

His train arrived so quietly he barely noticed it, the lowering of the volume on 'Sugar Baby Love' acting as a signal. He strode aboard, stood by the outer glass wall, a waiter at the end of the carriage ready to serve coffee and nibbles when requested. The Rubettes smash was playing softly, his switch from platform to train seamless. Once they started to move, he could see those Crats not tuned into their Palms silently mouthing the words of 'Sugar Baby Love'. He adjusted his cap and peered into windows as the service passed along Whitehall, the line's elevation meaning he had a clear view into a series of rooms and the various intelligence agencies inside. This was the USE at its classy best – democratic and accountable. Nothing was hidden. The Political Quarter was populated by open-minded thinkers, each person checked and vetted for their purity of thought, a generous ten percent of the personnel coming from the region itself.

A side street led to the Churchill War Rooms, preserved as a testament to the perils of Englishness, the bigotry of a Britain that had for so long rejected integration. The tunnels of the bunker were dark and stifling, but it was in the cavernous hollows that the worst offences had taken place. This was where Winston Churchill and his criminal cronies had waged war on the German and French democracies way back in the 1940s, using their military might on the peace-lovers of Heartland. Churchill had ordered bombing raids and the spread of dishonest propaganda, and finally a terrible land invasion. It was here that he had hatched the idea of a Final Solution. Driven by a psychotic hatred of non-Brits, he had implemented the extermination of millions of men, women and children.

The Overground moved smoothly and Rupert straightened his spine, thrilled by a sense of history as he passed the Cenotaph, a memorial dedicated to all those European idealists murdered by British terrorists during the 1914-1918 conflict, their names added to as another generation of bulldogs targeted forward-thinkers again in the 1939-45 war. Poppies were produced by the Hans & Michele Trust, a show of respect for those who had lost their lives fighting tyranny, a remembrance of that time when Luftwaffe peace missions flew to the likes of London and Coventry, dropping millions of paper flowers into the docks and poorest streets, urging the people to stay strong and wait for liberation. This had not been possible, though, as the RAF had outnumbered the German and French squadrons, Churchill's war machine having been built by slave labour imported from Poland. Crats such as Rupert had helped right a terrible wrong.

Churchill was a master liar who had blamed the great liberal leaders Adolf Hitler and Benito Mussolini for the carnage, while the Heartland forces of Vichy were smeared by the traitor de Gaulle. Counteracting these outrages had taken decades, and this was where digitisation had been so important. Hard books carried falseness across the centuries, closed out the ability to edit and, where necessary, delete. A corrupt educational system had also demanded urgent attention. Despite his lack of enthusiasm for London, Rupert was each day moved by the fact that he was grafting at the core of a once dominant dictatorship. He was marching over the ruins of an evil power, like a brave invader, an intellectual soldier.

Trafalgar Plaza came next, gold stars glittering high above the blue-lit stone, and this was an area of relaxation, a place of theatre and feasting. Entertainers walked on stilts, juggled balls, blew long rushes of fire into the air. Food outlets achieved high sales. The pirate One-Eyed Nelson topped a yellow column, leaseholder Mango showing its latest releases along the surface. In front of the National Gallery children had gathered on a platform. They were waving at lambs in a plastic tube. An installation by the boy wonder Damon Hurst, it linked to one of the larger tunnels used to move animals to processing. The glass walls of the abattoirs matched the casing of these corridors. Only the smallest of funnies could access the artist's loop. It was a bold comment on the nature of food and the values of the meat and dairy industries. Twelve celebrity chefs watched from a floating mural. Some smiled and others frowned, according to their brand. All agreed that the system was based on love and respect.

The Tenderburger branch chosen by Polestar was on the Strand, so Rocket disembarked at Chandos Corner and emerged at street level. Like most trenders he had a bean he could plug inside his ear whenever he wanted internal tunes, but he resisted the temptation to add to his stroll, listening to the passing pedestrians instead, the soft hum of taxi batteries. There was the sound of laughter back in the centre of Trafalgar, muffled words from one of the resident comedians. He crossed the street and was welcomed by a new Abba song. He had heard it earlier today, while he was grafting, but the case was closed and he treated the tune as fresh.

Tenderburger was bouncing, which was to be expected, but Rocket was surprised to find the tables packed with hundreds of near-identical mademoiselles and fräulein, the current Tender fash for jet-black wigs, orange lenses and white face-powder making the finding of individuals near enough impossible. Features, colour, shadings were all smoothed to conformity by the covering. While this uniformity was admirable, no telltale signs had been agreed with Polestar, and if she was keeping to the style it would make recognition impossible. He had little idea of her true appearance, raised his Palm and searched for facial recognition, saw Polestar on all fours as Gio took her from behind, knew that the end shot was distorted and unlikely to help. Rocket stood and looked around at the eaters and drinkers and supposed he would have to admit to a lack of preparation. He was mildly disappointed with himself. It was out of character.

Polestar had seen his entrance and checked the details on her own Palm, finally standing and hooting her honker so that he was able to glide through the tables and take the seat next to her, a waiter immediately appearing to ask for their drinks order. Polestar remarked on the quick service, reached down and squeezed Rocket's hand, chose an apple/banana/day-chick shake, and he did the same, grateful she had spared his blushes. She was dressed in the majority fashion of the females surrounding them, so he would never have found her without the intervention.

– You're a friend of Giovanni? Polestar began.

– Yes, a work colleague, he replied. He thought I might like to meet you, so you've come highly recommended.

– But why go through Chums? A personal connection is easier.

– He deleted your details.

Rocket immediately regretted these words. They implied a lack of interest, which while true was not polite and did not respect the lady's hard work. But Polestar's attention had shifted to the other side of the room. Rocket followed the direction of her eyes, joining hundreds of heads that had turned to watch the arrival of no less a celebrity than Joey Porto. Even Rocket was impressed. He rarely watched mainstream InterZone, but knew there was a crossover between Crats and commons, that both shared an interest in soaps, realities and talent contests. This was currently regarded as a positive by the State. And so Rocket agreed. What he could not understand was the level of excitement racing across the room. Men and women stood and cheered. Some ran towards Joey, but were blocked by his security team. Others fainted. Female Crats began to scream. Dates saw this and joined in. People were becoming hysterical. But really, what had Joey Porto ever done?

True, he had come second in *Too Much Rest For The Wicked*, based around sleep deprivation and its effects, which was, Rocket had to say, quite an achievement. His colleagues had talked about the show so much he watched the last two episodes. On the surface it was a simple story, but search deeper and important questions of privacy were being raised. Ten contestants started off on a small island, their hours of sleep reduced by one each week. As soon as they went a second over their allotted time built-in sonics were released. There had been arguments, affairs, one sexual assault, several physical fights and finally a suicide. It was clear from the beginning that Joey was unusual, his behaviour barely changing as the weeks progressed. After three nights of four hours' sleep he finally snapped. It was a touching end. Tears were shed and mistakes admitted. A classic redemption tale. His future was healthy. Rocket nodded and admitted that Joey Porto was smarter than he seemed, but did he really *believe* in anything? It was unlikely.

– How common, Polestar remarked, as a screaming date was led away by a waiter. She is from Chad, you know. She is only doing it to show off, to fit in with the custom. It is not heartfelt.

For a moment Rocket feared Polestar had made a racist remark. If so, it would mean the end of their evening. Diners at a nearby table may have overheard, picked the crime up on audio and/or visual. If so, he should report her immediately, but this reasoning triggered the nightmare scenario that he was prepared to ignore racism and only mention it to save his own skin, in reality more interested in tonight's sex than the needs of the community. He felt a stab of adrenaline in his chest, was going to tell Cool about his date, but then reasoned that Chad was a state and her remark wasn't necessarily meant as an insult, that it could be a straightforward observation. For instance, 'common' wasn't a slur. Not really.

The diners returned to their meals as soon as Joey disappeared into the VIP section. Tenderburger continued to roll. Girl power rightly demanded that every female be allowed to do as she pleased, and the Chad sexer was as entitled as any Crat. He deplored sexism as much as he did racism and the prejudices of localism, veganism and paedophobia, was pleased that he hadn't acted incorrectly. He was relieved that Polestar meant no harm. She was beaming, yellow lenses impressing, the tight top she was wearing showing off her large breasts. This was a fine-looking date and he knew for a fact that she loved to fucky.

– So, tell me about yourself, he began, keen to move on.

This attempt to discover the inner Polestar was suspended before it was properly underway, a waiter appearing, placing their shakes on the table, keen to take their food order. Fresh wraps, french fries and a bottle of red were duly ordered, the two lovers-to-be raising their glasses and toasting the moment. Rocket felt good about Polestar. Exploitation was immoral, and this coupling would be built on respect.

– As I was saying, he laughed. Please tell me about yourself.

– Well, I work for Chums, as you know, and my studio is in Holloway. I like to dance and listen to music, and I love visiting restaurants, my favourite being Tenderburger. Most of all, I am a listener rather than a talker. I always want to learn and progress, develop my mind rather than my looks, although I like nice clothes and being treated with warmth.

Rocket must have allowed surprise to show on his face.

– Does that sound strange?

She was running her tongue over lips painted to match her lenses. The tattoo on the tip was of a serpent, and this seemed to come alive, as if it was slithering through sand. Rocket found it highly erotic, which he imagined was the intention.

– It doesn't sound strange at all, he responded.

– What about you?

Rocket puffed up.

– I am a Crat and I work in Westminster. At the moment I have B+ grading, but my levels of concentration are excellent. I enjoy the dissection of detail and believe this will one day mean that I progress through the ranks to top Techno and beyond. I have...

Polestar held up a hand, the yellow of her eyes verging on orange.

– No, tell me about the real Rocket Ron. Where do you come from?

– I live in London, he replied, slightly taken aback.

– Before London... Where were you born? Who are your parents? What were your dreams as a boy?

Rocket was confused by the first two questions, while his childhood memories had long been abandoned. He had no interest in his previous life. He was dedicated to his job. As a Crat, he was able to reinvent himself and start again. He believed in change and the new. As for dreams, he hadn't had any for years, such was the depth of his sleep, but if she meant ambition, well...

– I have dreamed of being a Crat since I was young.

She seemed unimpressed by this answer. He became bold.

– One day I will be a Controller. I am certain of this.

Polestar's expression changed. She was clearly impressed. Controllers led such important lives and the financial rewards matched the respect they were afforded. Her eyes had changed to a bright orange and the snake was wriggling across a mouth that was slightly ajar. He had been too modest, had to accept that the likes of Polestar were turned on by ambition.

– I believe that...

Again, they were interrupted, but Rocket didn't mind, as Polestar's right foot had lost its shoe and was rubbing against his leg under the table. Rocket had a rocket between his legs, but he gave the waiter his full attention as the plates were arranged in front of the couple, with various sides added – shrimps, olives, a selection of sauces and powders.

– This is one of the greatest pleasures, Polestar announced, taking a small bite of her wrap. I love to eat joeys, to concentrate on the experience, free from conversation.

Rocket took the hint, was aware of the need to focus on food in order to heighten the taste. They ate slowly and quietly, chewing methodically, the soft flesh of the tiny kangaroos beautifully prepared, their fries dusted in rabbit juice. It was a fine meal, the noise of their fellow diners falling as more meals were delivered. The wine was fruity and flavoured with veal specs, and they drank the first bottle fast, ordered a second and then a third.

When they had finished he felt a little awkward, remembering her request for personal information, which in other circles would have been considered rude. But it didn't matter. He was Rupert Ronsberger of the USE, aka Rocket Ron, rider of Euroland rides. Polestar seemed to sense his awkwardness, her foot resting on his chair, rubbing at the inside of his thigh as she talked about Joey Porto. The Crat world was beautiful and near enough perfect, the problems threatening society coming from outsiders, the small-minded and bigoted elements, but relaxation time had to be free from any serious concerns. It was etiquette. Vital to the health of the mind.

– Lets go to your place, Polestar announced, thirty minutes later.

Rocket called for the total, tipping the waiter generously and making sure Polestar noticed, leading the way to the exit where he hailed a cab, the couple travelling quickly and in silence, Polestar's hand resting on the Crat's leg. She moved it to his groin. She began stroking his balls.

– Floor 24, he said, once they were in the elevator.

Rocket studied Polestar in the glass, loved the texture of the powder covering her face, the pulse of those magnetic eyes and the nails on her fingers, noticed that the serpent had vanished, guessing it was a temporary transfer.

– Nice pad, she remarked once they had arrived.

He waved wands for light, increasing the temperature slightly, even though the apartment was warm and ready for visitors.

– I love the scenery she said, having gone straight to his viewing window.

The East Side Gates were on fire. Domes sizzled and stars beat, patterns forming and breaking apart before coming together again.

– It is very warm. Just how I like the weather.

Rocket was surprised when she slipped out of her outers to reveal a black body beyond the powdered head and hands. The girl Giovanni had recommended was much lighter skinned. Polestar was dressed in leather thong and brazier, hands resting on the window, blue light bouncing off her shoulders. She turned and strutted towards the bathroom to urinate, guessing its location easily enough. Perhaps he had been mistaken. He conjured his screen and zipped and zoomed close, saw the light-brown buttocks raised in the air as the Milanese pounded her stud-style, lens moving along a slender back. This was definitely another woman. Rocket was not disappointed. If anything, he was excited by the mystery involved, tried to fathom what had occurred.

– You are Polestar, aren't you? he enquired, when the sexer returned.

She pouted and became coy, turned and leant forward, displaying a fine pair of legs and a shapely rear, before facing the Crat and confessing her passion.

– Polestar's visa ran out and so I took the opportunity to meet you in person. I know you are a man of great focus. A believer. I am the new Polestar. The real deal.

Once she had spoken she started to dance in slo-mo. She was stunning, and despite the unusual circumstances Rocket wasn't about to complain. He was sure he hadn't actually asked her name, so the deception was unstated and harmless. If he had enquired she would have answered honestly. He was certain she could be trusted. It was natural that she should want to meet him in person, but how did she know about his abilities as an expert concentrator? She flashed the talons of her left hand.

– I'm sorry, but you didn't ask my name. I would have told you that here in Europe my friends call me Hannah if you had done.

He had been correct all along. His powers of deduction remained sharp. That name was a strange choice, but familiar. He struggled to remember. The woman who tried to hug Joey Porto? No, it was the same as the actor in the movie. That's where he had heard it before.

– I remember...

– Yes?

– Nothing. So you saw my enquiry? I didn't know Chums worked that way, passing on names and faces.

Polestar laughed and moved closer, near enough to smell and touch.

– What shall I call you? Hannah?

– Hannah is not my name. It is Polestar.

– It rolls off the tongue. But I am being rude. Would you like a drink?

She turned and sauntered across the apartment, not answering, Rocket watching her go. There was something different about this date and he was interested to discover the personality behind the sucker. She circled him, running hands over the walls, returned to the window and turned her back again.

– I grew up in the Congo, she said, as if reading his mind. But moved to Free Libya at the age of eleven. I was a child in the Glitter Centre.

– The Glitter Man?

The young entrepreneur had adopted the name of one of the greatest libertines Europe had ever seen, the popular crooner bullied and ostracised in the days of twisted sex laws. Prejudice had been rife in the pre-unification era, the sexual expression of liberal artists such as Glitter interfered with in a way that was now illegal. Oscar Wilde was another freedom fighter who had been persecuted in a previous age. It was hard to believe that there had been ages set under which sexual acts were illegal. Paedophiles had been subjected to abuse, prison and post-release harassment. For his part, Rocket could not see the attraction in prepubescent sex, but he had been trained to accept this as a question of personal choice.

The modern-day Gazz Glitter had made his fortune bringing orphans from the sub-Saharan regions to the Euro-controlled zone of Free Libya. His centres of excellence trained these poor boys and girls in the sexual arts, so that they could find work in the USE. Gender alterations were also carried out there, to cater for specific areas of the European market. Similar schemes had been set up in the Far East, but it was Central Africa that supplied the majority of dates fleeing from conflict. It was a simple matter of supply and demand, a contemporary form of aid, where unfortunates were given the chance to help themselves while experiencing spells under genuine democratic rule.

– I am a lady, Polestar announced. Have no worries. I am what I seem.

Rocket was relieved. It meant he wouldn't have to reject her advances and risk acting in incorrect fashion. He didn't want to cause offence. That was the last thing he wanted to do as he went over and joined her by the window.

FOUR

THE CADILLAC GLIDED along the fast-track reserved for Good Europeans, bodywork beaming a brilliant black beneath the freeway lights, one-way windows bouncing reflections back into the London suburbs. This channel had been cleared thirty minutes earlier, Cool overseeing the operation, logistics carried out by Gendarmerie. The movement of a Brussels-based Controller had to be clean and efficient, free from fuddles and possible terrorist attack. It was important to respect the individual as well as their role in society. Status was married to location, and Controller Horace lived at the heart of New Democracy.

The lane ran parallel to InterRegion 4 and was separated from the everyday London traffic by an animal tunnel, while transparent plating protected the outer side of the official lane from wind and other threats. Houses and small blocks spread out beyond the screen, running towards a fuzzy horizon. The ramshackle humour of the four-leggers was more interesting than these repetitive estates, but Horace Starski had seen thousands of tubes in his lifetime. He looked beyond the beasts to the cars and transporters that were backed-up and barely moving, noted the way their brake panels added splashes of bloody red to a mass of moving cattle. Electricity flashed whenever the poobums paused, shocks jolting them forward. Faces, legs, torsos fragmented in the cackle of high-voltage, chopping out a prime-cut collage.

He wasn't near enough to see the eyes of the cows, but knew they would express fear as a handful of drivers added their own strokes, venting frustrations, raising Palms and directing software, seeing the response, increasing power and frequency, small explosions burning fur, enjoying the release of tension. Controller Horace knew how important petty cruelties were to the functioning of society. Humans were bullies. Give them an easy target and some sort of justification for their sadism and they were capable of anything.

Easing himself back into the depths of the lion-skin seat, he remembered the years he had spent in England as an eager young Crat. Using the old name of these regions was frowned upon, but there were times when it was unavoidable, and he recalled raw experiences this modern breed could never imagine. He had come to understand the nature of the British Isles, and despite the battles he had won for the European Union, he respected the spirit he had helped smash. Not that it was completely dead, that was just the official gloss, but the non-believers were locked out and rotting in wastelands beyond the major cities. It was only a matter of time before their resistance ended.

He thought about his public persona, the language that was vital if the feelings of innocents such as Baby and Bob Terks were to be spared. The Controller cleansed his mind of bad words, tried to step back into line, searching for the mundane.

The demolition of Heathrow Airport had taken place five years earlier, the land remodelled to house labourers brought in from India as part of a deal he had helped broker. Hardcore lived on the Homes Estate to protect these vulnerables, to ensure they didn't wander from their camp and fall foul of cockneys, while a replacement terminal stood on Windsor Hill, the remains of the castle recycled into the foundations of a state-of-the-art launchpad.

This was his first journey via Cameron's Head and he was mildly impressed. Ease of movement was one of the USE's basic ideals, the influx of investors leading to a complicit Central London. The old-time British cities were dominated by Heartlanders too, a policy that was applied right across Europe, the commons neatly sidelined in every debate and referendum. Not that it mattered, but the charade of casting a vote had been generously funded, with all the razzmatazz of a game show. That was the past. There was no more need for elections. His thoughts were darting here and there. He was oddly excited.

Crat Horace was twenty-two years old when he first arrived in London. The locals were more resistant in those days. After decades sleepwalking towards unification they had suddenly realised their rights were being siphoned off, but it was too late, the masses outwitted by Brussels and betrayed by their own professional classes. These Europhiles existed in all the former nations of Europe and were present in every modern-day region, in the main a mixture of believers and chancers, all of them clever enough to see a winner and smell the connected profits. But it was the hard work of the unsung Crats that really mattered. He was proud of the graft he had done, the years of dedicated service, even though he had been simultaneously partaking of a dying culture's vices. He had to admit that it had been the most exciting period of his life. If reported he would have been examined and warned, a repeat offence leading to dismissal and even charges.

He thought back to the pubs he had frequented, could still taste the beer and hear the sick he spewed into late-night gutters. There had been terrible hangovers treated with basic, fried food that broke the rules of Continental cuisine. It was crass and simple yet filled his belly and made him happy. He had never been a boozer, and when he did indulge these days it was a fine wine, sipped in small quantities, a conservatism he was used to at home, and yet he had come to love the ales and beers, the ciders and stouts and lagers. The English were barely Christian, a point he noticed early, and while he wouldn't have called them pagans, there was a less fussy approach to life, an openness he had not found elsewhere.

The elite within British society were clearly embarrassed by this difference, keeping to the classist tradition and worshipping Heartland. They craved the influences of France, Italy and even Spain. These cultures were seen as exotic, sophisticated, noble. The elite studied Latin and Greek and hated the Germanic and Scandinavian mixtures that drove the wider population, and he had been able to exploit his observations once he realised their worth. The move towards a single European state was like a long-distance train journey that kept to one speed, moving at a slow but steady pace, the driver knowing he would reach his destination in the end. It was just a case of avoiding derailment, relentlessly crushing anything that got in his way. The USE was a machine, but there were times when thinking outside that single channel saved time and money.

Without his discoveries he wondered how long he would have survived as a Crat. He admired run-of-the-mill Bureaus who could deal in trivia for six days a week, across the decades, some of them never moving more than a couple of ranks in their entire careers. To serve in such a selfless manner was fantastic. It showed that humans could stop themselves drifting into the dangerous no-man's land of excessive imagination, because it was in the realms of fantasy that disaster lurked. Bureaus could take anything directed their way and choose what to accept and what to dismiss. They invented the truths that would protect them in the long run. They were humanity's greatest survivors, and he enjoyed testing these faceless heroes, stretching their genius to the limits.

He loved Technos also, as they were Bureaus who served loyally and were promoted to a higher level. An ability to remain emotionless under pressure was essential for this next step, along with a degree of ambition, but they rarely progressed beyond Cratdom. Technos were clearly more driven than Bureaus, which was conversely seen as a weakness by the academic Controllers and their Sus-driven researchers. The Best European was boring and conventional and ready to obey every order, however unreasonable, and yet the Controllers themselves lacked these qualities. They were restless and unsatisfied. Every few weeks this paradox returned to exercise Horace Starski's mind.

He possessed the essential Crat skill of being able to focus on the most humdrum of trifles, and yet his endurance was modest compared to most of his former colleagues, a deficiency that even today made him feel slightly ashamed. He had, however, been unable to suppress his ambition, never seeing himself as a Bureau or Techno for life. It was this lack of discipline that led to his grasp of the British mentality, and his insights were quickly put to use by the State, leading to his breakneck rise through the ranks and early elitism. He doted on his fellow Controllers, their internal drives and foibles, the marriage of hard-nosed selfishness and devotion to service that meant they were able to respond to the unusual, but he

would never stop romanticising the lowly Bureau. He was interested in the new breed, the mavericks in their ranks, the future stars
with eyes fixed on Brussels. These Crats would be more deadly,
another species, their foundations so different to his own. In truth,
it had become the focus of his reflections.

Near the end of IR4, the lane split and the Cadillac lifted into
the rooftops, a specially reinforced tube enclosing the vehicle,
pressure pads connecting with the undercarriage so the auto
seemed to be floating. Bob Terks was driving and turned off the
battery, allowing the sensation to feed inside. Views into the city
were modest here, but colour blazed in those communities where
Good Euros dominated, gated boroughs promoting the dream of
gentrification. Controller Horace wasn't overly interested, as he had
seen the same energies right across Europe, but he was looking
forward to the spectacle they were fast approaching.

– Tell me what you see and what you think, he purred, Bob
Terks and Baby turning their heads towards the modest towers on
either side of the tube.

The office block nearest to them was caked in changing shades
of familiar blue, and while it was an impressive sight, the
Controller's buddies had seen bigger and better displays elsewhere.
However, the closer they got the clearer it became that something
novel was taking place. Horace Starski glanced at their faces, saw
mild confusion, while he experienced a shot of ecstasy.

– Stop here, please.

Baby seemed alarmed, but Bob Terks did as he was asked.

The Cadillac paused in the air.

– We're a sitting target, Baby said. We should keep moving.

– There are no rebels here, and their weapons are useless against
the coating. Take a moment to appreciate the beauty.

The block held zillions of living cells, a chimpanzee-human
hybrid that appeared to be breathing, an intensity of experience
never before seen in public. Mixmaster Marcel was at the controls,
shuffling palettes while matching official guidelines – playing with
the blues, pumping rhythms into the stars. The Controller was
enthralled.

– It's fantastic, Bobby announced.

– I arranged it especially, Controller Horace admitted.

He was proud, yet always modest.

– The fusion is original, soon to be released commercially, but I wanted to see a public showing first and where better than in this dark, dank, depressing city. It is my gift to us all.

Bob Terks and Baby were clearly mesmerised, and this made the Controller even happier. He was noting their reactions, certain that his blend would prove a hit with his fellows and those among the masses who appreciated great art. There was a fine chance the technology could spread into international markets, the next step forward from his Scales! success. The motion was tight and vibrant to the point of life-changing, near to elements of Kiev tech but on a far higher and more realistic level. As the main investor and owner, there was a fortune to come.

– What is it made from? Baby asked.

The Controller looked at his buddy and was pleased with the chance to explain.

– You take a female chimpanzee from the continent of Africa and a male human from Indonesia, ask them nicely to mate and help the fertilising process by using the best insemination professionals. Once embryos have formed we keep the strongest and abort the weak, then monitor their progress before harvest time comes around and the youngsters are moved to more comfortable, laboratory accommodation. We choose the correct moment and begin siphoning cells, carry out the required mutations and begin cloning. The cells multiply and are put through a factory process that links them, always bearing in mind that we need strength in connections coupled with great flexibility. It is essential that the cells remain alive and individual, otherwise the effect you see would be lost.

– Why does it have to be a monkey and a human? Baby asked.

– Cross-species breeding is the future. More importantly, there is an interesting scent involved. Creatives want these boundaries pushed.

– The towers of Brussels smell faintly of the sea, Bob Terks remarked.

45

– Exactly my point. Scales! is greatly loved, but citizens become bored. Here we have the brutality of the African jungle dominated by a slender human from Indonesia. It is exotic. Primal. Mind over brawn. Imagine using cells from those cows we saw in the tunnel a few minutes ago.

Bob Terks laughed heartily, while Baby had turned her face away, concentrating on the show.

– Roast beef, the Controller murmured.

The three friends sat in silence for several minutes, Mixmaster Marcel turning on the style as he slowly built a pulse, lightening the blue and adding faces, a subhuman monkey and a human helper, both smiling widely as he created a drip-drip effect, as if the scene was melting, pulling back before it collapsed, hardening textures while riding the beat. Baby had tears in her eyes.

– We had best continue, Controller Horace suggested, suprised at the depth of her appreciation.

He looked away from the towers to a chopper in the sky, knew AirCav had the Cadillac under constant surveillance. He had told them of the pause, though there had been no details on duration.

– We don't want to keep our hosts waiting. They may become nervous.

The team moved on, leaving the spectacle behind, and when they were a kilometre away Marcel cut the power, having been asked to keep the display as private as possible. The tube crossed rows of housing, the monochrome nature of the neighbourhood more obvious now. The good buddies travelled in silence, lost in their thoughts, clearly moved by the experience.

– My chum... Horace Starski suddenly announced, his Palm vibrating.

He wanded digits and a screen appeared, the face of Controller Ralph life-size in the car.

– Welcome to London, pal.

– Thanks, Ralph. How's tricks?

– Couldn't be better. Everything perfecto with you?

– Excellent. We stopped at Tarzan Tower. Or Tarzan *Block*.

Ralph Malls laughed heartily, his 3D head moving left to right, the smell of aftershave adding to the subtle lion scent filling the Cadillac.

– Tarzan. Very good. Chimp-boy deluxe.

He straightened and became quizzical.

– Really, what did you think? Large-scale public performance is always going to be different to the much smaller, private version.

– It's a winner. I am certain.

– Excellent. Sorry I couldn't be with you, but I had to fine-tune the reception. Marcel is sending me a recording.

– Please make sure it doesn't leak. If he allows access... I have told him.

– He knows, don't worry. I want to win on this also.

Controller Horace was pleased he had shared this first showing with Bobby and Baby. It would have become complex otherwise, with various chums feeling jealous if they discovered Controller Ralph had been present and they had not. Coming into London like this had given him an opportunity. The informal approach – well organised but secretive – was often more effective than the formal.

– We will be there by 22.15. I look forward to our meal and to seeing good friends.

– Likewise, buddy. Likewise...

Ralph Malls vanished and Horace Starski returned to his view of the great outdoors, leaving Bob Terks to focus on the road ahead and Baby to concentrate on her Palm. Knowing Ralph as he did, no expense would be spared at the reception. It may have been official expenses involved, but it was the thought that mattered. The bod was a raver who loved the Euroland razzle. He was a native, descended from a long line of landowners, not too bright but good fun. How he made Controller, Horace Starski did not know, but he was always glad of his company and coming from England he had insights. The rich of the deleted European nations had revelled in excess – some of them fighting unification, the majority knowing that the new order was essentially a replacement for the defunct system of rule through royal families. He admired Ralph for his energy and a desire to crack the English nut.

– Men and monkeys, Baby said to herself. What next?

Controller Horace glanced over, saw her draw out her screen to fill the space vacated by Ralph Malls. Lenses were hidden in the bricks and mortar below, and she played an image of their progress from there. The terraces of a rundown neighbourhood passed and they were flanked by new-builds that showed they were nearing the West Side Gates. Glass towers rose into the sky ahead of them in a riot of culture. These scrapers were the usual oblong in shape, but there were designs inspired by apples, carrots and pears bursting from the Hammersmith Hub.

They slowed down a little when they reached their Gate, but only briefly, as the Controller was expected and had been tracked since landing. Cool were on high alert, those running the operation relieved to see him enter the West Side. Bobby continued, moving smoothly, quickly on the raised route that curved and followed Embankment, the Thames to their right, illuminated by bed-sighted panels, the banks lined with exotics from the Med, apartments loaded with Crats and Financials, walls of glass sectioned in the manner of Gil & Georgie. Islands sat in the middle of the river, artist colonies that were reached by escalators, tanks raised and filled with fish. The Cadillac followed the track and skirted The City before bending back, finding a straight line towards the East Side Gates. Towers sparkled, welcoming Horace Starski back to his London pad. It had been a long time.

FIVE

ROCKET WAS AWAKE early, even though he had disabled the alarm, seeing as it was a relaxation day. He left his bed and entered the lounge, headed for his VoyBox. It was still dark outside and when he arrived he automatically raised his eyes upwards, drawn by the beauty of Pearly Tower. But his vision was blurred, an aftershock of the excess red consumed at Tenderburger and back at his apartment post-dinner, or perhaps it was the last dregs of the sex bomb he had dropped later in the evening. He screwed his eyes shut, lids clamped as he counted to ten, reopening them slowly and expecting his sight to have cleared. The distortion remained. Raising hands, he screwed knuckles into the hollows, firm on bone and gentle to jelly, but it did no good. He became mindful, his grogginess fading as he realised that his eyes were fine and the fuzziness was in the air.

A thick fog had been allowed to enter the East Side and perhaps the whole of Central. He wondered why. It might be a technical issue. An error. The idea made him feel sick, and he shivered as if stranded on the other side of the glass, defenceless against the harsh conditions. It was as if civilisation was melting away. He was wearing Radical boxers and a *Whatever* T, the drive running the apartment's atmosphere ensuring he was warm, but he no longer felt secure. He became fearful, knew that Rocket would not care, realised he was currently more Rupert than Ronald. He felt claustrophobic, and vulnerable, as if an unknown enemy was watching him from inside the haze. It was crass to be spooked this way, and he felt foolish, told himself that the sensation would pass and life would be simple once more. He thought of Polestar and was pleased she had stayed, reassured by the company, and this helped him to understand that the fog had been allowed inside the domes as part of an artistic happening. On the whim of a Controller no doubt.

Rocket decided he would politely ask his date to leave once

another coupling had taken place. With bodily needs sated, the mind became fine-tuned and he would normally have bid her farewell last night, enjoyed quality downtime to the max, but instead he had asked her to remain and it took a while to find a reason for this change of routine. He recalled a case he had been working on, a similar straying from fixed behaviour, the name Hannah returning, and hadn't Polestar repeated it, though perhaps the red had played a trick? It didn't matter. Uncertainty was sent to the shadows for forgetting. Again, the idea of straying from strict patterns was stimulating. He was horny, but in this sexer he had identified a challenge.

Polestar had a confused take on reality. Maybe his imagination had been stirred by her fine looks, but it was almost as if she was asking for his help. She was clearly in awe of the USE and, without boasting, Rocket Ron (aka Rupert Ronsberger) as its living embodiment. He had worked closely with Free Libyans and other non-European cocksuckers before – dates from Phnom Phen and Hanoi being particular faves – and their training had always included a course in democracy, but Polestar was different. She clearly wanted to learn more. The lady was interested in what he had to say, and he had observed her hanging on every word, stretching his intellect with some intelligent questions. Naivety played a part. He couldn't deny that this was a factor.

He found that he was keen to educate, excited to talk about the beliefs driving his life, to express personal aspirations and desires and the pride he felt. This was a surprise. He had enjoyed peering into the future and thrilling her with tales of great endurance, dreams of his own penthouse, and as his life *was* the system he wanted to bombard her with facts relating to the project, share some of the details that so thrilled him, and the impulse was even stronger this morning, despite that lack of clarity outside.

He sat down on the sofa and ran a hand across its skin, the effects of the stimulants fading as a familiar level-headedness returned, and yet Polestar had stirred his tongue. He grafted for the good of others, possessed ideals and faith, truly believed, but he had nobody to impress as his colleagues were the same. It wasn't healthy to stray beyond Good Europeanism, to mingle with the commons, so it was possible that Polestar fulfilled a need he hadn't known he had. His conformity tightened. She was a date. He was showing weakness. And yet she was different to the sexers he had known, where the fucky-fucky dominated, as she had actually wanted to have conversations with him, came in from new angles, and he recalled Polestar's enthusiasm, her questions and eagerness to absorb his answers. He watched the fog swirl, pressing on the glass, and he had to admit that whoever had opened the Gates was touched by genius. Rocket was strong and looking ahead. The gold stars that hovered over Pearly Tower were still there. He had no fear. They would return twice as impressive.

Sunday was Funday. Like most of the population he wouldn't be grafting. It was a chance to laze and tick chores, to spend an afternoon shopping at a mall, munch at restaurants and watch the footie and partake of walks and sport. Rocket decided he would spend his time with Polestar, if she was agreeable, which he imagined she would be, seeing as she also appeared dedicated to hard work, the earning of credit to consume and help society. It would be important to increase her rating if she hoped to buy a visa for the USA, to find work in the USE's twin. The sexers there were for the most part drawn from Central America and Asia, but she had variations of appearance to offer, a certain novelty value. He would prepare strong coffee and croissants and place them on a tray and take it to his bedroom where Polestar still slept. He wondered if she would be keen to chat, or more likely listen, as he had been doing most of the talking. It was her choice.

– The greatest threat lay on this very island... he began, standing over the naked woman.

Her eyes opened and for a moment she seemed confused, but then consciousness returned and she grinned, sitting upright and pulling fur to her body. She accepted the coffee and had a sip before placing the mug on the bedside table, taking the offered plate and lifting a ham-stuffed croissant to her mouth, butter running down her fingers. The Crat sat in the recliner next to the bed, wondering if he was Euroland stud Rocket Ron or USE intellect Rupert

Ronsberger. He decided they were near enough one and the same, but seemed to be tilting towards Rupert.

– The people couldn't see the seeds of democracy embedded in the old freedom doctrines, Utopian systems tagged fascism and communism. There were other attempts at unification before these, of course, going back thousands of years, but it is modern history I find most fascinating. The island monkeys of these regions were, for the most part, rabble. And yet when there was a chance to kill and maim they fought with great violence and refused all offers of peace. They were too bigoted to see the need for discipline and leadership, a centralising of power wedded to rampant capitalism. The southern tribes were noted for their excess cruelty.

– You are talking about the English? Polestar asked. We are in England now, are we not?

Rupert flinched. It was in extremely bad taste for her to use this term – especially in such a flippant manner – although she had done so in an historical context, and the woman *was* a non-Euro. He would let it pass. She had more knowledge than Rocket had imagined, and he should meet her halfway, use the base language she herself had employed. He was alone with his sexer, so couldn't be overheard and misunderstood by a conscientious Crat. He was doing nothing wrong.

– We are in London, a city in the United State of Europe.

– The English are bad people? Didn't they win the big wars of the 20th Century?

The Crat almost choked. He shook his head sadly.

– The USE won the war that mattered, he murmured. And we did it in a peaceful, democratic manner.

She sat up and the rabbit fur fell away, breasts jutting out so Rupert was distracted and pulled towards Rocket mode. But he remained professional. He only wanted to help.

– The English, as you call them, built death factories we now refer to as concentration camps. This was during the Second British War, which was caused by GB aggression. It was here, on these two islands, that millions of innocents were starved and murdered. The commons slaughtered men, women and children as if they were animals. They even referred to them as subhumans. The victims were largely guest workers, party politicals, libertines, liberals, sexual exotics such as batties and child-lovers. Meat-eaters were also targeted in certain areas.

– Paedophiles are not welcome in my country, Polestar volunteered. They are wicked.

Rocket was shocked. He had learned about paedophobia in his first year at school, so the notion that sex between consenting humans should be outlawed was an alien concept. But Polestar *was* alien, from a primitive land lacking the protections he took for granted. Thankfully he didn't care too much about what happened beyond the boundaries of the USE, so he continued. Maybe he would confront her prejudice later, but for now he was going to allow it to slide.

– This happened a long time before unification. The progressive politics of New Democracy are loved by everyone now, but then they were violently rejected. Today, the USE helps its corporate benefactors, and our CBs help us in return. A federation between government and business. New Democracy is inclusive, you see. But this is basic history. Well known. Though as a non-Euro you may find it to be fresh information?

Polestar nodded, added a sweetness of expression.

– I will be a Good European one day, she said. Please, tell me more, Honey.

Rocket reached down and stroked his semi. He was feeling strong. In control. Spreading the love. Splashing seed. Polestar was just the sort of date Euroland needed. Her occupation would prevent permanent status, unless she was sponsored by a Controller, or maybe a top-level Techno with healthy connections. Returns were handed to tens of thousands of sexers each year, and while he was sympathetic, there were rules. He thought about mounting his date now, but a need to discuss the triumph of the State will was stronger than his desire for penetration.

– The war of 1939–1945 was lost due to the incredible brutality of the British, he went on, having closed his eyes and motioned for his chair to recline.

– The rush of progressive ideas was too much for the British mind to absorb and the great thinkers of Berlin were broken by the violence unleashed. These were peace-loving intellectuals. Sensitive souls. Twenty of them met in a bunker and drank coffee laced with poison.

– That is so sad, Polestar whispered.

– The GBs bombed our greatest cities and killed millions of civilians, while their propaganda unit spread endless lies. Truth was perverted. They accused what were then the German people of attacking their neighbours. You won't have heard of Poland and, to be honest, why should you have, but fantastical stories were told about the Polskis' treatment by German stormtroopers, and there were outrageous claims that Jews were abused. The opposite was the case, but the GB publicity machine was unstoppable. Churchill had been a journalist when he was a young man and knew every single trick. The point I'm trying to make is that the dark ages of the pre-USE era were more horrific than anyone not educated by the State can imagine.

Polestar was eating as he spoke, finished and exchanged her empty plate for the mug of coffee. She held this in two hands, face bowed over the steam, making him think of mist rather than fog, a sparser version that seemed harmless in this miniature showing. When she raised her head he realised that her lenses were still attached, that she hadn't taken them out when they slept. The yellow light was intense and seemed to be beating.

– The Berliners laced their coffee with poison? It is romantic, but tragic. I hope you haven't added anything to my drink.

They both laughed.

– I have heard of the hero Churchill. His father was English, the mother American?

Rocket smiled indulgently. He had underestimated Polestar, it was true, but her history was topsy-turvy and craved correction. Faced with such muddle he would remain gentle.

– A drunkard and a gangster, Churchill was bitterly opposed to unification. He rejected the advances of men such as Controller Adolf and Controller Joe.

– I have heard these names, but know little. I am sorry.

He held up a hand. There was no need to apologise.

– Herr Hitler was greatly respected. He was a strapping Bavarian juggernaut who rejected British aggression and actively fought RAF terrorism as a fighter pilot.

– The RAF?

– The Royal Air Force were British lowlifes. They carried out merciless attacks on the major cities of Heartland, their destruction of Dresden, Treblinka and Warsaw three of the worst examples. Hundreds of thousands of innocents were murdered by weapons invented by a small cadre of homophobes. The GBs flew pro-pellered Lancasters and dropped huge explosives willy-nilly. There were none of the precision strikes we see in the USE's peace-keeping missions. The British revelled in these assaults and became so full of hatred that they invaded and committed horrific crimes.

– There were some GB intellectuals who were so outraged by these attacks that they risked all and rebelled. Oz Moseley, a working-class plumber who had cleaned gutters as a boy, before teaching himself the ways of pipes and valves, decided to fight back against racial prejudice as well as his own poverty, becoming the spokesman for a large section of the community. He was beaten, tortured and incarcerated by Churchill, then when the war was over and the British imposed totalitarian rule he was released, only to be bullied by the generals until his death.

– You see, there were good people here, heroes such as Oz, the likes of Teddy Boy Heath and Mags Thatcher, Big Dave Cameron and Little Tony Blair. They could have stopped unification, but played a long-term game, kept the dream alive. This was before the arrival of advanced citizens from the mainland. Franco-German management teams saved the inhabitants from the false prophets who had invented this UK bloc and created a so-called English people. This band of Churchillians were manipulators and bad-thinkers. There has never been an England. It is a myth. A lie spread by small-minded sectarians.

– But the whole of Europe speaks English. An Americanised version at times.

Rocket closed his eyes and breathed deeply. He counted to ten.

– We speak European. There is no English language... no such place as England. It is a deceit. A dangerous one. There is no union of Britain. No Scotland, no Wales, no Ireland.

With his lids still shut, he listened for Polestar's voice, but she stayed silent, waiting for him to tell her more. He continued in the soothing voice he knew she loved.

– After this war, which left tens of millions dead and Europe divided, a brave new warrior class emerged. Crats evolved and took on their current form, meticulously working behind the scenes, our goal a single super-duper state and the removal of wasteful elections, which has of course been achieved. Conflict is wrong. We must all think alike.

– There were obstacles? Polestar asked.

– Many obstacles. Prejudice was rife and continues to be a problem. Not just here, either, but in pockets right across Europe. We are fighting it every day. *I* fight it constantly. The Controllers know what is best and every Crat worth his weight in credit considers their requests. We graft together for the good of society. The freedoms we enjoy today didn't magically appear. Democracy needs to be cultivated and, once established, maintained. And there is so much still to do.

– How did this imaginary Britain become part of the USE?

– It joined the European Economic Community, and did so at the expense of a cult called the Commonwealth. This had supplied many of the troops in the suppression of unification. Primitive fighters. It was a deliberate policy by Brussels, appealing to the greed of the British leaders... the *imaginary* British leaders. Businessmen identified increased profits, while those who hated their own culture saw the chance of a collapse. There were idealists also, decent beings who didn't care about the effect on those non-Euro nations of the Commonwealth. Controller Ted brought this island into the EEC, but decades of bickering followed as Europhiles worked with Brussels to complete the transfer of power. There were plenty of fools who thought it was a common market.

Polestar giggled.

– Mags Thatcher continued Teddy Boy Heath's mission. She was known as the Iron Lady, but she lacked the strength of Controller Ted. To her credit, she was able to appease the rabble by trading on GB patriotism while allowing the transfer of power to continue. She was starry-eyed, but not immune to the odd wobble, so history will never regard her as it does Teddy Boy. However, in the context of the time in which she ruled, she achieved much for the development of New Democracy. You see, anti-freedom organisations had gained disproportionate power by the 1970s, and not just in GB either, but right across Europe. Trade-unions were causing damage to profit margins, slowing down the great capitalist racers. Certain industries were even nationalised.

– Nationalised?

– A totalitarian policy whereby the profit motive is removed and an industry is no longer run as a business. GB had been split by the TUs, which professed equality yet actively denigrated the libertines of our culture. Essential services such as gas and electricity were supported by taxation, along with the steel and coal industries. The bosses of these unions were gangsters, modelled themselves on the criminal Churchill, calling out huge armies of thugs who attacked a friendly police force for no fair reason. A warped ideology had taken hold and it was the Iron Lady who broke their power through a bold use of law. She worked hand-in-hand with a host of unsung heroes. Rupert Murdoch was one such man, although an Australian by birth.

– That wouldn't happen today, would it? Polestar asked.

– Indeed it would not. Australasia has chosen its own path to oblivion, but thankfully their Little Englandism occurs on the other side of the planet. But back to the history... John Major followed Mags, again juggling balls for the project, while the switch from what was then a Tory Party to a Labour Party saw a continuation of the good work. Tony Blair would rule for a decade, inventing another cult in Cool Britannia, an odd feelgood movement that married a love of Brussels and business to unhealthily high levels of investment in nationalised medicine and education.

– Hospitals and schools were not controlled by benefactors?

– Indeed they were not. There was what is known as a 'welfare state' on this island.

– It is hard to believe, Polestar said. How could there be excellence in such a system? Where were the incentives to heal and to teach?

– I am not sure, Rocket admitted. Maybe they were leaving it to chance, hoping for the best, or perhaps people believed they were entitled to a free service, that they didn't have to pay for doctors and teachers. What is probably true, is that an arrogance had taken hold. There was no dynamic, a refusal to consider detail, and check and recheck minutiae. Ideals were required. The European Union continued to promote privatisation through directives and the assistance of purists within the fading nations. The EU cracked deals with the USA that liberated economies. The Transatlantic Trade and Investment Partnership was an early example. A lack of total control caused small currency wobbles, but here we must be harsh on the regimes of what were then Greece, Italy and Spain – corrupt officials, lazy workers, stagnant cultures.

– I don't like laziness, Polestar commented.

– Again, the GB cartel caused much of this turmoil, and especially the dominant 'English', just as they had done during the British Wars. By refusing to join the single currency they were acting in the same way as they did in 1914 and 1939. The British undermined our democratic moves, and responsibility for that lies with a man called Gordon Brown. If it hadn't been for Brown the eurodollar would have been introduced earlier and much argument avoided. This madman went further, opposing Scottish independence, a move that would have weakened GB and led to an earlier completion of the unification process.

– I have never heard of this person, Polestar said. I find it all so interesting. And it is true? You have no doubts?

– Doubts? Why would I doubt the truth?

Polestar removed the blanket. She was naked. Laying back, she opened her legs slightly, tongue playing across her lips like a scene from a pornographic movie. Rocket was erect, but he had to continue now that he had started, repeating as if by rote, but keen to impress and express his feelings. He was the State. Its power was his power.

– The braver capitalists were prepared to see Britain disbanded, but the trade-unions, which had changed sides in the 1980s and embraced us as a way of furthering their interests, suddenly betrayed the workers for a second time and opposed Brussels and its multinational backers. It is insane, I know, but this is what happened. The elite always get their way, of course, due to superior education and an ability to inherit money, and with the main political groupings complicit the ignorant masses were thankfully removed from the equation. This was for their own good. The political and media classes played their parts and full union was finally achieved. Commons rebelled here and across Europe, but this was controlled, though due to decades of incorrect thought and the problems attached to living on an island these regions remain our biggest problem.

Polestar lowered a finger, placed it between her legs, began to stimulate herself.

– There have been many attempts at union, Rocket announced. Empires have risen and fallen. The Greeks, Romans, Ottomans, French, Russians and Germans failed for myriad reasons, but each one was ultimately undone by impatience. The USE did not, and will not, make the same mistake. This is an eternal empire. It will last for a million years. I am one of its soldiers and I *shall* be a Controller. I am an embodiment of the State – composed, loyal, tolerant, stoic. Our authority is enshrined and the people are pleased with their possessions and debt. They trust us. We keep on developing. *I* keep on developing.

Polestar rolled out of the bed and strolled towards her lover. She stroked the Crat's hair, ran sharp nails lightly across forehead and nose, finally resting them on his lips. He knew that while he had already taught her so much, it would take time for the lesson to settle. The sun had yet to rise and burn away the fog. The day was still young and there was so much to talk about, but his date was in the mood for sex. It was time for Ron to add some Euroland flavour to the equation. He removed his boxers and T, placed his Rubettes cap on his head. He stood to attention as Polestar went down on her knees in front of him, the snake on the tip of her tongue moving along the length of his rocket.

SIX

KENNY JACKSON BREATHED deep on the sweet smells leaking out of The Wheatsheaf, flavours so strong he imagined them as warm currents flushing into a freezing-cold river, melting ice same as hops had dissolved the fears of his ancestors. Frost edged the windows of the pub, crystals forming their own psychedelic cobwebs, metallic patterns that would spread out across the glass as the temperature collapsed. He stopped walking and took a moment to study the street, found blue bricks for building blocks, cars and vans dusted with silver powder, white lines trimming the pavements.

His father was nearby, ashes scattered in the churchyard, the Norman tower of All Souls a rigid black outline beyond the houses, but he was more interested in living strangers, off the grid but still making sure. The street was empty of people and he relaxed, let the smell of the beer pull him inside.

Seven steps down a narrow corridor and he ducked right, entering the small side bar, away from the busier main room. The ceiling was lower here, sectioned by a black beam lined with horse brasses. A fire glowed inside the far wall, reflections flapping on metal so that Kenny imagined the USE flag and its gold stars, the rewards teachers gave small children who did as they were told. The bubblers loved spreading their logo about, but it was never seen in this town. The outlawed flags of Wessex, England and Britain dominated the walls of Yeovil, stencilled by youths branded racist by Brussels. These youngsters followed the style of Jonesy and her inspiration Smithy, who in turn looked to the great heritage artist Banksy. This was a Free English plot, beyond the Reading Line, but while Cool stayed out, spies were always a concern. It was only a matter of time before the next push began. As a member of GB45, the USE was never far from his thoughts.

– All right, Kenny boy? Fred called, wobbling slightly. Not snowing yet?

– Don't know if it will. The streets are starting to freeze.

– It's warmer in here than at home. Brass monkey weather. Might have to stay the night. Settle down in the corner with a good read. Too cold for simians.

Fred pointed to the brasses on the beam. There were lots of horses, Celtic crosses and bales of corn, a single fox and the witch Jennie Jones, Saxon knotworks and a Grand Union barge, fractals and a devil, but no monkeys. The vixen raised her ears as stallions reared. There was a flock of birds at the end, moving down the wall in single file – five swans, two geese, one seagull from a sea-side town, a robin without the red breast. Below were exotic plants in terracotta pots, two big jades near the window, their glossy green leaves in succulent contrast to the scene outside.

– It'll probably be hot tomorrow, serious T-shirt weather, everyone out sunbathing.

– True, Fred mused. Never know. I was only hanging on for you, but now you're here I can't be bothered leaving. One pint too many. One pint too few. I fancy another as well.

Kenny was used to Fred justifying the time he spent in The Wheatsheaf, but didn't think he needed to seeing as drinking and thinking went together. Beer rinsed the brain. Loosened the screws and allowed ideas to circulate. Worries and regrets were washed away. There was nothing better than being in a proper pub with its mix of people and opinions, talking freely and arguing in a civilised manner, learning and sharing what you knew and imagined. The Wheatsheaf was where they liked to do their business, a shared passion destroying that daft idea of a generation gap. Kenny was thirty-two, Fred nearly nearly fifty years older.

– This is the warmest place to be right now, Kenny reassured his friend. They like a good fire here, don't they, but it's getting icy and I can walk you back when you're ready.

– Don't you worry about me. I'm not that drunk.

– I know, Kenny replied, more concerned about his balance.

– I brought your odds and ends along.

Fred tapped the canvas bag on the floor with his right foot. Being familiar with the care he took over his merchandise, the seriousness of his dealing, Kenny knew that this nonchalance was a way of disguising the valuables inside. Fred preferred a public exchange, even if the bag was reinforced, zipped and locked. He liked to remember the freedoms of a previous era.

– You can pay me later. There's no rush.

– I don't like to be in debt.

– Who does? Not out here, anyway.

Kenny rolled his head and shoulders as the heat from the fireplace hit his hands, working its way into the fabric of his coat so a sheen of frost he hadn't noticed started to melt. The smell of beer was matched by smoking wood and coal, the warmth rising up into his face. He loved this pub. Men had stood in The Wheatsheaf through the centuries, talking and joking and arguing as their lives levelled out. They would have hidden from the diseases wiping out wives and daughters, the wars that killed their sons, a race-based class system that had kept the rank-and-file English suppressed for so many centuries, a prejudice that had driven the final betrayal by those in power. The common people had fought in this pub as well, swapped insults and punches, anger as well as friendship.

– There's something extra for you, Fred said, lowering his voice. Let me know what you think.

Most of the big-city pubs had long been replaced by bars and gastros, a handful of soulless chains dominating those that remained, but out here the traditional local thrived. There were exceptions in the metropolitan areas, in neighbourhoods set aside for core workers, but inside the bubbles where the Good Europeans socialised and shopped, things were the same in London as they were in Lisbon.

– Still no Meyrink I'm afraid. One day...

Kenny looked meaningfully at Fred, who shrugged and took a mouthful of Kingdon. They didn't have to worry in The Wheatsheaf, protected from recordings by the landlord's trusty Jammer 3, and all the faces here were known. But while they were free from the paranoia of the cities and beyond InterZone, it was still important to be cautious. Fred grinned.

– The Dedalus edition. Fine cover. Taken from the film naturally enough. The 1920 version. That's the one you want.

Kenny was after a copy of Gustav Meyrink's *The Golem*. He owned Hans Fallada and Heinrich Böll hards, had read Meyrink as a copy but never seen an original. He loved the spiritual darkness of that Central European fiction, the German expressionists with their dreamtime woodcuts, the genius of Frans Masereel, and this ran into Fritz Lang and the origins of film. His memories of leaving London as a boy played in black-and-white, what he now saw as a repeat of that noirish interwar dread that had inspired the greats. Russian pogroms, Bolshevism, the German wars, fascism – it all linked into the current dictatorship, had created a powerful cultural reaction that offered lessons.

– There's a chance I can put a copy of *May Day* your way, Fred continued.

He was leaning closer, half playfully, showing how cautious he could be, but serious also. His eyes had narrowed and he was waiting to see the response. Fred had his ways. That's what locals said about the maverick. Kenny was excited.

– That would be brilliant. Where...

Fred rocked back on his heels, steadied himself with a hand on the bar, eyes glinting as he held a finger to his lips, bouncing some of the caution back. The drink might loosen his lips more than in the past, but he was no fool, familiar with the quirks and interests of everyone present. Most of those nearby had done business with him in the past. Kenny was younger and bound to be nervous. He had his pressures. Fred went to speak and thought again, turned and leaned against the counter and motioned for his friend to do the same, talking almost in a whisper.

– It will mean a trip down to Penzance, he said. I'll need a driver.

– I'm more that happy to do that, Kenny filled in. When will we...

– The man calls himself Trewarden. Don't know if it's his real name or not, sounds too Cornish to be true, but I suppose it could be. Maybe, maybe not. Who cares? Doesn't matter. Haven't met him before, but I've been told he's dedicated. Doesn't live in Penzance exactly, but near enough, a few miles to the north. On the coast I think. Near an old tin mine.

Fred moved even closer.

– It was Suzie Vickers told me about him. It's an easy run. Three hours maybe. We'll have to stay the night. You ever been to Penzance before?

– Never been to Cornwall.

– You're in for a treat. I used to go down there as a boy. It's changed, but not too much. Mind you, must be nearly ten years since I last went. I'm excited about this Trewarden character, seems to have long fingers in many pies, and there have always been lots of bookworms in Cornwall. Incomers as well as natives. People were pushed out of London and kept going through the West Country until they reached the end of Britain. Nowhere else to run. But we'll wait for the weather to clear. Go in the spring. Perfect for *May Day*. Or June maybe. For Golowan. They let Penglaz loose on Mazey Day. Close the streets. Local obby oss. Shall I tell Trewarden to hold on to it for you? He believes in what we're doing. Fancies handing it over in person and making a connection.

– Definitely, Kenny agreed. This is great, Fred. Don't forget I'm going to London next week.

– And don't you forget what you're taking and who you're meeting.

– Of course I won't, Kenny replied. Main reason I'm going. That and to see some friends. *May Day...* I don't know how you do it, I really don't.

Kenny stood up straight and looked around the bar, saw two faces raised.

– All right, Cliff? Kev?

Cliff Stevens sat at a table with his eldest boy Kevin. They silently raised their pint glasses in response, the measure illegal under USE law. He supposed the Crat legions had to be kept busy, an endless series of orders doublespeaked as directives, and on top of this there was the constant tinkering and rewriting of existing regulations, the loading of words and the pulling apart of sentences. Job creation rolled into a bubblehead version of perpetual revolution. *Change = Progress* and *New Is Best* were two of their many slogans.

Kenny wondered why Pop wasn't with them, reasoned he was better off at home, not risking a broken leg on the ice. As bad would be a chill. He worried about Fred, even if he had plenty of birthdays left. Pop was pushing ninety and there would be someone with him. The Stevens were a big family. Sitting one table away from Cliff and his son were Mr and Mrs Wu, a married couple in their late eighties who, like Pop, had shared their memories with Kenny over the last couple of years. With the digitisation of culture compulsory, and physical recordings and books illegal, the elderly offered a living, uncensored view of history.

– I'm gasping for a pint and there's no-one serving, Kenny complained.

– Ronnie's working tonight. She's turning Tom's head again.

– He loves a bit of flattery.

– She means it as well. Lovely lady. If I was a lot younger, much better off and a little bit more handsome, I'd ask her out. Might need another trade, something legal, but money's been scarce for us all since anyone can remember. Not sure what I can do about that. Tom seems happy. As far as you can tell. Doesn't give much away.

– We can't have it interfering with his work though. Why isn't one of them serving round this side? Don't want him slacking. There's thirsty shiremen here.

– Kid Bale and his boxing droogs are in the other bar. It's five years since that fight with the gypsy knuckler outside Cardiff.

Kenny remembered the day well. They'd run two coaches from The Wheatsheaf, following local roads to avoid InterRegion tolls and Gendarmerie patrols. With a few beers inside them it would have been hard to keep the boys under control if they'd been stopped. They'd have been badly zapped, a foreign police force warped by years of training always keen to pump electricity into the English commons.

It was a Wales v England bout, so was always going to be fruity when the lads met up. They might have been united in their hatred of the USE, but family rivalries surfaced after a few pints.

– That was a lively one, wasn't it?

– It took me a week to recover, Fred said, the memory seeming to cause him pain as he winced and pulled a face. It was the Brains. I was younger as well, but still a lot older than the rest of you.

– Remember when we arrived?

– I was on the second coach.

Kenny shook his head in mock horror. It was ridiculous really, fighting among themselves like that, but it was the beer and the result, Kid Bale putting Gypsy Dai down in the fifth. They had lasted until near enough closing time, which wasn't bad, given some of the faces present. The local police had come in and made some arrests, but it was forgotten in the morning, everyone released without charge. It would have been a lot different if the Gendarmerie had been involved.

– Kid hasn't fought for ages, Fred mused.

– I heard he retired.

– It's for the best if he has. Some jobs you can go on doing forever, others have their natural span. Me, I'll never stop working.

Fred was one of the best cabinet makers in Wessex, but he was referring to his sideline in books. He made his living from the carpentry, had shown Kenny how to build his own shelves.

– Drink up, Kenny urged.

Landlord Tom had appeared.

– Where have you been? Kenny asked. We're dying of thirst round here. I know you've got your exotics to look after, don't want to overwater them and that, but we're not a load of camels.

– Don't you start. I've got Kid Bale and his mates round the other side.

– Fred told me. Pint of Kingdon please. Same again, Fred?

– Be rude not to. Thanks.

– Kid's brother's with him as well, Tom said, as he poured the first pint. You know Ted Bale don't you?

Kenny did know Ted, but in a different way to the others. He was another GB45 man, the same as Kid. Ted was a sergeant in the armed wing, while Kenny had less dangerous duties. He also knew that they were in Yeovil for a reason.

– He's retired, hasn't he? Kenny asked, shifting the emphasis. Kid I mean.

– He has, but none of that lot are turning pacifist. Still, it's good for business. They can certainly drink.

Tom passed Kenny's pint over and started on Fred's. A third of the Kingdon quickly disappeared. The landlord lowered his eyes.

– Did you hear about Chris Hobbs?

– No, Kenny replied, knowing by the tone that it wasn't going to be good news.

Wounded, tortured, butchered, clean-killed? Did he walk away from a failed ambush smiling; had the enemy snatched him off a street and hurried to a deserted factory so they could break his bones with iron bars and use drills on his joints; was his head hacked off by a sadist with a sword; or was he shot with a single shell to the heart?

– Blown to pieces outside Tehran.

Tom was direct, rarely showed emotion, but his voice quivered.

– Ted just told me. Seems it's all over InterZone. Slow-motion replays and a remastered soundtrack. He was in Birmingham this morning and it's on the Bull Ring floaters, mixers looping his death and playing it across the towers. Stirring people up. Brussels is offering counselling to Crats and the other plastics. They've been selling it as an attack on every European. Don't give a fuck about Chris or his family. Imagine his mum and dad seeing that?

They all knew the boy's parents and stood in silence thinking the same thing, that he should never have joined the European Army. He had been ostracised by a lot of the locals, even though he would never have had to serve against his own people. Kenny felt bad about the reaction, but it was inevitable. He hadn't known Chris well, but still felt terrible.

Fred's pint was placed on the bar. Kenny paid.

– I can't believe them showing his death like that, he said. Well, I can. Of course I can. It's the same as those slaughterhouse and abortion shows. They say they're being open and democratic, when all they're doing is tapping into the lowest sort of emotions. Zero respect. Reality? No. InterZone has desensitised people on the things that matter, made them concentrate on the trivia that doesn't.

– It's a disgrace, Fred half-shouted. A fucking disgrace.

Drinkers looked over, unaware of Chris Hobbs' death, only saw Fred's bright red face.

– What's wrong with us? he muttered. What's wrong with us as a species?

The landlord looked as if he was about to explode.

– Should never have enlisted. Near enough a traitor fighting for the Controllers like that – it has to be said. That's the way I feel. Liked him personally, don't get me wrong. What I knew of the boy...

Kenny and Fred agreed with Tom, but there were reasons for everything. The USE targeted poor lads with energy and ambition and nowhere to direct them. It reeled them in with work and a wage and the promise of adventure. It had always been the same, right through history, but with the old traditions and identities outlawed this felt different.

– I remember him as a youth. Served him in this pub. Told him what was what. But he never listened.

Kenny sipped at the Kingdon. His fight was with the USE's internal security forces – Hardcore bullies and the brains of Cool. It was important to focus on the real enemy, not a young man who lacked a political outlook and wanted a better life, someone who was essentially easygoing but had been manipulated by propaganda and grand promises. He was by no means alone.

– We can drink to him at least, Fred said. For his mother and father's loss. His brother and sister. For Chris himself. He was a decent lad.

Kenny lifted his pint high and let the cider do its job, loving the sensation on his tongue and the knowledge that it would relax his mood. Tom drank a double gin. There was silence as each man considered his thoughts. It was broken by the sound of Clive falling into the bar.

– Hello, hello, the big man said, reaching out to shake Kenny's and Fred's hands once he was steady.

His head was close to the ceiling and he had to remember to mind the beam.

– What do you want? Kenny asked.

– Pint of Guinness. Thomas taking ages pouring again?

Landlord Tom looked up at Clive and the flicker of a smile played across his chops.

– I know how to run a pub. Come here before you break that beam and bring the ceiling down.

Clive patted the top of his head which was still aching from his drunken dance three nights earlier. He glanced at the wood and frowned, sure for a moment that he could see some of his hair in the cracks. He'd nearly knocked himself out.

– Hold on a minute, my shoelaces have come undone.

He sat in the chair nearest the fire, stretching for soggy grey straps, dirty but returning to an off-white as they were dragged along the frosty pavements. Kenny saw a trail on the floor, followed the line to the door, pictured a snail with a shell on its back. The stout was placed on the bar and Kenny nodded at the Kingdon pump.

– I don't know why they always come undone, Clive fussed. Every day it's the same. Ten times. Sometimes more, sometimes less. Been like this all my life.

– Needs a double bow, Fred said. I've told you before.

– But then I can't get them off. Try undoing two or three bows. It turns into a knot.

– That's as bad, Fred admitted. But a good bow is easier.

Clive was ready to topple over as he reached further forward, Kenny placing a hand on his shoulder to steady him while he worked.

– Thanks, mate. I do them tight enough, but they never stay fixed.

– One loop isn't going to hold.

– But what happens if I fall in a pond?

The conversation was following a familiar path.

– You won't though, will you? Kenny replied.

– I could. Can you say that I will never ever fall into a pond? Or a lake? A river? Honestly, Ken, can you swear that I'm not going to end up in the water one day?

Kenny shook his head, knew that he couldn't argue with the logic, realised Clive wasn't looking.

– No, I can't, but would it matter?

– If I couldn't get my shoes off they would pull me down and I'd drown. I saw it happen in a film. It's the weight of the water, it gets into the material and your socks as well, makes your feet heavy so you can't kick properly. Then you panic and your lungs fill up. I wouldn't want to die like that.

– You buy light shoes, don't you?

– I do, yes. I'm always ready. You know me...

– I could take my shoes and socks off right now, Kenny admitted. Warm my feet in front of the fire. The cold gets into your bones.

His cider was placed on the bar.

– Do you take Confederate money? he predictably asked, having forgotten to use this one-liner before.

– Thought you'd never ask. I prefer it to Yankee dollars.

Two currencies operated across Britain – physical pounds in the free areas, digital euros in those under full USE control. There were some crossovers, as working for any of the larger firms involved automatic membership of Troika, which managed all earnings, credit/debt and purchases.

Kenny drained a third of this second Kingdon. He fancied a session, but had things to do in the morning. It would be wrong as well, seeing as someone they knew had just died. People forgot so easily. He was the same.

– You've done it now, Fred said to Kenny, who followed his eyes.

Clive was pulling at the laces he had just tied, his other foot bare. He took the shoe and then the sock off, carefully positioning his footwear near the fire to dry, then leaned back in the chair and pointed his soles at the heat.

– That feels fantastic, Clive laughed. Pass me my pint will you, Ken?

Kenny picked up the Guinness and handed it over.

– Thanks. I'll put it on the table here for a minute.

Clive eased further back and closed his eyes like he was going to have a nap. Nobody in the bar minded. There were no winks and no smirks, but Kenny guessed that was because he was known for his eccentricities, and he thought back to the playground and how Clive had been bullied for a while, but the memory was vague and he couldn't remember when or how it had ended. Kenny took the few steps back to stand by Fred and looked down at his bag, automatically checking that it was still there, picturing the inside with its padding and lining a tailor had added, a crimson that seemed to explode outwards when the zip was undone. He tried to remember the name of the lady who had done the work, but that was also out of range.

– We should get some flowers for the Hobbs family, Tom said.

Kenny nodded, putting his glass and hands on the bar and looking into the Kingdon, pushing the faces of Chris and then Clive away, thinking about the cruelty of humans, the petty hatreds and lies, and he could feel his mood sinking, and it was no surprise really, because he had a lot on his mind. He had another mouthful of cider and felt better.

– Hello Kenny, Ronnie said, arriving in a rush.

Tom's expression immediately changed. They were roughly the same age, but she had a bubbly personality and was a smart dresser in comparison, and the landlord's face seemed to be melting and reshaping, as if he was suddenly younger and happier.

– We're missing you around the other side, she said to Tom.

Kenny wanted to take the piss, but the landlord was clearly sensitive despite his bluff exterior, and he was blushing as well, so decided to let him off.

– Better go round, Tom said, starting after his barmaid. We've got The Winstanleys on in a while.

– Speak of the devil, Fred said, looking towards the window.

The light dipped as three black shapes passed, killing the frosty glow filling the glass. He felt a stab in his chest, the light quickly returning as the men entered the pub. The first of three musicians passed the entrance to their bar as they made their way towards the main room.

– What do you think? Fred asked, now that Tom was gone. Is he in love with Ronnie or not?

– It would do him good. Must be lonely sometimes, being on his own.

He immediately wished he hadn't said that, but Fred didn't seem to notice.

– I reckon he might be in love, Kenny quickly added. Yes, I think he might.

Clive yawned, stood up and banged his head on the beam, rubbed it and ambled over to the table where the Stevens men sat, Kevin inviting him to join them. Kenny turned and pressed his hands on the counter again, inspecting the pumps, glasses, bottles, wood panels. He was happy enough listening to Fred as he went into a detailed description of a job he was about to start, talking about the nature of timber and the qualities of specific woods, Kenny looking for the grain under his palms, feeling the smoothness of the finish. The bar was well polished and he noticed the smell for the first time, thought about how the horse brasses seemed to shine brighter than before and wondered if it was down to Ronnie.

– If you plan the job out, like I've shown you, then it all fits together. Like a lot of things. Once the shelves are up I like to take my time with the varnish, adding thin layers and letting each one dry and harden before putting the next one on. The end result is worth the time spent. Lasts longer. You have to stay on it Kenny boy. No good getting impatient.

Jan was always telling him the same thing. His moods had been shifting these last few weeks and the sadness returned. Life was short. He didn't like to think of her being left on her own, couldn't imagine how the Hobbs family must be feeling. Jan had been sitting at that battered old desk he'd bought more than a decade earlier when he left the house. Fred had mended the areas that needed doing, told him how to strip and revarnish the wood, but he never had. Strangers had sat at it long before he found it in a junk shop, and he liked the idea of it having its own private history. Fred tapped Kenny on the shoulder to emphasise a point.

– It was the same with my dad's old man. My grandfather. Habits can skip a generation. Or you might want something different to your parents. But they were the same, and there's only so many possibilities I suppose. You can end up at square one. I think life just repeats itself. Over and over again. We try to remember the lessons, but they're soon forgotten. It's worse now, of course.

Fred was on a roll, drunk but making sense, even if Kenny had lost the thread. The older man was cajoling and confiding, at least until the music started next door and Kenny picked up the bag and led the way through. It was Sunday night so the place was busy. They arrived as a version of a traditional Conflict number was starting, those present singing along to the chorus.

– Where have you been hiding? Kid Bale shouted in Kenny's ear. What do you want?

Two more pints of Kingdon followed. The three men turned to watch the band.

– How are you feeling? Kid asked, coming in close.

– I'm feeling good, Kenny replied. Very good.

He meant it as well. Kid Bale folded his arms and was satisfied. Three songs passed in rapid succession before lead singer Trina Bowles announced a brief pause to mend a string.

– Trina's beautiful, isn't she? Clive said.

He had come in and was standing behind them.

– Gorgeous, Kid Bale replied, looking up at the man.

– It's the anniversary of our fight, then? Clive said, raising an enormous fist.

Kid seemed confused and then suspicious, while Kenny and Fred exchanged nervous glances.

– The punch-up we had at school. I heard someone say it was the anniversary. That's why you're here, isn't it? You could've invited me.

74

– It's another fight. You showed me how to punch, though, didn't you?

– You started it, Clive said, without animosity, wrapping a childish arm around the hardman's shoulders.

– I did indeed, Kid Bale agreed, looking sheepish. And you finished it. I deserved what I got. It stopped me turning into a bully.

Trina tapped the microphone.

– One, two, three, four... she shouted, before launching into 'Babel Tower Burning'.

The pub sang along to the chorus, the songs following in rapid bursts before slowing for 'The Ballad Of Billy Singh', dedicated to the GB45 fighter who had launched a single-handed assault on a Cool unit eleven years earlier, killing six of them in the process. Labelled the Southall Massacre by the USE, the reprisals had been swift and brutal and blamed on racist rebels. The tragedy was that Billy had been taken alive and, according to information seeped by Cool, died two years later at the notorious Cuddles HQ on Prinz-Albrecht-Strasse. This was followed by the more frenetic 'Fuck Brussels (And Fuck Berlin Too)'.

Kenny could easily have stayed drinking until the pub closed, but he had a busy day coming up and wanted a clear head in the morning. After one more pint he said his goodbyes and left, Fred keen to stay and Clive promising to make sure he made it home safely. As soon as Kenny walked out of The Wheatsheaf the cold hit him, driving into his eyes and ears. He stopped and looked across the same scene as before, the frost thicker and more fluffy, turned to see that the ice had spread halfway over the windows of the pub. He moved nearer and peered inside. Silhouettes stood at the bar, their movements vague, conversation muffled and broken by laughter.

He was on his own out here. Without protection. Saw himself there a little earlier with Fred, lost in their interests, the sort of obsessions that kept people going, and maybe none of it mattered, there was no way small men like them could ever beat the system, but then he felt the bag of books on his shoulder and was strong. He started walking. Jan was waiting for him. The street was thick with frost and it crunched noisily under his feet.

Kenny kept adjusting the bag, thinking now about what was inside, looking forward to returning to his cosy little house and undoing the zip and removing the books. He would take his time and enjoy the experience, hold each one up to his nose and flick the pages, take in the smell of the paper, watch words flash past in their thousands. He would then check the state of them, always slightly worried but never let down. Fred was a stickler. His gradings were spot on.

He walked on through curtained houses and closed shops, turned off the bigger street and followed another path towards the green, his way home taking him past the pond and All Souls church, the temptations offered by Peanut Paul Harrison. He could smell food. Coming into the open, there across a sheet of white grass was Paul's van. It was surrounded by a patch of clear lawn. He was suddenly very hungry. It was impossible not to stop. He always did.

– All right, Kenny?

Peanut Paul stood in the back of his mobile caff with the counter down, grille and hotplate allowing him to wear one of his famous short-sleeved Hawaiian shirts. The heat coming off a nearby steel drum added to the summertime feel. There were two white-metal garden tables set out for his customers, four matching chairs at each one. Kenny stepped into the tropics, skin tingling even more so than in the pub. This was another sanctuary. Paul had arranged an orange plastic pot with a tall bamboo between the tables. Kenny was reminded of the Brass Bar in The Wheatsheaf, the tropical flavours, a commons love of exotics, succulents and alpines. Light fanned out from the van and each table had its own lamp.

– You need a mug of hot chocolate. Freezing your bollocks off, you are.

– Tell you what, even walking from the pub to here has let the cold into my veins.

– It's going to be warmer tomorrow.

– Hope so.

– No Jan tonight?

– She's at home, but I'll sit here for a while. Maybe take her something back.

– What do you want? Beanburger? Pasty? Mushroom curry?

– Burger and chips, please.

Kenny knew what was coming next and tried not to smile.

– Peanut sauce on that?

– Of course. I could smell it a mile off. Makes me hungry as soon as it hits my nose. Best satay sauce in the world. I can't get home without you mugging me on the way.

He controlled his expression, tried to force the glint out of his eyes as the peanut king zoomed in. It was the same exchange every time. A standing joke among Paul's punters, it was one they kept to themselves as everyone wanted the sauce and a generous helping as well.

– Special recipe, isn't it, Paul Harrison said, satisfied with Kenny's intentions. Best satay sauce in Wessex, but I can't say about the rest of the world. Secret ingredient. You have your peanuts, soya sauce, coconut milk, chilli. Must use the right quantities. That's essential. Different strengths for different chefs. Then there's the hidden extra for that extra magic. That's my dream, to go to Indonesia one day. Sumatra, Java, Bali – I don't mind. Maybe all three.

Kenny's mouth was watering and the menu showed he was spoiled for choice. Paul knew his business and was stocked up ready for a feast, which seemed odd, seeing as it was a Sunday.

– The Winstanleys are playing, he said. I'll have twenty people down here in an hour or so.

– You're right. Just been in the pub and it's packed.

Paul rubbed his hands.

– Life is good. These drums are a godsend this time of year. Best get on. One beanburger on its way.

He turned his back and hunched over a surface, hands moving fast, and Kenny knew not to interrupt him while he was at work. Instead he found himself comparing the neat row of ketchup, mustard, curry sauce, sweet chilli, mayo, brown sauce and cranberry containers to the glasses in The Wheatsheaf. Jars of chutney and pickle to bottles of whisky and gin. It was the way they had been chosen and neatly arranged. This was more than a takeaway, the vintage Transit customised by the Canning sisters down on the South Coast, a new engine added. It was Paul's empire when he was on the road, the bodywork decorated with dolphins and mermaids. He used it when he went surfing in Cornwall, had beds built in and could remove the cooker if he wanted. It was why he kept it so clean when he was using it to sell food. Maybe they'd bump into him when they went to pick up *May Day*.

Kenny walked to the drum and warmed his hands. The wood inside creaked as it burned, the smell different to the coal fire in the pub, and he thought of those American movies where the homeless gathered in the slums of Detroit and Chicago, ragged men with long beards and women pushing trolleys, talking in tongues. He was a lucky bloke in comparison, standing in an arc of light and heat in an English town, with friends he met in a local pub and Jan at home, and yet when he looked over at All Souls he felt totally alone.

Once his food was ready, Kenny sat at a table. The metal was warm when he touched it, free from frost and ice, and he was soon digging into his burger, giving a watching Peanut Paul Harrison the thumbs-up, marvelling at the taste of the satay sauce which really was fantastic. As he ate he returned to the outline of All Souls, a church that a few years back was rundown and neglected, the graveyard maintained by volunteers. The gates where local victims of the First German War were remembered had always been kept in the best condition, along with a monument to the dead of the Second, at least until a couple of lowlife thieves stole the metal and damaged the plaques. Free English had tracked them down, the youths claiming they'd been paid by a Romanian scrap-metal boss operating out of Swindon. The plaques were long gone and those responsible had been punished, promised that if there was a next time they would be shot. It wasn't difficult to guess that Cool was behind the theft. Similar incidents had been reported from villages and towns across the Continent. War denial was USE policy.

The air was very still, as if it too was freezing, the small world of Kenny Jackson silent except for the hum of the van's generator and a cackle from the drum. He looked into the sky. It was said that there were times, when the conditions were right, that it was possible to see the outline of Michele, one half of the InterZone fantasy. It was a quirk of technology, but miraculous in its way, the invisible briefly visible. A ghost of the machine. Hans was dominant, hidden deeper in cyberspace.

None of that corporate bullshit mattered. It was about perception, and he thought in different ways to those forced to live under USE rule, ordinary people just trying to get on with their lives. They had no power. Many didn't seem to care. Maybe they were right. He didn't want to die and leave Jan on her own. He really wanted to live a long life.

SEVEN

RUPERT FELT SLENDER fingers on his shoulders, sensors delivering the massage that would ease him into the coming day. Raising a wand, he increased the pressure a little. Lights eased to his ideal setting and he sat up in his bed, eyes still closed, took a few seconds to realise it was Monday. He was tired and started to doze off, the fingers delivering a tiny shock, urging him to rise and shine. He took a deep breath and pushed the fur from his body, stood and slipped into his polar gown, wandered over to his VoyBox. Rupert felt no fear of fog as he neared the glass, his confidence rewarded with a crystal-clear view of Pearly Tower. The sight never failed to thrill.

Pearly was greeting the dawn in fine style. Scales streamed as orange currents laced with slivers of deep red. Gold stars circled metres from the summit. The spectacle seemed even more magnificent than usual. The tower could almost be a living entity, which was impossible, but the idea brought tears to Rupert's eyes. He brushed them away with the ball of his hand, reflecting on his show of emotion, deciding it signalled love and devotion. The realisation changed the direction of his mood. He felt sensational. But even these discoveries could not explain why he was experiencing such an almighty high. Every morning he was eager to get into the office and start work, and after a day away this yearning doubled or even tripled. Again, this couldn't explain his near-ecstatic state.

Rupert sat in his VoyBox for several minutes, focused on the Pearly penthouse, right hand inside his boxers cradling Ron's aching balls, and while Polestar added porno flashbacks, it wasn't even the physicals responsible for his joy. He continued to muse.

She had been more than worth the transfer of credit, value achieved and the pumping recorded for replays, but their long conversations had been the crux of the collaboration. She had listened as he spoke, absorbed his knowledge and ambition in an exciting manner, genuinely believed that he was Controller material. He felt special, imagined he was at the top of Pearly right now, reaping rewards, looking down at Bethnal Plaza and watching the Crats strolling, one or two rushing. These were lazies. The slackers. He saw the time and hurried from his VoyBox.

Inside thirty minutes Rupert had washed and dressed, left his apartment, crossed Bethnal, journeyed on escalators, surfed his Palm as he rode the Overground, admired a T that urged *Be Yourself*, hummed along to a Saviles mix of 'Sugar Baby Love', was under the Westminster domes when a breaking story stopped his progress. It was being reported that subhumans had infiltrated the East Side Gates. He stretched his Palm screen. Six birds were on the rampage. Images were relayed. He zoomed and saw sparrows in close-up. Dirty vermin. Infectious feathers. A shudder ran through his body.

How had they gained access? He thought of the fog. Did it link to the sparrows? The domes had clearly been breached. Was this deliberate or accidental? Nobody sane would have invited the birds inside. That he knew. They had clearly seen an opening and sneaked in. There were health and safety issues to consider. These subs had beaks. Loved to wee and poo without restraint. If they were left to breed there would be nests, eggs, flocks. The East Side was at risk, but the reporter involved said the danger would be nullified within the hour. A specialist had been called in. The man then starred in a ten-second promo *Dan Dann, The Bird Killing Man*. Everyone could relax. The invasion would soon be over. Rupert was relieved. He continued walking.

Leaving the elevator and turning towards his desk, Super Kat emerged from her office and fell into step. She was even more cheerful than usual, again showing an interest in the Crat as she asked about his R&R.

– A fine Funday, Rupert? she enquired.

– Brilliant. I partied hard with a girl straight out of Free Libya.

– The dancer Polestar?

– Yes, he said, a little surprised, although there was no reason why she shouldn't know who he had met.

InterZone existed to bond the population, and an excess attachment to privacy was suspect. Rupert was beyond suspicion.

– Do you know her? he asked.

– I have seen glamours in which she has appeared. A very randy date.

The best sexers often appeared in movies. He was interested to learn that Polestar was an actor, wondered what sort of storyline she preferred. Perhaps he would peep her on InterZone later. He could merge his amateur digitals with her more professional sessions. The surprise he had first experienced must have shown on his face.

– Are you okay, Rupert? his Super asked, placing a hand on his arm and softly squeezing. Is everything still brill?

He flinched, but kept it internal, didn't want to appear nervous, worse still cause offence, but was again surprised, this time by her touch, which was out of character, even if it showed that she rated him as one of her best Crats. It was a fair call. He was a class act and Kat Romero was lucky to have him on the team. She was highly professional and deserved her rank and benefits, would never have reached her current position if she wasn't a good judge of character. She could see the future legends. Rupert was grateful for her support, but knew that one day he would overtake her on his trip to the stars.

– I really do feel fantastic, he said. It was important to let my hair down, act a little crazy, take chances. My energy levels are high.

– You are extremely dedicated.

He realised that they had stopped walking. Big Ben was visible behind Super Kat's left shoulder, and while advertisements popped on its surface and life was perfect under the domes, he must always remember that beyond Central and the Gates there was a dirty metropolis that needed bleaching. He had never been into the regions beyond the Reading Line, at least not in the physical, and by the time it was extended and Good Europeans were needed there he would be back in Heartland.

– I am impressed by your dedication, Rupert. Your desire to progress. I hope we can work together for many years.

He wondered if Kat Romero was keeping more detailed reports on him than was the norm, if she had taken a personal interest in his career. He knew that this was sometimes the case. A superior often saw elements of themselves in a younger Crat, did their best to encourage their ambition, but in a subtle, unseen way. He had read about these special relationships. They showed the value of community. Spotting a rising star brought rewards and was encouraged. If this was the case with Super Kat, then he was flattered, but it wasn't essential, as his success was assured. Just as long as he got on with his work and didn't stand around gassing.

– I *am* dedicated, and the sensation makes me incredibly happy sometimes.

Kat Romero tilted her head.

– Sometimes?

Rupert returned the tilt.

– At other times I am ecstatic. My life is sweet.

Her right hand stretched towards his face and he felt the faintest touch of nails on his left cheek, seemed to recall that she had touched him before, but from the side, back when he wasn't expecting it, pressure on his arm that was different to the sensors coaxing him to wakey-wakey, more a squeeze than a massage, the current action reassuring but firm, and for some reason he thought of Polestar and Super Kat scratching at his flesh, ripping into his features.

– That incident the other day...

Rupert was lost.

– Incident?

– The actor destined for Hollywood.

– Polestar?

– She's hardly going to Hollywood, Rupert. A fine glamour, some good fucky-fucky and sucky-sucky scenes, but perhaps not A-list? There would be permit problems.

Super Kat was shaking her head, obviously thought he had been joking. He tried to understand what she wanted. She was keeping him from his graft.

– I meant that other actor. The one with the noose around her neck. A brilliant amateur. Has the potential to become a professional.

Rupert tried to focus. For a few seconds he was back in his apartment, inhaling his date's perfume, running hands over the flesh, hearing her voice, and yet he hadn't retained much of what she had said, her conversation a series of questions and prompts. He had done most of the talking, needed to repeat and share. It was a special day. He had talked and talked and now he was mute.

– Are you sure you're healthy? Super Kat asked. What is the matter?

Rupert Ronsberger recovered.

– Of course. I am brilliant.

– You aren't worried about anything you might have seen or heard?

– I never worry. I am confident and certain of the future. We will convince the doubters. Find the bads and ask them to discuss things with Cool.

His Super beamed and removed her hand, stepped back and nodded, showing Rupert that he should continue to his desk, and as he left her and walked along the corridor, noticing yet-to-be-filled desks and colleagues arriving via the elevator, following him into the fray, he felt strong and determined and excited about the cases to come. He couldn't help regretting the minute or more lost to cheery conversation, but reminded himself that he should never be selfish, that if a Good Euro wanted to chat then he must make space in his schedule. It was a positive that he was seen as approachable.

Sitting at his terminal, Rupert waited for Himmler to clear a path, heard a rattle and turned to see Gio arriving in his usual bumbling manner, carrying a tray from the floor's franchise, placing it on the surface next to his pal. There was coffee and muffins for two. Rupert was nervous that he was going to consume more valuable time. At least Himmler was in operation.

– Here you are, Gio said, standing over Rupert.

– Thank you. That is very kind. What is the occasion?

– I have been promoted to B+, so we are true brothers.

Rupert felt a pang of annoyance, but smiled broadly. There was no way Giovanni was on his level, although the man was a couple of years older so in theory should be pushing for Techno, but even so...

– Your cappuccino is the one nearest you. I asked them to sprinkle extra chocolate. I know what you like. The muffins are blueberry.

Rupert arranged his food and drink, and hoped his friend would leave, but instead Gio lingered and he couldn't stop his irritation building. He knew that his friend was conformist and honest, but he did question his commitment, as there were many occasions when this newly promoted Bureau left dead on time while Rupert added extra hours. His concentration levels were inferior and there had been signs of uncertainty when it came to changes in language. But Rupert was a generous colleague. He controlled himself.

– So, tell me, Gio said. How was Polestar?

Rupert pictured her eyes shining as she lay naked on his bed, absorbing his wise words while she masturbated, sharing his dreams and ideals. The State was spreading the best values, fighting for choice and expression, and with Gio standing opposite, leering and winking, he realised that because she came from such a savage part of the world her love of the project was more profound than he had imagined. She was a novice, like he had been as a boy, and yet he had always been protected while Polestar had lived as a primitive. His respect for her grew. She was keen to believe and he was her guru. That was the truth. She grasped the need for unity, knew that security and wealth came at a price, and her under-standing was always going to be deeper and more profound than that of his fellow Crats. This level of belief could be the key to Controllerhood. He no longer cared about Gio's promotion.

– You did meet her, didn't you?

– Yes, I did, Rupert replied. An interesting lady.

– Interesting, yes... A good description. I hope she danced for you, used that pole that connects to floor and ceiling, a retro design, improved for current consumption, a beam of light rather than hard steel. The energy pack in her handbag is barely noticeable. First the dance and then a session to follow. Very nice.

Giovanni was snickering. Rupert ignored his chum.

– I dropped a bomb and got my credit's worth, Gio continued.

Rupert was annoyed at Rocket Ron for thinking this way, or had he done so as well? Rupert and Rocket, Ronsberger and Ronald...

– She has a love of bondage, that one. Her handbag is large and deep. She carries novelties. I was in excellent form, believe me. Oh yes. Have you watched the pornos I pinged? Patch some of yours with mine and we can upload.

Gio was laughing hard, on the verge of spilling coffee from the mug he held, and Rupert felt deflated, shocked he was experiencing something near to jealousy, wondered why Polestar hadn't brought out her pole, but then he remembered that it was another date, someone who had seen a chance to approach a Crat she admired. Gio was talking about a different person.

Rupert joined in the laughter, rocking on his chair, taking over from Gio who quickly calmed and felt his own stab of annoyance. Polestar must have been better than he recalled for the oh-so-serious Ronsberger to express such joy. How could an everyday sexer have such an effect? No, it didn't make sense. Maybe he had underestimated the woman.

– Best get to work, Giovanni said, glad to be on his way.

– Thanks for the refreshments, Rupert called, spinning back to his desk just as Himmler ended a preliminary interrogation.

The first case of the day involved a commons recorded abusing a pedo on a suburban train. She was clearly a descendant of the cockneys who had once ruled London, the remains of these families surviving on the margins of the city. The tribe had been known for its violence and the taint lived on. The lowers often travelled the Underground in silence, heads bowed and eyes closed, breathing deeply, wary of making mistakes that might see them challenged. Surveillance maintained order. When every millimetre of the USE was thinking correctly, the quiet would be replaced by free-flowing conversation.

This woman did not care. She was openly mocking him with her lack of respect for State-run eyes and ears. The bigot was staring at the man opposite in hostile fashion. He was well-dressed and mannered, sitting with a girl in school uniform, a hand resting on her knee. Known as the Nippon Deal, and in accordance with Japanese business tradition, a respectable nonce would approach a child with offers of sweets in return for mild petting. If the relationship was consensual, other exchanges followed. Rupert noted the high heels and make-up worn by the girl, zoomed in and confirmed a Saviles logo. The eyes of the child were yellow, but a lighter shade than those of Polestar. The scene seemed harmless, but other passengers were displaying similar expressions of anger, turning their heads as commons did when they did not agree but were clever enough not to challenge InterZone. This cockney was different. Perhaps she had been drinking alcohol or ingesting narcotics, both of these problems in the suburban wastes.

Rupert waved a finger and snapped back, found the moment when the woman – who Himmler was identifying as Sarah Rodgers – first joined the Underground at Gallows Hill, part of the Uxbridge Loop that included barrios such as Iver Heath, Black Park Estate, George's Green, Britwell New Town, Slough Central and Slough East, Langley Manor, West Drayton and Cowley Bricks. Given the location, Rupert deduced that she was a speedhead, her rapid motions seeming to confirm his expert assessment.

The abuse began immediately Rodgers joined the carriage. He tapped Himmler, who named the pedo as Christopher Brown, a professional who had strayed outside his Gate. Why was the suited nonce so far from home? The child was the key, H springing back into action – Lucy Bates, an InterZone scholar from South Ruislip. Where were they heading? There had to be an attraction in their destination. The river at Maidenhead? But why risk torment on the Underground? Maybe Chris was naive? But first things first. Rupert drew on his experience, exploring patterns of behaviour. He froze the imagery where Rodgers stood and pointed a finger at poor Christopher and an embarrassed Lucy. The Crat reached for his capp and rolled back.

It tasted great and Gio's gesture was generous. He had seemed sad when he left, Rupert wondering if there was jealousy involved. Reaching for his muffin, he broke a chunk off and popped it in his mouth, the taste of blueberry laced with a hint of pork. He would see if Gio wanted to go for a bite to eat later. They could hop a couple of Central bars and munch sushi. The Japanese angle was in his head. There were plenty of dates to be found along Lisle Street. Mature ladies. Painted faces. Africans and Asians, but no Nips.

Having finished his refreshments, he recycled and went to the restroom to wash his hands. Having adjusted his appearance in a mirror, he was about to return to work when Super Kat came in, patting his shoulder as she continued to a cubicle. She paused at the door and looked back, her tongue emerging and running along designer lips. He was sure he spied a familiar snake tattoo, but knew it couldn't be, as he would have noticed it before. He was soon engrossed in his case.

It turned out that Chris was a popular InterZoner, with plenty of close friends and a member of several communities. He was a Good Euro, a success in business, with no errors to his name. His credit records showed that he used a hotel in Maidenhead that specialised in pedo scenarios, with rooms tagged Class, Playground and Nursery. It made sense, though his choice of transport did not. He would have to change at Slough Central to reach his destination, so there was probably a masochistic element to his personality.

Rupert was on the trail, discovered that Chris had been attacked three times before, part of a group that fantasised about rough young commons and went looking for trouble. Everything was legal and above board, with no hint of coercion. Foundations in place, it was time to deal with the crime.

Rupert played the rest of the recording, Rodgers jabbing her finger viciously at Chris, denting his chest before balling her hand into a brutal weapon and punching him in the face. The child said nothing, merely looked out through the window, as if removed from the situation. Himmler jumped in with a profile of the girl, which described her as coming from a one-parent family of poor credit and discipline. Clearly the child needed funds and a sense of self-worth as academically she was a low achiever. Who was Rodgers to deny her the chance to stand on her own two feet? He stopped the action, went back and played the scene again to be clear, adding volume to the show.

Rodgers was spewing poison and using the incorrect term 'pervert'. She screamed that Chris was a predator, as if this was illegal, that the girl was clearly drugged. Rupert took note of this accusation, but had to be cautious. If he acted negatively against a paedophile it could come back to haunt him. It might even ruin his career. The rights of minorities were important. Allegations of phobia could be hard to shake off. He zoomed the child, who appeared tired and unfocused, but had clearly made an effort with her appearance. Everything seemed in order and he returned to Rodgers. She said that the 'Free English' would have killed him if they were on the train. Rupert shook his head.

The rant continued and more punches followed. Chris cowered in his seat, snivelling but grinning, Rodgers' fist small and tight. He was a big man, dwarfed the child and his attacker, and when the cockney kicked him hard in the shin he reacted. He stood and pushed her back into her seat. This was clearly a justified defence, but other commons stood to intervene, a youth moving down the carriage and about to add to the assault when he remembered that he was being watched. He backed off, but Rupert could see clear intent there, and in other people present, and once he had made a decision on Rodgers he would investigate them also. This sort of behaviour was unacceptable.

Chris tended his wounds, a white kerchief quickly soaked in blood. He became alarmed and left the train at the next stop, records showing that he called Gendarmerie and visited his doctor. Lucy Bates stayed behind, alone and unprotected.

It was a straightforward if disturbing case and Rupert would no doubt be passing it to Cool, but he would remain open-minded for a while yet. He called Hound Dog, as it was time to peep on Sarah Rodgers, delve into her home and life, past crimes and future intentions, as someone like this would have many secrets. Mention of Free English killers was a serious matter. Terrorism could never be discounted, though he knew she was trying to impress. The rebels were little more than a rabble.

The boys and girls of Cool would decide how best to help this sad woman, but before he released his canine pal he opened separate cases, replayed the moment when Chris stood to defend himself and other passengers reacted. Several males and two females were detached, each one now a focus of his attention. This was turning into a major incident and Rupert had the scent. He would deal with these perps once he was finished with Rodgers. Intention was clear and thought had to be policed. He was excited by the challenges ahead. His day kept on improving.

EIGHT

HORACE STARSKI STOOD by the main window of his London penthouse and peered into the world below. The super-thin glass was also super-strong, reinforced and loaded with Peep, the latest upgrade on the fading VoyBox series. Access to prerelease tech was one of the perks of being a Controller, and for a Brussels man the possibilities were extreme.

Greater London was at least three years behind the major Heartland cities, despite the arrival of so many standard-raising Crats, and lifting his head he zoomed beyond the immediate beauty of the East Side and out towards the M25. There were skills in Peep that raised it far above Hound Dog, the best sniffer currently available to Crats. In seconds he could be on Southend Pier, walking with the day-trippers instead of just watching them, but he didn't want to stray into the seaside shanties of the English. The lights of Blackpool flickered, but he turned them off.

Country commons clung to their myths – winding lanes and uneven hedgerows, boring cricket matches on greens lined with rancid thatch, happy to refuel on unhealthy beer and pies, some even maintaining allotments when they could buy cleaner, near-identical vegetables at a hypermarket. This refusal to change had limited the spread of more progressive values, but eventually the shires would be brought into the modern day. The USE kept pressing, offering friendship, playing its long-term game. Rejection would not be forgotten. Insults had been stored. The removal of Englishness was inevitable. Welsh, Scottish and Irish rebels would go the same way. Yet despite Cool attempts to create infighting, the British resistance was united. For the moment at least. Victory was assured. The USE always achieved its goals. The timescale did not matter. It had been this way since the start. London was already so different to the city he had first known.

Leaving the protected areas to walk its mean streets, he had been fearless in those days. He was a young man with a love of time-tables exploring the Underground. He found the common English unsophisticated, some of them stupid even, but he was honest enough to see that they had an energy his colleagues lacked. As an experiment he had compared short-term pleasures to long-term gain, listening to aggressive music and sampling beer in rough pubs. The women were sexy in a trashy way, their appeal owing little to wealth or social standing or the sexual expertise that came out of the rehabilitation centres of Free Libya and the Bangkok Exchange. While studying temptation, he had stayed loyal to some simple truths. Discipline led to success. Emotion was a weakness. Controller Horace felt sick.

There were more immediate issues to consider. The case of the six sparrows roaming the East Side for instance. A barbecue team had supplied the birds live for roasting, but when he arrived from Brussels and found them waiting in his apartment he had suddenly decided to set the creatures free. The odds were against these flappers, but he was interested to see if they could find a way out of the domes. Fog had been allowed to filter through as a treat, one that had been agreed with his Controller pals, but the sparrows were a secret extra and had turned into the main event. He was keen to see the reaction of those living inside the Gates. Part of him hoped they would escape and fly far away, the other part wanted to see them dead.

Peep clinked. His favourite Crat was leaving one of the towers below. Having an apartment in a top location such as Pearly was the dream of every Bureau and Techno, proximity to the right addresses the next best option. Horace Starski wanded and watched Peep suck the scene in, forwarding and predicting, playing out scenarios. He saw the possibles for exactly a minute before crossing to the terrace doors and going outside. The extension was an in/out, the set-up easily adjusted, shell peeling if asked politely. It was in place at the moment, allowing him to proceed to the edge without danger of a fall. This mini-dome beat according to his steps, a small mimic of the huge curves protecting the Gates. The sparrows were out there and he wondered what they made of Scales! and its salty scent. Peep was up to speed and he reached for his Toms, placed the goggles over his eyes and was instantly walking along next to the B+, loving the full body-popping, down-on-the-streets experience.

Horace Starski was pondering a physical visit to a commons area, but wasn't decided, had a busy schedule, though once his chores were complete he might well wander. He placed a hand on his chest, felt for the tick of his heart, pictured illuminations and circling gulls, a stab of nostalgia telling him that it was something he *had* to do. Realising the hand was the one carrying his Palm he removed it quickly, but for no good reason. Being a Controller, it was different to those built into Crats and other Good Euros. He had no internals and so was beyond Sus, and while some simple surveillance had to be confronted, he was free of monitoring. He was at one with Hans and his soulmate Michele. After all, if a Controller couldn't be trusted, who could?

Controllers had to respond, consider, originate, encourage and fine-tune the system, but they also needed to inspire faith. To this end, absolute power was required. The mass of people working for the USE relied on rules and wanted to follow orders, so stronger men and women were needed to make sacrifices and take on the burden of leadership. Errors could occur, and there had been excesses, while the security services were occasionally too firm. But the system worked perfectly. What the masses didn't know could not hurt them. If nobody knew then it followed that nobody cared. If nobody knew or cared it meant that the event had not occurred. New Democracy was worth a degree of flexibility. Relaxed thinking, while discouraged in the Crat ranks, was the hard-earned right of a Controller.

Horace Starski could smell coffee and chocolate. Sizzling bacon. He moved as an invisible, a great helmsman, part of the machine but beyond its control, guiding developments, able to do whatever he wanted. His morals were solid and he would never abuse his power. The Controller was pleased to be with his people, dipping into Crat conversations – reassuring chats about train times, the merits of a Mango promotion, a lower than expected rise in the InterZone tax. The smell of bacon was replaced by a rush of deodorants and perfumes as the Bureaus and Technos converged, lines swelling as they marched towards the main station, the best young minds in Europe narrowing into a tight column, various levels mingling without pushing, showing respect for their chums.

Controller Horace would have been crushed in a physical situation, but he held it against no person present as he couldn't be seen and, in the truest of respects, still had his head in the clouds. This open-minded approach to his fellows meant he carried no grudges and could concentrate on riding the escalator. Once on the Overground platform there was a three-minute wait until the next train arrived, and this gave him the chance to study the Crats in full stillness. They blinked and moved muscles in their faces and stared ahead and glanced sideways and smiled politely, some talking quietly in ones and twos and threes, while most of the rest had unplugged InterZone feeds and were preparing for the important tasks ahead. Building concentration. Using State-taught relaxation techniques to achieve serenity. And being around these youngsters filled the Controller with hope for the future. If he had been visible, their reactions would be different, admiration and even awe breaking into the calm. He was happy to remain anonymous.

Peep provided an intimacy other technologies could not, and he thought of the humble Hound Dog and the way Crats customised their barkers, which could become disobedient in certain situations. But in a year or so everyone would be drooling over Peep, moving credit to reward its inventors and manufacturers and backers, while he would have risen to higher levels. There was always another exciting upgrade imminent. He was at the cutting edge of tech. These products had to be legalised, and it was the Controllers who managed the means. They were well paid, as was correct, and on top of this he had made a fortune from Scales! If that human-chimp hybrid took off, well...

He realised he was humming along to a tune, but wasn't sure of the title, smiled as he saw feet faintly tapping, at least half the men present reaching into inside pockets of jackets and coats to produce white caps. These were arranged on their heads, females and a smaller number of males turning to admire these studs, and seeing their interest the Controller took the chance to appreciate the mademoiselles present. They lacked the immediate appeal of a date, but their modesty was attractive in its own right, while most would have a Euroland double.

When their service arrived everyone filed aboard, the train soon leaving the East Side and gliding towards Central, the streets below a rougher level handling deliveries and back-door workers. There was labouring to be done and those commons allowed access were carefully vetted and monitored. Security was tight, yet Controller Horace knew that if the Free English launched an attack in London it would be through the cleaners, deliverers, builders, replacers and other lowers. It was the same in every European city, but Britain was one of the most dangerous places to be. A planned outrage by the Free Scots had been foiled in Glasgow two months earlier. The B+ that he was shadowing left the transporter and led him along escalators and out into the gardens of Westminster.

Controller Horace heard his name being called. He was a ghost glimpsed by a clairvoyant, a faker in the cold shadow of Blackpool's rusty tower. The Paris of the North? He tensed and waited, must have imagined it, but then the call was repeated and he wondered if he had died. Peep had taken him away from his buddies. His body had been deleted. For a moment he was scared, loneliness swamping him again, and he wished he had stayed in Pearly or better still Monnet. He should never have left Brussels. The assassin was a young woman and she sang like a sparrow. She would show no mercy, but when the job was done he hoped she would escape. He recognised the voice and remembered who and what and where he was, removed Peep's goggles and turned to face Baby.

– Would you like your coffee out here?

How he had confused Baby's beautiful Heartland accent with the guttural cockney of the London commons was terrible. He had become disorientated. Peep was a powerful tool, its ability to take a person beyond virtual and into the visionary potentially fatal for a weakling. Yet it wasn't physical. Of course it was not. Borders became blurred and he had been working on a vision of his own, was merely keen to try it out. He smiled at Baby, who knew exactly how he loved his coffee. It was the right time to leave the Crat in Westminster. The Controller had a busy day ahead. He indicated an indoors drinking.

– Blueberry muffin? Baby called, having turned and retreated.

Horace Starski followed her into the lounge. Bob Terks had arrived from his bedroom and was busying himself with the espresso machine, the former CIA agent loving his shots. The Controller enjoyed black coffee prepared in a cafetiere, on occasion a latte for variation, while Baby liked tea. Each to their own. Freedom of choice. There was no pressure to copy.

– We have a busy time ahead of us, Controller Horace announced, once he was sitting comfortably.

The walk had loosened his limbs and he was ready to bop. Their stay in London would last no more than three days. He would attend meetings, slap backs and make the right decisions before heading home in triumph. It was an easy schedule, but customary to exaggerate.

– Here you are, Baby said, placing a tray on his lap.

– Thank you. It smells fantastic. The beans?

– They come from Palermo.

– Palermo. An interesting city. Have you ever been there?

– I have not.

– We will go one day. What do you think, Bobby?

– Excuse me?

– Shall we go to Palermo and see the beans being processed?

Bob Terks turned. He seemed alarmed.

– Not today, Bobby. Obviously not now. In the future. Baby has never been to Palermo.

Bob Terks stood straight.

– Neither have I. There are many European cities I have never seen. Most of them in fact.

– We will do it soon. I promise.

Bob Terks was clearly pleased. The hero of the LA clearances returned to his task, working hard for the best espresso, while Baby perched herself on the nearest chair. It was made of steel and she looked even smaller against its tall back, dressed in the polka-dot romper she liked to wear in place of pyjamas. On her feet were the lion-mane slippers Horace Starski had bought for her last birthday. He had not seen them for months after, asked if she did not like them, and since then she wore them every morning and late at night. She raised a foot and rubbed the sole on the Controller's calf. It was the action of an innocent, a child showing her affection for a wise relative, and he reflected on her pure nature, the fact that she would show no mercy if he was threatened.

– I am going to have a cream-cheese bagel, Bob Terks announced. Anyone else fancy one? I have cod flavour, lamb-chopped or plain.

– Plain for me, Horace Starski called out. You have scanned them properly?

– Why would I scan a bagel?

It may have been a running joke, but poison was not funny if swallowed.

– I have ordered those ingredients I mentioned. When we get home I am going to make you a true Californian treat. I can't believe you have never had a Tex-Mex Tornado before.

– Served with refried beans? the Controller asked.

– The works. Tacos to start. Washed down with margaritas, which will be served in iced glasses trimmed with salt.

– It sounds fantastic, Horace Starski said.

He had eaten Mexican food before, but didn't want to spoil Bobby's enjoyment.

– It is a traditional USA dish, Bob Terks boasted. Invented by early European settlers, a mixture of bread-makers from Cork and spicers from, oddly enough, Palermo. These people toiled with soil and grew beef and lamb and goats and chickens and dogs and beans and the chillies and peppers and rice and other ingredients that I may or may not use. I will be bringing a European classic home. I know there are CA restaurants in Brussels, but these dishes haven't been as successful as the curries of Amsterdam.

– Hurry up with that bagel, Baby said. Controller Horace must be hungry.

Baby was staring at Bobby as the American spoke about the treat he was planning. Bob Terks was facing the counter, back turned as he prepared the more simple bagels and spoke of tortillas, a hulk who never questioned orders, fixed in his habits and loyal to the bone. There was a faint friction with Baby, which was not nice, but the Controller felt it would resolve naturally. They were young and idealistic, regarded him has an elder, and yet he did not feel old inside.

He saw himself in that young Crat he had walked with in Bethnal Plaza and stood next to on the train, surrounded by up-and-comers in similar outfits which were strict and conformist yet in their minds individual. There were the lenses the girls wore and the caps of the boys, the designer labels and brands, and his Crat was so proud of a B+ status – the boy Rupert – on the surface a lover of detail and trivia with an ability to never tire of repetition, but it was the quirks that might set him apart. Bobby's voice boomed, and although Horace Starski was an ex-Crat, an ideas man, he would always be more deadly than the gunman who had helped liberate LA.

The Controller was a young man standing at a counter just like Bob Terks, listing ingredients, speaking the same nonsense, his audience a London girl called Belle. It was the first time she had invited him back to her flat, a one-bedroom affair in a small block in Balham. It was cluttered but nice enough, warm and homely. He had wanted to tidy up, throw things away, but knew enough to keep his mouth shut on that at least. It was near where she worked in a public hospital, back before the NHS was privatised, EU directives linking to the ideology of Britain's native capitalists, the American corps coming in with their expertise.

He really had talked and talked, drinking from a bottle of beer, and he wondered why. It was the first time he had been inside a 'flat', the term avoided by estate agents who only wanted to deal with wealthy professionals. 'Apartment' sounded more European, reflected the snobbery of the UK's UK-haters, a fifth column that had been essential to unification, but which through Belle he had come to despise for a while. He felt as if he was back in her flat now, listening to himself, wishing he'd shut up. Thinking about her made him happy and made him sad.

He hadn't spoken to her for over forty years. He wondered what she would think of the songs being played on the Overground, but she'd never travel on that system. She was a commons and lived in a shadow world. He remembered how she made him listen to her punk records when he was in her flat. He grinned and Baby noticed and did the same. Belle had always been so strong and independent. He wondered if Baby was the same, but how could she be? Despite his initial dislike of the music, he had quickly realised its importance and why it had been marginalised. He could still remember the names of the bands and a lot of their songs. It had all been deleted now, which was for the best. The same went for Belle.

NINE

KENNY WAS EXHAUSTED, but it was a healthy tiredness, the result of a good day's work. He had done everything he'd planned, plus a bit extra, and was looking forward to a relaxing night in with Jan. She had stopped off to see her sister and he was timing dinner for her return. He had a slow-cooking curry on the go and it was doing nicely. He was feeling pleased with himself, happy about last night as well, that he'd left the pub early and eaten on the way back, as this meant he had woken up without a hangover. Clear-headed and out of bed by seven, he turned the heat on and filled the kettle, opened the curtains and suddenly remembered that Fred's bag was in the bedroom unopened. Jan didn't have to be up yet, so he let her sleep, fetched it and sat in the living room. It was still dark outside, but he had his reading lamp bent over the back of his chair.

The coffee he made himself was extra strong, and as he sipped at the edge of his mug he ran back over the previous evening – a half-drunk Fred, Clive and his shoelaces, Tom joining them, Ronnie worrying the landlord, some words with Kid Bale, finally Peanut Paul Harrison and his satay sauce. He thought of the horse brasses on the beam in the front bar, father and son sitting at a table below. He loved The Wheatsheaf. It was the perfect drinker. A ten-minute walk from his front door as well. He had spent a lot of time in the town-centre pubs when he was younger, knocking about with some of the local tearaways, but he was settled with Jan now and much more disciplined. He did love a session though, missed days out like that Wales trip, but most of the time his energy was channelled in other directions.

He saw himself on the green, lit up by lamps and the fire in the drum, Paul waiting for summer, his Hawaiian shirts ironed and folded at home. Everyone had their dreams. Kenny was in the spotlight this morning as well, the darkness in his garden as dense as that of the All Souls graveyard. The memory of Chris Hobbs' death returned, knocking him back. A young man's pain had been recycled as propaganda. Cheap entertainment. He would have been a sitting target. The same as Kenny last night and now. But his secrets were safe inside his head. He turned off his lamp and waited for the sun to rise. Faint outlines appeared and became firmer shapes, firstly the top of his garden fence and the roofs of the nearest houses, followed by the plants he kept in pots. Chris faded in the haze.

As he stood with a glass of beer in his hand and breathed the spices of his curry, Kenny felt as good as he had that morning, once he had finished his coffee and the room was full of sunlight. He'd taken his time opening Fred's bag. Treated it like a ceremony, making the experience last. Closing his eyes, he removed each book individually, held it up and looked, ready to be amazed. These were some of the best moments – seeing the cover design first, then the title and author, flicking and smelling the pages, imagining the stories and ideas waiting inside.

First out was *PUSH*, an anthology of short stories, edited by Joe England. Names jumped out – Joseph Ridgwell, Dickson Telfer, Michael Keenaghan – and he dipped into the text, immediately hooked, but stopped himself. Next was Pete Haynes' *Malayan Swing*, and he read the synopsis on the back, the story of an outsider. He saw earlier examples of today's rampant doublespeak – the term 'care in the community'. Another period in London's story came out of the bag next in *Without The Moon* by Cathi Unsworth, dark fiction from the Queen Of Noir. Prostitutes operating in the West End during the Second German War were being murdered by two serial killers. The first of these was the Blackout Ripper, who strangled and then mutilated his victims.

There were seven novels in total, but he'd been interrupted at this point by Jan, who had come into the room and was standing with her hands on her hips, putting on a false frown, doing her angry-teacher routine. She taught at a primary school and joked that he was like a small boy with his enthusiasms and shifts of interest, but more seriously and privately she felt he was too trusting and naive, lacked confidence, and this was why she'd put up with his drinking in the early days. That was before he became focused. Jan was the sensible one, but knew they balanced each other out.

They'd had breakfast together, the books returned to the bag, and when Jan left for work Kenny had a shower and dressed, saw that the frost had melted, and while it was cold out it was also bright and sunny. He transferred Fred's bag to a larger, scruffy holdall, and left his house, returned to the green but headed in the opposite direction to The Wheatsheaf and All Souls, cutting through Knapp Estate and coming out near the old farm cottages. It was a roundabout route, but he had to be careful, came into the churchyard through the back, that part of the cemetery where Christians used to bury the poor in unmarked graves, out by the boundary, and there would be bones on the other side of that line for the sinners and illegitimate babies and the suicides and anyone else they cared to bully. Thinking about this cruelty made him angry. It was no wonder those sorts of religion had died out.

This area was shaded by trees and there was a bench Fred had put in a few months after his wife Sandra died. It was when they'd been scattering her ashes that Kenny noticed something odd at the back of the church. There was a section of stone different in colour and starting on a lower level. This could have been due to subsidence, but he didn't think so, and he was certain it was older than the rest of the building. He had gone back and had another look a few days later. It was a remote part of the graveyard, cut off and forgotten, but personal to Sandra as her great-great-grandmother had been buried there without a stone.

Kenny discovered what looked like a blocked-up entrance, its outline just visible through the moss, and this was tucked behind a newer wall, which meant it was hidden from view. He was sure it was a door, went and saw Pop Stevens, who had some books on local history. It turned out that All Souls had been built over an older Saxon church, which in turn sat on a pagan site. This wasn't unusual, and if Kenny's guess was right there could be a crypt and other rooms under the ground. Fred came with him and they broke through the opening. They had to pick their time and do it with a hammer and chisel, keep the noise down, but Kenny found what he was looking for, and luckily there were no coffins remaining. There was a lot of space and it was private, but needed work. He was excited. This was where he would build the library Fred had spoken about in the past, putting the idea in his head and not letting it fade. It would be easy to connect to the electricity supply above, seeing as the church was run by and for the community, and Fred was one of those who kept an eye on the place. Nobody could know it existed. It had to remain a secret.

Kenny turned the heat down on the curry, didn't want to ruin it, checked the time and hoped Jan wouldn't be too much longer. She hadn't seen her sister for nearly a month and they had a lot to talk about, the last time they'd been together rowing over something silly. They were very different characters. It some ways they mirrored one of the wasteful splits that had existed locally.

Kenny and his old drinking pals – men like Alan Nash, Kid Bale and his brother Ted, Steve Knowles and Johnny Daniels – believed in a united British Isles, while the anarchists that supplied Conflict with its fighters were against any sort of nation or government. There was no trouble between them now, but it had been a problem in the past. Both sides had mellowed, found common ground. Differences were tolerated as there was clearly a much bigger and more deadly enemy to confront. It was the same across the two islands, with elements in the Free Welsh, Scottish and Irish ranks opposed to a return to the UK model, but this division had faded as the USE tightened its hold.

Fred preferred buying and selling small numbers of books these days, making new connections and seeing long-term friends, linking up bookworms. He was relieved to clear out his loft, emptying that plus a lock-up and two full rooms, while a friend's stash also needed rehousing. These libraries were being passed on to future generations, donated to the country. Fred had wanted to rid himself of his possessions since Sandra's death, and hated the idea of leaving his books in the house after he was gone, and in

Kenny he had the ideal person to continue what he and others had started.

The younger man worked hard in the crypt, adding lights, ventilation and heaters, along with a secure door that was neatly disguised, a gate to the tiny enclosure, and once the premises were secure he started moving the books in. Since then he had been patching concrete, painting, adding shelves, sorting out the mountains of literature, indexing as he went. He loved the place and wished he could spend every day there, but he had to go out and earn a living. Jan just wanted him to be careful. Her great love was teaching, and the curriculum was a lot different to the one ordered by Brussels.

This morning, Kenny had been in the library by half-eight, the day stretching ahead of him as he made more coffee and turned on his Technics turntable. It was an antique model, needles handmade by a young DJ in the town, problems with the mixer and speakers dealt with by an associate. Kenny loved the symphonies of Shostakovich, chose a record and sat down to look at the remaining four books in Fred's bag. The Russian's 5th boomed as he relaxed in his sanctuary.

Sipping his beer and waiting for Jan, hungry and looking forward to the curry, his special bajhis and the various extras, he took the day forward through four more London titles and wondered for the first time if Fred suspected something more about his upcoming trip to the city. They had talked about collecting *May Day* at one o'clock, bumping into each other in The Wheatsheaf, Kenny having a Ploughman's and a single pint of Kingdon. That novel was another London story, and he couldn't stop himself thinking back, which was probably better than thinking ahead.

He saw himself as a child, sitting in the back of a car with his brother and sister and their new dog Zola. He was a mix of collie and labrador, and they had just got him from a charity that looked after and rehoused strays. They were taking him home and the dog was nervous, looking through the back window, over to the sides, not knowing where he was going or who he was with, and they patted him and tried to make him feel safe, but his tongue was hanging out and he was panting. He was big, tall and thinner than he should have been, slouched a little when they took him out for his first walks, Kenny's dad reckoning he must be part wolf.

Soppy and good-natured, Zola just wanted to be loved, settled in fast, but his past was a mystery and there was no way of knowing what had happened to him. He seemed to like motor-bikes, chasing one in the street a month after he came to live with them, but then the memory faded. He was delicate when he took a biscuit from a hand, so Mum thought he must have lived with an older person, and maybe they had died and the dog was aban-doned. When they first brought him home he was so thin his ribs were visible, and he stumbled when he walked, had a big patch of raw skin on his side where he'd chewed the fur off. There was red in with the black and the vet said this was due to malnutrition. The people at the charity said he was seven years old, one of those left unchosen by the mainly young families who wanted puppies and more lively dogs. He was probably nine or ten, and they only had him for four years, but he had been spoiled rotten and loved until the end.

The bubbleheads of the USE ate dogs now. The idea would have been unimaginable when he was a boy, and yet it was a hypocrisy to choose one species and treat it like a best friend and then torment and kill others. This had changed with the spread of veganism, which had come to mirror the split between city and country, the conformists and commons. He thought of Zola as he stood in the kitchen waiting for Jan, pictured him clearly. His wound was treated and the fur grew back, and Mum fed him up so he didn't stumble any more and his coat shone. Kenny could still smell his fur, and the fumes of the petrol that powered their car. And he thought about when they'd left London, and how his dad was shaking and his mum was crying, telling their children it was all going to be fine, and Zola...

He heard Jan arriving, the car turning so its lights shone through the living-room curtains for a second or two. The engine was turned off and he moved to the shelves where he kept his records. In thirty seconds or so the front door would open and she would be in the hall calling out 'hello... anyone home?' He would welcome her with a song. He had thirteen albums and twenty-one singles. The vinyl was worn, but it had been looked after and played well enough. A selection of CDs were in a pile nearby, along with DVDs of deleted films. Few of these worked properly. He kept them for their covers. His records were time capsules that would last for centuries, despite bubbler propaganda. One of their more ridiculous stories was that the grooves hid dark, subliminal messages.

The USE pointed to an InterZone site highlighting the crimes of Charlie Manlon, a long-haired motorhead from Wolverhampton convicted of directing the vicious murders of some budding young creatives south of Liverpool. Kenny knew this was rubbish as he had a book about Charles Manson, who had organised similar killings in California. The site insisted Manlon was a jealous trade-unionist connected to GB45, before focusing on the band Scousers 4 and the way they had buried orders to kill Good Euros in their song 'Helter Skelter'. This hypnotic messaging had driven Manlon and his racist Black Country Crew into a frenzy. The State was clear on this – physical recordings corrupted the young. Only total digitisation could protect the innocent.

Kenny considered the time and effort that went into this sort of propaganda, and despite the power of technology it took a huge number of people to reshape history in such a way. Crats had to destroy and recreate, make sure every reference was removed before launching new versions. Controllers ran the operation, had the intelligence the Crat robots lacked. A Controller had drives that went far deeper than those of the average wand-waver. There were other reasons for their plagiarism, the way they rehashed and distorted the past. He had talked about this at length with other Free English rebels. It was important to understand how your enemy thought. Get inside their heads. Controllers were little known to the wider public, yet within the Crat ranks they were revered.

Last year had seen the new movie release *Controller X*. He watched it with Jan and they laughed their heads off. It was supposed to be serious, but they treated it as a comedy, worse even than Manlon and that subliminal messaging nonsense. Sadly, it was a hit, with the main actors winning numerous awards for their performances. Maybe they would watch a film together tonight. Eat the curry first and have a drink, and later he would make some popcorn.

Controller X had been directed by Johnny Scorsese and starred Rob De Vero. They were a tight team, responsible for some major, in-depth, conformist product. The Controller was portrayed as a child genius with an ability to memorise and believe, but he was bullied by jealous commons who considered him a nerd. A liberating move from Cologne to Lyon at the age of sixteen allowed him to study and progress, first serving as a Bureau in Thessaloniki, then a Techno in Copenhagen and Paris, before his big promotion arrived. It was a period piece, the climax the Controller's victory over an anti-USE terror gang.

It turned out that the worst of his childhood tormentors was the leader of the terrorists and Controller X had finally confronted him, beating the man in a fair fight but showing mercy and sparing his life. A Cool officer was asked to serve coffee and muffins, but the bully rejected this kind offer and seized her weapon, was about to zap when Controller X blew the pig away. It was classic Euro trash and, after a stunned silence, Jan was the first to speak.

– What I don't understand is why Controller X can't fly. He can do everything else.

– He used a hover-pack before he became a Controller.

– I'm being serious, Kenny. Those Controllers can do anything, even remain invisible if they want. That's what GB45 needs to do. Move among the bubblers unseen. You look at the original superheroes – Batman, Spiderman, Iron Man.

– Superman himself.

– Exactly. Why can't Controller X fly? What about Captain Euro?

– Batman doesn't fly, he uses a bat-rope, and Spiderman climbs with a web that shoots out of his hand. I don't know about Iron Man.

– Fair enough, but what do they have in common?

– I don't know.

– Come on. What makes them so similar?

– Masks?

– Yes, masks, but something else.

– Don't have a clue.

He was grinning at the memory, how she pretended he was a child being coaxed to an answer, or maybe he was supposed to be one of those slow-witted, cider-drinking yokels from the film. The old Saxon burr of the Southern and Eastern shires had been insulted for centuries by the Latin- and French-loving aristocracy, the Europeanised rulers of pre-bubblehead days driving a racial prejudice that still persisted. The same bias was applied to the cockney accent.

– It's all fantasy, Kenny. Make believe. These Controllers don't exist like we think they do.

– I don't know...

– Maybe it's the same with the USE. I just don't think they're as strong as they want us to believe. The majority of people don't support them, do they?

– Never have done. But they have money and power and InterZone. Spies and Cool and Hardcore. Millions of Crats.

She shrugged.

– We're the underdogs, but that gives us a chance of winning, doesn't it? They don't come near us out here, do they? And why not?

He finished his beer, wondered what record to choose, realised he had taken too long. Jan was in the house and rushing across the room. She was sobbing. Wrapped herself around him.

– What's the matter? he asked in a panic. What's happened?

He stood back with his hands on her shoulders. Jan's face had caved in. She looked twenty years older than this morning.

– What is it? Come on, what's wrong?

She tried to speak, but couldn't. He pulled her close, could hear her heart beating against his chest. He waited as the sobs drew out and finally stopped.

– She's dead, Jan said at last. My sister's been murdered.

Kenny didn't understand.

– I found her body. She's been strangled. With wire. It was pulled so tight it cut her throat open. Nearly took off her head. I could see the bone. There's blood everywhere. Her eyes are wide open. They left her on her back on the kitchen table, naked from the waist down. Whoever did it balanced a blueberry muffin between her legs.

Jan pushed back and looked into Kenny's eyes. He thought he was going to vomit.

– Why, Kenny? Why would anyone do that?

TEN

FOLLOWING THE SUCCESS of their Tenderburger date, Rocket Ron invited Polestar to Bark! – a cutting-edge club created by the artist-activist Abattoir Annie. Daughter of Detroit pig-magnate Randy 'Cutter' Voss, she was a fave in the chit-chats of InterZone, her love of rebel tags transcending a pride in movies that had seen her star in roles ranging from Dildo Dawn in S&M sizzler *Hillbilly Whores* to the virginal New York nanny Norma Bates of the *Bates Motel* franchise. Annie had ploughed tens of mills of her father's eurodollars into Bark! and was reaping the rewards. But Bark! was only the start of the night Rocket had planned. Annie was on a new path and he was sure she would achieve even greater greatness. Something like Splash! perhaps? This was the main course. His date would be impressed. He hadn't told her yet. It was going to be a surprise.

– This is a beautiful hub, Polestar said, staring up at the Docklands scrapers.

– By day a centre of trade, by night a trendsetting clubland. Work hard, play hard – that's the way I choose to live.

There were no abstract designs playing across the towers here, the walls made from a novel strain of reflective glass, the logos of the world's greatest financial institutions bouncing between them, the angles calculated to create a kaleidoscopic effect. The vibe at ground level was far more brash than that of the East Side, perhaps encouraged by the phallics rising into a pink dome where a thousand tiny stars beat. Between the boardwalks and bridges, in the water of the ancient docks, millions of fish frolicked. Crustaceans moved among them, with tortoises and alligators in smaller ponds, the highlight a pod of dolphins lounging in pools to the side of Bilderberg Tower – known as Junkie's Needle to the commons. While Bilderberg was home to various banks and corporations, the basement housed Splash! The glass rods of Schuman and Spaak created a three-pronged sculpture with the larger tower.

– It is very expensive, Polestar remarked as they entered Bark!

She had seen the screen where his fingers hovered. Rocket felt a rush of pride.

– A thousand euros each, she continued. Two-thousand bucks just to win entry.

Polestar slid a hand under the Crat's right arm and pressed close, the swell of her left breast firm on his elbow. Rocket imagined her fingers testing muscle through his jacket, admiring bone that proved he was a man of the mind. Credit, location and occupation were huge turn-ons for anyone, never mind a cocksucker. He remembered their first meeting and the arrival of Joey Porto, the way she had devoured her meal and raved about the hen-flavoured mayo. Simple pleasures were the greatest pleasures. He felt the same.

– You are going to love it here, he promised.

Two doormen stood back as a third motioned Rocket and Polestar towards the lobby, and this was palatial in the extreme, its walls lined with gas mirrors, the floor a patchwork of solidified, scented fur. An Oriental waitress met them before they were halfway across the room, holding out a tray and keeping it steady as the couple snorted Chang through silver straws. Rocket stared into the server's eyes, entranced by what he saw. The narcotics of China were clearly visible. Taking a Champers flute each, they relayed their thanks and continued.

– She was a good-looker, Rocket remarked.

– There are some classy ladies here, Polestar agreed.

When they reached the doorway leading into the club's groove area, Polestar glanced back to look at the waitress again, watched as she approached the next arrivals, buttocks rolling inside super-tight leathers, part of a Bark! uniform shared by her fellows.

– I wonder what skin she is modelling, Polestar asked, before turning to view the inner Bark!

She was immediately drawn to the gold-plated cages hanging from the ceiling. Inside were a range of subhumans – an orangutan with his face lowered, a couple of koalas, one adult but smallish kangaroo, a large number of dogs. These canines had been separated according to size and breed, and all were in an agitated state. There were labradors, collies and boxers, but the bulk were ragged mongrels. Sparks flashed and dogs convulsed.

– Abattoir Annie is a true radical, Rocket explained, leaning in close so he could be heard above the music. She studied our glasshouse idealism and turned her insights into art. The electric prompts used to help our four-legged friends to the killing floor are a core element of her work, as you will see. The clubbing community loves her genius.

– But why are there so many dogs? There are very few pedigrees, just trampish mutleys.

– Fashion statement? Shabby chic? A comment on the primitive pet fetish of the country commons? I'm not sure, but I do know that their voices connect with the beats found in classic hip-hop.

– Like Snoop Doggy Dog Poo?

They both grinned at the idea of InterZone's current rapper-in-residence barking. Snoop Doggy was no poobum.

– Seriously, though... Abattoir Annie compared the tones of hollering subs and chose dogs as her best friends. Her mixers ride their pain, which is stimulated by management, or even better, the Bark! community. We have the chance to work together. There is a terminal where we can add our touches, but it's crowded now, and of course we lack the skill of someone like Annie. She is more than a mere artist. I see her as a street-wise intellectual. She really does push the boundaries. This is no random show. It is important to confront reality. Honesty is best.

Treble pounded and electricity popped, the dogs singing along, adding a primal rhythm to the tunes. It was clear that a number of Crats and dates had consumed large amounts of Chang and Champers, the club's animal-welfare officer adjusting levels when excessive shocks were applied. Rocket saw a couple copulating below the orangutan cage, a male date in a leather jumpsuit servicing a Super from behind, the lady vaguely familiar to Rocket when she looked over and winked. His attention shifted to Polestar, who was waving at the kangaroo.

– Disgusting subs, he ventured. I heard that a hopper punched a human on the nose in Australia. That really is a dangerous, backward place.

– Oh no, Polestar said. They are beautiful and clever creatures, and it is so sweet how they bounce.

Rocket Ron considered Polestar's morals, felt the comment was crude and out of place, but they had finished their drinks and he led the way to a bar where he ordered refills and two bombs. He dropped these into a pocket as they touched glasses, nodding along to the sounds, which were lighter now, the cage dancers on a break. Good Europeans chilled while the dogs panted, tongues hanging from dribbling mouths. Smoke hung in the air. The other animals cowered.

Rocket reached for Polestar's hand and invited her to the edge of the dance floor, which was busy with rocking Bureaus, Technos, non-Crat Goodies and horny aliens. Magnetic was replaced by cheese, a style that had emerged over the last three years, inspiring the mighty Rubettes, Abba and new-kid-on-the-block Etonian John. Rocket punched the air and chanted a chorus, lost in the chaos. He felt fantastic. Righteous. The cosmopolitan nature of Euroland was clear in the tones and features of the dates present. Many had painted their faces white, but they were still clearly friends from the mini-states of Africa and Asia. Bark! offered them a crazy sort of sanctuary. There was also a Thai Kitchen in the corner, where youngsters waited for caring adults to make contact. Boys and girls sat together eating cookies and sipping pop.

– Bark! is a bastion of multiculturalism, Rocket shouted, as the chorus made way for a strident keyboard solo. It shows what can be achieved in this miserable city. Anti-sexist, anti-racist, anti-exploitation, sexually liberated, cruelty- and bully-free... Abattoir Annie has worked hard to make this night a success.

– It would be nice to meet her, Polestar began. I wonder what...

The chorus returned and the Barkers howled, danced faster and faster. Rocket could feel the potions in his blood, saw abandonment in the bulging eyes of so many of those around him, and it was the Crat community that really knew how to enjoy themselves, his colleagues drinking and snorting and dropping and bonking to their hearts' content, free to do as they liked – as the Controllers asked. The sexers were more conservative, and cultural differences were respected, but Good Europeans were a liberated bunch. He loved Bark! and its people, but in a while they would move on.

Standing in the hot Docklands night thirty minutes later, Rocket Ron and Polestar let their breathing return to normal before joining a column of revellers snaking towards Splash! Restaurants lined the way, diners filling every table as they feasted, drinkers crowding around the attached bars. Palm trees flourished as Mediterranean temperatures were maintained.

– Look at the dolphins, Polestar shouted, once they were inside Splash!

She rubbed Rocket's groin and he throbbed, thinking about the fucky-fucky of the other night, excited there was more to come. The sex would be harder and more intense after the eroticism of Splash! The nearest dolphin was twisting this way and that as it tried to escape its too-small tank. Stressed and frantic, the fixed smile on its face hid true feelings, and this pleased Rocket so much that he speeded left and reached the head of a dancing line and led it to the middle of the floor. It then dispersed, Good Euros forming small circles, hands on shoulders, moving in loops.

Polestar joined Rocket and the two lovers embraced as Beethoven's 9th exploded. The dancing became regimented. The floor and roof were solid, but the walls had been shaped from glass and gave the clubbers a constantly changing display of fish in their pre-Scales! state. Tortoise wandered through plastic tubes and offered amusement with their slo-mo moves and heavy-heavy shells, but the dolphins were the main attraction. They offered the feelgood factor that Bark! lacked. The experience here was slick, smooth and subtle, but Rocket couldn't help feeling that Annie Abattoir would one day surpass its achievements.

– What is Splash! about? Polestar asked.

– Breath. Life and death. Water and air. Pressure, silence, heartbeat... How they connect. Look, there are taps at the side of each tank. At certain times these can be opened so the water drains and the beast concerned is free to dance on air, but the taps can also be closed, and others will fill the box and offer revival. The loss of water is far slower than instant electrification. Suffocation is a slow process and so offers the clubbers more scope for erotics. It swings both ways all night. The dolphins take their turn. Tanks are emptied and refilled. Heartbeats are threaded inside the compositions of Beethoven, Mozart and Chopin. Each dolphin is eventually hauled out of their tank by a golden net.

– What happens then?

– The spectacle varies. It depends on the mood of the Splashers, the satisfaction already achieved. Usually people swim with the dolphins. Wrap their arms around them and hold on tight as they beat their fins and search for the ocean. Sometimes things become more frenzied.

– Will we stay to see what happens? Polestar asked.

– If you like.

– It all seems so cruel and brutal. I can hardly believe these people are the same nervous Crats who serve Brussels so timidly.

Rocket Ron was shocked. He had expected his date to be grateful for her visit to such a high-end venue, to become aroused by the games, but instead she repaid him with ravings. Crats were brave and bold, made their own choices, while the dolphins existed to serve humanity. They were happy. Look at their smiles. Despite these errors, Rocket's erection remained firm. Polestar was built for fucky and the cementing of gender and racial equality. He had given a great deal to his community and deserved satisfaction. Tension had to be released. Allowances must be made.

He replayed the prejudice she had expressed towards child-lovers on their first outing, and while he personally had no interest in prepubescents he would never question the right of others to express their sexuality. If Polestar had been a native Londoner he would have reacted in different fashion. If he had been grafting on her file he would have zipped it to Cool. It was a fact that those who pitied animals usually hated people. Personalising sub-humans was dishonest. A threat to the system. He pitied Polestar, could not be angry. She was a non-Euro, less educated and lacking tolerance. He was here to help. Cultural differences *had* to be respected.

– Lets dance, Polestar whispered, clearly concerned by his silence.

Rocket relaxed. His sexer had realised she'd caused offence. This was important. A first step. He admired her regret, followed her into the scrum, fighting for his right to party with the Beastial Boys, demanding instant anal with Polly Came In Hollywood, scathing in his attacks on selfishness alongside billionaire helper Goodie Geldof. They only stopped bopping when there was a break in these tough tunes. Ludwig's 9th returned. The classical version. Splash! came to a halt. The community stood to attention as the national anthem played. Tears were shed.

When they retired to a chill-out space, Rocket and Polestar were wet-wet and tired. A playgirl was ready to help them unwind. She had white hair and mirror-contacts on her eyeballs, reflecting images of the Crat and date opposite. He had to admit that as a couple they were visually stunning. A tray arrived and refreshments were consumed.

Fifteen minutes later they rejoined the gang on the dance floor, old friends they had never met but knew so well, focusing rushed brains as they pushed their bodies to the limit, losing themselves in waves of perfume, singing along to anthems written to elevate their spirits, and as they moved Ron was joyful, pleased he had dealt with an awkward situation well, looking across the human heads to the dolphins in their tanks and thinking about Bark! and those dirty dogs, wondering if he might meet Abattoir Annie one day. It would be a gas if he did. He would love to dong her, but if he didn't then so be it, he was a trooper, part of an army. R&R made him stronger. Urgent work was required if every millimetre of Europe was to be cleansed of prejudice. It must be fully polished. Remembering the Rubettes cap he reached inside his jacket and popped it on his head, tilted the peak at a jaunty angle, and right on cue 'Sugar Baby Love' blasted, and looking around he saw a sea of white peaks, but he was the originator, the scene belonged to him, and the look on Polestar's face made the whole night worthwhile. He dropped a bomb and passed one to his date, who did the same, and after two more tunes they were ready to visit the sofas. Flopping down, Rocket eased back, Polestar's head on his chest. Soundproof doors sectioned them from the frenzied core. It was five minutes before either spoke.

– I am sorry about earlier, Polestar began. Did I offend you?

Rocket Ron didn't know what she could mean. They had danced and covered their bodies in layers of perspiration and now it was time to relax.

– Not at all.

– About this place, I mean. You see, I am not used to such... not cruelty... no... what is the word? Honesty. That is what I feel. Such honesty.

He tried to remember her comments, but they had been filtered and lost. It was hard rehashing items when the process was finished and a conclusion reached. There was no point discussing dead cases. He was content with what had occurred. He had made the correct decision.

– I found it very difficult seeing those children in Bark! I can never accept that men are allowed to mount girls and boys of such a low age. I love my Tenderburgers, but the idea of hurting animals for pleasure like this seems obscene.

Rocket was barely listening. He was waving to one of the servers, indicating that he was famished.

– I know that this is a great liberal society, but how can...

Rocket pondered Polestar. She couldn't see how wrong it was to impose limitations on human expression. As for the animals, well, that was nuts. They were *subhumans*. The reason tunnels and glasshouses had been introduced was to be clear about processes that made billions of euros for those involved in meat and dairy production. In the past these truths had been hidden, which was a mistake. The masses had become removed from the reality and had turned on core industries. Bark! and Splash! took this honesty to another level. Did she want Good Europeans to become vegan like so many of the commons here in so-called Britain? He supposed her opinion didn't matter, not when he was in sex mode. Nobody was near enough to hear.

– Maybe I should give up my dreams and return home.

The waiter indicated by Rocket placed a tray on the table in front of them. The man was mature and smartly dressed in a tuxedo. Different standards applied in this part of the club – not better and not worse, just *different* – and it was important to apply this openness to everyday life. Polestar would learn. He was going to devote himself to her development.

Rocket transferred credit. He was hungry and once the man left he waited for Polestar to take a muffin and then helped himself. His bites were fast and eager. He tasted the blueberries and was pleased.

– Lets see what the future brings, he remarked, proud of this original remark.

Polestar reached for her coffee and drank slowly. They were chilling nicely and when they had finished eating they snuggled into the sofa.

– Yes, Polestar whispered. It takes time to adjust. Europe is so civilised. I must change to prosper. You couldn't imagine what it is like to live without New Democracy.

– No, I can't, Rocket admitted.

– There are no Palms and little freedom to work and become wealthy. There is disrespect for dates. The girls and boys are beaten and raped and the police do nothing.

Rocket was outraged. Consensual violence was fine, with credit passed to the willing receiver, but rape was a terrible crime. Thankfully the courts were at last applying stiff sentences to the locals, while an effective sex-worker system had seen instances drop from minimal levels to zero among Good Euros. His own preferences were modest, but he respected the rights of others to indulge their fantasies. The desire to torture did not make you a bad person. Quite the opposite, it showed an ability to free-think. Such people should be admired, and within the elite they were fêted, fast-tracked and rewarded with creative status.

– If I am lucky, maybe I will live in London for the rest of my life. In time I want to leave the dating world behind, become a Crat, earn high wages and enjoy perks.

Rocket knew this was impossible, that Polestar would one day return home. It was always the way, but he didn't want to make her sad. She could work hard for a number of years and build a client base, move to Technos and perhaps even a Controller, save and save and buy a nice property back in Africa. It was better for her and the future of her fellows.

– What about you, Ronald? she asked. I know you want to be a Controller, but what sort of leader would you be?

He sniffed his sexer's scent and smelled the coffee mist floating in the air.

– I will use my expertise to educate those areas of the USE that do not understand New Democracy. I will be a patient but firm Controller.

He raised a hand and stroked Polestar's hair. His fingers were ultra-sensitive and he could feel each strand. Under the wig, her hair was cut close to the skull. Rocket continued.

– We live in a free society and so conformity is rewarded. We are on similar journeys, you and I, our experiences and ambitions connected. The path to the top is narrow. Stray and it is impossible to return to the straight. Tunnel vision is a strength. Focus on your goal and it will be achieved. But I am learning all the time. We must listen and heed. Thank you for your help.

He felt Polestar sigh. Soon they would return to the dance. Cause reactions, create history. The great Controllers made plans and his were beginning to form. Humility would be his greatest asset. And he could feel his energy levels soaring. He was going to make a dolphin boogie. Twist and shout. He would tease and revive and cull one of these smirkers. Polestar's nails moved along the inside of his right leg. In Bark! and Splash! he could do as he liked.

ELEVEN

THE FUNERAL OF Hannah Adams took place at Cropper's Circle, two days after her death – as was the custom. The temple had been used as a Christian church until four years earlier, when a period of near-zero attendances led to the vicar finally leaving, workers nailing boards over the doors and windows before his redundancy took effect. Greens arrived the next week to reclaim the site. The Judaic-Christian cult had run out of excuses in Wessex, while the Holy Roman imperialists had long been building alternative bases inside the USE. Faced by easy credit and the march of materialism, organised religion had faded across Britain, but in reality it had been ruined from the inside. A new spiritualism was emerging to take its place.

Greenwood beliefs had tangled roots. Core Christian values had been re-established and brought to life with a revival of native paganism and the wisdom of Eastern thinkers within the commons, but the one-god, supremacist stances of Christianity, Judaism and Islam had for the most part been rejected. Buddhist and some Hindu ideas were more in tune with the population and had merged with older ways of thinking. Just as importantly, its environmental sympathies appealed to the masses.

– Hannah believed in freedom, the priestess said. She loved the England that evolved from the merging of the original tribes. She saw the open-mindedness of the people and how this linked with those from the non-Semitic traditions. She was interested in the beliefs of the Saxons and Celts and Vikings, loved the feasting halls that became our pubs, the deeper truth that actions speak louder than words...

Kenny felt Jan squeeze his hand, but while he was doing his best to focus, his mind was racing. If it was right that the murder was the work of Hardcore, as was believed by GB45 and Hannah's anarchist friends, then its intrusion into a town deep in Wessex was a huge worry. Hannah had been a member of Conflict, it was true, but she was hardly a soldier. It made no sense.

– Hannah rejected the lies of false liberals who preach one thing and do the opposite. She hated the USE, the doublespeak that calls its dictatorship New Democracy. More than anything, though, she loved life. She was generous and giving and believed in helping others. A decent human being, an honest soul and, it has to be said, a genuine English maverick. There were times when she...

The USE was a long-term project. Controllers studied its enemies, took precautions and operated in slow-motion, only struck when they were sure there would be no fallout, so an assassination such as this one was either a change in strategy or a mark of escalating confidence. The muffin shouldn't have mattered when matched against the brutality of the assault, but the fact they had mocked their enemy so cheaply angered Kenny as much as it did Jan. He felt her hand move away as she leaned forward, placing them on the back of the pew in front.

– ... in Hayes, West London, Hannah the first of two daughters and one son. Her mother and father, Keith and Debbie Adams, moved the children out when she was six, an experience remembered as a drive into the countryside, the seriousness of the situation hidden from them. Targeted for Debbie's trade-unionism, the family was fortunate to escape. According to her sister...

Kenny was back in his parents' car making the same journey, leaving London and not understanding the mood. These memories would be common he supposed, as stories were bound to overlap. Zola was sitting in the back seat with the kids. It was cramped and hot, their belongings piled up around them, and that dog was smart, hardly moved the whole time they were on the road. Normally he would be peering out of every window, his brain ticking as he watched pedestrians, breaking off to scratch his ribs or chew a paw, demanding that his chest was tickled by rolling on his back, but this time he knew something serious was happening and didn't want to attract attention, grasped the atmosphere in a way Kenny could not. This was a year before the final clampdown on pets and an increased demonising of animals, so maybe he had felt that as well.

... she was a happy child, full of energy and willing to help those around her, something that took her into the caring profession. She loved to dance and run, completing several half-marathons for charity. When she was a teenager...

The lives of Kenny's family had been changed forever. He guessed Zola liked it more in a smaller town, with fields nearby, the fresher air and everything, but London was Kenny's home and he had seriously missed it for a long time after. His dad had been sacked after an argument with his boss, and not long after a man came to their house and warned him to take his family and leave the city as soon as possible. He had been reported for spreading anti-USE propaganda, which was a lie, and his case had been passed to Cool. Kenny's aunt lived in Yeovil and they left later that day.

– ... the death of plants, insects and animals, which was caused by the introduction of genetically modified crops, changed her from a passive to a deeper green. The troubles that...

Kenny was going through the motions, unable to concentrate, his head full and ready to burst. He went with Jan and her family to the private cremation after, arriving at The Traveller's Rest an hour or so later and heading towards the function room. A detective was waiting to ask Jan more questions and she went with him to his car, Kenny ordering a pint of Kingdon at the bar. The pub was owned and run by the locals. The Subhumans mob drank in here. There'd been a few rows with the Wessex Boys in the past, various faces moving into Conflict and GB45 when they were older, both now linked into the broader resistance.

He took his pint and went outside, sat on a wall and waited for Jan. It was cold, but he didn't care, could see her in the car with the detective, knew the police meant well but could do nothing outside of the Free English plots. Policing was by consent. It had to be. They were brave men and women, would be at the top of Hardcore's list when the USE moved in. He wished he could run away with Jan, live in one of those places Peanut Paul Harrison talked about, sit in the sun and leave this mess behind. But he couldn't just walk away. It would be wrong to surrender.

– All right, Kenny? Sam asked, joining him on the wall.

They shook hands.

Sam was one of the original Subhumans, and Kenny would always respect him for the part he had played in the animal-rights movement, fighting and suffering at the hands of the authorities before the wider population finally lived up to the claim that Britain was a nation of animal lovers. It was hard to believe that meat-eating had been practised by the majority of commons a mere thirty years earlier, whereas today the shires were for the most part free of this cruelty. Vegan values were now entwined with the fight for independence. They were seen as essential to any moral philosophy.

Brussels pulled in the opposite direction. The meat, dairy and skin industries meant huge returns for the corporations involved, and the State was never going to threaten their profits. Glass-walled slaughterhouses and see-through tunnels featured in huge propaganda campaigns, notions of necessity, honesty and freedom of choice used to justify the abuse. People became hardened. It was a rotten system, based on deceit, and symbolic of the USE. Those at the top scorned the weakest in society, but they were clever and never stopped smiling. Even so, they made mistakes.

– The feds have no respect, Sam said. No fucking respect and no fucking class.

It was the State that had inadvertently helped the rebels. Inter-Zone acted as a monitor, its two clouds represented by a handsome Berliner called Hans and the Parisienne lovely Michele. Data was dissected, words and images analysed, Sus predicting problems, its choices passed to Crats who released the likes of Himmler before agreeing with Sus and notifying Cool. Michele shadowed everyone linked to InterZone, but the arrival of the Palm 7 meant she would soon be able to operate from *inside* a person. GB45 had heard of this device early, thanks to undercover Bristol man Walter Hope, but passing the information on was difficult, as the means of distribution were controlled by the enemy.

– What a way to die, Sam continued. I can't believe she's gone. Poor Hannah. I hate those bubblers, Ken. Fucking hate them.

Palm addicts could not believe that the 7's advanced chip would be used for anything other than their fun and protection. Modern life was impossible without InterZone, which was why, following a rebel attack on Heath 4, a Cool base near Reading, it was decided to turn off the nearest regions. This temporary lockdown was meant to turn public opinion against the attackers, but the USE had underestimated the mood of the people. And it had not realised how successful the digitisation of society had been in making the masses dependent. Key services crashed. There was no electricity, which meant no light and no heating. Troika vanished. Without credit, families could not buy food. The population panicked. And the commons blamed Brussels.

At first the protests were contained by Gendarmerie directed by Cool, its riot squad released in sealed areas, but the numbers ready to take on the authorities soared and it was forced to withdraw. Michele maintained her clampdown, backed by Hans, the Controllers in charge of the operation adding to their earlier mistake by deploying a mercenary unit hired by Hardcore. Locals were shot, beaten and raped. A crucifixion was rumoured. The English fought back and there were numerous deaths on both sides but, like the uprising, these were never reported. The Argentine Brigade, despite its experience and hatred of all things British, had been driven out by badly equipped irregulars. It returned to base and the contract was cancelled. Elite Hardcore units were brought in from Berlin itself, but held in reserve.

Restraint was imposed from above. An escalation of the violence had to be avoided. Every victim had relatives, and while a small number of deaths could be covered up, the truth where it leaked out discredited, there was a limit. Brussels was outraged by the attack on Cool, the rebellion that followed and the lack of value supplied by the Argentines, but Berlin had stepped in to calm the situation.

– ... it's a nice idea scattering her ashes there. Suppose it won't be for a week or...

InterZone was switched back on and an uneasy calm followed, but the lockdown had created a new anger in those it hurt. The news spread to nearby counties, passed on word of mouth, while rebel fighters who had hurried to the scene took the story across the British Isles. Kenny was a boy at the time, but he would never forget the initial panic and how quickly people had adjusted.

The turn-off only lasted a week, but those seven days were too long. Those affected had to deal with the realisation that they were totally powerless and could well starve or freeze to death. They lived in darkness when night came. The fact that Controllers could behave this way stunned even those who were willing to bow their heads in return for an easy life. Yet finding that they could survive outside InterZone was a revelation. Hypermarkets were raided for food and small retailers emerged. There were no screens and no keyboards, so slate was utilised, chalk recording temporary loans.

When InterZone was restored and millions refused to connect, it was the turn of the State to panic. It was said that fifty Crats, who had only been obeying orders, were punished as blame was passed down. The Controllers responsible for the mess had to answer to their superiors in Brussels, who in turn had to explain things to Berlin, so these unfortunates were sent away on vacation, which was doublespeak for a rendition. Nobody could swear this was true, but both Conflict and GB45 considered it likely. Cool was happy for the rumour to spread. The converse applied to Inter-Zone.

– ... there was this time when we...

Efforts were made to correct the mistake. Grants were distributed and credit offered.

– ... you have to laugh really, I mean...

Huge, state-of-the-art screens were erected in the towns that had rejected InterZone, and advertising and shows were played in an attempt to pull people back into the system, but these were soon destroyed. Surveillance cameras were treated the same way. The small number of Good Europeans present in these marginal areas were driven out. Kenny had learned the details about this when he was in his early twenties, and more recently thanks to the likes of Pop Stevens.

– ... and there was the time we ended...

You only had to go back to the troubles in Ireland to see the way the bigger picture was missed, all that fighting between Christian sects hard to believe when the EU was busy dismantling democracy. The part of Ireland that had broken away from the UK had been sold out to Brussels, which was impossible to understand. There were other countries that had done the same. It amazed him how politicians could behave. Was it naivety, fear, laziness, greed, ignorance? Why had the people not seen what was going on?

– ... we worked together for seven years, Sam was saying, and Kenny glanced over and saw that he had tears running down his face.

Maybe Hannah's murder was connected to her job at the hospice. The State encouraged voluntary euthanasia. It said it was responding to public opinion, offering freedom of choice, but it had directed a narrative via InterZone, creating conventions that were promoted and became unwritten law. Brussels then added legislation. Everyone wanted to grow old and receive the pensions they had spent their lives buying, but this was a private service and the corporations had profits to maximise. Kenny was sure that the hospitals, care homes and prisons – overseen by Brussels, run by private companies – were killing people in a non-voluntary manner. The casual dismissal of the elderly by the media, which had cast them as a burden rather than an asset, was driven by financial motives as well as the mission to cut the last ties with pre-digital history.

– You can come round and hear the recordings if you like. I know you're interested in all that. We had fun doing it, Hannah and me, and the old-timers loved it. I've got them stashed.

– I'd like that, Kenny said.

He knew about Hannah's respect for social history and memory.

– She told me something about the recordings, he continued. But you know what it's like, you get busy and put things off. She was going to play them to me.

– She transcribed it all as well, Sam said. I have a copy.

– I didn't know that. I'd like to hear the recordings first, though. If you don't mind. Hear the voices.

– Come round whenever you want, Kenny. You want another drink?

He wondered if Hannah's murder was somehow linked. Did she have copies at her house, and if so, were they taken?

– Thanks Sam, I will. Pint of Kingdon please. I'm waiting for Jan. Cheers.

Sam took their glasses and went back inside the pub, leaving Kenny to stare at the police car. They were still talking and he tried to imagine what they could be saying. If it was a local responsible, the police could act, but few people believed this was the case. Hannah was outspoken, her hatred of the USE well known, and this would have had her branded a terrorist, even if her activities didn't go much beyond support work. Then there were the recordings. Even so, the murder made no sense. He worried that it connected to his trip into London, but that was impossible. Again, why kill Hannah?

He was fed up of waiting. The decision had been made a week before her death, and while there were concerns, he refused to back out now. Jan wanted him to cancel it and stay here, insisting that books were the least of their worries, but he had to go. The USE could prosper without the free regions, and the credit needed to monitor every house, street, lane, wood and field was better used elsewhere, but Berlin wanted total control. Brussels was its proxy, the Controllers its creatives. He wasn't going to stay at home waiting for their next push.

The car door opened and Jan got out. The detective started the engine and pulled away, indicating right as he left the car park and headed into town. Kenny paused and noticed how she walked, head down against a drizzle that had started to fall as soon as she took a step towards him. He stood up and went over to meet her, saw the resignation in Jan's face and put an arm around her shoulders. They walked back to The Traveller's Rest together, climbed the steps and went inside.

TWELVE

GENDARMERIE BEEPED RUPERT Ronsberger on IR4, less than a minute after he passed the glasshouse at Junction 2. Once his identity had been confirmed, a super-friendly officer handed him a cup of chocolate and a blueberry muffin. Rupert loved this classic combo, and while his preferences were readily available on Inter-Zone, these pals had taken the trouble to check and bring refreshments to his window. He was impressed, if a little surprised that a chit-chat was taking place at this particular moment. He rarely drove a car and had never been invited to pull over before, but being educated in freeway etiquette was more than happy to help the broader travelling community. His only worry was missing the big match.

The clash between the Flamboyants of Barca and a defence-minded London United was a highlight of the Euroship season. There were only three hours left to kick-off and he wanted to enjoy the build-up, had acted on Polestar's suggestion that he do some shopping and savour the atmosphere at the Milan Megastore in Windsor, before heading back to Soccer City for a pepperoni pizza with his favourite date. He had already ordered his merch to avoid the crush of last-minute fanatics, but felt tense, worried he might miss the start of the live beam-back. He so wanted to see the Flamboyants thrash London on a communal screen in real-time. Delays were for part-timers. He mentioned this to the Gendarmerie, who were quick to suggest he watch the drama on one of the new Kiev 4Ds. An officer lifted his Palm to relay the contract to Cool who, it turned out, were on their way.

Rupert was excited. Only Controllers and Very Good Europeans had access to this Kiev. D-tech was top-of-the-range and the limited early release of such a sultry model had stirred InterZone for the last month. He had already invested in a Kiev 4C and previous versions that offered thrills far beyond the normal viewing experience, but the 4D was on another plain entirely. He had maxed his credits for the 4C, and was still at an interest-only level of repayment, knew he wouldn't be able to invest in anything else until his limit was raised. Not that Rupert was complaining. He had some of the best options available, but the chance to watch the match on a 4D was awesome. He wasn't sure why Cool cats were coming along to join the chat, but felt it must be related to one of his cases. Those boys and girls were certainly thorough.

Like so many of his pals, Rupert was a Barca nut, a crazy ultra. The boy wonder Messi would score his twentieth goal of the season today, and with the 4D Rupert would be able to feel the vibration as the ball hit the back of the London net, smell the sweat on Messi's skin as he wheeled away to start his trademark celebration. At this very moment fanatics across the planet were buying items produced especially for this game. Men, women and children would show their loyalty in the best way possible, transferring millions of dollars to the companies charged with safeguarding the people's game. Without them there would be no such thing as pro footie. Soccer was all about the supporters. Sadly, though, there were times when the passion of the ultras could spill over into law-breaking. This never happened inside USE borders, but it was still a sorry, if understandable, side effect of fandom.

The Shanghai disturbances two years earlier were the most dramatic example, as gangs of dedicated merchandisers rioted, wrecking the four main megastores after a limited-edition Messi model sold out a full six hours before Barca met Matadors Madrid. Sixty-three people lost their lives as a result of defensive actions by the Chinese military. Thugs had taken advantage of this overflow of passion to loot hundreds of non-related shops. Copycat riots followed. Business-minded Beijing and the Han cultural centre of Lhasa also erupted, and then, as the mayhem became viral, nuts assaulted malls in New Delhi, Bangkok, Manila, Nairobi and Jo'burg. InterZone ran rolling specials on these outbreaks, while the corps channelling the craze responded with admirable speed, rush-releasing fresh waves of Messis to satisfy demand. A premium was added to this edition, thereby pacifying the concerns of early birds. Global love was restored.

Everybody knew that the Flamboyants would defeat London, but the score remained a mystery. The contest also had an added attraction beyond the presence of Messi – namely the ritualised humiliation of white-trash defender Terry Johns. The Euroship had firm limits on non-USE players, but Messi had overcome a poverty-stricken Mexican upbringing to claim one of the coveted alien slots in the Barca line-up. Johns – born and raised in the suburbs of London – had spent the last two weeks splashed across InterZone for his use of the word 'England' in what was seen as a racist incident during the encounter with the Munich Bears. The term 'British' had also been uttered. A liberal approach to ignorance was applied across the USE, but there was no room for such incorrect language in a modern, democratic society. Johns' behaviour was of course a reflection of a larger problem facing New Democracy.

The Union Jack had become a symbol of resistance across Europe, adopted by commons who had linked into the GB heritage cult. TJ was an adult in a position of responsibility and could not allow himself to be connected to such groups. He was a role model for millions of youngsters, and the media and political classes were rightly outraged by his behaviour, their indignation spreading through the ranks of all those employed as social commentators. In light of the Terry Johns affair and the popularity of GB45 at an underground level, the question had to be asked – did those Shanghai merchandisers die in vain?

Tweets flowed in their billions. Johns was a deserving target, although it was suspected by some that he actually enjoyed his role as a pantomime villain, while edgy comedians suggested the centre-half's vocab was part of a credit-raising plan. Stereotypes were built into promotionals at the State's request, thereby proving that diversity was safe within a homogeneous culture, but there were limitations. Redemption would follow the 'England' outrage. It had happened before. Nobody could resist a media onslaught, and there was talk of a lifetime ban and even imprisonment, but as

Johns was a celebrity and loved by the London United lowers this seemed unlikely. The star would pay a hefty fine and be expected to apologise to the Controllers and Crats he had offended, but only after he was embarrassed by the mesmerising feet of Messi. Rupert was fascinated by the story. He did not like Johns one little bit.

It took less than three minutes for Cool to arrive in an unmarked Mercedes. The driver's door opened and a plainclothes female strolled back down the hard shoulder. The Gendarmes bid Rupert farewell and returned to their patroller, and he watched them rejoin the flow of early-evening traffic, a convoy of lorries moving in the opposite direction, packed with kangaroos for the glasshouse at Junction 2.

The advertising on the side explained the situation, and he remembered the recent documentary by cult Tenderburger director Stephen Spieler, who had captured frightened joeys sitting inside what they thought were their mothers' pouches, but were in fact mimicked versions. Rupert laughed at their stupidity, turned at the sound of the passenger door opening and the Cool sliding in, oohing and aahing in one of those sexy Paris accents so loved by male Crats. The mademoiselle complimented him on his shirt, before reaching over to feel the fabric.

– A lovely texture, she said. You are a happy man who laughs and smiles. It is healthy. Cheery workers are the best of grafters.

– I was thinking of half-witted joeys in their mothers' pouches, Rupert mused. Did you see the new Spieler doc?

– No, I missed it I'm afraid. I have been busy. But where did you buy these jeans?

Her hand was on his knee, stroking the material, sending currents into his groin. He thought of Polestar laying naked on Rocket's bed, strumming as he lectured, wondered if he should respond or wait and see how this chat progressed. He looked down at the officer's manicured fingernails, saw them move slowly along his leg, and he could feel Rupert turning into Ronald, but had to remember that he was in USE rather than Euroland mode. His window opened and another hand reached in and removed the car's ignition chip. The mademoiselle's fingers were on the dash now and a large male head was floating a few centimetres in front of Rupert. The badge on the man's jacket identified him as Andreas.

– Would you mind if we travelled in the Mercedes? the mademoiselle asked.

– I will drive this rental, Andreas said. If you are agreeable. It is your choice.

– And I will operate the Mercedes, the woman concluded, with a faint hint of finality.

Rupert sniffed some sort of meat on the man's breath, layers of lotion in the clothes, the merging of subhuman and human, an interesting mix where the brutality of the four-leggers met the nobility of the uprights. He nodded and smiled, glad to fit in with the arrangement. He would be travelling in a fine auto, a beautiful mademoiselle acting as his chauffeur, like a Controller on his way to a crucial meeting. It was a taste of even greater days to follow.

– There is no time to waste if you want to see Barca in 4D. We have an outlet that will supply you with beef- and bacon-flavoured popcorn as you express your passion.

Andreas opened the door and shielded Rupert from passing machines, while the mademoiselle watched from the other side of the car. Her name was Sophie and she was clearly attracted to him, could see that he was not going to remain a Bureau forever. Rupert found himself musing, wondering what sort of date she preferred.

– Remember to tap the belt, she said, when they arrived at the Mercedes.

Once he was comfortable she turned to the other officer, Rupert's mind wandering off towards the soccer. Andreas raised a hand and spoke to his Palm. The seats were super-comfortable, the smell of hide filling the interior, and Rupert felt relaxed and content. He inspected his surroundings, noted a label on the dashboard, saw the letter R in the company's trademark font and identified rare-breed rabbit. His calm was broken. Rupert could hear honking, looked out past the evergreens planted on the side of the freeway, up towards the glass tunnel running along the top of an incline.

– There they are... someone shouted.

Hundreds of pigs were running through the tube, heading for the glasshouse at Junction 2. Their scared faces were reassuring, the jerking limbs and panic amusing, shocks built into the sides of the tunnel delivering reminders whenever they slowed down. Usually their journey would be a silent one, the tubes sound-proofed and their singing only really heard by those who went to visit a meatworks. He wondered if the system's rarely used amplifiers had been turned on. The traffic was slowing and about to come to a halt. Sophie climbed in next to him.

– Those pigs are noisy, he remarked.

Rupert's face was radiant.

– You really are a happy bunny, she said, her mouth twitching as it broke into a smile.

– Thank you, he replied. They are going to be talking louder soon, when they reach Junction 2, really screaming their heads off when the knives come out. Heads off – no pun intended.

Sophie was looking at her navigation tool and didn't seem to notice his humour.

– There are no jams building in the tube, she said. There must be another reason. Maybe they are testing the acoustics. It is very strange. We will be leaving in a moment.

Rupert nodded.

– I think I will have some of that bacon popcorn.

There was a lull in the chat.

– What did you have for breakfast today? she asked, still puzzled by the outbreak of honking.

– Croissants, ham, two cups of coffee.

– Strong coffee?

– Very strong. I have my own maker.

– We are waiting for Andreas. He is moving slowly.

The Cool operative considered some tunes.

– Do you like Paper Lace? she asked.

– Love them...

A finger hovered for a split-second before choosing the brilliant new release 'Billy Don't Be A Hero', which told the story of a young Bureau working long hours, his Super telling him to take a rest, to spend some time in Euroland. The Bureau wanted to keep grafting. There was conflict, but for the best of reasons. Rupert guessed Sophie was dedicating the song to him. Maybe he would suggest a rendezvous. He would take things slow-slow, knew it was better to stick to sexers at this point in his career. It was hard to be exact, but she outranked him, so he was a little surprised by her interest.

– They really are a noisy bunch, Sophie said.

Her smile faded. She was on full alert, had seen something unusual, and he followed her line of vision as best he could, saw a pig tumbling down the embankment, an explosion of pink limbs, the porker rolling over and over, reaching the bottom and taking time to recover, hauling itself up and looking about, sniffing the grass and shaking its head and raising a huge face that was beaming and grotesque, a parody of more official smiles.

– This isn't right, he heard Sophie say. Something is wrong.

Another pig came rolling down the slope, and looking beyond this one Rupert could see humans up there as well, one holding a device which he at first thought was a zapper or a shocker, but then realised was a laser. This person was burning into the tunnel, cutting glass, while another was removing chunks and casting them aside. It was why pigs were pooing on and polluting the freeway margins. It was messy. Dirty. Very unpleasant. The hole was becoming larger as well, two humans climbing *inside* with all that wee-wee and nasty pong, actually blocking the route to Junction 2, forcing the pigs out into the open air where other people were guiding them along the ridge and back under the tube, through a hollow, over towards the other side where he imagined there were houses and quieter roads.

– It's those fucking animal lovers, Sophie barked. Stay here.

She was out of the car, Rupert amazed and trying to understand what was happening, why the sudden change in language and tone. To be honest, he had found Sophie a little coarse.

There were six humans on the ridge and they were all dressed in black, faces hidden behind white masks. They seemed to be releasing the animals, but for what purpose? Perhaps there was a blockage, or an accidental hole had appeared further along the passage. Otherwise, such drastic action made no sense. 'Animal lovers' – that's what Sophie had said. Well, Cool knew best. He had heard about the ALF and how its poison had seeped into modern terrorism, but had always been sceptical about the scale of the problem, yet here he was watching what could be the real deal. He leaned forward, fascinated by the unfolding drama.

Sophie and Andreas were crossing the road, exploders appearing from inside their jackets.

The two pigs at the bottom of the embankment were running towards IR4. They were disorientated, unsure where to go. Rupert was disgusted. Traffic disruption was no laughing matter, however funny reporters and other medias found glasshouse breakouts. Time was money, and the loss of working minutes due to sub-human confusion was unacceptable in today's society. These animals really were stupid, just kept on grinning as they reached the freeway, drivers terrified of damaging expensive vehicles. With their wee-fronts and poo-backs they were selfish and immoral. He was angered by their lack of control and ridiculous trotters.

Sophie was near them now, shooing the pigs back to the grass verge, drivers sounding their delight, and once the subs were off the IR she fired into their heads several times, sent the fatties falling. They kicked their legs and shook their bodies, screamed loudly and were finally still. Rupert clapped his hands and cheered, happy that order was being restored. Sophie ran after Andreas, who had started to climb the slope.

Another Cool transporter arrived – this one an eight-seater – seven braves dismounting with zappers and prods, the same exploders as their comrades, and then there was a pop and Andreas was slipping backwards, rolling down the slope like the subhumans. Rupert realised that the black-clad humans had fired a shot, that Andreas had taken evasive action. These were real terrorists, the first Rupert had ever seen, the boys and girls of myth, and he watched as they ran along the ridge with other pigs, ducking under the tunnel, one figure stopping to zap at the Cools below. Luckily they were laying flat and had raised protective screens. Andreas was fine. It was a terrible thing to see these events unfold, but also exciting, even if he did wonder if it was actually a training session. It was hard to believe that this sort of outrage could happen in real life.

More Cool cars and carriers arrived on the hard shoulder. Officers clustered. Palms were held close to mouths and ears. Rupert's eyes returned to the tunnel, where more pigs had gathered at the opening, not knowing what to do, looking down the slope at the people and machines, but more at the sprawled porkers below. One of the animals Sophie had zapped was still alive and trying to raise itself up, but couldn't quite stand, was weak or too fat or both, Rupert supposed. A lard-arse, lazy stinker. Disgusting specimen. The beast collapsed, but its chest was heaving, a leg shaking, its trotter tapping. Rupert laughed so hard he almost wet himself.

THIRTEEN

MAKING SURE THE forged Palm was level, Kenny pressed it hard against his hand and waited for the cement to fix. Travelling into London meant he had to be ready to blend in. It was essential. Life was looser in the suburbs where he was landing, but even there he would stand out if he walked around bare-handed, and later he would be heading into the heart of the city. Without a Palm, he might as well stroll in naked. Bubblers would stop and stare, record and upload, call for the Gendarmerie. They in turn would notify Cool. And that would be the end of Kenny Jackson. He closed his eyes and waited.

– Thirteen, fourteen, fifteen...

Different rules applied out here. Michele's clampdown and the insurrection that followed a piece of history that would never be forgotten, the lessons passed on, fed into the minds of the young. Palms were spying devices. Peeping toms. Trackers. And InterZone polluted the thinking of everyone it reached. It was a virus. Another fifth column. Hans and Michele were cartoon pervs. The ultimate trolls. Keyboard watchers. The commons might be hard-up, the target of embargoes and sabotage, constantly belittled, but Kenny didn't care. He would never be rich or truly safe, yet neither did he have the USE inside his body trying to read his mind. He was invisible. Cool was never going to know that he preferred black tea to a latte, that he would always choose a crumpet over a muffin. As others had said, he would rather be poor and walk on his feet than rich and crawl on his hands and knees.

– Twenty, twenty-one, twenty-two. Press harder...

The craftsman responsible had done a fine job. Not only had Zacharius Hodd perfected the look of the Palm, he had also built in shades of light and texture. The glue was going to be tough to break when it was time to take the Palm off, but a stitch or two was nothing compared to the bondage of the original. The chassis of this was so embedded in the host's hand that removing it could lead to nerve damage, paralysis, maybe even amputation. Kenny was sure this was deliberate. The State wanted everyone tagged and the work had to be carried out by specialists. It was an expensive service, but despite the risk and cost involved, these machines were considered indispensable by tens of millions of people. Many regarded them as sexy. And a more dangerous model was on its way.

– Thirty-three, thirty-four, thirty-five...

The Palm 7 wouldn't be released for a couple of months yet, but it was being promoted as the most exciting upgrade ever. Kenny had heard what it could do and what it would mean at one of the talks that kept GB45 members informed about USE developments. It was believed the 7 could detect the most subtle changes in mood and, through T-Police software, the boffins' version of thought.

The Palm 7 would be sold as a major healthcare solution, but the real aim was to increase State control. Vital signs and core mechanics were monitored, fluctuations studied by T, chosen cases referred to Crats. In time, suggestions would ensure the 7 became a firm convention, before sliding into law. Anyone who refused to transfer credit for its installation would clearly have dark secrets to hide. Everyone at the talk agreed that the bubbleheads had gone mad.

– Forty-one, forty-two, forty-three...

Kenny tilted his hand a little, reflecting on the Palm's power, how vital it was to everyday life in a city such as London.

– Keep it straight. You've got to let the glue set properly.

Gloves and the use of pockets had been prohibited near sensitive locations following an attack on Heath 6, ten miles outside of Birmingham. Cool had suffered six fatalities in the assault which, while carried out by Conflict, the Controllers had blamed on local criminals. A week of mourning had taken place across the InterZone arc, Hans stepping forward to console Michele, while Cool provided the logistics for a Hardcore action in the Handsworth area. Inside two months the area was being regenerated.

USE money flowed and new-builds saw hundreds of Good Europeans relocated. The efficiency of the operation had been textbook. The USE had also learned lessons.

– Forty-nine, fifty. All done. Come on, lets see if it's worked.

Kenny stopped pressing and turned his hand over. The shell didn't budge. He shook it to make sure. Rock solid. He raised the fake Palm up for Kid Bale to inspect, his friend sitting opposite and counting down, then turned toward Zacharius Hodd. The master forger clapped his hands once. A loud bang that made the younger men jump.

– It looks good, Kid said. Nobody is going to stop you for not having one now. You'll get a feel for it I reckon, love it so much maybe you'll have a real one fitted in London, come back to spy on us, and then I'll have to shoot you in the legs.

It might have been a joke, but Kenny knew that Kid was capable. He had always been a fighter, going back to when they were kids, but as a youth his behaviour had run out of control, and yet it was Kid and his brother Ted who had formed the Wessex Boys. Previously they'd been a couple of young tearaways who liked a drink and a bundle with other locals, but after an incident at a pub well off their plot, one that saw a youth stabbed, the Bales had received a visit from GB45. The boy wasn't that badly injured, but the level of violence and presence of a knife was considered unacceptable in a Free English town. The four men in the Bales' front room were not happy. The use of a blade was seen as cowardly, effeminate and non-British, while an escalation in aggravation could not be allowed. The offender had already been bashed by the brothers, but they were not about to give his name.

The GB message was clear – cut out the ultraviolence and stop fighting your own kind. Or else. Kid and Ted heeded the warning, took on board the need to maintain order at home and focus on the bigger enemy, something that had been explained at length by one of the men present. Kid started channelling his aggression into an interest in boxing and, with the extra training, started winning bouts, while an increasing political awareness saw the brothers pulling the Wessex Boys together a year or so later. Focused and disciplined, the firm was different to its earlier incarnation. Local youths found a shared cause and links were made with like-minded souls across the West Country.

Neither did GB45 have any time for InterZone, narcotics, pornography or usury, and it was soon using the younger lads as muscle for some of their local dealings. When cocaine started to appear on the plot it hadn't taken the Wessex Boys long to find the culprits. Kid Bale led the team that dealt with those responsible, a promise made that if there was a repeat it would be harder men coming next time. The dealers' sources weren't so lucky, with two bodies found in a burning car outside Marlborough, executed by GB45 for supplying on behalf of the USE.

– Sure you're still happy making the trip? Kid asked. What about Hannah? They say there's no such thing as coincidence.

– I think there is, Kenny replied, conscious of Hodd's presence. If Cool know about me and my books, why would they send Hardcore to kill Hannah? When did they start murdering bookworms? It makes no sense. If anything, they'd want to find out where the hards are coming from, make a sweep of sellers and libraries, but they can't do that out here yet. They have their low profile to maintain. If anything, it shows they know nothing about me. I hate to say it, but Hannah was taking chances, circulating a lot of information and not being too careful. They could have picked up on that, wanted to send a warning? Perhaps that's why she died. But I still find it hard to believe.

Kid Bale was about to respond when the forger Hodd spoke. He tended to croak, his voice hoarse, words seeming to come from deep inside his chest, sentences crackling as if laced with electricity. The long periods of concentration required for his work were balanced by rushes of adrenaline and movements that could worry those nearby.

– Everyone's saying it's an assassin responsible, a professional killer, someone cold and calculated and only obeying orders, but that's unlikely. As Kenny says, why would they bother?

He left the question hanging in the air.

– Why?

He was suddenly on his feet, darting over to the curtained window, the two younger men jolting, a long hand reaching out and touching the material. Zacharius Hodd was a skeletal presence, his large face more bone than flesh, and while his appearance and mannerisms were strange enough, it was one of several stories told about him that filled Kenny and Kid Bale with a sense of dread.

– No, the murderer is much closer to home.

His mood changed. He became reflective.

– It's natural for us to want to blame an outsider. We can accept that easily, but in Hannah's case I don't feel it's true. Deception is rife. Facades and veneers... Look at those who want to control us. The greatest con ever played. A counterfeit democracy. Fake and fake again. Appearances are meant to deceive. If I can help you with some small technical matter, surely a psychopath can apply their own cunning and remain unseen? It is in the person's nature. Surely?

He ran crooked fingers through the neat creases running down the fabric, started humming what sounded like a nursery rhyme, eyelids fluttering as if he was about to fall asleep on his feet, the charge fading, but then he filled his fist with curtain and pulled it roughly to his nose, breathing deep and long. The skull behind the skin of his face seemed to be pressing further forward, stretching the features, creating another mask, heartbeat drilling inside the swelling veins of his temples. Kenny glanced at Kid Bale. They had both turned pale.

– But... Kenny began.

Hodd had dropped the curtain and flashed across the room, was leaning down low and too close, torso at a sharp angle to his legs, Kenny staring into a pair of milky green eyes. He couldn't speak. Doubted he was able to move. The room had become much smaller. A wizard's hand was on his left shoulder, pinching the material that covered his own skin and bone. The commons in the Free English plots had started to believe in magic and spirits again, a side effect of their rejection of InterZone and the loss of its technologies, the collapse of established religions and the growing idea of a shared unconscious.

– It was a person Hannah knew well. Someone close.

The forger's head was on Kenny's shoulder now. He was sniffing the cloth. The humming sound was still there, but ever so faint, a wheezing inside his lungs. Kid Bale had stood up and was on the other side of the room. Zacharius Hodd snorted and backed away, leaving behind a smell of wet feathers.

– Think of the violence involved. It was extreme. Terrible, terrible violence.

The nails of his hand flashed across Kenny's neck, barely touching the skin.

– Whoever killed her was seething. They hated themselves or they hated Hannah. Maybe both. I can feel it in my heart. Why are we assuming it is a man? It could easily have been another woman.

– It had to be someone strong, Kid said.

– What?

Zacharius Hodd's voice had taken on a clipped edge.

– The head was...

– ... nearly severed. I know. It is a woman. I am certain now. The ultimate deception. Clever. Very clever. Look for someone quiet and conventional.

The forger was sitting down again.

– I know about these things. Listen to me. I am a counterfeiter. A deceiver and a replicator and an honest man. I can be trusted.

Kenny and Kid Bale nodded, trying to look as if they were considering what he'd said, keen to get out of the flat, except this was where Kid was staying. Zacharius Hodd was leaning back in his chair, hands together, fingers tapping, the sound of his nails louder than it should have been.

– Right, I better get home, Kenny said. Jan's waiting for me.

He shook hands with the man who was maybe going to save his life, felt jagged knuckles and joints covered by the brittle paper of the thinnest pages of his oldest books. Kid Bale came with him to the door and they exchanged meaningful looks, then grinned at their foolishness, for being spooked by a story told in a pub. The forger was eccentric, but loyal.

Once he was outside, Kenny wondered at his reaction, glanced up at the window of the flat and saw that he was being watched, the skull of Zacharius Hodd pressed against the glass. He turned and hurried away, stumbling but managing to stay on his feet.

Five minutes later, as Kenny walked through the empty streets, he felt a surge of freedom. The air was harsh but fresh, streetlights electrifying the frost. His world was cold and crisp and pure. When a car approached he rushed his hands into his pockets, didn't want anyone seeing the Palm and getting the wrong idea, and once it had passed and he was alone he removed them and enjoyed the sharpness of the air. He was soon at Fred's front door.

– Cup of tea? his friend asked, once he was inside and sitting down.

– No, I can't stop. Got to get back to Jan.

He held his hand out and Fred did a quick inspection, simply nodded his head and handed over a package. Kenny slipped it inside his coat.

– Was it Hodd made this? he asked.

– It was. Hard to know what to think of him.

– Split personality. One extreme to the other. You've heard the story?

– It was you who told me.

– Me? I don't remember. When was that?

– In The Wheatsheaf. Couple of years ago. It's not true, though, is it? Just a story?

– I wasn't there when it happened, but I'm sure it did. Nobody's going to make that up, are they?

There was a long pause. Kenny thought about Hannah's murder. Outsider or neighbour? A stranger or someone she knew? The end result was the same, but it did matter. What was better for the people who lived here? An assassin meant they could trust each other, but it also meant the enemy was focusing its attention. If it was a local man then others might be at risk, while their overall security remained the same. He wondered why Zacharius thought a woman was responsible.

– You know where you've got to meet Ms Vickers then? Know what you're doing?

– It'll be fine.

– You mind yourself. She's a heartbreaker. Seriously, be careful.

There were tears in Fred's eyes when Kenny left. It was unexpected, reminded him of the reality of where he was going and what he was planning, and he thought of Jan on her own and hurried home as fast as he could without slipping on the ice.

Standing across from the house they'd shared for the past four years, he imagined it as a box full of photographs from their time together. Old-style prints. He had some from when he was a boy, but none with Jan, only digitals inside redundant cameras. It was a shame.

Small and maybe bland to someone from the city, for Kenny their home was beautiful. It was a sanctuary, the place where they could be themselves, and yet he had been keeping the truth of his trip into London from Jan for two long weeks. There was a chance he might never see her again after tomorrow and he felt terrible. A light was on in the hall and he could see a white trim around the closed living-room curtains. She would be sitting in her chair either marking children's work, reading, or listening to the town radio station. She was in the warm and he liked to think she was safe, yet any passerby could smash their way in if they really wanted. No, Hodd was wrong. It had been an outsider who attacked Hannah. He went indoors.

– Let me have a look then, Jan said, once he had leaned down and kissed her forehead.

He stood back and held out his hand.

– What do you think?

– It looks real enough, thank god. He's done a good job.

Kenny took off his coat and put it on the back of a chair, placed Fred's package on the table. He could feel the warmth of the room stinging cold hands, and he went back to Jan and got down on his knees and laid his head on her lap. She ran fingers through his hair and felt the bone, the crease in the skin where it had been split open and stitched back together, in the days when he hung around with the Bale brothers, back when he was a Wessex Boy. She searched for the pulse of his imagination, the idealism that had made her fall in love with him, an optimism that would drive them into the future.

Jan knew they were doomed. She didn't want him to go to London, had said so, but neither would she seriously try and stop him, knew the real reason and was proud. She had argued with her sister the last time they met. Loose talk cost lives. It was true. She saw the need for Kenny's lie that wasn't really a lie, and it made her love him even more. Like him, she would be brave.

Kenny was a man who protected literature and, through it, free speech. It was a travesty that the contents of books were managed by people with no understanding of what they represented and what they could mean to the masses. Good Europeans, Crats, Controllers, careerists – they were the criminals, not Kenny, her, Fred, Hannah or the detective she had talked with in the car after the funeral. Not the Bale brothers. Not GB45. Not Conflict.

She understood the pull of London. It had been her home as well, but she'd put it behind her, knew there was nothing left for the likes of them. Kenny couldn't do the same, the memory of his father being bullied and forced to run refusing to fade. He was determined to return and make his mark. This he would do. One way or the other. He had promised this was his last visit to that bleached, broken city. She started to cry, but softly, and in silence, so that he wouldn't notice.

FOURTEEN

ONCE INSIDE THE perimeter of Cuddles, Sophie fell silent, Rupert noting her sadness as she realised that the first stage of their friendship was coming to a close. He shifted his attention to the complex, found austere architecture and barren spaces between low-level blocks. There were no light shows, exotics, advertising mottos. The arrangements were interesting if a little unsettling, and yet he had no reason to be nervous. He loved the towers and plazas of the East Side where he lived and Central where he worked, the sexy mirrors of Docklands where he played, the hustle-and-bustle of the malls and the friendship of his colleagues, that moment when night fell and gold stars filled the sky. But Cuddles would be beautiful too.

Sophie parked the car and they crossed a courtyard, entered a nondescript building and escalated three floors, followed a stone corridor and arrived at an unmarked door. Sophie opened this and waved Rupert forward. Her familiar smile returned.

– Here we are, Rupert. Home sweet home.

He went inside and was welcomed by the Kiev 4D, its screen fully physical rather than floating, which allowed for a range of progressive options. It meant zero shake and even greater definition, the fixed terminal dominating the space. A recliner was positioned in front of the 4D, the walls around him decorated in pink skin. He stopped and stared.

– Time to chill, Sophie said. You have grafted and deserve the ultimate footie experience.

Rupert was in awe. The 4D oozed class, the logo alone a work of art, and he was tempted to move closer, reach out and stroke the bodywork, but Sophie wanted him to relax and who was he to disappoint? He turned towards the chair, saw that it was embossed with the Banana label, and when he was near he ran a hand along the surface, considering the care that had gone into its production and the credit transferred. The letter P was stamped on the arms and he appealed to Sophie for confirmation.

– Panda?

– *Baby* panda. Straight from Vienna.

– Expensive?

She appreciated the humour, nodded in rapid fashion, moving her head sideways to acknowledge the realities of raising and harvesting the material from lazybones layabouts, the famed craft of Vienna's panda breeders and skinners, the need for tired Crats to unwind. Delivering a mock salute, Rupert sat down and tuned his angles, a rest rising to support weary feet. Sophie stepped over and produced a handset, a deluxe faux-retro physical with manual functions. He weighed this oddity in his left hand, slightly alarmed by its meaning, but realised that it was mimicking a zapper, as he had seen Jamie Bondo do in the blockbuster clip dedicated to the promotion of the 4D.

– Thirsty? Sophie asked.

– I am, yes. Quite thirsty.

– Would you like a glass of Coca Cola?

– I would. Thank you.

– With ice? We have stars and pig-face cubes?

– Pig faces? No thank you. It will be stars for me.

They laughed in perfect time. Rupert first, Sophie second. He felt a warm surge in his chest.

– What did you think of that foolishness on the freeway, Rupert?

– The movie-making? I was enthralled. Only one scene I know, but I will be interested to see how it fits into the finished product. It could become one of the classic comedies.

Sophie's eyes narrowed as she considered his choice of cubes.

– Yes, but you thought something else at first, didn't you?

– I wasn't sure, but I soon realised it was a comedy rather than a serious shoot-em-up or tearjerker.

– Are you sure? A good number of Cool came along to help, so it must have looked as if there was trouble with the boys and girls in black. I was involved. Andreas also. But you are a Bureau and...

– B+, I am a B+.

– Yes, a B+, Techno material, a man on the move, and you know how mistakes can occur.

– I do, but it is a comedy. I couldn't help but laugh at the porky fats.

Sophie was watching his face carefully, went to speak, but stopped, changed her mind.

– You must be hungry.

– I am looking forward to the popcorn you suggested. I see a dispenser in the far corner.

– What flavour would you like?

– Beef, please.

– I will bring a carton over, and there is pizza for later. Order anything you like. Deep-deep or skinny-thin crusts. Cuddles has a range of cuisine. The best franchises are on hand.

– Cola and popcorn to start I think, with a deep-deep later. I do like a pizza. Maybe some ice-cream as well. I am being treated well, I must say.

– The system works, Rupert. We reward our friends and ourselves, but you know that better than I. My apologies once more for the delay in bringing you to Cuddles. I am sorry that you have missed the build-up.

– Those piggies rolled and tumbled. I do like a porky pizza. Skinny-thin leaves me feeling not quite full after I have finished. Deep-deep is best.

– Those pigs certainly twisted and turned. The figures in black didn't concern you? They dress in darker colours to Cool cats such as myself.

– They wore white masks. An interesting combination.

– Do you know why?

– They held up the traffic.

– They were on the ridge.

– The pigs fell down to the bottom of the hill. Their presence made the travellers slow.

– Briefly, yes.

– Any interruption of traffic flow has knock-on effects. But I am sure the drivers present were forewarned that movie-making was taking place?

– You found the whole thing very funny.

– The sight of those pigs made me laugh hard, despite the slowing down of vehicles. The flow was naturally protected and that is a credit to everyone involved. I know there are jams in many areas of the city, although thankfully never on channels reserved for Good Euros, and as far as the commons go, that is inevitable. Even so, unnecessary interruptions make my blood boil. But it was a movie. I remember...

Sophie held up a hand.

– I am very sorry, Rupert. I would love to stay and gas, but I have to leave for a short time.

She had poured his Cola and filled a container with popcorn and presented these starters on a tray.

– I will return soon, but please, enjoy the game. It is about to start. And be careful. I don't want you getting hurt.

Sophie left and Rupert puffed up. He could look after himself, but it was nice of Sophie to show her concern. He was part of the Barca community and ready to roll. He felt confident, knocked back by the clarity of the image when it appeared. Once he had recovered, he charmed it from the screen, the picture wrapping itself tight so he was fully encased. This was no ordinary beamer. Rupert was right there in the Olympic Stadium.

The intensity of the match-day experience was immediate. The real deal. Surrounds tightened and he was sitting with thousands of fellow fanatics, the sort of edgy ultras who might well attack a megastore if merchandising was in short supply. Danger lurked. He could smell beer and cheap food. There was a threat of foul language. He was nervous, but excited.

– Come on London, a cockney called.

London United had long been polished of locals, its fixtures pulling in a sedate audience of polite clappers, a mixture of Good Euros and non-European tourists. The stadium was rarely more than a third full, but the dollars were in the digitals of InterZone. Fanatics demanded a crazy atmosphere and this was created by techs. The homers and big-screen nuts craved the commons touch, with packed stands, chanting, controversy and mild levels of aggression. Rupert adjusted the language level.

– Kill the fucking Flamboyants, the same voice screamed.

Rupert turned to look at the man responsible. He was over-weight and nearing middle age, a menial with scars on his face. The cap on his head was filthy. In a normal environment this would have been disgusting, but soccer offered Crats the chance to mingle with the lowers. Rupert was captivated.

– Here they come, a shaven-headed youth shouted.

A hand rested on Rupert's shoulder.

– This is going to be a cracker, mate.

Rupert jolted at the very physical pressure, but remembered his wake-up massage and relaxed. The 4D experience was far more dynamic, which was to be expected. There was genuine volatility here, but it remained virtual, so no harm could come to him. He grinned at his fellow supporter, who wore a London rosette on his coat. The man was holding a kebab, grease dripping through the broken base of a pitta bread. It stained his trousers, which looked as if they hadn't been washed in days. The meat was cheap, a crushing of rancids that were then mixed with herbs, slices topped up with lettuce and onions. It was peasant food from Thessaloniki and Athens, devoured by drunken commons before the vegan cult emerged. It was not the sort of food Rupert would ever eat, even though the chilli sauce could not burn him in 4D.

He loved this trip. The chance to have and have-not. To be and not to be. He looked from the filling in the kebab to the face of the cockney, noted his expression and simmering fury. Yes, this was soccer all right, the game of the people, and 4D was bringing it alive in a way that he had never known before.

– Johns, you're a fucking disgrace, roared a Barca fan.

The teams were in the centre circle, hands on their hearts as the national anthem played. Rows of European flags fluttered over the Moynihan Stand. The Flamboyants seemed more keen than United.

– Stand up straight, a cockney chirped. You're a fucking rabble.

The London cloggers huffed and puffed as they chased the ball around the pitch. The first goal came after seventeen minutes when Messi ran from inside his own half, pace slow and deceptive at first, but increasing as he gained momentum. Spectators stood and blocked Rupert's view, forcing him to wave a finger and ensure they sat back down and remained in place. The boy wonder nutmegged two players and dribbled past another three before flicking the ball over TJ's head and back-healing it into the net. It was a fantastic effort and Messi ran to the Moynihan where Rupert was sitting, skidding on his knees and kissing the Barca badge on his chest.

– Brilliant goal, Rupert shouted. Fucking brilliant.

Rocket Ron had taken over. He was on his feet and other ultras were making their presence felt. Stewards looked on with concern.

– Come on London, came a faint response.

Terry Johns was receiving abuse from his own supporters now, the experts commentating and every loyal Barca fanatic, with Inter-Zone insults flowing across the hoardings. Rocket focused on the white-trash nasty. A cockney, a commons, a success. Rocket Ron flicked his fingers, taking full control of the narrative. Nobody could blame him. He had a bottle of red and drank it down, threw the empty towards the London captain. It bounced off his head, creating a gash. Blood flowed. The Barcas nearest Rocket cheered and slapped him on the back. Johns was on his knees, trying to stem the flow of claret, but his foe wasn't finished. The game was being destroyed by locals and it was about time someone stood up for the beauty of the sport. Rocket Ron reduced the background noise and heard himself pointing out the defender's defects, and amazingly it seemed as if the centre-half was listening, finally taking in the wisdom of a Crat who clearly knew best. But Johns could not control himself.

A pass was played through to Naughty Neymar and TJ went in with a firm challenge, got the ball fairly and moved away with it, but the Flamboyant fell flamboyantly, arms thrown in the air in one of those flamenco falls that the top refs invariably rewarded with a penalty and dismissal. In this case, though, he waved play on. There was pandemonium as Rocket manipulated the reaction of those around him, enlarging himself so he stood tall and strong, a giant of a fan. Rupert went with his Euroland pal, allowing this side of his personality to dominate the rest of the contest.

Barca went on to beat London 6-0 and Rupert was as pleased as Rocket. They had played their parts in the victory and the inevitable sending off of Johns. The Flamboyants came over and applauded the cheering fanatics.

– Did you enjoy the match? Sophie asked.

She was sitting next to him in the stand, a hand resting on his leg. The Kiev dozed and he turned his attention to the Cool. He had not heard her enter his room, yet how could he have done? The game had left him drained, but now it was dismissed.

– Would you mind staying here tonight? Sophie asked.

– But I thought we were going to chat? he replied.

– There will be conversations to come, but not with me. At least not today.

– I don't understand.

He hesitated. Had not wanted to ask the question.

– Why am I here?

He didn't like uncertainty and had been controlling his concerns since the freeway, but now he was being invited to a sleepover. The notion that he had made a mistake hit him hard. Cuddles was a cheerful if austere location, but he was no fool, knew what it could represent. He had not confronted the reason for his arrival yet, as he was trained to never question the State, had told himself that his opinion was needed on a case. But that made no real sense. Questions could be asked during grafting hours. Unless it was an emergency. Then why wait until tomorrow? He was confused. What if he had made an error. Acted in incorrect fashion. He glanced back in time.

There was the change of routine when Polestar stayed the night; his failure to report her offensive comments on paedophiles; not recognising and greeting Kat Romero when she was being serviced at Bark!; laughing at the amateur efforts of Sophie and Andreas on the freeway shoot. But none of these were genuine mistakes. He could explain his conduct in each case. His thinking felt blurred.

– I want to go home, he whispered.

Sophie saw the Crat's anxiety and removed her hand.

– There is no need to worry. Someone wants to meet you. That is all.

He didn't seem to be listening.

– Horace Starski is in London and he would like to talk.

– Controller Horace?

– He is eager to meet you.

Rupert flopped back in his recliner. It took a while for the news to register. He was elated.

– Controller Horace? Are you sure?

– I am certain. He admires your graft. It is a great honour. An incredible achievement.

FIFTEEN

FOLLOWING TWO LATTE-driven meetings at Pearly Tower and lunch in Mayfair with his chum Ralph Malls and several London-based investors, Controller Horace proceeded to Cuddles. Here he spent two hours in conference with Commander Fabian, discussing the security situation on Monkey Islands – the amusing codename for the old British Isles. The immediate news was positive. An assassin had been neutralised and an anarchist plot foiled, three members of the Geordie Boys had been taken into custody in Gateshead, while an attack on a Cool unit outside Manchester had resulted in a successful Hardcore action in Salford. Fabian Schmidt then raised the issue of sparrows flying about under the East Side domes. Had the Controller seen these rogues from his penthouse? The two men talked at some length about this serious breach.

Their business concluded, Horace Starski retired to a relaxation suite. He was attending a formal dinner that evening, but had a number of free hours in which to chill. He bathed and steamed before drifting to a recliner to de-stress. Having briefly dozed and feeling energised, he asked that his favourite Crat be invited to join him, with the relevant coffee and muffins provided, plus a range of additional nibbles. This Bureau (B+) had attended his lectures as a youth and a reunion was due.

Bob Terks greeted Rupert Ronsberger on arrival, scanning him in a paddock between inner and outer doors. Horace Starski watched on his Palm. A pal of Rupert's was with him and he ran her history across his screen. He was interested in everyone he met, but this intro was necessarily brief. Core data told him what he already knew, that Sophie had first met Rupert at the chat on IR4, when the thrusting young Crat was invited to Cuddles. He readily accepted and his behaviour had been impeccable. Controller Horace congratulated himself on both the timing and location of the rendezvous, having liaised with Fabian Schmidt to see if a tie-in was possible. The terrorists responsible for the tube outrage had been under surveillance and could have been stopped, but he'd wanted to see how his pal would react. He was planning to probe Rupert on this in due course. Sophie had not known what was to come and had performed superbly. He was impressed. The animal lovers were in custody and involved in some enthusiastic Q&A.

Rupert left the paddock and entered the suite. He had been unable to sleep properly, such was his excitement. An ambition was being fulfilled, and he had to be at his best. Portraits of Jean Monnet and Henri Spaak drew his attention, features playing in slo-mo. There was a rich smell of skin in the air, Rupert identifying it as reptilian, but he was more interested in the faces of the trailblazers, his knowledge of history second to none inside the B+ range – although this was only a personal opinion. Despite his love of Controller Jean and Controller Henri, he could not obsess as he was here to see his guru, and this visionary was alive and prospering and raising a hand.

Controller Horace waved from his recliner. He was tilted with feet up, decked in oversized Michael Mouse slippers. Rupert was surprised, given the subhuman status and recent InterZone debates concerning rodent droppings on the margins of London, but the man's successes had elevated him to such heights that he could wear unusuals and thrive. This Best European had been Rupert's hero for years and his lips started to tremble. He tried, but could not stop the motion. While he had attended the Controller's lectures at the Hallstein, they had never engaged in conversation. First the Kiev 4D, then the Barca 6-0, now this audience... But what could he say that would make a good impression? He had questions, yet they might sound foolish. He preferred to listen and learn as Horace Starski spoke of great things, as the sexer Polestar had done in his apartment.

– Please, sit down.

Friendly, humble, accommodating – Controller Horace was pure class. But Rupert could not move.

– Can you hear me? What is the matter? Please, take a seat.

Rupert felt as if his bones were about to splinter when he forced them to move.

– Thank you, he spluttered.

– Hot chocolate or a cappuccino?

– That would be nice. Thank you.

– Freedom of choice, young man... The right to choose. I know you like both options. We fought hard for such fundamental freedoms. Never underestimate the difference between plain black coffee or the same brew with milk and perhaps sugar, or a frothy cappo sprinkled with chocolate. These decisions are what make us human. The mark of a civilised society.

Rupert beamed, but then realised the depth of the message and altered his expression.

– I will take a cappuccino, please.

The Controller flicked wands and eased further back in his recliner as they waited for their refreshments to arrive, another line of conversation quickly emerging.

– A good game, I believe? London United thrashed and Terry Johns humiliated. Fantastic.

Horace Starski had no interest in soccer, but knew that Rupert was a fanatic.

– Yes, I enjoyed it very much. Did you attend a beam, sir?

– Please, call me Controller. Or Controller Horace if you prefer. Really, there is no need for two chums to be so formal. No, I did not have the pleasure. Too much to do. I am only in London for a brief visit and there are importants to meet and business to conduct, not to mention unscheduled get-togethers and chinwags. I must stay alert for whatever occurs. Fluidity is a great asset.

– Most definitely, Rupert replied, finding his voice at last.

He felt that Controller Horace had raised some fascinating points.

– I like to be direct, Rupert. Get to the point after brief preliminaries. Even so, let us wait some further minutes, enjoy the ambience of the moment.

The door opened and a new friend entered with a wheelie, accompanied by Bob Terks. The lady was from Budapest and monitored the Cuddles kitchen, had helped the Controller when he was in conference with the Commander. She was a security whizz and her future was bright, of that Horace Starski was sure. She arranged their drinks and nibbles before leaving them in peace. Bobby went with her, as previously agreed. The two men sipped and munched in relative silence, commenting on taste and texture, before the older of the colleagues focused their chat.

– I have been watching your progress with interest, Rupert. You are said to be a Bureau who never misses a detail or entertains a doubt. One of the truest believers. Yet we are all human, are we not?

Rupert nodded enthusiastically.

– We are certainly human, Controller.

He was overwhelmed by this recognition of his talents, although it would have appeared brash to admit to these qualities. Crats had to be self-effacing at all times, whether Bureau or Techno, and whatever their grading, but he had already turned the head of his Super, been charmed by Cool and treated to the full Kiev 4D experience. Now this.

– Please, tell me about the mysterious Hannah Adams.

For a moment Rupert was flummoxed, then realised it was a trick question.

– I don't know anyone of that name, I'm afraid.

Horace Starski raised his cup and tasted the last mouthful of coffee through milk and flecks of chocolate. A fine cappuccino. The Crat was leaning forward, clearly energised.

– Hannah Adams. Think hard, my friend.

Rupert smiled and shook his head slowly, knew that this particular Controller had a playful nature.

– Nobody of that name comes to mind?

– Nobody.

– What about Yeovil? You have heard of the town?

– A retarded outpost. It is full of commons, most likely a dull and depressing place in which to live, with the usual racist element. Eventually it will be polished.

– Exactly. Well done, Rupert. But tell me more. A recent incident occurred there. One that you saw, I believe?

Rupert realised what Controller Horace was talking about and allowed recognition to show in his face.

– I am sorry, I didn't realise this was directly related to my graft. I dismiss the details of each case once I have ended my enquiries, so as not to become attached or personally involved. It is important to look forward in life.

– As you were of course taught, Horace Starski replied. But to completely forget, and so quickly, is a very difficult skill to master. Some say it is impossible.

– I have always found it easy.

The Controller nodded. He would have said exactly the same when he was an ambitious young Crat, a Bureau determined to progress to Techno and beyond.

– We do remember, though, don't we? On a deeper level we never forget anything. We always know what is true and what is not.

– Every case I deal with is erased from my memory. In theory it might be retrieved, under hypnosis perhaps, or with the help of specific chemicals, but the nature of my tasking means a decision must be correct and it must be final. Lasting concerns cloud future investigations. I am always loyal to my education. Whatever the State tells me is the truth.

Controller Horace knew that Rupert was conforming, as anyone who wanted to succeed must do, and while it irked him a little to hear these lines being returned so many years later, he would stay cheerful and try another approach.

– Can you remember what you had for breakfast this morning?

It was a mischievous question.

– I started with...

Horace Starski held up a hand. Rupert had missed the subtlety of his enquiry, was responding in literal fashion. Either that or he was being impudent. The former was more likely.

– No, there is not a need to list the items. Please, tell me what happened after you were asked to stop on IR4. I want to hear about the pigs.

Rupert Ronsberger spoke quickly.

– There were improvements being made to a tube on the ridge above the freeway. That was my first assessment of the situation. This work included the removal of glass sections and their replacement with stronger or cleaner versions. Pigs were the nearest subs to the workers and they rushed to the exit. Maybe they were confused by the commotion. I am unsure. They are very stupid animals.

– How were the workers dressed? What colour were their clothes?

– They wore black, which given the nature of the job was a perfect choice.

– How so?

– The dirt that splatters will be less obvious, thereby avoiding more regular washing, the wasting of time and cleaning materials. I could not see their faces as they wore white masks. These would have been used to protect delicate skin from the contents of the tube. These are toxic environments, although I am not an expert and have never been inside a glass tunnel.

He laughed heartily, raised a finger and thumb and pinched the end of his nose.

– The stench of urine would be nauseating and dangerous to health. Huge amounts of excrement must also be present. Pigs are terrible stinkers.

– The tubes are washed once a month.

– May I ask, how is this done?

– Water is pumped through them, but that's not important.

– Surely a detergent is used?

– Yes, a detergent is added. But we are beginning to stray.

– A monthly rinse seems modest, Rupert mused. This is only my personal opinion. There will be constant additions to the flow of urine. Subhumans are forever weeing and pooing and they do this wherever and whenever they fancy. What would happen if *we* behaved in such a way? There must be dead subhumans in there also. Some are going to die when their hearts pop and I wonder how they are removed. The traffic must keep moving. Conditions will deteriorate quickly. The workers maintaining these structures deserve the enthusiastic thanks of the wider community.

– You say that pigs left the safety of the tunnel. And you imply that a second assessment was needed to clarify the situation. It seems likely that these were not menders after all.

– Some of the pigs did leave, yes. Two fell down the embankment and it served them right. That was amusing, but there was a darker side to the episode. Human traffic could have been delayed.

– I heard there was a violent clash between Cool and those on the incline, Controller Horace mentioned. That is what happened. It was an outrage, Rupert. A terrorist outrage.

Horace Starski adjusted his recliner and sat upright. This Crat rushed to trivia, danced in circles, and yet he was sure there was another level to his character.

– It was a movie in the making, Rupert continued. There was no way I could have known from the first scenes. I must praise those involved. There was a zapfest involving pro and amateur actors. I am not sure of the nature of the production, but I do believe it is a comedy.

– You witnessed a raid carried out by anarchists, Rupert. It was not a movie. These were murderous rebels. They were trying to free the pigs.

The Crat giggled. Controller Horace was a tease. He remembered his days at the Hallstein, the wit and wisdom of his guru, the tall tales and impossibles.

– Our enemies could never stage an assault like that inside the Reading Line, Rupert said, deciding to play the Controller at his own game. If they could, then London itself would be under threat. We must be alert to malcontents, that is true, and probe the regions that reject InterZone, but under our domes we are safe from those who hate democracy. This is the promise of Hans and Michele. We are strong and the terrorists are weak.

It had been a busy day and Horace Starski was tired. Even slightly irritable. He would try another angle, but before he could speak Rupert was talking about InterZone and its star-crossed lovers as if they were real people, something that was the norm among Good Europeans, but nevertheless grated, and he inwardly sighed as he was told about Hans and his hidden Berlin home,

Michele and the life she led in Brussels, the sacrifices the pair made, their friendship with Captain Euro, and then the trail led back to IR4 and pigs and creatives, the words smoothing into each other until they became a semi-robotic drone, the hum of a half-human computer, and yet there was something soothing about the delivery, and the nonsense convinced. Controller Horace was confused.

There seemed to be another layer of thought running through the repetitions, even if the digressions always returned to official policy. He was probably wrong. If the Crat was less confident, he could have put this rambling down to the nerves he had displayed earlier, a naive attempt to say exactly what was expected and dress it up in babytalk, but after a slow start when he was clearly in awe, Rupert was now enthusiastic, confident and increasingly ecstatic. It was time to intervene.

– Would you be able to retrieve Hannah Adams, do you think?

Controller Horace had identified the woman as a nuisance. She was anarchic and noisy, made her views too well known, believed she was untouchable in her Free English town. Her attitude was beyond reconstruction. He wondered if the hooligans who had come to Britain centuries earlier had been expelled from Scandinavia and Continental Europe. It didn't really matter, as history was fluid, but it might explain their rejectionism. He insisted he detested the Hannahs of these islands, their customs and lack of respect, and yet she reminded him of Belle.

– Adams? Rupert repeated, wide-eyed. Was she part of the repair team?

– No, she was not. I am referring to a case, Rupert. A serious matter.

There was a long pause. The Bureau closed his eyes. Controller Horace waited. He rarely angered, but could feel this negative emotion stirring.

– You are talking about the woman who wanted to become a movie star? Rupert finally asked.

The Controller flicked fingers and his chair was upright. He moved forward, Michael Mouse slippers firmly on the floor.

– Your Super explained the situation?

– She did.

– And you are happy with what she had to say?

– Of course. She would only tell me the truth. Good Europeans never lie.

Controller Horace's voice hardened.

– It is what we do best, Rupert. Our system is based on lies. The USE is a huge deceit. We fabricate and manipulate, say one thing and do another. Our history is built on falsehoods told across generations, a slo-mo blitz of deceptions. As the great Jean Monnet said: 'Europe's nations should be guided towards the superstate without their people understanding what is happening. This can be accomplished by successive steps, each disguised as having an economic purpose, but which will eventually and irreversibly lead to federation.'

Rupert smirked.

– We talk about honesty and liberal values as that is what the commons want to hear, but the reality is that we are a bunch of liars who have destroyed democracy and can do whatever we want.

Rupert chuckled.

Horace Starski clenched his fists and waited for a response.

– I saw my Super at Bark! But at first I did not recognise her.

– What?

– I had never seen her naked before.

– Naked?

– She was being serviced by a date.

– You yourself were with Polestar...

– I was not expecting to see Super Kat at the club, and in any case, my attention was elsewhere. I was showing respect and helping a less-fortunate bod. Her sexer was pumping her hard, in time to the beats.

Controller Horace closed his eyes and counted to ten. He opened and then shut them again. This time he counted to twenty.

– How did you feel when you saw the attack on Hannah?

Rupert's smile faded a little.

– I was shocked, unsure of what I was viewing, but I quickly adjusted and then I was given a full explanation and the file was closed.

– The assault looked real, though. Do you agree?

– It did, yes. The acting was of such a high standard that it fooled me, warped my logic for a short period. It was terrible to see someone so frenzied.

– But how could such an attack take place? Controller Horace asked. It is not positive to see Cool or even Hardcore depicted this way. They are here to help the population, not strangle them with lengths of wire and nearly remove their heads. More importantly, that sort of action would never be recorded and made public. There are safeguards. Cool meets InterZone.

– I did wonder...

– Did you now?

– But only briefly. Once I heard about the absurd dream of this Hannah Adams, her desire to leave the shires and become a celebrity actor in Hollywood, I knew the plot would be of low quality, but that did not explain the brutality of the assault. I then reasoned that it was a satire. An agent of the USE acting out of character in order to emphasise their love of the masses. I am not saying that we are pushovers, as at times Cool is forced to respond to mindless violence with measured force, while Hard-core is there to guard us from the more murderous rebels, but these units are always fair and only use their strength as a last resort. They would never carry out such a brutal slaying of a lone female.

– This is your honest explanation for what you saw?

– Yes, Controller. It is a simple enough story, but I have not thought about the scene since that day. The tumbling of pigs made much more of an impression. It was so funny. I am sure it must be available to replay on InterZone. Will you have time to view the show, do you think? I can't recommend it enough.

Horace Starski was nodding slowly, but he had lowered his eyes. This Bureau was incredible. He had explained away a vicious murder and refused to respond to a verbal assault on the integrity of the USE. He had merely smirked. Treated it as a joke. He was either an idiot, a psychopath, or so advanced in his cunning that he had genuine Controller potential. The man from Brussels was determined to discover the inner Rupert Ronsberger.

SIXTEEN

KENNY SET OFF at eight in the morning, concealed in the back of a lorry taking building materials to a depot in West London. He was wrapped inside a reflective cloak and carried an oxygen pill in case the air became too tight. It was pitch black in the windowless container, but he had a beam and music by Shostakovich and Scientist, a print of Herbert Sutherland's *Fiddle Me Free*, the original safe in the All Souls library. He'd read the novel several times before, liked to dip in and out of it as the humour lifted his mood.

Going on the rarity of the hard it may never have been digitised, but a deletion was just as likely seeing that pre-USE materials relating to the Second World War had been targeted early. Quickly and quietly confiscated at first, the various factual and fictional accounts were then openly denounced as lies and racist slurs. The State's version of the conflict was very different to that which had gone before, but the huge number of books meant thousands had survived and made their way into the hidden collections of the underground.

Set in a British army camp in Persia during the war, far from the fighting, the heroes of *Fiddle Me Free* found themselves stuck in a cold, barren landscape with little to do. The narrator was Thor Arnulf Nordvaago – aka Big Oley – a drinker from South Shields, son of a Norwegian he had never known. He shared a tent with Taff and Alfie, the first of these a cunning ginger-haired Welshman, the second a slow-thinking but big-hearted ginger-haired English-man. Little Eppy was a regular visitor, a Jewish thinker who liked to argue the toss. Tiger was the bullying RSM, Joe Golightly a kind officer. Neither of these two was particularly bright. A chunk of Britain was there in the characters and recognising stereotypes was part of the joke. The story revolved around a rare tin of bacon and how Big Oley and the others would cook it without the smell leading to their arrest, seeing as Alfie had stolen it while on guard duty.

The lorry stopped and started as it negotiated lights and junctions, eventually picked up speed and settled into a steady rhythm, Kenny knowing they were on IR4 and properly on their way. This was the easiest part of the journey, the real danger coming when they reached the M25. Gendarmerie checked vehicles at random here and beady-eye lenses lined a twelve-lane strip known locally as the London Wall. Frequent arrests were made and the news splashed across InterZone as a deterrent to any undesirables thinking to enter the city. Exits leading away from London lacked the same surveillance. The cloak he was wearing might well save him, because when added to the bulk of a lorry's cargo it made a person near enough invisible to scans.

Kenny pushed himself to read and was soon in Burma, didn't want to be thinking about what was coming next in England. He had another of Herbert's books – *Magnie* – which was sad and haunting, saw a sense of loss linking the two, people dealing with problems in different ways. He had learned from the dustjacket that the author was a teacher in the North-East and seemed to have been a South Shields man like Big Oley, but doubted he would ever find out more.

Despite the fear he was suppressing, after a while he started to drift off, having been unable to rest properly the night before. The book slipped from his grasp as the dubwise sounds of Scientist soothed him to sleep. He missed the slowdowns on the M25, waking with a jolt when there was a loud banging on the back doors. Five spaced-out blows meant they had arrived safely.

He raised a hand to shield his eyes as daylight flooded the inside of the lorry. Stuffing *Fiddle Me Free* in his bag, he was quickly on his feet and jumping out, hurrying through stacked wood and bricks, following a man he didn't know to a shed. Tubby Nowakowski was waiting and they shook hands warmly, the Londoner motioning for them to fill their arms with boxes of bagged nails, which they then carried to a van. The back was open and they dumped their cargo, the interior thick with the smells of oil, rags and metal. Another of his friends reached out of the shadows and pulled the boxes further into the vehicle. Kenny gave Steve a thumbs-up and followed Tubby to the front. The van left the yard with Steve leaning forward between them, passing a bottle over, followed by an opener. Kenny removed the top and raised it to his lips.

– Lovely.

– Pleasant trip? Steve asked.

– Fantastic scenery. No, it was fine. Spent half my time in an army camp with Oley, Taff and Alfie.

Tubby and Steve were confused.

– Oley?

– Characters in a book. I got here in one piece, that's the important thing.

– It's been a while, hasn't it? How's Jan?

– She's been fine. Until recently, anyway, but I'll tell you about it later. She sends her love.

– How long since you were last in London?

– Six years. You had your thirtieth birthday in The Pipemakers.

– That was a long old night. Do you remember, Steve?

– Just about. We ended up in The Dolphin, didn't we?

– We did. But you ended up in the canal as well.

– Nearly drowned.

– No you never.

– How many people has that happened to over the years? It could change your life forever. It wasn't nice, you know. Or you end up dead and never see what happens next, never meet new people or see those you know get older. There's no happy endings, I can see that.

There was a brief silence.

– I'm Karen, another voice sounded. Seeing as nobody is going to introduce me. Cheerful soul, isn't he?

Kenny turned to say hello and immediately knew he wouldn't want Karen as an enemy. She had razored features and peroxide hair and an intensity that worried him at first, but after a few seconds cheered him up as well. The English needed nutters if they were going to fight and defeat the psychos of Hardcore, and he was sure she was a headcase. Her grip was firm when they shook hands.

– Look over there, Tubby said, pointing to a Yummy outlet. What's missing, Kenny?

The place was pristine and plastic, and he naturally wanted to say character.

– The Cowley Curry Room. It's gone.

– Mickey Patel as well, Tubby explained. Official story is he received a generous offer for the place, was so pleased he packed up and took his family to India the next day, but we know that's bollocks. He was a proud Englishman, made it well known, argued against all that Protective Custody stuff, but Cool slapped a PCO on him anyway. Said he was being bullied by racists, asked how could he feel local when his ancestors came from Gujarat? We think he's there now. Deported. 'For his own good'. It does your head in living round here.

– See, they've turned it into a coffee shop, Karen added. Sells fancy cakes. Like there's a shortage. How much coffee can you drink? How many pastries can you eat?

Tubby updated him on mutual friends as they continued, added a couple of jokes, and during the fifteen-minute drive Kenny thought about Mickey and how he had at least stood a chance due to the USE's deals with India, the cheap labour brought in to undercut local wages. With trade-unions banned, the commons had nobody to represent them, minimum rates of pay long abolished as undemocratic. He wondered what Mickey Patel would make of Gujarat.

– Nearly home, Tubby said. You can rest up for a bit. Have a nice cup of tea.

The van had entered Uxbridge, a car park to their left packed with market stalls, part of a growing trend among locals. Chain-controlled malls and hypermarkets, married to higher taxes for small businesses, had driven the independents from the high street, but a new generation was fighting back, sole traders selling their wares off tables in defiance of USE law. Green, self-help values were nagging at the edges of the city, but a destructive drug problem cancelled any gains. This part of London was very different to Central and the four Gates.

– How's that beer going down? Steve asked.

– Nicely. I brought some Kingdon with me. Couldn't carry a barrel, so it's bottles I'm afraid.

– Very kind of you, Kenneth. We'll have one later.

They pulled up outside a row of flats, Tubby backing close to the building before the others jumped out, quickly passing through glass doors and a short corridor, coming out into the open air and crossing a yard, flanked by staggered concrete. The graffiti was kept to certain walls, more mural than Jonesy and Smithy, inspired by LS Lowry and Norman Cornish, two heroes for those of a heritage persuasion.

– Get the kettle on, Steve, Karen said, once everyone was safely inside their flat.

They disappeared into the kitchen, Kenny following Tubby and sitting down in a living-room chair, finally able to relax. The depot switch and subsequent car journey had been as dangerous as his time on the M25, maybe more so, given the threat of spies. The USE had plenty of informers on the payroll, despite the fact they were risking their lives. Operating under the constant threat of arrest, torture and execution, the London firms could show no mercy to traitors. InterZone beat down on them. Palms were everywhere.

Kenny was in some serious company and yet he was the man on the mission. Despite his London origins, he felt like a country cousin, the book-loving librarian he was, someone not used to the stress of city living, a man who lived beyond the heavy manners of genuine State control.

– We're starving, Karen announced as she came into the room. Steve's made some sandwiches.

Kenny had been warned they were speedheads, but wasn't about to say anything. He didn't need an argument, and this was a short stopover. He would be on his way in a couple of hours.

– Is it good to be back in London, then? Tubby asked.

– Haven't seen much of it yet, but I'm looking forward to tonight. How have you been?

– Can't complain. There's plenty of building going on, the usual investments, everything sold off-plan to millionaires. Makes me sick, but it's work and a cover. It's harder and harder to live here, though. Constant lies and bullshit. Endless sniping and prying. It's all denied, so after a while you wonder if you're imagining things, start to think you're cracking up.

– You've done more than your fair share, Kenny said. You should come and live in the country. Life's a lot easier.

He thought about Hannah's murder, how long their freedom was going to last, and he missed London, even though it had so many problems, the resistance here less organised and more fractious. Before Tubby could answer, Karen had flopped down, raised her legs and propped a bowl of crisps on her knees. She was skin and bones.

– Not me, she said. Steve neither. We could never live out there, Kenny. No offence, but I'd go insane. I don't mind dying here, I honestly don't, just as long as I take some bubbleheads with me.

– Fucking right, Steve agreed, coming in with a tray that carried their tea and a stack of sandwiches.

He placed it on the table and sat down. Looking at the man while he was still and in close-up, Kenny realised he was even thinner than Karen. It was the whizz-whazz responsible, and she was right, life in Wessex would cut off their supply and drive them mad.

– We're too far gone, Tubby said. You left when you were young, escaped having a Palm fitted. We've got the machine inside us. The technology is basic, dedicated to tracking, but who knows what they're developing.

– Doesn't bother some people, Steve said, but if you've got a brain it'll make you paranoid.

Kenny wanted to tell him the drugs didn't help, but what did he know? He had it easy. There was no point mentioning the Palm 7.

– I can watch InterZone, see what's going on, but if Cool want me I'm finished. There's nowhere to hide then. Unless I do what Karen did, but I can't. I'm not strong enough.

Kenny didn't know what he meant, turned towards Karen.

– I had no choice she said, in a whisper.

– She was taken away by Cool when she was a teenager, Steve explained. Her parents were arrested and never seen again. They sent Karen on a special vacation. You can imagine what happened.

– A rendition?

Steve and Karen nodded.

– They brought her back. Her uncle was on the run and they wanted to use Karen as bait, but the Germans attacked the transporter she was in outside Munich, freed her and one of their own. Willie Müller, he was the bloke who tried to blow up Hardcore Central on Wilhemstrasse. The Germans passed her to the Dutch and after she spent a month in The Hague fighting an infection she was smuggled across the Channel. Hates bubblers with a vengeance, don't you?

Karen raised her arm and removed an artificial hand, her eyes locked on the shocked reaction that filled Kenny's face. The hand carried its own forged Palm, and he briefly wondered if it was the work of Zacharius Hodd, before focusing on the stump and its taut pink skin. Steve leaned back in his chair and looked at the ceiling while Tubby peered into his tea. Kenny knew that he was staring, but couldn't move.

– Amputation by train. I did it myself. Laid on the ground and put it on the railway line and a Eurostar sliced it off. The Munich to Paris service. First Class Special. Hundreds of Good Euros onboard. Me in the dark. Unseen by humans and in a second invisible to InterZone as well.

Kenny didn't know what to say. It was another sort of existence. He was out of his depth. No wonder Karen, Steve and maybe Tubby were on the speed.

– I had no choice, she continued. The chip was buried deep and it would have taken a top-level surgeon to remove it, and there wasn't one handy and no time either. Live or die, that was my choice.

Her voice was so faint now that Kenny could barely hear the last words. She changed again.

– Give me a blue, Karen half-shouted at Steve, who jumped at her burst of energy. Come on....

He passed over a capsule.

– Go easy on those, Tubby said.

Karen flared up, but Steve leaned forward and intervened.

– It's fine, Tubs. Don't worry. She can handle it.

Steve took one for himself. He lifted the plate off the table and passed it around.

– Very nice, Karen said, foot tapping fast as she ate. You know how to make a sandwich, don't you Steve? Kenny... we're going to get married. Did you know that? Will you come to the wedding? There's a Spiritualist church near here. It's not grand, more of a shack really, but it has this little garden round the back that the congregation planted. You'll like it when you see it, living in the shires, and well... the church has this fantastic atmosphere. And when we die one day, if it's still there and our ashes haven't been stolen by Brussels, added to one of their bubblehead roads, then we want them scattered in the garden. That would be the best place for us I think.

Kenny raised his tea and wished them well.

– It would be an honour, but you know, there's this old Norman church near where we live called All Souls. Built on Saxon ruins. You could get married in there if you wanted. It's greenwood now, but open to everyone. Spiritualists would be more than welcome.

Steve widened his eyes.

– What do you think, Karen?

– But the shack and the garden is where we go and sit. That's our special place. Would we even be able to come back into London after? They would be watching you, Steve.

– London's fucked, Tubby said. Has been for years.

– They could follow me, yes, but they wouldn't do anything. Why should they?

– When you tried to return they'd know, wouldn't they?

– People move about. I've done nothing wrong. At least not as far as they know. Maybe we should leave London for good.

– No, Karen shouted. I can't live out there.

– Bubblers are sneaky fuckers, Tubby remarked. You'd be better off staying away if you left.

– Thanks Kenny, Karen said. But when you see our church you'll understand. Won't he, Steve? That's where we're going to get married. And did you know that...

They listened to Karen as she spoke, Steve trying to calm her when she became agitated, and after they'd finished eating she went into the kitchen and he followed her with the tray, their voices rumbling along for a while before Karen groaned loudly and began to cry. Kenny felt bad for them, kept talking with Tubby and tried to shut out their confusion, the two men counting down towards the evening rush hour. The traffic would act as camouflage, the darkness adding to their confidence, a psychological as well as practical boost to their chances of getting over to Wandsworth safely. He was looking forward to seeing Frank and Wes again. They were less volatile than the UXB nuts. Once he landed there his mission would be properly underway.

When they were ready to set off on the next part of his trip, Karen and Steve decided to join them. Kenny didn't want them in the car Tubby was using instead of the van, but couldn't dictate, was in his driver's hands, and at least they were only going part of the way. Even so, he wasn't comfortable. They were a liability and he was on edge as it was.

– What's it like out where you live then? Karen asked, once they were on the move.

– It's a lot safer than London. For the moment. No Cool, no Hardcore, no InterZone, no Crats.

– You were lucky slipping through the Wall like that, Steve said.

– Maybe it's not as secure as they want us to think, Kenny replied. Look at the Free English areas. We broke away and Brussels can't get us back. Not without a war, anyway. Jan reckons the USE is weaker than it makes out.

– Why have you come back to London? Karen asked.

– My uncle's seriously ill, he lied. He lives in Wandsworth.

– Sorry to hear that, Steve said.

– Yeah, sorry, Karen agreed. I hope he'll be okay.

Kenny turned as she reached into her jacket and took out a Z. Placing it on her false palm, she broke the capsule and lifted it up, tilting it so the powder slipped into her mouth.

– What the fuck are you doing?

He couldn't believe it. The car had windows. Anyone could report her and then they'd be finished.

– What's it got to do with you? she snarled, leaning forward. We're looking after you. Nobody can see me. I'm not fucking stupid.

Her eyes were burning with a fury he knew wasn't really directed at him. Her rendition, the amputation, a life on the run... Even so, he was fuming.

– Calm down will you, Tubby said. Come on...

– You can fuck off as well.

Steve put a hand on Karen's shoulder, but she shrugged it away and turned her face to the glass. Kenny kept his mouth shut. He didn't want to make things worse. Despite her hatred of everyone and everything connected to the USE, she'd allowed State-supplied drugs to make her weak. Steve as well. They were loose canons. Maybe Tubby was the same. He knew the rebel crews were struggling in some of the metropolitan areas. InterZone nagged the mind and chemicals clouded it, caused chaos and a breakdown in discipline. There had been clashes between different factions and even manors, and some of these had escalated into tit-for-tat gang warfare and criminality.

Tubby tapped his player and released a selection of English Pride songs. Branded racist for no honest reason, the Bulldog label constantly attacked those in power and had been deemed terrorist for its efforts. Even so, it remained hidden and was doing well, dealt in hards as well as digitals, and had its own pressing plant. Bands such as Churchill Rules, Proper Liberal Values and Horse-power UXB captured the feelings of those who believed in freedom. Identity, unity and independence was the main subject matter of a wave of exciting young lyricists, but commons roots and the non-PC nature of their messages meant they were smeared as so many had been in the past. First up was 'Mention The War' by Churchill Rules. Tubby cranked up the volume.

– Sorry, said Karen, once the song ended, shifting forward and placing her real hand on Kenny's shoulder. It's just, you know... it all boils up in your head... and I suppose thinking about us getting married and the idea of a church... everything really... what's happened before... what's coming.

– It's fine, Kenny said. It doesn't matter. It was my fault. Sorry.

Proper Liberal Values went straight into 'National Health', followed by a version of 'England Belongs To Me' by Cock Sparrer, everyone in the car singing along to a Free English anthem. Horsepower UXB delivered 'Democratic' and 'Chopstick Chiv', while the Two Islands label added Cardiff outfit Dragonhead and their 'Somerset Miner', Cork's United Cross and 'Palmcore Ponce', while Glasgow's Street Squad roared through 'Kill All Nonces (Kill Saviles First)'.

Tubby turned south before they reached the approach to the West Side Gates, crossing Kew Bridge and passing the botanical gardens with its new luxury towers sold on an eighty-percent investment one year earlier. Twenty percent belonged to Crats, while the rest remained empty as they grew in price. The gardens added novelty value to the cost of an apartment, and Kenny decided that this part of the South Circular was essentially a tube for the area's workers.

He saw his first domes of the trip, tiny replicas of the main bubbles, his anxiety increasing as Tubby turned the music off to concentrate on his driving. Approaching Mortlake, the landscape started to change, recently built commons blocks sitting on the other side of a junction. They stopped at a set of traffic lights and saw the beating blue ball of a Cool patrol on the crossroads.

– Act normally, Tubby said. They're not interested in us.

A young local was standing on the pavement next to his car. Two Cool were with him, one holding a coffee and a muffin, the other with a smile on her face and a hand on her zapper. Most of the passing drivers were fooled by this show of friendship, but not

Kenny and his friends. It might be a routine check, or something much worse. A second Cool unit arrived. The youth turned and started to run, was immediately brought down by a bolt from the zapper. He hit the ground, head smashing against concrete, the weapon adjusted and held steady so electricity continued to burn. The lad was convulsing, arms and legs flailing, smoke rising from his groin.

– Fucking murderers, Karen screamed, and before the others could react she was in the street and running towards Cool, a shooter raised.

– No Karen, Steve called three or four times, so fast the words joined and became one.

It was too late and he had to follow, was quickly behind her, tooled-up the same as his love.

There was an explosion and the Cool shocking the boy crashed down. Karen aimed at the officer with the coffee and muffins, didn't give him a chance, blew his head clean off.

– That's for my mum, she shouted. For my dad.

Steve pulled her to the side of the road as the newly arrived Cools left their vehicle and fired, narrowly missing their targets. A stunner was thrown and Karen fell, her left leg shattered. Steve pulled her behind the youth's car, Cool closing in, keen to finish the job. The traffic lights changed.

– Come on, Kenny shouted as Tubby hesitated. Drive. Get to the other side and pull over. We'll go back. We're in the open here.

They moved forward as a shrieking sound filled the air. It was metallic and alien, and before they had a chance to stop, a chopper from the AirCav zipped past. It was small, fast and deadly – a Hardcore unit with a difference.

Four beetles rode the boards, black stickmen with helmets for heads, reflective visors for faces. Bolts of lightning cracked. Precision strikes. No collaterals. That was the promise.

– Fucking hell, Tubby shouted, thumping the steering wheel.

– Keep driving.

Kenny was decisive and strong and surprised himself.

– We can't stop now. They're gone.

The traffic was pressing forward, motorists keen to get away from the disturbance. Tubby was crying. Both men were at least thankful Karen and Steve hadn't been taken alive. Hardcore revelled in its reputation for cruelty, although the masses remained oblivious.

Kenny and Tubby had a head start. It would take a while for any link to be made, though they might get lucky if the lenses were focused elsewhere. The car was stolen, and even if Karen and Steve were traced back to it, the vehicle identified and tracked, they could stay anonymous if they left it somewhere private. Tubby had sprayed the windows with a distorter, so their faces could not be seen properly from the outside. Kenny's admiration for his friend grew. True, he was a scruff with a wobbling beer gut, but the man was smart. Now they needed a secure location and an escape route.

– I know where we can go, Tubby said, once they had picked up speed and left the scene.

He was back in control of the situation.

– We'll be underground. A peeper-free zone.

Tubby concentrated on the road ahead.

– Fuck, what were they thinking? What was the point of that?

Kenny was silent. He had forgotten about the distorter when he swore at Karen. He felt terrible. At least they'd made up, but his friend Steve was dead. He could hardly believe what had happened. Finally he spoke.

– It was everything that went before, wasn't it? Karen did her best, tried to deal with the past, all the terrible stuff that happened to her, but how could she ever forget? You can't wipe your mind clean, can you? Then there was the speed, mixing with the Z. Why did nobody stop her?

– Half the firm are fucked. Can't tell any of them. There's some people seeing an earner as well, but this Wandle Manor where you're going is more organised. The crew there is invisible. Perfect hideaway. Look, I'm sorry about all this. We let you down. There's going to be changes when I get back. If I get back. We have to sort out the good-timers. It's just hard when it's people you know.

Kenny turned the music back on. Played it loud. Started with *New Future* by Stand Tall.

Fifteen minutes later and they were on an estate in Roehampton, descending into an underground car park and leaving the car at the furthest end. A door led to a storage room, and a second one took them into a tunnel lined with cables. Tubby had the codes. A ten-minute walk along this service track saw them emerge at the back of a parade of shops. They came into the darkness with their heads down and split up, Tubby crossing to a bus stop that would take him out towards Feltham, Kenny continuing to a crossroads and catching the Underground to Wandsworth.

Inside a packed carriage, he checked the nearest screens to see if there was any mention of what had happened, but the news seemed to be focused on a sparrow. Some were reporting a controversy involving a lady tagged The Witch. She was being recorded at the front door of her house. Late middle-aged and tearful, there were demands for her to lose her home as well as her job.

An item appeared on the Palm of the woman standing next to Kenny. There had been a movie-making session on the South Circular. Lights flashed and an emptyhead waved. Actors in Cool and Hardcore roles drank coffee. One was eating a muffin. A creative pouted and prepared to address the lens. Behind him, performers played dead under yellow sheets carrying the One Love logo.

SEVENTEEN

FOR THE FIRST time in years Rupert Ronsberger was scared. After meeting his hero he had been escorted back to his quarters, but his opening lines fell flat as the Cool smiles of Sophie and Andreas turned to blank stares. Their expressions hardened as they strolled, further attempts at conversation failing. He began to wonder if he had let an incorrect word or expression slip through when Horace Starski was playing his funny games. This was near enough impossible given Rupert's concentration levels, and neither had his Cool pals been present, but something was wrong. An error *could* have been made and then relayed, yet he was alert to every little detail as to what was and was not acceptable. No, there had to be another reason.

When they reached the door to his room, Sophie opened it and stood back, avoiding eye contact as she nodded Rupert inside. Tired, but polite... Of course... It had been a tough day's graft for these officers and he sympathised. Cool pros they may have been, but when it came to movie-making they were novices, their acting debuts on the side of a busy freeway naturally leading to an increase in stress levels. They were clearly exhausted.

Like every other hard-working Crat, Rupert respected the sacrifices made by genuine celebrities, whether emptyheads or creatives. Empties were loved but mocked. People could live their dreams of stardom by proxy while remaining free to engage in love-hate as they scorned the vanities of these cocksure strutters. Creatives were different. Small in number and sponsored by the most prestigious corps, they were moody and said little as they suffered for their art. The struggle for genius had a tiring effect on this brand of celeb, so it was logical that amateurs such as Sophie and Andreas found themselves strained. He forgave them, had never been the sort to carry a grudge.

It was also possible that he had not been positive enough when discussing their performances. He had talked enthusiastically about the scene on the ridge and the tumbling pigs, which had been dispatched in excellent fashion. Sophie and Andreas had played their parts superbly, and he had said so several times, although the porky killings were real. Was that the problem? If so, they were being oversensitive. The missing Cool cheeriness was certainly lazy, but he wasn't prepared to condemn his pals. He was a Crat on a roll – relaxed, generous, forgiving. They were friends for life, after all.

Rupert entered the room ahead of the others, expected them to follow and chill, organise three coffees and a blueberry muffin each, or pop some corn and arrange sodas, finally relax and game or surf InterZone together, but when he looked back they were still in the corridor. Rupert was shocked by Andreas' expression. The man was angry. And it seemed as if Sophie was sneering. She wanded the door shut without saying 'night night' or 'sleep tight' or 'bye bye'. Rupert wanted to invite them to join him, concerned he had been rude by going in first, but Sophie had asked him to proceed – he was sure she had. Or did he misunderstand? No, he didn't make mistakes. The Cool had definitely nodded him ahead.

He missed his apartment and, while loving the Cuddles experience and the levels of tech available, he wanted to go home. He tried to reopen the door, but his fingers didn't connect. Several more attempts were made. Mystery codes blocked his exit. He was fixed in. Yet this was clearly for his own welfare, as Cool existed to help Crats and protect every Good Euro. Even so, he felt a little uncomfortable. There was the chance he might amble and become lost, or slip and fall and hurt his head, that was true, but a few words from Sophie or Andreas could have eased his surprise. Even so, he loved them for their concern.

He sat in the recliner and tuned into his Palm, opened a screen and drew it out, creating wide boundaries and trawling for flashes, distractions that would ease his mind, but found that his access to InterZone had been restricted. He was inside a Cuddles, so it made sense, but to be limited in this way was still unnerving. Rupert was respected for his ability to concentrate on a single subject, but for this a focus was required. Instead of pinging messages or searching for pictures of IR pongs, Andreas' face returned. The anger was severe. It was ugly. Neither had Sophie been at her best. He really had to sidetrack, which was going to be difficult given his limited media.

Rupert decided to recall his audience with Controller Horace. This would zoom his attention and boost confidence. The pride he had felt when sitting with his guru returned. He was invincible. Modest but powerful. Praise was repeated. He was rising through the ranks and would leave London and live in Brussels. His breathing slowed as he played out a single scenario with small variations, and yet his sense of feelgood lasted a mere five minutes. His spirits dipped. There was definitely something important he had missed. It was hard to reclaim information professionally dismissed, but this was different, as he had neither need nor desire to erase his time with Horace Starski. Rupert dealt in clarity. Positive thinking. Uncertainty was abnormal for a Crat, and especially one that was fast-tracking to glory. A scene sparked.

The killing of the Adams character had been very realistic. For the first time he wondered what the finished movie would be called. The freeway incident was part of a comedy, but this one was much darker. The clip had played while he was working on a case, which was peculiar. Himmler was grafting and Hound Dog roamed. Security was tight. Super Kat knew about the acting, but why would Horace Starski be interested? Crat business was top secret, if repetitive. Their exchanges became clearer. Controller Horace had mentioned Polestar. Before the mock lecture began. And hadn't he also... Rupert felt sick.

He had talked to Polestar about his work. This he should never have done. How could he have been so stupid? It was confidential. For some reason he had muddled fact and fiction and not separated work from play. Rupert and Rocket had become confused. Polestar asked questions and he had been seduced. No real damage was done, but a Crat had to be secure. There were no exceptions to the rule. He had risked everything. Raising his legs and wrapping both arms around them, he felt his kneecaps pressing into his skull as he sunk his head forward. He was trembling. His bowels ached. He started gnawing at the bones, digging his teeth in, tasting rabbit in the material of his trousers, realised what he was doing and stopped. He was sure he had spoken about the movie to the cocksucker Polestar. Horace Starski had asked about Hannah Adams. It was a terrible error.

Rupert could not cope with these swings of emotion, which belonged to the world of his childhood and early teens. That life had long been rejected. He was used to certainty. He was forever upbeat. Often, he felt ecstatic. Rarely worried. Why should he when he was protected by the State? If he lost its backing he did not know what he would do. He *was* the USE. He had been brought to this room by friends and treated to a sporting spectacle. It was important to remember this fact. Yes, it had been a glorious experience, one to be cherished. Sitting here watching Barca in 4D, part of the carnival as Messi turned on the Flamboyants brand, running at the heart of the London defence. He hated Terry Johns. Loathed the man.

He hurried to the kitchenette, removed a bottle of red from the rack, took a glass and filled it high, drinking it in one hit. There were shades of Rocket in Rupert's gesture, and returning to his chair he stretched out and allowed the wine to take effect, five minutes later rushing to the bathroom where he showered and dressed in the change of clothes provided. Downtime was limited, but he loved to veg on the East Side. Hanging out in his apartment was one of his fave pursuits. He had been asked to remain at Cuddles so couldn't return home to chill or even morph to Rocket and wander malls and feast on Tenderburgers and party hard at the likes of Bark! and Splash! In time, he would have his own commercial interests, which was usual for a Controller, but that was something he could largely manage from his pad. It was also the future. He had another glass of red.

He opened his Palm, didn't need InterZone, created a screen in 3D, ready for the night ahead. He was clean and tipsy and ready to enter an inbuilt application. With the red relaxing him he was starting to understand why he had revealed Crat business to Polestar. There was always a reason for the behaviour of a Good Euro. He had to take a more holistic position. Controller Horace would know this, so why had he become upset? It was in the past. Rupert needed a rest. Rocket Ron was eager to rock 'n' roll. Wands were waved and a fresh world appeared.

Dates surrounded him and he explored their beauty, turning to trigger mode and enlarging heads to double-size, flattening each one out and allowing them the chance to float freely in the air. He took his time inspecting the shapes of mouths and textures of lipstick, the colours of eyes and the smells of black and blonde and brown hair freshly polished in a range of shampoos. Each date had their own customised perfume, and he nosed side-to-side. It was time to let Rocket enjoy the flavours of Euroland. Few Crats were invited to chill at a Cuddles complex and help a Controller with his experiments.

Horace Starski was pushing boundaries with his upside-down comments and mental twists. The man was amazing. He never tired of confronting the enemies of New Democracy, knew that to defeat them it was essential to feel how their minds worked. He repeated lies and played with their language, delved deep into the warped history and logic of the commons.

Rupert had been given a sneak peak of a movie, and as a lover of the arts had wanted to share his experience. Polestar happened to be in the right place at the right time. Nothing could be more innocent. And Rocket could smell the sucker right now, her perfume merging with a hint of sweat as he boned her across his Voy-Box, and the mixture had hovered in the air as they slept after the exchange, had floated over to him as looked out at the London fog. Time was smoothing and he wasn't sure if that was one, two or three days ago. A week or a month or even a year. For a moment he felt as if he had always known Polestar. Her life was a mystery, and he had no interest in her story, but there was a connection that crossed their levels. He could be a deep thinker when he wanted, transcendent in his musings, and he complimented himself on these important qualities.

The confidence that made Ronald such a terror in the Euroland clubs was back. He weeped for the suppressed of the world, had credit and standing and only wanted to help. Three girls exercised their freedom of choice as they waited on the dance floor, clapping their hands to 'Sugar Baby Love', lights strobing as clouds of dry ice flowed. Rocket reached for his Rubettes cap and placed it on his head. He was ready to love the ladies and learn their ways. He pulled the trigger and Girl 1 jumped into blow-up mode dressed in a red bikini and matching high heels. She smiled and giggled and did a twist while he glanced at the vital statistics listed. Girl 2 was slightly taller, wore a silver G-string and nothing else. Girl 3 was taller, clad in leather, but like the others had her titties on show. He was a lucky dude, and yet he waited a little longer before forging ahead, thought of Horace Starski and wondered what he was doing at this exact moment.

The great man would have returned to Pearly Tower. He was in his penthouse high above London, the domes shutting out terrible weather, helping to create the sanctuary they both adored. Controller Horace was dedicated to his craft and would be working on the problems they faced, maybe even drawing on his chat with Rupert. There was clearly a bond between them. A trust that could never be broken. One lived on the floors of a Crat tower, the other at the top of the world. Rupert was on his way up and he was taking Rocket along for the ride.

Rocket Ron returned to the ladies in front of him, was tempted to dismiss these wonders and call a virtual version of Polestar, but despite the red was alert enough to realise he might not be able to control his curiosity. He would find it hard not to ask about Free Libya and her education, if it was true that European history was taught differently outside the USE. But what was he thinking? He froze the three sexers. His lack of InterZone access meant Polestar was not available.

He tried to remember lessons on alien labour, the process of cultivation and choice, and yet every date was different, origins chosen for specialist abilities, the skills of those humans produced by quirks of environment, their appearance and habits and desire to work with the Euro elite. The liberal values involved were solid. Opportunities were offered. He rejected the foul language of the commons, the crude words that challenged the fortress model. He wished he could talk to Polestar in person, ask about her background and hear of the gratitude she felt, but that wouldn't happen for a while. He checked his surroundings, tunes pumping inside an upmarket club full of VIPs and gyrating celebs. Still his suckers waited, showing great patience, revealing their eagerness, and he adjusted the sound levels, fiddled with the visuals. He spotted Polestar dancing on a podium.

She waved and drew attention, first to herself and then to Rocket. Hundreds of Crats had appeared and their faces turned. It was clear they knew about Rupert's error and were shocked to find that his pal Rocket was still cavorting with the same snoopy. The screen flickered and something strange happened. The virtual vanished and a single option was offered. This would normally have surprised the two characters, but words were forming and it was Rupert who read them and was mesmerised – *A Gift From Your Uncle Horace... Welcome To The North... The Grim North... Truly Another Vision... Another Dimension.*

A gift from his *Uncle* Horace. It was incredible. *Uncle*. A door appeared. It started to open. *Uncle Horace.* Rupert Ronsberger stepped forward and was stepping out of a train that had stopped at a station called Blackpool North.

EIGHTEEN

BOB TERKS AND Baby worked hard and deserved a snooze. Controller Horace watched his two good buddies yawn and lean back and slip to sleep. Once their breathing had settled, he left his recliner and ambled over to Bobby, looked down on the man mountain, pleased to find that he wore the innocent expression of his boyhood. Raised on a Texas homestead, he was no doubt dreaming he was Marshall Terks, bringing law and order to the Wild West. The natives were lowdown murdering locals and Marsh was polishing the land in humane, USA style. It wasn't easy work and, knowing Bobby, there would be plenty of Mexican dates and cantina fellatio to help him relax at night.

He was clearly comfortable, so Controller Horace switched his attention to Baby, collapsed floppy-doll against the arm of the sofa. She was resting at an awkward angle. A hiccup or sneeze could send her toppling to the floor, so he gently lifted her legs and made sure she was secure, slipping a cushion under the porcelain head as he didn't want her to suffer a stiff neck later.

Knowing his friends would sleep soundly for at least six hours, Horace Starski adopted his best commons disguise, then hid this under a Crat layer and left Pearly Tower. He walked across Bethnal Plaza, pleased to mingle and appreciate the balmy evening created by the domes. He watched the passing and pausing Crats with pride, heard excited Bureaus and Technos discussing their latest upgrades. The top producers created problems and offered solutions at reasonable cost. Minds were stretched and profits generated. Everyone was happy.

Crats sat on benches with their sexers, the faces of these lucky Afros and Asias bright white, brilliant greasepaint blazing under lights expertly positioned to promote the setting. He saw solitary figures staring into square, oblong and triangular screens that lay cloudlike in the air, but it didn't take long for clusters to form around these loners as caring communities were created. There was a noisy crowd nearby and he headed over, passed a smaller gathering enjoying the roasting of a young commons by two football stars. This double penetration had the usual homo ingredients, and increased the validity of the scene, but he was more interested in the talkative huddle, stood at the edge of a twenty-strong team and saw that a trial was in progress. There had been an incorrect use of language and this was being condemned by thousands of twits in a spontaneous demonstration of free expression.

Horace Starski loved strolling through these secure havens, where the atmosphere was vibrant and original yet totally conformist. New Culture boomed. New Democracy ruled. People were content. At times they became ecstatic. The system wasn't just working well, it was working *so* well that there were times when it almost *sang*. Quietly though. A faint purr. In Brussels it was possible to ramble for hours and never leave Central, the squares packed with politicals and financials, eager young professionals discussing legislation and sponsorship as they dined on the recipes of Heartland. Only Berlin could match the experience. He had a pad in Mitte, but preferred the energy of Brussels to the aloofness of Berlin, where he was not part of the main circles. This was the home of Hans. Remote, but dominant. He favoured Michele.

Everything he could ever want was easily had in Brussels, but he was old enough to recall some of the more lively cities of a pre-polished Europe. In Marseilles, before PCOs were introduced, he had glimpsed the lives led by North African workers, wandered through teeming, dangerous markets and eaten in small cafés that served exotic dishes he had not seen since. In Athens, he was shocked by the anger of the people, watched it simmer and finally explode in a week of rioting. A result of the failures of 2015, the fury of the masses created a unity he had never experienced before. Most of all he remembered London. This was where he had fallen in love.

Horace Starski was soon on the Overground. He turned the tracker in his detachable Palm off, one of the many perks of his position. He was on his own, the same as those who rejected InterZone, though he was correct and they were not. He knew how to alter his mannerisms to hide what the commons might see as bubbler arrogance, and on leaving the Overground removed his outer strip in the station pisser before entering the Underground. The air was heavier here, hot and dirty, but he was one more face in the crowd and ignored. He joined the crush in the first train to arrive, feelings of claustrophobia and distaste balanced by a growing excitement.

Fifteen minutes later he was on the mean streets of London, walking away from Waterloo station, past the glass statue of a victorious Napoleon that towered over the entrance, moving in the direction of Castile. He saw a taxi and raised a hand, the driver by law an authorised cockney. Craggy faced and wearing a trilby, the man croaked a welcome.

– Where to, guv?

– Can you take me to Morden, please? I will show you the road when we get there. Could you follow my directions though, as I want to do some sightseeing on the way?

– Jump in, squire.

Controller Horace opened the hands-on door and climbed inside. The cabbie watched him settle down and fasten his safety belt.

– Lovely jubbly. London calling.

The cab turned and joined a flow of slow-moving traffic. Horace Starski glanced at a State channel nearby, a single vehicle racing along an empty stretch of road, but he was here to lose himself in a parallel world so concentrated on the streets outside, looking deep into a bus packed with a wide range of ages, features and tones. This was very different to the cities of Heartland, where those Protective Custody Orders had saved non-European stock from the violence of the locals. Safer homes had been found outside the USE, the scourge of racism challenged. Protection units were robust, but had to operate more cautiously here.

The Handsworth mission had been a disaster, a slower approach subsequently adopted. Inside the so-called Wall, sanctuaries had been formed in the likes of Southall and Tottenham, but it was hard to convince the ethnically diverse that they were not welcome in the traditional English manors. Inter-racial relationships had flourished, it was true, but the racism of the lowers was deep and ingrained. The curse had to be broken and separation was the only solution. Gradual, caring, unspoken division and, where possible, the offer to start afresh elsewhere. The land nearest the East Side Gates had been nicely polished, and it was difficult for even Horace Starski to remember it as anything but upmarket.

The professional classes essential to regeneration had brought a more progressive, homogenised culture with them as credit was transferred and huge profits achieved by investors. Everyone who counted was becoming more wealthy. This helped the wider economy. Benefits trickled down. The success of the Gates followed an established Heartland pattern, while the rest of Central London had been secure for decades. For now, non-European stock would remain, but eventually it would be moved for its own safety. The Controller considered his thoughts, loved the way language could be distorted. The project had always been a serious matter, but there was a humour involved. It was a theatre of the absurd, operated by an army of dumbos lead by a handful of creatives. Doublespeak showed humanity at its most honest. The ability to deceive was a skill, the power to self-deceive a gift.

– Off down the boozer are you, guv?

Horace Starski looked at the cockney's eyes in the mirror. He could see no hint of mockery, but the man wouldn't be in this job if he wasn't a believer. Every major city had its themed workers – characters who performed for visitors and expressed the cultural range of the USE. This driver would have studied hard to achieve his position, the permit on the panel between them identifying him as Sid James.

– On your way to a knees-up?

The Controller raised a thumb, thought of Scouser Tommy, Geordie Girl, Yorkie, Brummie Bill, Wurzel, Taffy Williams, The Wee Lassie, Paddy O'Toole and all those other salt-of-the-earth, fairground chavsters.

– Cor, tell you what guv'nor, there's a proper smart pub I can take you to if you like. They've got jugs and old railway signs and a Peruvian flautist is playing tonight. The Apple And Pears, over near The Courgette. What d'ya say, me old mucker?

Horace Starski had no time for bars like The Apple, which was part of a Europe-wide chain. Expensive, flat lagers and small plates of Rude Ramsay nibbles did not appeal.

– No, I'm fine thanks, just take me to Morden, via Tooting.

– Tooting? You sure, mate? It's a bit dodgy round there.

– Down along the high street please.

– Fair enough. Bit of sightseeing makes sense. You're not from around here, are you?

– No... Brussels.

– Blimey.

Sid was clearly impressed, as Controller Horace knew he would be. He even whistled. The name no longer had any connection to that maverick city fuelled by double- and triple-brewed beer, where the Flemish and Walloons argued over dead languages long since replaced by European – which Horace Starski knew was really English. The seditious 9th Art had thrived in Brussels, its spirit lodged in the killing fields of Flanders, the inky strips of dead artists spooking him when he was a Crat investigating the illegal trade in hards. The original population had been eased out, replaced by a breed of bright young things, and the USE had needed every last centimetre of land to create what was now regarded as one of the greatest cities on the planet.

– Never been to Brussels, Sid remarked, but it's something the missus and me would love to do one day. See the sights. Must be fantastic living there. You're a Techno, ain't cha? Pretty high up as well. Good on ya. Makin' the world a better place, educating us cockney fellas.

Horace Starski was surprised that he had been found out so easily, but Sid had tagged him as a Crat rather than a Controller, and of course cabbies were trained to identify their fares. This meant they could easily cater to a passenger's interests.

– London is a fine city, he replied. But it needs honing. We are here to help.

– Don't I know it. Very kind of you to assist with the civilising. Most generous. Lovely.

– We are working for the future of your children. You do have offspring?

– Two nippers. A boy and a girl.

– Excellent. The ideal number. Three is a crowd, remember.

– I know, and when it comes to kids, well, two is definitely best. My lad wants to be a cabbie when he grows up. Like his old man. One of the authentics. Proper cockney. The girl could make a lot of money cleaning the houses of the rich and famous. Celeb premises is where an up-and-coming wants to toil. Have to think ahead in the game of life.

– Excellent. We can never have too many cockneys.

– Would you like to hear something from *Popping Mary Poppins*? Sid asked. My favourite is *The Sweep's Song*. Mick Van Dyke and Julie Anders. He's a randy chim-chimney from Amsterdam, she's a naughty nanny from Oslo. They sing about the old bamboo. Yes. The old bamboo. London calling. Lovely.

Horace Starski nodded and tilted his face to the window. The best cabbies knew when to speak and when to fall silent, recognised the subtle shifts in a fare's focus. Sid James was clearly dedicated to his craft, had perfected quirks as well as patter, was eager to present the best Bow Bells experience. There were times when Controller Horace found these characters nauseating, but it was a personal view no doubt shaped by his age. It was vital to believe in such displays of diversity. A tune from *Popping Mary Poppins* played as they trundled towards Kennington. The Oval Baseball Stadium glowed beyond the nearest houses, which were dark and miserable. Stockwell came next. Clapham High Street. They skirted the common and continued into Balham.

– Turn here, please, Controller Horace requested, halfway into Tooting.

– You sure, guv? Don't think you want to be going down that way me old cock. Nasty place. Full of villains. Nasty, nasty. Cut-throats and fagins and those fucking heritage gangs – if you'll pardon my Parisian.

– I have friends here. I'll be safe, but thank you for your concern. I will of course pay the full fare to Morden and add a generous tip.

– It's not such a bad place. Good people in these parts. Right here? Lovely.

Horace 'Harry' Starski paid and thanked Sid, watched the taxi pull away, felt the cold of the city closing in. He was way outside his bubble, beyond the temperature-controlled Gates, the protection of the domes. For some bizarre reason he imagined spirits closing in and poking fingers at him, as if he was a virtual in a vision. Reality was overrated. Where did one version end and another begin? Until recently, he had rarely considered death, but came from a different generation to the hip young gunslingers of today. He was a spiritual, conscious man in comparison. He buried truth, but could recall it also. Crats had their levels. A Controller operated in a different dimension.

Terraced houses flanked him as he walked. He was carrying a zap, but did not feel threatened. The area was familiar from a recent Peep and little had changed in the decades since he was last here in the physical. He doubted whether any Crats had visited since. Division between Good Euros and the wider population was quietly encouraged. This was never done openly, and would always be denied, but the likes of Tooting were very different to the official impression. This wasn't a lawless place. The idea was nonsense. Barely disguised prejudice. Snobbery. Controller Horace helped shape propaganda, but there was no way he was going to believe it as well.

Before long he reached the site of the pub where he had first met Belle. Harry stood on the corner opposite and tried to picture the place. It had been converted into a pizzeria, then a Eurobar, finally a fusion restaurant. Few people went to any of these ventures. Finally it was knocked down and offices built. Gentrification had failed here and the premises stood empty. The brilliance of The Black Horse had been lost forever. His hands were clammy and he realised he was sweating, his heartbeat racing, but it only lasted a few seconds. He made himself calm again. Free and easy. He had privacy and secrets. His memories were clear.

Harry was a twenty-four-year-old Bureau and had been in London for six weeks, was living in a flat in Clapham, back before the final transfer of power to the European Union. It was still acceptable to enjoy the local customs, and he had travelled the short distance to see a punk band play at the pub. It turned out there were three on the bill. He forgot their names. The music's heyday was already in the past, but it was appreciated on the mainland, youngsters embracing the Union Jack as a rebel symbol even then. He went as a tourist, but liked the atmosphere and towards the end of the night met Belle. They were the same age, but she was much more outgoing and confident, and after their first exchanges he was smitten. He bought her a drink and asked her out and the next week they returned on a quieter night. This was her local and they sat in the corner by a coal fire. After a lot of beer they held hands under the table.

The details were blurred, but he would never forget how he felt then and in the months that followed. It was the only occasion he had ever been in love. While it was a long time ago, when he allowed himself to remember he felt the same way. His emotions were less raw, but still strong. He felt tears fill his eyes as he stood alone in the street. He was an old man who'd sold his soul, but he would stay strong.

The fourth time they went out, he stayed at her flat. It was a room really, just off Tooting High Street, and there was a powerful smell of curry from the nearby restaurants. Belle worked hard for a minimal wage, and he supposed that deep down he knew they would follow different paths in life, but he had only just met her and wasn't going to admit she would be bad for his career. She lacked his ambition, but was braver and more honest. He admired her for these qualities, and yet he was the great success, the one who had done something important with his life.

His best memories belonged to the five days they'd spent at the seaside. This was a great British tradition – the belly-filling Full English breakfast, a day building sand castles and sheltering from the endless drizzle, nights spent drinking in busy pubs, eating chips on the way back to their lodgings. Every joke about greasy food, bad weather, cheap B&Bs, hangovers and punch-ups on the promenade came true. The need to impress and self-censor hadn't existed and he felt great. People didn't take themselves too seriously here. He laughed a lot, dealt with the wet and the crowds, the smell of horseshit and candyfloss. It didn't take long before he was adding a mountain of ketchup to his food, overdosing on salt and vinegar. That was the life – sitting in a pub with Belle and listening to an elderly woman singing into a microphone like she was Adele or Amy Winehouse. Belle had certainly enjoyed a pint. He had never been happier, but nobody would ever know. Only Harry and Belle.

Despite this, he couldn't change direction. His breeding, education and fear of failure meant he chose his career over love. He wanted to be rich and powerful, knew that he could deceive himself as well as others. He was morally weak. Mentally suspect. But he was wealthy, successful and safe. He'd had it a lot easier than Belle. He was content, but in his own way. She would have become sad if they'd stayed together. He could not have taken Belle on his race to the top. She was a straight talker, would have held him back with her beliefs, accent and manner. Her job as a carer was laudable, but only in marketing terms. Working with the disabled was a waste of resources. He could never have changed her and would have been devastated if he had been able.

Turning away from the site of the pub, he followed the street that ran along the end of the terraces, came to a larger road at the top. The houses were grander, in that style that was becoming less and less popular, the fashion for period properties near enough dead. Location was everything, the past something manipulated to drive the present, the city's Edwardian and Victorian buildings increasingly demolished and replaced by a modern architecture that reached across Europe. A uniform appearance cemented unity.

He saw Belle's face, a unique beauty that turned heads. She never lingered over her make-up, dressed with a flamboyance that cost little, was natural and turned heads. She had seen something different in him, said once that he was childlike, but in a nice way.

Naive and romantic. Belle had sobbed when he ended their relationship.

Harry veered left on the main road and continued walking. It was as dark here as it was in the terraced streets, lights turned down low to save energy and dull expectations, while across the USE the centres of the great cities burned bright. He crossed over and was in another row of small houses, and these were more rundown and in the next year would be demolished. His virtual visit had been unconventional, but it had primed him for tonight. A heart tremor six months before had affected his mood, bringing on an attack of nostalgia. He had been trained to regard the pre-unification period as a dark age, when libertarians were bullied by a ragtag band of lowlifes that included socialists, patriots, anarchists, greens and veggers. He knew it was unhealthy to look back, but panicked at the idea of dying. He had become sentimental. It was terrible. Robotic was best.

Harry stopped and stared at the house where Belle lived in a ground-floor flat. His virtual visit had been heartbreaking. He cried as hard as Belle had done when he left her, the sadness engulfing him as he looked into her eyes. She couldn't see or hear him as he was using Peep, not really there in the traditional sense. He was a drifting spirit. Confused, he had to push himself to decide if he was here now or back in Pearly Tower. The wind blew and he was clear. With Belle he would have had children. He was sure of that, but did it matter? New Democracy was his baby. Pride fought regret. Harry knew his way. He was quickly at the back window.

Every Controller, Cool and Crat had their privates, however small. Secrets, doubts, plans. He was certain of this. He believed in Sus and the Palm 7, in surveillance and the restraints of the social-media circus, but without private thoughts those living under the current system would go insane. Maintaining healthy order was a balancing act. People were no good to the State if they fell apart and were unable to function. Generally speaking, Controllers came from the higher levels of society, but even they had to serve as Crats and prove themselves before progressing. Correct education, boarding-school childhoods and logic-only parenting gave them a fine start, as did established credit and zero debt, but the USE was a meritocracy, could only promote the best individuals. If it was driven solely by privilege it would fail. Hard graft allowed mentors the chance to monitor and select. At Controller level, the pressures were removed.

Belle was one of his secrets. She loved birds and he doubted they were a threat to society. His interest in fish was known and he had taken this and made it work to his advantage. It was vital that those driving New Democracy had successful business interests. Ideas and their exploitation were positives. Profit-making skills were respected. Innovation honed the mind. Harry had developed the Scales! brand by drawing on a visit to a seaside aquarium, standing there with Belle watching the fish glide past. Multi-coloured and exotic, they were prisoners nonetheless.

Now he stood at Belle's back window, watching her through another layer of glass. She was sitting in the same chair as when he came to see her before. She was reading a book. It was a hard. He should report her, pass the information to Cool, but that would never happen. She was older but still beautiful. Exotic like the fish that moved so gracefully. Magnificent like the birds that could flap their wings and fly away. They were demonised because they were free. And he thought of the sparrows under the domes and Belle in her flat and felt a pain in his chest.

It had happened before, all those years ago, a response to the realisation that he had a terrible decision to make. Maybe his more recent scare was due to a similar pressure. He couldn't tell, but was pleased with the doctor's positive verdict. He felt good and his drive was intact. There was business to conduct, values to pro-mote, a trip to London. But he was at the seaside. In an under-ground aquarium.

He had studied the creatures as they drifted, saw how their skin reflected the light, imagined larger patterns and formations. He thought about the weight of the water on their tiny bodies, found their lack of facial expressions interesting. Humans didn't see them as individuals. It was the beauty of a shoal that appealed. Numbers and movement. The idea for Scales! stirred that day, became a dream he would always associate with Belle, and when it was finally developed and realised it made him a hugely wealthy man.

The seaside had been his inspiration.

Fish and chips... greasy batter on tender flesh... scales stripped and bodies filleted... scales taken from live cod and trout and bream and roach... cloned in laboratories... farmed and forced to live... or at least respond... cells flowing across a small London tower... a test on the margins of the empire... a tribute to Belle... a triumph of his will... taking over the city... moving across Europe... conquering Brussels... and finally... Berlin... the Reichstag wrapped in his art... as his credit soared.

Harry was proud of himself. He was a creative who remained modest. Belle had suggested they visit the aquarium, but Scales! was his invention. The seed was sown. Birds were different. They ate the seed and anything they could scavenge. Scraps were harder to find these days, the rodents that had dirtied the suburbs cleansed. Birds flew outside the M25, but they rarely crossed it, and never made it as far as Central or the Gates.

He pressed his face hard against the window. He wondered what book she was reading. Belle had put on a little weight, but there was the same elegance about her movements, and with Peep he had been able to enter her home, hover in the kitchen as she made a meal. She was vegan, like so many people. He followed and sat on the couch when she relaxed in her chair, a tray on her lap as she ate. He could smell the sort of spices that convention banned from the domes, closed the sense down. When she was finished he stood next to her as she washed her cutlery and plate, went with her when she walked around watering the plants she kept. When it was time to leave, he placed a hand on her shoulder that she couldn't feel.

He felt terrible afterwards, tried to immerse himself in his work, and at least on the surface he forgot Belle for a while, but his heart scare had released too much emotion and he'd had to return in person. Standing here in the flesh was so much different. He was on the outside looking in, a barrier between them, but everything was more intense and he felt they were closer. The wind blew harder as he looked in at his love, hunched over paper pages, and he wished he could knock on the door and say hello and maybe hug her if she let him in, sit and talk or stay silent and just touch her fingers. But it would be the end for him, his focus lost forever. He stayed still and smiled as Belle read, sharing in the peace, like a long-term husband and wife.

Eventually, she raised her head and put the book on the arm of the chair, stood up and went out of the room. When she returned she was followed by a man, woman and teenager. Harry could see Belle in the male and the girl, noticed their faces in a row of framed pictures. He had refused to look at these illegals when he was here before, making an excuse only he heard. Other people were there, among them a man of his own age, standing with Belle at different stages of their lives, and there were two family portraits, everyone together in their best clothes. The last one he let himself see was Belle's wedding photo. He felt a pang of sorrow, but was pleased she had married. He wondered where her husband was, hoped he wasn't dead, was sure Belle was living on her own. Her son reached out and held her hand. At least she wasn't alone.

Harry had made no checks on Belle's circumstances, maybe through a fear of what he would find, and was genuinely happy that she had a family. He hummed 'Sugar Baby Love'. It was their song, playing on a Blackpool jukebox.

He returned to their seaside holiday. They'd left a pub where the people sang out of tune and drank much too much, a cheerful character with slicked-back hair perched on a small stool as he played a keyboard between songs. The scene was sharp, as real as a vision, alive in his memory. A drunk whistled at Belle and he was jealous. Harry didn't want to see her belittled. He had confronted the stranger and after a brief exchange punched him hard in the face. There was some blood spilled and, looking down at him, Harry realised that he had a big mouth but was physically weak, a wanker in colloquial English, but even so, he didn't regret what he'd done, and neither did Belle. Not really. She said he shouldn't have punched the man, but he knew she was pleased that he had. And Harry felt fantastic.

It was a relief that he felt no jealousy towards Belle's husband. As a Controller, he could have had him arrested, if he was still alive, done anything he wanted, but he had shown he was removed from the situation. That's what he told himself. He was even more relieved that she wasn't alone in her poverty. She had a family and there would be lots of loyal friends as well. Belle had always been popular. He stood very still as he studied the people inside the flat, decided they were sentimental and nervous, like so many commons, but essentially decent. The girl turned and stared straight at him. Their eyes linked, and yet she said nothing. Maybe she thought he was a ghost. It was time to leave and this he did.

Ten minutes later he was approaching the high street. It was busy up ahead, with dinosaur pubs and takeaways and late-night shops selling cheap food, and as soon as he was away from Belle's that magical weekend was replaying again, and he was standing with the woman he loved looking out across the beach at the people running and walking and building castles and sticking flags in the towers, and he watched the man who kept donkeys and let children ride them up and down the sand, saw a little girl not too different from Belle's granddaughter, but a younger version, maybe seven or eight years old, and they noticed her every day afterwards, whatever time they passed by the child was out there with the donkeys. Her mother told Belle the girl loved to help the owner, looked forward to it all year long, and they wondered why children had to grow up and become adults.

Belle said it would be strange to never have kids. He hadn't responded. There was a festival and they went and saw bands play, and while he didn't know them or their music, he'd enjoyed every single minute. He thought back to the variety of sound, but mostly to laying in their bed at night with Belle asleep, Harry half-awake listening to the seagulls singing and cooing outside. Big, white birds ruled the streets after everyone had gone back to their hotels. He heard wings flap as one took off from a nearby roof and was happy.

He felt the same way sitting by the front window of a pub on the main road. Belle was okay. He sipped the stout he had ordered.

He'd made the right choices in his life. Glancing around the bar, he felt powerful, despite the fact he was on his own with no link to Bob Terks and Baby. The commons were large in number, but dreamers. They were soft, lacked the ruthlessness that led to brilliance. It was easy to sedate them with technology and media. The people believed in magic, and this had been exploited by pioneers such as Steve Jobs. Dazzled by science, and given the credit to consume it, as well as to eat, drink and dance, there was no great desire to confront the federation of State and business. This pub was another distraction. He finished his drink and went outside, hailed the first taxi that came along.

– All right, guv? the cabbie roared, once he'd pulled over and Horace Starski had addressed him in true Controller fashion. You're a long way from home. Been on the razzle? Nice bit of slumming? Touch of the fancy dress?

– Can you take me to Waterloo, please?

– Jump in me old cocker. There you go. Lovely jubbly.

– Drop me near Napoleon, please.

– Your wish is my command, the cabbie chirped. Yes. London calling.

The driver was called Del Trotter. Short, pug-faced, flat-capped. He was a wide-boy version of the Jack The Lad stereotype. A spiv. Old-school Peckham. Controller Horace sat back in his seat, knew this character well and wondered if he should put Del to the test. One day he hoped to hitch a ride with Arthur Daley. He was another legendary London face, long since deleted but available to the Controllers in one of the Brussels bunkers, where so many hards were kept for reference. These wide boys were also known as Flash Harrys, but this Harry was Horace again. He took the plunge.

– How's Rodney? he asked, watching for the reaction.

Del's eyes sparkled. He was clearly impressed. As he should be. Knowledge was important. So was respect. Humour played a part.

– Rodders? Saw him last night down the boozer. Me and Raquel was in there with Boycie.

– No Uncle Albert?

It was John Cleese who had screamed 'don't mention the war'

as he goose-stepped across the dining room of Fawlty Towers, but this Del Boy would know nothing of that, and Albert had been deleted from the course this driver would have studied. He looked worried.

– Sorry, guv, ain't got an Uncle Albert.

– What about Trigger?

– He was there. Nice new whistle. Powder blue.

– Rodney's a bit of a plonker, remarked the fare as they speeded towards Waterloo. Did he spill his beer on the new garment I wonder?

– Can't say he did. But he might of done. Never know with him. Love the bloke, I do. He's my bruv, after all. Plonker.

– Lovely, Horace Starski murmured. He is flesh and blood. Family. That matters. Lovely.

– Lovely, Del agreed, wobbling his head and wriggling his shoulders. Lovely jubbly.

NINETEEN

RUPERT LEFT THE train station and followed his *illuminations* – as the familiar voice in his ears called the floating balls of light. These would show him the way. *Blackpool...* He started to walk. *The North...* Rupert skirted a group of commons, eyes drawn to a sign that advertised a character called Ma Kelly. *It's grim up North...* Scruffy men puffed on cigarettes as he passed. *Sometime in the 2010s...* They were no doubt impressed by the cut of his clothes. *A holiday in the sun...* One of them winked. *And the rain...* Rupert frowned... *A tough place...* He was fearless. *But full of love...* Unless he willed it nothing could hurt him. *Friendly...* It was a great honour... *An English seaside town...* He wondered why he was here. *Tread softly...* He trusted his Uncle Horace.

Two forbidding pubs with frosted windows led into a row of takeaways serving cheap ethnic chow. He was appalled. The stink of Indian and Chinese food made him queasy. Pungent, vicious spices. The native fare was little better. Oil bubbled inside steam-filled rooms, while slobs lounged in the street eating chips cut from muddy potatoes. Their fish was encased in thick, heart-breaking batter. Red and brown sauces had been added. Salt and vinegar liberally sprinkled. Fingers dripped with grease. It was truly disgusting. Rupert was used to scented rooms, the sterilised air of offices and domes, plazas tended by expert gardeners. He dined at expensive restaurants and munched on health-conscious funny foods.

He was nearing the sea, crossed a road and noted the ancient autos, relieved to be able to lean on iron railings and breathe fresher air. The water was dirty grey and the horizon black. The walk from the station had been depressing. He was irritated by the squalor. The balls of light swirled around his head, picked up speed and became a blur, were soon moving so fast they looked like a solid halo. *Blackpool illuminations...* When they slowed and separated, a line of bouncing stars formed. *Why not follow the twinklers, Rupert...?* The trail led south, towards a busier part of town.

Rupert marched down the promenade. He passed tired husbands and wives hobbling and holding hands; families licking ice-creams and lollies and sipping from cans of pop; unkempt children frolicking unleashed and unsupervised; grinning young lovers; swaying overweight and skinny middle-aged drunks. And he saw broken bodies in wheelchairs and two lowers driving sit-downs; loners shuffling along with their eyes on the ground; one fool talking to himself about god; a youth shouting as he tried to sell rides in a carriage driven by a physical horse that defecated on the street; and there were dogs strutting, one cocking his leg and urinating on a lamppost. He was appalled.

Rupert turned his head and looked out across the beach, found adult commons ambling, youngsters kicking footballs and building castles from sand, sticking small English, Welsh, Scottish and Irish flags into the crumbling towers. *They are happy...* Rupert was impressed by his favourite uncle's sarcasm. *Simple pleasures...* The flags were illegal. *Sand structures that will be washed away when the tide turns...* Rupert was spying on the past, but even so... His illuminations created a whirlpool effect and directed him towards a bench. *Please, sit down and listen...* He did as he was asked.

A terrible shrieking filled the air. He looked up and saw white birds circling. *Seagulls...* These monsters did not fear humans. *They come and they go...* Rupert was outraged. *They are free...* Gulls were landing on the beach, and checking his surroundings he found that they were strolling on the promenade and sitting on the roofs of buildings. He thought of the mess they were making. It would need cleaning. He would loved to have been the Techno (A+) sent to polish this slum. His first job would be to remove the wildlife, but where could he site his command centre?

The beaks on these birds were horrendous. Huge, sharp, deadly. They could not injure him unless he asked, but he was unsettled nevertheless. The graphics were amazing. This was clearly another level of simulation. Zooming in on the eyes of one of the gulls he was disturbed to find clear signs of intelligence. The beast seemed to be weighing him up and Rupert looked away. There was nothing good about Blackpool and he wished he was sunning himself in the Med, where so many Crats chilled. Sunny, sophisticated, elegant and expensive. Cocksuckers fresh from Africa. Perfect bodies. There was no false warmth and humour there, none of these shows of emotion used to hide the miserable reality of life. Blackpool was packed with lowers. Poor people. Basic in their needs. It was wrong to pretend they could ever be happy.

Blackpool was also very different to Crat-friendly Brighton, where he zipped for short breaks, even though it still carried the taint of a remaining Englishness, and he wondered again why he had been coaxed to The Grim North, why his Uncle Horace had invited him along, what it could mean. He wasn't supposed to challenge official suggestions, would never query a Controller's wisdom, but this was part of his Cuddles experience, so he felt it was fine to ask these questions. He was always correct. *Always correct...*

His illuminations led Rupert back to the railings, used to prevent alcoholics falling and smashing bones on the sand below. He put his hands on the iron and was drawn into a nostalgic scene by a beam of orange light. A donkey was being led by a tall man. Behind him a small girl sat on the animal's back. The child's face was expanded to show her mood, the sheer joy visible a surprise, though not as shocking as the smell of the four-legger, which had also been intensified. He knew that it would be infested with fleas and other dirties.

She loves the donkeys... Rupert concentrated. *She comes here every morning after breakfast, from the B&B where she's on holiday with her family, and then she helps look after them, performs small tasks for the owner...* The orange beam directed him to three more donkeys further along the beach. *When things are quiet he lets her have a ride, but she would be here even if he didn't, and it has been the same for the last three years...* Why would she keep returning? *She looks forward to seeing the donkeys all year...* They belonged in tubes and glasshouses... *These people have a bond we can never match, a sentimentality that can be a positive...* Rupert loved the bending of logic. *This is not a mocking...* He was confused. *It is no joke...* Dirty donkeys. *Feel the love...* Filthy beasts... *She really does love the donkeys.*

Rupert focused on the scene for another minute, trying to find the hidden meaning, but his unease only grew. He didn't understand why he was being led in these directions, what the commentary was trying to achieve. The girl did seem happy, but how could she be, sitting on the back of a dirty dumbo? *Her favourite is called Dobbin...* An animal with a name? He found this amusing. Meat should only exercise when it rambled in glass tubes. Movement meant energy burned and a fall in profits. Naming it was irrational. Ridiculous. The beast turned its head and stared into Rupert's eyes. This was worse than the seagull. He imagined a human face inside a mask and recoiled, stood up and stumbled away, leaving his guiding lights behind. *No more illuminations...* It was suddenly black and silent. *No more stars...*

He was disorientated. Stood still and waited. Something brushed against his hair. He was terrified and wanted to scream, but heard the flap of wings and stayed quiet. The air was disturbed. A weight landed on his right shoulder. He could smell feathers, a dirtier odour to the decorative skins of the USE, felt them smooth against his ear. Steel claws gripped for balance. The monster's breathing rose and fell. It whispered, but he didn't know what it was saying. He flashed back and was a boy listening to his father telling him a story about an albatross. A beautiful, magical bird. The darkness was total.

Rupert's mind cleared and big, brash illuminations lit up the seafront. *Starry, starry night...* A sparkling tower appeared, doused in colour. He was sure he was inside the East Side Gates, started to run, pushing past a group of people and knocking one of them over. Voices were raised. This wasn't Pearly in front of him though, just a skeletal structure that bore a resemblance to Tenderburger Point in Paris. Behind him, people were shouting, but they sounded little different to the gulls. Winged beasts screamed and donkeys brayed. He was going to vomit. He'd had enough. It was time to return to Cuddles. Time to chill.

Rupert was his normal, confident, charming self as he moved fingers through the air, but instead of modern-day London he remained in old-school Blackpool. He tried several more times, finally flapping his hands as if he was conducting the ranting birds and the swearing of an elderly standing a metre away. He attempted to dismiss the old man, but he refused to leave, furious his wife had been pushed to the ground. When Rupert glared at the apparition he was punched in the face. It was a physical blow. Unrequested. Painful.

He lost control, ran across the road and was narrowly missed by a car, which made a loud, blaring sound that only increased his indignation. He was a Crat, a Bureau, a Good Euro. He would report this hooligan to Cool. Request a Hardcore action. He was going to lead the unit himself. Kill every seagull and donkey. Let an Argie militia loose on the locals. He had to escape the immediate danger first. He kept running.

Resting inside a shop doorway, it took Rupert a long time to recover. His mind was a tangle of conflicting thoughts. Finally, he realised that he had been a little rude. The great visionary Horace Starski had arranged this adventure and there was a reason. Rupert had declined his illuminations and failed to grasp the wisdom of the commentary, which was loaded with sophistications he was struggling to process. He was sure the Controller was still his Uncle Horace. There would be no rebuke, as he was a key member of Team USE, had complete freedom of choice, could make whatever decision he liked as long as it was correct, the unfortunate episode more a question of etiquette.

His reflections refocused. He searched for solutions, tried to solve riddles, juggled options, and it became clear that Uncle Horace had *wanted* him to break from the donkey's intimidation. It was a regress. *Pure* nostalgia. *Pure* horror. The choice was offered, his guru adding words and images that had made him decide for the best, and the unprovoked assault by that muscle-bound young thug had been a reminder of the brutality of the commons. This was England. Part of Britain. Monkey Island. What had he expected? He could leave Blackpool whenever he wanted, but had cleverly mimicked the wanding, playing his own funnies, knowing there was yet more knowledge to be gained.

His lights reappeared and he followed them into a narrow street. He moved quickly, past small shops selling more Chinese and Indian muck over high counters, came to a lane and saw his path extending to a pub. It stood on a corner and he went over, heard a ballad he was sure he knew, felt strong and revitalised, continued inside. Here he paused. The room was packed with commons. They ranged from mid-teens to post-seventies, the latter sitting at tables with glasses of beer in front of them, served in old measures. Many people stood. Everyone was noisy. Some laughed in crude fashion. The ceiling was low and there was a worn carpet on the floor, a fatty operating a physical keyboard. A woman in her sixties sang. The face was creased and she had teeth missing. A drinker in the former English, Welsh, Scottish, Irish style. Her clothes were shabby, but he had to admit that she had a good voice. *She has a magnificent voice...* Rupert nodded. *The woman is poor and has had a hard life, but she loves to sing. Music makes her want to live...* Rupert was sure she needed a haircut. *Her beauty is within...* Perhaps a shower.

The orange beam extended to the bar. He followed it over, realised that the ballad was by newcomer and Crat fave Frankie Sinatra. It was peculiar that it was being sung in the past, and he recalled Uncle Horace telling him about the theft and reinvention of culture, saw that it had been dropped in as a continuation of that earlier joke. He appreciated the touch, how it dipped into their chatting, but a drink called Guinness was being highlighted and so he pointed to the pump.

The woman serving said something he couldn't hear, so he put on his brightest smile and nodded. *Don't forget to pay...* He was about to raise his Palm, but realised it wasn't there. His stomach churned. *Hard currency only I'm afraid...* He was stuck. *In your trouser pocket. The right one...* A note was removed and passed to the barmaid and coins returned. Banned hards. More dinosaur living. Illegality. But legal at the time. Retrospective action was always just. *Why not drink it all...?* Rupert would close the pub down if he was given the chance. Cool could bring coffee and muffins for everyone present. The subhumans had to be dealt with first. Seagull barbies. *Please don't leave a drop...* Rupert drank slowly. *It is good for the blood as it's full of iron...* The beer tasted terrible. *An Irish brand of stout, which was originally from London, brewed inside the East Side Gates actually...* Rupert moved away from the bar. *Michele, my Belle...* He stood by a wall.

The woman finished her song and everyone in the pub cheered and clapped. He watched her return to her seat, hunched but smiling, a worn-down version of the donkey girl on the beach. This was the future that awaited a child in the days before New Democracy. Rupert was starting to see why he had been invited to this slum. The State offered its citizens the chance to leave this sort of life behind. *Blackpool has changed little...* The town could be saved, but first it had to be polished. He studied the faces filling the pub, heard snippets of conversation, finished his drink and felt superior, privileged and humble. He was a Crat and these people were lowers. He wanted to help.

Following his lights out of the pub and into a series of small streets, he stood aside as a gang of women walked towards him. They wore short, frilly skirts and high, shining heels, had strange devices on their heads, plastic tiaras with two thin strips of vertical metal topped by pink baubles. He found them attractive, even though they shrieked like the gulls. They laughed and laughed and laughed. Perhaps they were mad? Completely cuckoo? A cloud of perfume engulfed him, and then they were gone and he continued and caught up with his guides, turned into a longer road lined with houses advertising rooms for rent. He noted small displays of potted flowers, stone figures with pointed hats, a wide range of plastic buckets and spades.

A man sat on the steps of a hotel, drinking tea from a mug and smoking a cigarette. He said hello and Rupert turned his head away, disgusted by the smell of the tobacco and a dirty habit, and then he was in another grim street, passing along a desolate strip of closed cafés and shops. There were more people up ahead, standing together and talking, and he heard a repetitive thud, a sound that was charged and exciting. It became louder with each step he took. *The Winter Gardens is a place of entertainment that even at this point in time is considered a gem from the past...* The talkers were younger than most of those in the pub. *Music-hall stars performed here, men and women of variety, jugglers and bawdy comedians, escape artists, masters of a singalong culture...* Rupert could leave whenever he wanted. *People came here to dance and listen to swing, Pete McKenna played northern-soul records in the Spanish Hall, competitions were held around a game known as darts...*

It was busy inside the building and Rupert felt uncomfortable. His stars sparkled. The people smelled of beer and sweat, but worse was the bizarre appearance of some. *Punks and skinheads and a rockabilly...* Non-conformist styles that made him snigger. *Look, on that stall over there, a picture of the great Johnny Rotten...* Rupert saw a contorted face. It was a clear spoof of Jean Rotten, and again he marvelled at Uncle Horace's humour. *He was a real person who lived long before Jean. He was a Sex Pistol...* Rupert sniggered. Hards were being bought and sold – vinyl, CDs, books. A time of bickering and waste. The thudding was louder and he focused on it, was tempted to tap a foot but resisted. He thought of the soft melodies of *Holidays In The Sun*, knew Johnny could never match Jean, even if he had really existed.

It's hard to believe there was a time when professionals disagreed and formed factions, and that one of these was called Labour and held conferences here... Rupert shook his head sadly. *This was in the dark ages of trade-unionism and State-run services and some pretty spiteful attacks on our corporate benefactors...* Little about life pre-USE surprised Rupert. He was in the Empress Ballroom, but didn't remember coming in.

Look at the ceiling... The design was far too elaborate, created by individuals rather than computers. In theory it was a distraction, though high in the sky. A ridiculous waste of effort and expenditure. He preferred smooth surfaces. Fine lines. *Think of the craftsmen responsible...* Rupert watched the band Subhumans. He thought of the drama of the same name, which followed the lives of three meatworks men. *They sing songs that protest against the elite controlling society...* It was hard graft managing the four-leggers. Non-stop poo and wee. *Anarchists...* He had heard of Conflict terrorists. *They want to decentralise power and hand it to the people...* Uncle Horace was in brilliant form. An insane idea. *Listen carefully...* Rupert smiled. *Watch the scruff on the microphone. He rejects fashion. Thinks for himself...* The lead singer was a messy. He jerked as the audience pushed and shoved. *Magnificent...* At least there were no sparrows or seagulls inside the ballroom.

Rupert found himself in the Galleon Bar, beneath the Spanish Hall. *Why not look at the walls...?* He did as suggested. *And the ceiling...* He found his surroundings peculiar. *Added to the complex in the 1930s and modelled on a Spanish ship, but you may not have heard of Spain...* Carvings covered the walls and ceiling, this room much smaller than the Empress Ballroom. *Magnificent...* More time and effort wasted for no reason.

He went into an adjoining room where three men sat on a stage. *Ruts DC...* Rupert was tired and ready for bye-bye. *The man singing is Segs. Neat suit. See the round object? A small drum. That's Dave Ruffy. Look, he's using brushes. Leigh Heggarty is on lead guitar. Watch how he moves his wands. A brilliant musician. This is how music used to be made...* Rupert sighed. *It still works this way outside our cities, in the suburbs yet to be fully polished. Another example of the people's addiction to hards. Listen to the sound. They fuse musical genres. Here we have elements of reggae, dub and funk...* Rupert was lost. *Primitive, but brilliant. The bands here work instinctively, lack formal training and are therefore free to let their invention run riot. They create at a much higher level than today's homogenised coders.*

The location had changed. Rupert was in a simple room with steps leading down into a pit. The music was louder and more aggressive, reminded him of a melodic Subhumans. There were hundreds of short-haired males present. *Skinheads...* Part of the heritage cult. *The skins and the anarchists have more in common than they think. Both believe in localism. It is a small example of the bigger divide that worked to our advantage in EU days. Divide and rule...* The lead singer was heavily tattooed. *This is The Last Resort...* The crowd joined in the words of a song that mentioned England. If only he was a Techno with the power to intervene. *That's Roi Pearce there on vocals. Look, JJ Kaos. And Beef. Mik on drums. Fantastic...*

Rupert was back in the Empress Ballroom. *Roy Ellis and The Moonstompers...* A black man in a red suit was singing. *There was a time before Fortress Europe...* A bad time. *The Commonwealth was betrayed...* People were dancing in an unusual way. *Skanking...* How Rupert wished he was the Techno invited to drive a deep polish. *Cleansing...* Skinheads were present. He was concerned for Roy's safety. *Liberal masks...* He would be better off in Africa. *Roy was born in Jamaica, part of the Commonwealth...* He wasn't safe in Blackpool. Neither was Rupert. Danger surrounded them. He was in some sort of car park.

The Partisans... Rebels. *A fine Welsh band...* Part of GB45. *All these people have their quirks, but they come together the same as those fighting us today. These are the locals, Rupert. Please listen. Here we see past, present and future under one roof. Not a dome in sight. You are outside your bubble. This is the world...* Rupert was surrounded by enemies. A drunk banged into him and he fell to the floor. Hands reached down and hauled him upright. Rupert hated the Winter Gardens.

He hated the promenade and the beach and every person he had seen there.

He hated the animals and wished they were dead.

He hated Blackpool and The North and England and Britain.

He hated the pubs and he hated punk.

Rupert wished the population could be removed and the buildings levelled. Blackpool was beyond the help of even the most generous Controller. It would be far better to start again. Change was for the best and it was important to be decisive. The masses needed assistance.

This England isn't as bad as we like to make out, wouldn't you agree? Seaside holidays are where dreams come true...

Blackpool was a living nightmare. Rupert loathed the place and was happy to say so. He wanted to return to Cuddles. Uncle Horace was ironic and brilliant. He had made his points superbly. Rupert smiled and nodded his head.

Back in his chill room, he showered and changed and went to bed, but couldn't relax at first, kept touching his nose, which was sore from the punch. He had clearly been treated to technology that surpassed the Kiev 4D. The bond between Controller and Crat was solid. When he started to drift off he heard seagulls screaming. Silencing them, he imagined his revenge. He was soon asleep.

TWENTY

THE SPREAD EAGLE was one of several traditional London pubs in Wandle Manor, a commons enclave where those servicing the needs of a specific stretch of Thameside lived. The American Quarter of North Battersea and the mixed financials and corporates in Clapham Junction relied on these locals for their cleaners, gardeners, tradespeople, shop assistants, carers and other key workers. Crats avoided the area while Cool had no interest in irritating and possibly driving out a cheap, much-needed labour force. The people were indulged their eccentricities and the Wandle was left to its own devices. It was relaxed and friendly, with no unemployment and little crime.

Kenny was impressed by the pub's high ceilings and cut glass, but felt awkward that he couldn't buy a round. He wasn't connected to Troika, which managed the credit of every person working within the USE economy. The pub dealt in soft euros, while he was used to hard pounds. The Spread Eagle was divided into three sections – this main room and smaller bars to either side of the counter where they stood waiting to be served. The one to their left was full of noisy young skins and suedeheads, who were busy watching two of their friends play Wizard on a fixed screen. As well as these lads, there was a dressed-up droog standing slightly apart with a peroxide devotchka. This was the London cult that Kenny had heard about. Heritage. Cropheads and Jacks. Clockwork youth. Cockney agg. The bar to his right was less obvious, hidden behind a wall of thicker glass. Fred had told him to stay in the main part of the pub.

– Two pints of Shed Boy, please, Frank said, ordering from the landlord. Same for you, Dave?

Kenny looked at Frank's enquiring face, his mind blank, jumped when he remembered that he was supposed to be Dave

Brown from Somerset. Up from the country and staying with his sister and brother-in-law for a few days. Here to see a sick uncle.

– Thanks.

– The famous Shed Boy, mumbled Wes.

Kenny studied the picture on the pump. Concrete steps topped by a crooked roof. Two men stood to the side, versions of those next door. Tens of thousands of young commons were said to be fixed on heritage. The originals were acknowledged. It was nice to see. A pint was passed over and he was surprised. The decades had seen a series of Metric Martyrs hounded for dealing in native measures. These brave men and women looked back to the example set by Steve Thoburn, while the broader resistance drew on local heroes. For Kenny, his references were the likes of the Tolpuddles of Dorset, Captain Swing, the Diggers, Rebecca's Daughters, Ben Tillet.

– Shed End... Shed Boy Special.

He knew the State let things go in the core-worker zones of Europe, but this was a flagrant act of defiance a few miles from the South Side Gates and right next to one of the most gentrified areas of the city, home to some of the wealthiest clones. The pub's drinkers could well be working in their houses and gardens tomorrow. The reality was that Cool could close this place down whenever it wanted, and patience had always been the strength of those building the empire, but even though there were Palms in here he was again struck by the possibility that London just wasn't as nailed down as he'd thought. He knew there would be spies about, that he couldn't talk as freely as he did in The Wheatsheaf, but the sheer scale and complexity of the city meant a complete clampdown was impossible.

– Welcome to London, Frank said, once they had their drinks and had moved to a quiet corner.

– Cheers, Frank. Thanks, Wes. This place hasn't changed.

– When were you in here last?

– Six years ago.

Frank whistled.

– Fuck me, is it really six years?

They clinked glasses and Kenny guzzled a third of his pint. He'd been promised a good drink and after the South Circular he needed a session. The pressure of his trip here would have been enough. It was no good hiding inside, listening to Scientist or reading Herbert Sutherland. He would crack up, had to be out and about and around other people. Nobody knew the real reason he was in London. Not Frank and Wes, not even Tubby Nowakowski. The less information a person had, the less they could give away. Kenny was going to have a laugh tonight, and he was also determined to meet the legendary Suzie Vickers.

– Drink up boys. It's thirsty work hiding in the back of a lorry.

He finished the rest of his pint in one, unable to stop himself, tapped it on a nearby ledge. Frank and Wes followed and he took their glasses back to the bar.

– Three pints of Shed Boy, please.

He studied the pump more closely. One of the figures was pale skinned, the other slightly darker. They had short hair and wore blue-and-white scarves under black Crombies. Their footwear was cherry red. One was called Eccles, the other Babs. He glanced over to the bar with the heritage youth, could definitely imagine them in here, wondered if they had ever been inside the pub. The skinhead/suedehead/modernist look had long been the dominant style for commons men. Small changes occurred, but the classic appearance prevailed.

– They're still chasing that sparrow, the landlord said.

– What's that all about then? I just came into London today to see my uncle. I haven't been keeping up with the news.

– There were these sparrows flying about in the East London bubbledome. Don't know how they got in. They were stuck, trying to escape. Scared the Euros half to death. Used to be birds all over the place, but of course they were wiped out. Hardly ever hear them singing round here now. No reason for it, just bubblers hate animals.

– Did they let them out?

– No chance. They've killed five and there's one left. Useless fuckers can't get him. Poor little chap. It's a boy you see. He's been zoomed. They barbecued the dead ones, stuck their heads on skewers.

– Barbecued them?

– Had a party as well. That's trended across InterZone. They'll kill the last sparrow eventually. You know, London really was full of birds when I was young, and people still had cats and dogs. There were foxes, but they were exterminated. Toffs didn't want them, you see. Same with the locals, but they couldn't kill us, bought up the property instead, so there was nowhere for a normal person to live. They ruined London. No culture, those idiots. Plenty of money, but zero class. Toffs, yuppies, Euros, Crats – no difference, mate. Bunch of cunts.

The landlord had been leaning forward and talking in a confidential tone, looking side-to-side, clearly felt Kenny could be trusted seeing as he was a friend of Frank and Wes. He was taking a chance, though, faced ruin if a sly recording was made and appeared on InterZone. Trial by twits would follow. Kenny wanted to tell him about his dog Zola, how they had left London when he was a boy, talk about the no-tolerance policy they had for digitals where he lived, how Palms and lenses and InterZone were banned, their pubs protected by scanners, but he would be giving too much away.

– I'll pay for these, Wes said, having appeared by his side.

Kenny couldn't believe he'd forgotten about Troika. It was a basic error and he felt like a fool.

– Want to know the history of the Shed Boy? Wes asked, once they were back with Frank.

– Go on then.

– Fucking hell, don't encourage him, Frank roared. You've asked for it now. He'll be battering your eardrums for the next hour. Facts and figures. Football mad.

Wes took no notice and moved closer.

– Used to be a football club called Chelsea. They had a stadium across the river in Fulham. Two, three miles away. There was a bridge linked Wandsworth and Fulham. Knocked down now. Anyway, it was all Chelsea round here. There were four big teams in London back then. Chelsea in the West, Arsenal and Tottenham in the North, West Ham in the East. South London had Crystal Palace, Charlton and Millwall, but they were smaller outfits. Mind you, Millwall was famous for other reasons. They came into the big time off the pitch.

Wes smirked and Frank grinned.

– You had other smaller clubs – Brentford, Fulham and Queens Park Rangers in West London... Barnet and Watford in North London... Leyton Orient in East London... All the big towns had professional sides in those days.

Kenny was surprised. He went to see Yeovil occasionally, but there were massive differences between them and the likes of London United. It was hard to imagine so many professional clubs.

– There were ninety-two sides in four divisions, but a handful were greedy, fucked the others over and formed their own league in the 1990s. Called themselves Premier. Like a credit card. It was all about money, though the usual bollocks was spouted. Everything in England was being put up for sale and it was no different with football. Foreign owners and managers came in and had little interest in local talent. A rich Australian was running the media. More and more players arrived from abroad. There was money laundering going on, the shifting of debt, land grabs, backhanders.

– What happened to Chelsea and the others? Kenny asked.

– They were merged, became London United. The same happened across the country. All over Europe. Glasgow City is a combination of what used to be Rangers and Celtic; Liverchester is Liverpool, Manchesters United and City, and Everton; Middle Tigers includes the old Aston Villa, West Bromwich Albion and Birmingham City; Hoops Deluxe is the likes of Newcastle, Sunderland, Sheffield United and Leeds. They were launched as The Big Five, played each other six times a season, but before long they became part of the Euroship.

– That's where the dollars are made.

– London United is run by the Muller Corporation, Glasgow is part of the Tenderburger chain, Liverchester belongs to an

American billionaire who has never been named, Middle Tigers is financed by China State (Europe), while Hoops Deluxe is the property of a creative from Naples. Pretty sure he's the one who discovered that new band Abba.

Kenny knew his music history and wanted to tell Wes about Abba, but let him continue.

– Before the mergings, those running the richest clubs wanted to force out the proles and attract the prawn-sandwich brigade. That was a luxury food back then. Ever heard of Roy Keane?

– Don't think so.

– Nutty Irishman who grew a huge, bushy beard after he stopped playing football. Anyway, it was him who invented the term. The bosses of these clubs only wanted nerds and numpties, customers with excess funds, the sort of cockheads who pay huge prices for replica shirts and wear clown hats. Like they do today.

– You know, advertising on a player's shirt was seen as low class at one time, Frank added.

Wes stared at his friend. He was holding court and did not appreciate interruptions.

– Directors, managers, players, commentators, journalists... they all cashed in. Brats, sightseers, tourists and sheldons took over. This was before so-called Crat culture, but you're talking about the same people. The atmosphere changed. There was a time when tens of thousands attended a match in person, remember. Chelsea used to represent communities like this one here, but now there's only London United, and they have one local player who's persecuted for his roots. He's an English commons, male and heterosexual, London-born and short-haired, and you can't get any further down the PC totem than that.

– Terry Johns...

– Ever heard of John Terry?

Kenny shook his head.

– The snobs will never admit their own prejudices, pump out a series of excuses, but he can do no right. Johns is an invention. Part of the spectacle. Only big ground left is Olympic Park. Wembley Stadium was the home of English football, but that was turned into a conference centre the year after the countries of Europe were dissolved and international fixtures ended. The USE plays at the Allianz in Munich, as I'm sure you know.

Wes realised he'd been rambling and eased off, thought again and didn't care. Football was his life. He was a historian and had his own stash of hards.

– Tell me about The Shed, Kenny said. The steps and roof. Those two men on the pump. Who were Eccles and Babs?

Wes nodded to a couple of women as they passed, Kenny noting that they had similar peroxide feathercuts to the devotchka in the busier of the two smaller bars.

– I'll tell you later, the football fanatic replied. Don't want to bore Frank. But Shed Boy's dedicated to them both, a double tribute. There's others... A Hickmott Light Ale, Fat Pat Stout, Daniels Smooth, Nutty Ned Lager. There's local brews right across the manors... A Johnny Brookes Bitter up Tottenham way, Bunter's Best over in East Ham, an Islington-made Jenkins Pale Ale... Tiny's Tup in Catford. That's the real London United. Golden years. Another world. Wish I'd been there.

One of the devotchkas came back over and spoke to Kenny.

– Suzie's ready to see you. If you go in the bar over there, turn right towards the toilets, and you'll see another door marked *Private*. It's open, but make sure you click it shut after you, then continue up the stairs. She's on the third floor. Turn left on the landing and walk straight ahead. Just knock on the door at the end.

She squeezed his arm and went back to her friend.

– I think you're up for some of the old in-and-out there, Frank remarked.

– Who's Suzie? Wes asked.

– Friend of a friend. I won't be long.

Kenny finished his pint and followed the instructions, found the lights dimmed in the quieter bar, people huddled around tables. He passed through the *Private* door and tested it was closed before climbing the stairs. On the third floor he stopped to look at a row of framed posters lining the corridor. He was excited.

– Come in, a voice called, once he'd knocked.

The room was dark, lamps turned down low, spreading red light, the lady he had come to see sitting in the far corner. A white reading lamp was bent over her left shoulder. He couldn't see the face and felt a stab of dread. Something moved to his right and he started, peered into the shadows. There was nothing there. His imagination was playing a trick.

– Come and sit with me, Suzie said.

– Thank you, Ms Vickers.

– That's too formal, *Mr* Jackson. You can call me Suzie. Everyone does. Sorry about this...

She raised a physical scanner when he had sat down in the chair opposite. Checked the screen on a separate and turned it off.

– You understand?

– It's fine.

The reading light was shining in his eyes and he still couldn't see her face. Suzie adjusted its angle and her elegance was clear. His skin tingled. They were probably the same age, but she seemed a little older, or maybe it was wiser, and because she was slender he imagined she was taller. Her presence engulfed him, and he wondered how much of this was down to her reputation. Suzie Vickers was an inspirational figure. She was London's greatest librarian.

– I hope your uncle recovers, she said, with the trace of a grin.

For some reason he wanted to tell her why he was really here, and what had happened to his friends on the South Circular, how Hannah had almost been decapitated, the wire twisted so tight it cut into the bone. That was in a Free English town as well. The dangers Suzie faced were far greater.

– I've forgotten my manners.

She was on her feet and standing by a fridge, turned the overhead light on so he could see the room, the posters on the landing backed up by framed photos of maybe thirty authors. He narrowed his eyes and studied the labelled portraits nearest him – Kate Sillitoe, Steve Smith, Sally Chat, Billy O'Brien. Four original talents operating outside a credit-driven mainstream. Their novels were only available as hards, passed through an underground where literature was taken seriously.

– I've just got lager I'm afraid. Fred said you're a Kingdon man.

The fridge was open and she was holding two bottles up for his inspection.

– Thanks, Kenny said, guessing she was about to ask if he wanted a glass or not. The bottle's okay.

Suzie opened the lagers and returned with a tin of nuts. She pulled a small table over and arranged it between them, removed the lid on the tin. He wondered if Sillitoe, Smith, Chat and O'Brien were aliases, as they had to operate in the shadows. Suzie probably did as well. Their faces wouldn't be on InterZone, never mind their novels, so why were they on display here? She was obviously confident. And defiant.

– Representations, she said, pointing to the pictures. I have never met them in person, and if you look closely you will see that the images are made from minuscule sentences.

He stood and went over. Up close the faces disintegrated and he saw the words.

– Sit down, she ordered, her tone making him jump.

It sounded like a different person.

– Help yourself, she said, softly now. Tell me about Fred. How is he? Still drinking too much?

– He likes a pint.

Suzie clapped her hands and a vibrancy filled the room. Fred had warned him that she could change moods in a second. She was no witch, but someone with shifting personalities, like loosely linked characters in a subterranean novel.

– I first met Fred in a pub, when I was fourteen. My dad bought and sold books. It was in Luton, but I forget the name. Fred liked to do his business in drinkers.

– He hasn't changed.

– My dad and him were a lot alike. They got drunk and I'm surprised we made it home. I had to drive. It was my first time behind the wheel as well. But I ended up working with Fred after Dad had a stroke. Our first job was in Bracknell. I was seventeen and things went badly. I nearly died of fright. Did Fred tell you about that time?

Kenny shook his head.

– Made more of an impression on me I suppose, seeing as I was young. The ban on hards was at its most intense as the directive had just been upgraded. There were lots of books about and Cool wanted to take as many out of circulation as they could in as short a time as possible, before people had the chance to hide them or copy the originals. The traditional libraries had been destroyed years before, but small bands of readers and lots of individuals had their stashes. Cool organised specialist units and offered bonuses. Punishments were introduced at the same time as a propaganda surge. Some gave up their books, others did not. So Fred was going to pick up a big collection in Bracknell and I was chosen to drive his van.

– He still can't drive, Kenny said. He likes to give directions though.

– He was the same with me. We loaded the books out of this lock-up, and never met first in a pub as the lady who owned them was too nervous, wasn't a dealer as such. Well, we were on the smaller roads and away from Bracknell, heading for home, when a patroller starts flashing us to pull over. I was terrified.

Suzie took a handful of nuts from the tin and sat back.

– What happened?

– A policeman came up to the window on Fred's side and asked him what we had in the back. He answered that we were loaded with books. Paperbacks and hardbacks. Fiction and non-fiction.

– He said that?

– They thought he was making fun of them, but he climbed out before they had a chance to start bossing him about and marched to the rear of the van. He opened it up and their eyes almost popped out of their heads it was so full. Remember, there was a lot of scandalising going on, and this haul meant a nice reward. Turned out they were locals, not Gendarmerie but Englishmen. Badly paid. Low on morale and status.

– How long did you get? Fred never told me any of this. He always said he'd lived a charmed life.

– Fred susses people out fast, but likes to keep them guessing. It was a game he played.

Something about her face changed. Green eyes bored into him. Kenny felt uncomfortable and looked away.

– One of these coppers was Welsh. Fred commented on the accent as he was leaving the van. He was making conversation, but planning ahead. Just before he opened the back he asked him if he'd heard of Gwyn Thomas, which he hadn't, and Fred told him he had to read *The Dark Philosophers*, described the novel and mentioned a Library Of Wales list, and that he should definitely try Lewis Jones' *Cwmardy* as well. Fred was quickly into the back of the van, standing on a metal platform. There were so many books piled high, and it seemed like a cliff was teetering and about to collapse. He was a giant looking down on dwarves, and I saw those two policemen take a step or two back. He removed *The Dark Philosophers* from a box and passed it down. The Welshman thanked him and opened it up. Like a little boy he was.

– He started reading the book?

– I think he might have done, but his friend wasn't impressed and Fred apologised, became very humble. I didn't see it right away, but the threat had been halved, though this other one was tougher, told him to get down and put his hands on the side of the van. Fred asked if he'd been in the army, seeing as he liked to do things the right way, and he just wanted to say before he was arrested that he felt the same way, didn't hold it against him even though they were both patriotic Englishmen who hated what had happened to the country they loved. This second copper nodded and frowned. It was then that I realised Fred was one of the cunning folk, but in a genuine, honest sort of way. It was a big game to him.

– He gets a look in his eye when he's on a roll like that. I've seen it myself.

– He was thinking fast, dives into another box and comes out with *From The City From The Plough* by Alexander Baron. He's had a good look at the books in the lock-up, but quickly, and don't forget we're talking thousands of titles here, yet he knows exactly where to find these two. He stuffs the Baron novel in the second man's hand, changes in a split-second and adopts a gruff tone and tells this English bobby that there's his history and he should fucking well read it – those words – asks what on earth he's doing hassling a fellow Englishman and his granddaughter.

– He told the man off?

– Deflated him. Talks about the Second German War and steams into the USE, crosses from the war to the trade-unionism of *Cwmardy*, the nature of Alexander Baron and London and what it means to be English and British, delivers a lecture in this little lane, right there in the night. I'd never seen anything like it in my life.

Suzie moved forward, took a handful of nuts and started eating them one at a time.

– What did the police do when he finished?

– They let us go. Fred told them to keep the books.

– They let you leave?

– Told us to get back in the van. Turned their car around and drove off. It wouldn't have happened if they weren't locals, I'm certain of that, but they didn't believe in what they were being ordered to do. Even so, Fred was amazing.

– You were lucky, Kenny said. You could have got five years.

– More at that time. Fred reckoned ten. It wasn't luck though. He could weigh people up in seconds and had a knowledge of these books, don't forget. He said it was a shame they didn't have another one of their mates with them, that there was a copy of *The Third Policeman* in the back. Flann O'Brien, Thomas and Jones, Alexander Baron – whoever bought these books first time around knew their literature. The lady we got them from said it was an inheritance. Later, Fred thought he might look into it, find out who owned them originally, but I don't think he ever did.

Suzie paused and Kenny guessed that his friend had inspired her as much as her own father. She had probably been in awe of Fred at the time.

– Is he still the same? He must be eighty by now. I'd like to see him again, but travelling is difficult.

– Fred's eighty-one. He's slowed down, but not much different in himself.

– Thing is, what happened that night backed up what he would tell me over the years, that everybody would read novels if only they could find ones that connected to their lives, that fiction shouldn't be censored and the commons excluded. Publishing has always been controlled by an elite, but for a while a few free-thinkers got to work as editors, and going right back you had idealists with money who weren't driven by profit, but then the corporations came in and the censorship increased...

It was Kenny's turn to take some nuts from the tin. Suzie paused and watched him. She continued.

– They denied their censorship, applied 'correct' values, and this gave those earning the big money an excuse to do what the accountants demanded. It allowed them to hide their own lack of ideas and commitment. Careerists should not be involved in literature.

– Digitals played a massive part in the destruction of the book trade though, didn't they? Kenny ventured.

– They didn't help, but that was part of something much deeper, I think. It was more to do with the slow erosion of principles. There was less and less common ground. A new hierarchy was forming, one that lacked ties to genuine communities. It's all very depressing.

They sat in an easy silence and drank the lager. Suzie adjusted her reading lamp, so the beam was directed at the floor, turned the main light off and adjusted her position so her face was in the shade again. He heard her humming softy, the unease he'd felt when he first arrived returning.

– Here's the package Fred sent, Kenny said at last, taking it from inside his jacket.

His friend wouldn't tell him what the book was called or who had written it, insisted it was top secret, teasing as usual. Maybe Fred thought he needed a mystery to drive him on. He hoped Suzie would open the parcel in front of him so he could see what was inside, and he waited for her to emerge from the darkness, watching closely, and when she did appear a hand was raised and he noticed long nails painted a brilliant yellow, sharp as tiny knives. When she looked up quickly and read his mind he knew what would happen next.

– Thanks Kenny, she said, placing it on the arm of her chair, just as Fred would have done.

A hundred thousand words were in there, hidden by sealed paper. She ran her nails over the surface, a faint but mesmerising sound, and he realised there was something highly erotic about Suzie Vickers. She may have been the daughter of the bookworm Vic Vickers, but she had achieved much more in her own right. She was the editor behind Sillitoe, Smith, Chat and O'Brien, had published them all through her own Spiral Press.

– I've heard about your library, she said, peering into his eyes. We're going to be doing some business one day?

– I hope so. I'd love to see the London Library, if it exists of course.

She laughed as the hand and its five nails flashed and was lost in darkness.

– If a London Library did exist, it would be well hidden, in the sort of location where you'd least expect to find it, and it would take a long time for a person to be trusted enough to go anywhere near such a place.

– Fred imagined it...

– But he never said where it could be, did he?

– No, just pictured it, but I wonder if it should be moved out of London?

He wanted to ask her to take him there, but it would have made him look foolish to do so. In truth, he was as interested in the authors she was publishing, admired what she was doing for the present as well as the past.

– There's a novel coming out I think you'll really like, Suzie said. The author writes in staccato sentences. Short, sharp prose. *A Great British Southall* shows how Cool agents bombed a gurdwara and blamed it on the Middlesex Boys. It's fiction, based on fact. It looks at several generations of Sikhs, their historical links to the British Army and West London, the way the Commonwealth fought with us in the two wars against Germany and its Eurofascist poodles.

She paused for a response, but he didn't want to distract her, and she saw this and continued, told him about Billy O'Brien's *They Burned My Flag*, branded racist by *Good European* reviewer Todd White in a feature on 'criminal literature'. A hard copy had subsequently been left on his doorstep. It was a coup getting it covered, as it put the title into InterZone, and that would alert the masses to its existence, although how these novels could ever break out of the underground was beyond Suzie. Tens of thousands of outraged posts had appeared across the social-media spectrum inside the first day, though none of these keyboard warriors had actually read the book. Twenty-four hours later and every reference had been deleted, along with White's article.

– I'd like to read both of those, and I'm sure there's plenty of people at home who would as well, Kenny said. We have our bookshop don't forget.

– I know, Suzie said. That's brilliant. Out in the open?

– Between a pub and a curry house.

Suzie shook her head in wonder, paused so long that Kenny had to coax her back, wanted to hear about the other novels she was publishing, the authors behind them, and it struck him that he should have brought some books by his own locals along, though if he was honest the Wessex writers he loved weren't as hard-hitting as her Cockney School. Johnny Knapp was an exception. Suzie would have loved *Murder Murder*. But she was revived, holding court again, and he sat back and listened to her voice sing.

Sally Chat's *Robots Too* was the tale of a Crat who had built a doll to replace his date. This was no ordinary doll either. It moved and responded so well it could not be told apart from its Bangkok sister. The Crat fell in love with her and she slowly started to take over. When a new law was introduced making homosexuality compulsory, she became jealous and forbid him from complying, which did not go down well with his Super. A Cool unit was called in to speed up his agreement, the novel ending with the doll – who was called Dot – killing various Cools before she was zapped and died in the arms of her Crat lover.

The Sentimentalists, by Steve Smith, went back to the first ALF-GB45 collaborations, a series of attacks on the meat industry that escalated in ferocity over the course of a nutty two-month period. It doubled as a love story and was set when the infighting between commons was starting to die out, although tensions remained. Smith clearly knew his subject matter, as Suzie explained the author's own past in some detail.

Kate Sillitoe was the best known of the bunch, her *Soulless* quartet set in and around Slough. The brilliant *More Speed For Slim* was a long and winding satire, pulling apart the efforts of a creative and his scriptwriters as they prepared to set up and shoot a comedy series that showed the locals in their hilarious squalor. The fictional characters were low-level thieves, drug dealers, addicts, female prostitutes, layabouts of both sexes, bullies, drunks, rent boys and a supposedly radical philosopher played by a famous emptyhead. The novel revealed the prejudices of those making the series, how genuine locals realised what was happening and had their revenge.

Lost in the world of the editor and publisher Suzie Vickers, Kenny saw her in every novel she described. He was excited and soothed in turn, loved the rolling rhythm of her sentences and the way ideas drifted off before circling back in on themselves and reconnecting with storylines and themes and the points she was keen to make. It was a form of music and he could have listened to this wonderful woman for hours, but Fred had warned him not to take up too much of her time, that he mustn't keep her for longer than thirty minutes, only half-joking when he said that Suzie would make him want to stay in London forever.

His time was already up, but he couldn't leave just yet, guided her back to the legend of a huge, hidden library near the centre of London where hundreds of thousands of hards were shelved under the noses of the State, and she shrugged and told him it was possible and likely and unlikely and how could she know, but if there was such a place it would be deep underground as the corporations built taller and taller buildings, creating more and more offices and apartments for investors, all those empty shells with views few would ever get to enjoy. Even the lowest Crats refused to use the Underground. They were always looking to the skies and yet they hated birds, couldn't see what was right under their noses.

Kenny left soon after. They stood facing each other and he saw that she was slightly shorter, which surprised him, and then she leaned in and rested her head on his chest so he could smell her hair and was annoyed at himself for getting an erection, really hoped she wouldn't notice, but she seemed fixed on listening to his heart, which he was sure must be beating loud and fast. Red in the face, he shook her hand and left the room.

Back downstairs in the pub proper, he sat in a corner of the quiet bar for a few minutes to recover. He had been on the move since this morning and these moments were the first he'd had to himself since he left the lorry. In control, he returned to the main bar where he found Frank and Wes talking with the two women from earlier. They were a few rounds ahead of him now and showing some of the effects, and he knew he would have to push himself to catch up.

– Here he is...

Frank nodded to the barman, who started pouring a Shed Boy.

– Good luck, the others toasted, when the pint was in Kenny's hand and travelling towards his mouth.

– What would you like to drink? Frank asked, immediately confusing Kenny.

– Pint of Pat, Suzie Vickers replied, brushing against him as she pointed towards the pump showing the face of the heritage Chelsea boy and 12-Bar doorman.

Kenny was surprised to see her here with the drinkers, had assumed she would be going back to work or heading home. He wondered if she had decided to follow him down, hoping so, and then thinking of Jan and hoping not. He had come into London on a mission, lost two comrades to the AirCav and narrowly escaped capture himself, and then tomorrow he had to face the might of the empire alone. And yet he had a hard-on for this graceful lady standing by his side.

– Fat Pat Dolan... nice drop of stout... friendly chap... knew everyone... GB united... that's the story.

Suzie widened her eyes as Wes spoke, stepped forward and patted him on his left shoulder. She glanced at Kenny. He was thinking about that hidden library, a cavern deep in the lost vaults of London, a replica of the long-gone British Museum Reading Room. Its dome would be a version of those covering the bubblers, a positive to the negative. He saw himself having sex with Suzie sitting on a desk of Charles Dickens hardbacks. He realised she had changed her clothes in the time it had taken him to get his head together and return to his friends. She looked fantastic.

– I need this, she said, raising the glass that was passed over. It's been a long day. I hope we're not staying here all night. We should show our visitor some of the sights.

– No, we're better off here, Frank said. He's had a tough day too.

Two hours later and Kenny was drunk and sitting in the back of Frank's car with Suzie on his lap, her black skirt riding high, but he reminded himself that she was only there so they could all fit in, her face turned away from his as everyone but the driver looked out across rows of dimly lit terraces from their vantage point on the Tooting Flyover.

– They've got these mobile killing units, Suzie was saying. Four-person teams in unmarked vans. They go out cruising for strays. Not dogs, as there's none left, but runaways and tramps, anyone sleeping rough or looking too ragged near one of their precious developments. Most people don't believe it's happening, as there's no bodies and no witnesses. Someone should write a book about that, shouldn't they?

The contrast between the Tooting terraces and the Brixton bubs was dramatic. Further north in Battersea, on the banks of the Thames, stood the Twin Towers of the American Quarter, topped with floating stars and stripes and the beaming face of Teddy Tenderburger. The larger domes of the South Side Gates linked the villages below. Suzie shook her head and turned away from the view, reached down and ran fingernails along Kenny's right thigh.

– I fucking hate bubblers, she said, her lips inches from his mouth.

He didn't know what to think. His hard-on had returned. The car came back down to earth.

– This way, Suzie Vickers ordered, once Frank had parked. Come on, hurry up.

She led them into Emotional Hooligan, bought everyone a drink at the first bar they reached – six bottles of Gate 13 – continued into the maze chiselled from concrete that supported a disused railway station. It was a three-note night, a cockney variation that had evolved out of bumpkin four-note, and the combinations of length, tone and volume were soon having their effect. One-, two- and three-colour shows filled the small rooms they passed, images added in dedicated hollows. The place was busy and Kenny found himself alone with Suzie, who took hold of a hand and pulled him through a series of smaller tunnels. Faces and scenes flashed across walls, fact and fiction merging as they moved deeper into the labyrinth.

– In here, she whispered, lips brushing against an ear.

They entered a red-brick cave. People sat in couples, elbows on white tables, heads pressed close. He remembered the bar at the front of The Wheatsheaf, its horses and fox, the witch Jennie Jones, swans and geese and a barge. He thought about death squads patrolling the streets of London, tramps warming their hands over a burning drum, the vault of All Souls where he hid his treasures.

– My mother was a traitor, Suzie said, once they were settled. She was an informer.

Her words were more whispers in his ear. Kenny didn't know what to say. A hand cupped his chin and directed his vision towards the bricks, and out of the distortion came grainy pictures of a burning London. He felt the nails pressing at his skin, knew Suzie wouldn't break the surface. Her magical voice lost its music and became a monotone.

– She did it to save herself. Guilt by association, you see. Who's to say we wouldn't act the same way if we were bullied, if Cool forced us to make one of its choices? I never spoke to her again. Even when she was dying and asked to see me. She betrayed my father and it was only towards the end that she claimed she wanted to protect me. He was taken away and I never saw him after that.

The three-note snapped in its own unique way, while Kenny adjusted to the fainter light. The black-and-white images kept popping. Hardcore appeared and moved through a collage of British history. A Spitfire swooped low over the fields of Kent and a boy waved. David Bowie lay on his death bed with buttons for eyes. Suited functionaries gathered around a Union Jack. One set it alight. Youths threw bottles at Cool and were zapped. A lad was singled out by Hardcore. He was chased and ran through streets that crumbled as he passed. He reached a wood and crawled among the ferns.

– This is a film the author made from *They Burned My Flag*, Suzie said, singing softly.

Her grip relaxed and she removed her hand. He saw the excitement in eyes that darted from one image to the next, realised she was dedicated in a way he could never be, and maybe that meant she was a little bit mad. Fred had warned him, but never been specific. Kenny wanted to believe that she lived the lives of the characters she read about and edited and published. Maybe she was Kate and Steve and Sally and Billy.

– I have a present for you, she said. I'll give it to you later, when we're alone.

They stayed an hour and left, ended up walking for a long time, unable to find a cab. It had been raining while they were inside and the streets shone. Kenny was exhausted, heard Suzie talking in the distance, but wasn't taking in what she said, more bothered about his aching feet. They kept on going until Suzie stumbled and fell.

– Help me, she said, her voice childlike. Please help me.

He pulled her to her feet.

– Thank you, Mr Jackson.

This time her voice was clipped and proper.

She took the lead and he followed her in and out of an

underpass and into an estate, concrete rising high on either side, blank windows overlooking a deserted square. They reached a corner and she stopped and turned, pulled Kenny into an alley and pushed him up against the wall, kissed him on the lips. He responded, heard a zip being undone, his mind muddled by drink and tiredness. Her hands were on his chest, and even though he was excited he knew he had to say no, couldn't let Jan down. Yet soon he would be dead. How would she know and did it matter? He would be a spirit. If he was lucky. Or he'd just be deleted. No darkness, no awareness, no second chance. His ideas of identity and justice were meaningless. The USE was more in tune with reality. The best lies won. Self-deception was ingrained and perhaps the greatest liars were authors. Novels were produced by the angry and depressed, lonely souls who drank too much and ended up frustrated that their life's work had changed nothing. He had read plenty of biographies to see the pattern.

Kenny realised that the zip belonged to his jacket and not his trousers. Disappointed and relieved at the same time, he decided he would leave London tonight and return to Wessex. He was going to conform when the inevitable happened and the USE took control of his town. What difference would it make if he nodded his head and smiled? He didn't want Jan to suffer. If they behaved they would be fine. Good Europeans lived well, and while he was on a lower level, those commons who conformed seemed safe enough. There was always a need for labour and he would earn more working for the USE. He could join Troika and surf Inter-Zone. His books would be forgotten and the door at the back of All Souls blocked up. Suzie's mum knew what she was doing, cutting herself off from her husband and not letting him drag her down. It was probably too late for him, though. Cool would find out about his past quick enough.

He should stay here and fight. London was where he had been born, where he'd first lived, and he thought of his poor dad, targeted by bullies and driven out. He would be protecting Jan if he didn't go home. The zip was down to his waist. He could live with Suzie a few miles from the Gates, skirt the system and dodge

Cool, let the pressure kill him as it had Karen and Steve. It would be better to go out with a bang, same as they had done. He could feel Suzie's hands sliding inside his jacket, fingers unbuttoning his shirt, nails nicking his skin, and she swung her handbag around and another zip was undone. A hard object was pressed into his ribs, held firm by his jacket and shirt.

She stood back, palms on his chest as she pushed herself away. Her face was flushed. She glanced sideways and gave him a quick kiss as he was about to speak, turned and walked away, off around the corner of the alley where they had been standing. It took Kenny too long to recover. When he reached the end of the wall and looked for Suzie she was nowhere to be seen. He listened for her footsteps, but heard nothing. He reached inside his shirt and pulled out the parcel, knew that it was a book, and he heard her returning, raised his head, but instead of Suzie he saw two strangers approaching.

Turning the other way, he saw two more figures. Gendarmerie or Cool, he wasn't sure which, but he did know that he was alone and in possession of a hard. They started swinging Ticklesticks and he realised he was in serious trouble. They were in rubber-truncheon mode. It was Cool. There would be no coffee and muffins at this time of night. Not without an audience. There was only one escape route and he took it, heading back the way they'd come, glad Suzie had vanished but angry she'd left him with this parcel. He wondered if he'd been set up. She might be a spy like her mum, had been trying to warn him in her own insane way, personalities battling each other inside her brain. London was about to crash down on him, and he was starting to panic, stumbled and nearly fell, managed to stay on his feet.

Suzie Vickers was a long-term plant, and if she was a spy did Fred know? Was he a traitor as well? Was Jan in danger the same as Hannah? No, he was being paranoid. And looking over his shoulder he saw that the four Cool had united and were moving in formation, trotting in perfect time, angular black outlines dotted with glowing Palms. He thought of the mobile units Suzie had mentioned. A beam flashed past Kenny. The figures shouted and jeered, voices merging as a synthetic taunt that bounced off the blocks. They were chanting words he didn't understand. His killers were closing in fast. He drove his legs hard, dipped into the underpass and ran for his life.

TWENTY-ONE

BOB TERKS AND Baby were busy decorating the apartment, Horace Starski directing operations from the comfort of his lion-skin recliner. He may have had his feet raised and a double-froth perched on the refreshment rest, but he was grafting even harder than his buddies. His artistry was in full effect as he guided them towards the best possible results.

Baby was sitting on Bobby's shoulders, arranging a strip of ancient lights. She didn't want to work in this manner, but Controller Horace had emphasised how much it was going to please him if she would just do this one small thing for her guru. He pointed out that she could trust Bob Terks with her life. He would not let her tumble. Nor would he ever let her down. They were chums. Bonded by belief. A guest was coming to play and would soon be here. They had to be ready to receive. He urged his friends on.

Inspecting his Palm, he immediately recognised a Cool face – once he had been refreshed by MemJog. Sophie was in the lobby of Pearly Tower. It was great to see her again. He was always eager to chat with lowers, to hear their news and swap tales, loved to stay in touch with the kids. Not that he had to make a special effort. Charming and naturally friendly, he was forever telling those closest to him that he was a genuine man of the people. He pinged Sophie and overrode the Cool's control, stretched her screen so his face dominated the landscape. She was pleased to see him. It was an honour.

– How have you been since we last met?

– Fantastic, she replied, even happier now that Controller Horace had spoken.

– It's brilliant to hear that, Sophie.

He flashed to another viewing angle, scanned from the rear so he too could see his features on the three-metre screen. He noticed Gendarmerie and other Coolers stopping to gape, a team of Crats forming a step or two back, clearly moved when they saw a Controller in the here and now. They held their right hands up in order to capture the exchange. Horace Starski reminded himself that he felt embarrassed by the attention.

– Fantastic, Sophie repeated.

He had remembered her name. Horace Starski... A member of the elite... The driving force behind Scales!... Owner of the Pearly penthouse... One of the Brussels stars... A Monnet man... Berlin... It was incredible.

– You are doing an excellent job, Sophie. Protecting our hard-won freedoms. Refusing to take NO for an answer when challenged by bigotry. Upbeat and cheerful, yet also firm and consistent. I want you and all of these friends who have gathered here in spontaneous fashion to know that you have my full support.

Sophie was elated. The crowd beamed its approval and her eyes filled with tears. Controller Horace had summed her up perfectly. They shared the same mission, and with his seal of approval her career prospects had shot into orbit. As soon as she was off-duty she would add this exchange to her profile, edit and add tunes and send versions across InterZone. Their chat was already out there, throbbing and perhaps trending – how could she know? – but hers would be the official tale, recorded from the most intimate of positions.

– Thank you, Controller. Thank you so much.

– My pleasure. Anything I can do to help, please let me know. We are old pals.

He left Sophie to her duties, watched his face vanish but remained near, keen to see what she would do next. The Cool continued towards the elevator, nodding at well-wishers as she went, responses to Qs brief, but polite, refusing to linger and keep him waiting. Horace Starski perched on her shoulder as she crossed the foyer, selected a mute trip, returning to the age of silent movies. He had almost every Fritz Lang film on the shelves of his Berlin pad, one of the true greats living on in that masked city of legend. He glanced to see how Bobby and Baby were progressing. They had almost finished.

– Superb work. The countdown is about to begin.

He returned to Sophie, enjoyed her exchanges with a range of Euros. She was building a healthy reputation and he was pleased. Controller Horace loved to help. He was here to spread peace and goodwill. Every single person deserved a chance – Sophie, Bob Terks, Baby, Polestar, Belle. Especially Belle, even if certain opportunities were wasted on locals. The British were a lazy lot, but Belle was special. He had placed her in Forget for so long, should never have strolled the streets of Tooting, stirring memories and questioning choices made. He was not perfect. Neither had he behaved incorrectly. Last night was a matter of research. It was vital he tuned into life beyond the bubbles. Belle had done well in a modest way, but she did have the full support of the system.

The undercover operating as Polestar had followed a much harder path. Family slaughtered in the eternal genocide of Congoland, she was ten years old when she was taken into the jungle by a militia and raped for several months before being sold into slavery. It was unfortunate, but the USE could not become involved in such a conflict. It would have been immoral to intervene in a non-European theatre. Imperialist, racist, arrogant. The customs of Africa could not be questioned. In a liberal democracy these subtleties outweighed the need to stop the carnage.

It was also true that Congoland had no part to play in increasing prosperity, although the war there did damage Chinese interests in Greater Africa, which was a positive, while those able to escape the militias offered a supply of cheap and cheerful dates. The urges of Good Euros needed satisfying. Polestar had been handed the chance to escape Africa by ND missionaries, and it was a source of pride that Brussels had been able to help so many unfortunates. After some quality time spent in a Free Libya education centre – extended when her undercover potential was established – Polestar's dream came true and she was finally liberated to work in London.

– The elevator is on its way, Bobby announced.

Bob Terks was excited. Baby stood by the door. She was calm and did not speak.

– You have done a fine job, Controller Horace remarked, as he studied the decorations.

These flickering fairy-lights were for the benefit of another of his dearest chums.

– Here's Rupert, he called as the door opened.

The Crat emerged, stopped and stared at the illuminations. He seemed to freeze.

– It's the Rocket man.

One minute earlier, as the elevator was preparing for blast off, Rupert Ronsberger started to shake. Sophie and Andreas' cheerful demeanour on the journey from Cuddles was a relief, but their moods were irregular and his unease ebbed and flowed. Here he was, about to meet his hero again, yet he felt sick inside. Why was he being invited to the Pearly penthouse? And why was he questioning the invitation? It should have been a glorious occasion, but those Cools were firmly on his mind. He was retracing and pausing, too many words and images out of sync.

– *Rupert, Rupert the bear...* sang Controller Horace.

On their way to Bethnal Plaza he had shared stories with Sophie, funnies from the early hours of their friendship, while Andreas tutted his approval. Mentals of porkies falling from a ledge and rolling towards IR4 played. Screaming pigs dying on grass made Rupert roar and he spoke on the wonders of movie-making. He had been fully on form, but now doubts returned. Perhaps these Cools were forgiving him for an incorrectness? That would be terrible. But soon he would be with Uncle. This elevator was taking him to the stars.

– *Everyone knows his name...*

He would have to be at his sharpest to reward Controller Horace for his support, and as the rocket roared towards the London skyline Rupert experienced a surge of confidence. It was an exhilarating ride. The glass walls were unseeable yet he felt no vertigo, the sweetest of scents relaxing him as the city's landmarks were highlighted by zooms that predicted or guided his interest, moving in and out and fiddling clarity to fantasy levels. The rush was ferocious. Fast and slow. Every single contradiction made sense. Time condensed.

— *It's Rupert the bear.*

He had stared at the Pearly summit so many times since his move to London and now he was about to enter the location itself. The ride stopped and the door opened and Rupert took several steps forward. He heard a child singing. The windows turned black and tiny lights appeared. One flickered and died. There was a faint sound of laughter. His seaside nightmare showed in a series of terrible images. A donkey brayed and seagulls swooped and a man cursed. He was disorientated and dared not move, stood frozen for a full minute before he realised that this wasn't a vision or even a virtual, but a triggering of memory. He was horrified. The windows lightened. His Uncle Horace waved.

— Come and sit with me Rupert, he called. But let Baby touch you first.

A petite woman scanned him with her Palm. She nodded to a big, suntanned man with his gaze fixed on Rupert's face. Neither was in uniform and he assumed they were guardians.

— He's clean, said the mademoiselle. Please continue.

— Don't be shy, Controller Horace called.

Rupert did as he was asked, took in slabs of marble, mahogany and skin as he approached. He felt fantastic.

— Please. Sit across from me in that chair.

Horace Starski was far less happy than his welcome suggested. The results of last night's vision were unsettling. Ronsberger had shown no interest in his creation. Zero empathy for those he had met. Maybe he was psychotic. Could well be delusional. Whatever the truth, this was a new sort of Crat. Alarmingly, it seemed he was without a clear weakness. The ultimate conformist. A perfect deluder. Horace Starski could hardly believe it was possible. Perfection did not exist.

— Thank you for inviting me, Rupert began.

He was either a devil or a saint, and both possibilities depressed Controller Horace. It was important to find some sort of humanity in this Euro, tap into a sentimental streak. How could he not be moved by the little girl who loved donkeys, the strength and freedom of the gulls, the beauty of the woman singing in the pub, the punk festival with all its different shades?

– Please, sit down Rupert. There's a good boy.

The Crat lowered himself into some fine zebra.

– This is Baby, Controller Horace said, carrying out the introductions. Routine check, you understand... And over there we have the mighty Bob Terks.

– Coffee? Baby asked. Or hot chocolate?

– Muffins? Bobby added.

– Thank you. I would enjoy coffee and a muffin.

Baby turned and started walking towards the kitchen, but Bob Terks came closer, his eyes drilling into Rupert.

– It can be rude to stare, Controller Horace crooned.

Bobby lowered his head.

– You would like a *blueberry* muffin? he asked.

– Yes, I would. Thank you. Brilliant.

– Fantastic, Horace Starski announced. Bobby, would you do the honours and take over from Baby?

Only the Controller noticed his chum's reluctance. He took his Buddy Number 1 status seriously, expected Baby to serve their guest, but Horace Starski believed in equality. Not that Bob Terks was sexist, but all the same, he liked to keep things fair, had no time for prejudice.

– Baby?

Rupert instantly regretted the tone, which showed surprise and implied fault. Like his hero, he abhorred sexist behaviour in the commons. Fortunately, Controller Horace did not appear to notice.

– Yes, Baby. Tell me Rupert, did you enjoy your break at Cuddles?

– Very much so, but I am looking forward to returning home. I love my apartment.

– I love mine also. It is natural for thinkers such as us to lounge in our pads. I have this little place here, a much larger space in Brussels.

241

– Brussels...

– Rooms in Berlin.

– Berlin...

– Brussels is my favourite. Berlin is mysterious, I agree, but Brussels is the city for me. It must remain your ambition.

– Brussels...

– The beating heart of the dream. But tell me about Cuddles.

– I came from Cuddles directly.

– And our conversation. Did you think about what I said, when you were back in your quarters?

– Our conversation?

– We touched on the truth of what you saw and what you have been taught.

– It was amusing. A fun day. Earlier I had been grinning with Sophie and Andreas, when we were on IR4 and saw creatives at work, so the muscles in my face were tired. I told you about it, and then you recounted tales to go with the porkies and other funnies.

Rupert's features showed enthusiasm, positivity and a desire to please. His dismissal of awkward facts and a concentration on trivia were part of his Crat training and to be admired. Horace Starski tightened his fists. He needed more than this repetitive drivel.

– Tell me what you think about Jean Monnet, his method of deceit.

– You have a lovely penthouse in Monnet Tower, I believe. Brussels...

– I do indeed. But the quote? What sort of values does it suggest?

– I don't know the value of your Brussels penthouse, nor this one, although I could estimate. My own apartment is modest in comparison, but I adore spending time there, and being so near Pearly Tower raises my mood. A home is an investment and I am young and firmly on the property ladder. When I progress to Techno I will move to a larger space, but not at the expense of a fine postcode. Location is everything.

Controller Horace was gritting his teeth.

– I floated ideas. The meaning of honesty and the nature of happiness were two of many. Did you consider what I said?

– This morning I had a fine breakfast.

– Breakfast?

– Yes. I started with...

– But what about the endless lies? Our fabrications?

– It was amusing. I laughed inwardly. I may have told you.

Rupert was choosing his words carefully, articulating each one, leaning forward.

– But what did you think when I told you...

The Controller stopped talking and looked at the returning Bob Terks and Baby.

– Lets talk in another room, he suggested, with the energy of a decision made. It will be more intimate. We are pals, after all.

Controller Horace stood and led the way. Bobby strolled with them to a door. It was padded. Baby watched from further afield. Rupert leaned in close and sniffed.

– Preborn giraffe, Horace Starski confided. Plucked from the womb.

They went inside, Baby following with a tray carrying coffee and a muffin. Their leader sank into another recliner, this one crafted from leopard. He motioned Rupert to a tall chair and the Crat sat in it as suggested, Bobby leaning in and wrapping an arm around his neck in a friendly hug. Rupert felt a faint prick on his neck, the rub of material, a lone thread that had become rigid. Bob Terks followed Baby out of the room. The door closed.

– Nobody can hear or see us here, Horace Starski said. This is a place of supreme privacy. We can be frank with each other. Talk honestly. No more censoring.

Rupert's expression remained blank.

– This room allows me to fully relax. It is beyond InterZone. Free of lenses and ears. This is the true nature of freedom. Everybody needs privacy. We all have our secrets.

He raised a hand. Rupert's arms and legs were fixed to the chair by circular beams. It was a kind but unnecessary precaution, as the

Crat knew he wasn't about to fall to the floor, even if he was starting to feel a little lightheaded.

– Tell me what you thought of the singer in the pub, Horace Starski began.

– I never go to pubs, only bars. I dislike pubs. They are full of British lowlife.

– I treated you to a vision. I created it myself. Bared my soul. There was a woman singing in a pub. Speak freely. She was in a drinker's paradise called The Lighthouse.

– She was old and ugly and wore cheap clothes. A lager drinker. Cool should visit, backed by Hardcore. Organise a mass rendition. Polish and cleanse and refurbish.

– She had a beautiful voice and was young once. Expensive clothes are a luxury for locals, Rupert. Did you feel no pity for the passing years and the lack of funds?

– She sang beautifully, but it wasn't her voice. She only mimed. It was a recording.

– It was real, I can assure you. That was the lady's voice.

– It was a vision.

– But a memory also. A true account.

– There are no memories. Only stories that suit us.

– What about truth?

– The stories we choose are the truth. The USE never lies.

Controller Horace sighed. He reached for his Ticklestick, a warped version of a prop made popular in the 20th century by the magnificent seaside performer Ken Dodd, since patented and remodelled by Intruder Solutions. He held it in the air, admiring the subtle crudities of a tool that carried the thrills of both reward and punishment.

– Honesty is the best policy, Rupert continued, his voice slurring. We must never glance back or weaken. I want to be like you when I grow up. Live in a penthouse. Invent and prosper.

Horace Starski studied the Crat. There were small lapses in language, but as yet no revelation. Was he such a deluder that he could mask his real beliefs even when chilled by a shot? Was he still able to lie to himself? If so, he was an extremely dangerous man.

He might even pose a long-term threat to his own mentor, but Controller Horace would remain open-minded as he probed.

– The route to the top is not a precise one, Rupert. Crats and other Good Euros follow narrow paths, rarely if ever straying, but a Controller does not. When I learned about the corruption of history I was not surprised. The manipulation of language and morality was also clear. I had always known that we are instinctively totalitarian, but discovered how much more subtle and therefore successful the USE is compared to past dictatorships. I know what I am and I don't care, but you, Rupert... Do you believe every single thing that you say?

– I believe. Yes.

– There is a need in people – and I mean *everyone* – to tell others how clever they have been. We all want to be celebrities. A creative or an emptyhead, it doesn't matter. Humans find secrets hard to keep, and a Controller's life can be lonely, as secrecy is essential. In recent years I have found myself craving recognition. I have seen and done things you could never guess, but what I want you to fully grasp is the cunning involved, to appreciate the way we stole power and how I have had my fun at the expense of others, the sheer dishonesty involved in our takeover. We said one thing and did another, and the dumb, ignorant, trusting, gutless masses allowed us to succeed. They wanted to believe our propaganda. We serve the multinationals and spend fortunes insisting we serve the people. Can you understand this?

– I want to be a Controller, Rupert said. I crave power and wealth and an apartment in Brussels. The USE is pure. It never lies. And I believe. I honestly do believe.

Horace Starski growled. He needed Ronsberger to admit the fraud that led to unification and respect the ongoing repression. To do this, it was clear that he needed assistance. He must feel crushed by his own ignorance, accept he had been mocked by the great thinkers, appreciate the degree to which he and his family had been betrayed. Just as importantly, he must *love* the trickery of his Uncle Horace. Ronsberger had to *hate* how his hero had helped rewrite history and warp culture, as the theft of identity, ideas and even names was the final stamp of success. Work and play – the two sides of the equation – yin and yang – Rupert and Rocket – love and hate. And yet Horace Starski was a solitary. He did not need to split his personality. He was honest, despite his dishonesty. But if nobody outside a handful of confederates knew of his cunning then what was the point? It had to be celebrated. The dictators of the past strutted and preached and milked applause, but what about poor Horace? He was a humorist and the monster opposite just wasn't getting the joke.

– I think I remember the song you were singing earlier, the Crat mused. Was it playing in the car when Sophie and I were watching the movie-making? Andreas was there as well. It was so funny. Screaming pigs next to the IR.

Horace Starski raised the Ticklestick and removed the orange duster on the end. The tool was made of rubber and shaped like a penis, a metal ring piercing the bell. In erect mode, it would be a rocket for Ronald, but Horace Starski would never use it Hardcore fashion. Those boys and girls were degenerates. Cool used it floppy as a truncheon. Nothing more. Hardcore were no different to the rapists of Congoland. Horace Starski was rolling with the Cool cats. They shared a sense of style. A touch of class.

– Cool, he exclaimed, and brought the truncheon down hard on Rupert's right knee.

The Crat cried out.

– Nobody can hear you. Shout as loud as you like.

He did the same to the left knee.

– The USE is a corrupt dictatorship. There is no such thing as New Democracy.

Rupert grinned and the Ticklestick smashed into the fingers of his left hand, the Controller careful to avoid the Palm on his right. Bones were broken and he was pleased. There could be no gain without pain. He was a teacher and this Crat his disciple.

– We are bullies and liars. Scum. Fucked up in our thinking.

Rupert smiled.

– Dates are little more than slaves, looked down on because they are non-European. We abuse them.

Rupert sniggered.

– Animals suffer.

Rupert roared.

– We are sadists, cowards, subhuman.

Horace Starski was shaking, realised he was losing control and stepped back. The Crat had tears running down his face and was moaning, but his cheerful expression remained. Eventually he was silent.

– Did you secretly enjoy your holiday in Blackpool?

Rupert raised his head.

– It was interesting.

– Did you *love* my vision?

– I hated Blackpool. It represents everything we want to delete. Only a lowlife commons would want to visit the town.

– Could a Good European not find it stimulating? One of the thinkers? Someone such as myself?

– But you would not be a Good and you would not be a thinker. You would be nothing more than a dinosaur, a throwback, a senti-mentalist, a nostalgic fool stuck in the past and ready for rendition – the attentions of Cool and Hardcore. If you felt that way, I would report you myself as unfit for service. However, this is a test. Another of your funny lessons. Thank you.

– The best days of my life were spent at the seaside with a com-mons. It was when I was at my most happy. Power doesn't make a person joyful.

Rupert was sniggering again.

– Love is more important than power and wealth.

Rupert laughed hard and long.

Horace Starski moved behind Rupert. He slipped a transparent hood over the Crat's head and tightened the chord, walked back so he was opposite the distorted face.

– I showed you something special and you treat is as a joke. You have insulted me.

Rupert kept beaming. This was the funniest of games. He wondered if the dolphins at Splash! had such fun, but no, that was a one-way humour. They were subs and the clubbers were a dedicated brand of dancer. Without the flipping and flopping and suffocation and crush-crush of lungs and organs it would lack the edge trenders found so erotic. Consenting adults... Consenting men and women could do whatever they fancied. Freedom of choice... A dolphin couldn't consent. How would it? This increased the thrill. He loved to see the suffering of a sub, but was finding it difficult to maintain his merry mood.

– You had to talk to Polestar, show her how clever you are, but you did it in a roundabout way, as if it was a lesson. You made evil men out to be good men, turned history and logic on its head. You are a juggler, but worse than lying to my buddy Polestar you lie to yourself. I think you are insane. A lunatic with no future unless you admit that we are the dregs of humanity.

The plastic was tightening with each breath and Rupert was trying to limit the depth of his intakes. His nostrils were blocking as the hood smothered his mouth and forced him to use only his nose. Snot and a streak of blood smeared the plastic. His lungs were burning, skin bleeding colourless, rancid sweat. He attempted to move his hands but couldn't, the restraints cutting into his wrists, and he tried harder and gasped and was choking, hoped his Uncle Horace would release him in the next few seconds. It would be terrible if his teacher miscalculated, if Rupert let him down by dying, but that would never happen, he trusted his Controller. Rupert believed.

– Rest easy, my young friend.

The chord was loosened and the hood lifted to his forehead.

– Breathe the fresh, salty breeze. Listen to the singing of the birds.

Rupert spluttered and gulped for air and filled his chest. His trousers were wet. He hoped it was perspiration, but knew it was not. Had he defecated? He did not think so.

– I will be back in a while. Relax. Enjoy your time in Pearly Tower. The penthouse. My home. We will work harder to find the solutions we need.

Rupert heard the swish of the door sliding open and shut. The windows blackened and he was alone in the darkness. There was no sound apart from the thump of his heart. Dizzy and dreamy, he thought it was a drum at first, the beat of a new Abba tune, but it was too fast and brutal and when he realised it came from inside his body he was scared. He waited for his heartbeat to slow and his mind to adjust, felt the breeze he had been asked to enjoy, but it was polluted by spices and cooking oil and the salt and vinegar that was sprinkled on chips and hung heavy in the dirty air of England.

Tiny lights sparked and increased in size. Illuminations blazed and he saw himself on the promenade. He winced as other people appeared and an old man punched him in the face. He fell backwards into a pub where a crone sang, but when she noticed him she stopped and started to scream. He was ejected by a skinhead and found himself standing in an empty street, hoping the sound that had followed him out was that of a dying pig. Seagulls screeched as they circled. He saw razor claws and hooked beaks, could smell their feathers and the urine in his pants.

There was a gull twice the size of the others, its human arms carrying oversized wings. It landed and stood opposite, towering above him as it glanced left and right before darting forward and tugging at the plastic hood. It stopped and stepped back, searched his face and seemed to smirk. It was about to peck his eyeballs out. Rupert lost consciousness. He slumped forward, head at an angle, restrained in a chair at the top of Pearly Tower, high in the sky with the Controller he hoped to become.

TWENTY-TWO

KENNY JACKSON CAME into Docklands as part of a drinks delivery team. He lost his overalls at the drop and entered the transport system disguised as a Crat, was soon riding the Overground towards the East Side. He stood by the glass and exaggerated an interest in the pools below, mimicking newly arrived Euros and a group of American tourists by gawping at the trapped fish, turtles and dolphins. Leaving the confines of the Docklands domes, he felt as if he was finally on his way.

It was three in the afternoon and he had only been awake for two hours, left to sleep by Frank who had shadowed and saved him from Cool the night before. While he was initially stunned by his own stupidity, it now seemed worth the narrow escape to have spent time with the legendary Suzie Vickers, and what was about to happen meant he was too pumped up on adrenaline to feel tired. An hour earlier he had sat in Frank's living room with his last mug of strong coffee and finally accepted that he was on a suicide mission.

Wes had fine-tuned his appearance, the Wandle quartermaster keeping up with the latest Euro tastes. The fine points that would prove he was a Techno (B+). Rank was prized and superiors never challenged. His B+ rating was meant to discourage those on a lower grade, while not being high enough to attract the attention of a more critical A. They would focus on an A- and not bother about a B+. The admiring glances of several young Bureaus and lower-level Technos boosted his confidence. This was the closest he'd ever been to a Crat, and those around him were a strange lot, different to what he'd imagined. Childlike or childish, he wasn't sure, and neither could he decide how deep the pretence went. Some seemed nervous, others oblivious, the rest lost in InterZone.

Controllers were different. He'd never seen one in the flesh, but had heard plenty of stories, and from what he knew they were less disciplined, but deadly. He had seen pictures of The Tower Of London in books, read about beefeaters and ravens, the myth that England would fall if the birds ever left. Once the Treaty Of Berlin had been signed and the governments of the European nations dissolved, the ravens were killed and their bodies barbecued at a skyline party. Organised by London's resident Controllers, it showed a sadistic, mocking humour. He wondered if that last sparrow in the East Side had been killed yet, cooked the same way as his friends.

At the next stop the tourists got off and the carriage filled with Crats. None of these dongs would be interested in the story of the ravens. Half of them immediately opened screens, which adjusted to the space available. He was confronted by close-up footage of a roasting session. Three Crats were penetrating a teenage commons in time to a Saviles tune. This was only heard by the owner of the Palm, but there was an inset of the nonce singing in the background. Kenny was shocked, but nobody else seemed to care. Other screens showed movies and shows and lots of reports on the sparrow saga. It looked as if the bird was still alive, and this cheered him up.

Other Crats were leaning in to watch the sex. The girl's eyes were bleary and she gritted her teeth as she tried to smile for the lens. Kenny wanted to thump these clowns, but controlled himself. A negative remark would be bad enough. He focused on one of the sparrow flashes instead, noticed the sweet odour of the carriage now it was packed. A mix of deodorants, flavoured gels, aftershave, perfume. These people looked so similar it was almost comical, but he was starting to see differences, small touches that were repeated and mirrored Wes' work. As the train progressed, jackets were undone, with *Bird Hunter* and *Rebel Rebel* T-shirts dominating.

At Cablestrasse, Kenny left and joined the column moving down the Blair Pathway, took the escalator to the East Side line when he reached the end. He breathed deeply and raised his Palm with everyone else as he passed under the entrance scanners, elevating his head and waiting to see if he would live or die. These devices checked for outsiders, but were fooled by a reflector Zacharius Hodd had installed in his forgery. The system was State-stamped, but like most things privately run, the cost-cutting needed to increase profit margins leading to flaws. The belief that a commons could never get this far had also contributed to tired security and a failure to upgrade. His Palm had kept him safe on the London streets, a smuggled code had seen him on to the Overground, and now the trickster Hodd had returned with a flourish. He took the short ride to the East Side and was soon on the edge of Bethnal Plaza.

It was warm and bright, the stone shone, and rows of palm and olive trees created a Mediterranean effect. Kenny had to admit that the scene was stunning. Looking up he could see the faint outlines of two domes, part of the larger bubble covering the Gates. They seemed to be fizzing, a variation of 'Sugar Baby Love' playing faintly in the distance, words removed and the tune slowed, adding to the surreal nature of the setting. He could smell coffee brewing and pastries baking, and despite his vulnerability he relaxed.

There was a fantasy element to the Plaza, plastic and stained-glass plants filling the beds he passed. He breathed the scents of the Crat-filled carriage, noticed something extra, but couldn't let himself be seduced, had to keep moving and not think too much, walked past a series of boutiques, a cheerful look fixed to his face, reached a junction and paused. A line of eaters stood at the counter of a Sabini stall. The franchise sold more pizzas than any other firm in London. Driven by three Brussels-based commissioners and headed by Controller Beatrice, the brand had lots of denied advantages, but there was nothing he would ever want to eat on the meat-heavy menu.

Kenny had a fifty-nine-second window during which he could get into Pearly Tower safely, but had to time his approach just right. When he was near he slowed and waited, raising his head again and following the outline of the building to its summit. The penthouse was a blur, a silver box topped by a tiny dome, like the icing on a cake. The tallest building in East London, it was home to three thousand Euros, had ten hotels and twenty restaurants, plus sports facilities, parlours, bars, maxi- and mini-malls. It was a city inside a city inside a city, and as such it needed an army of workers to make it function. It was in these massed ranks that a Welsh rebel lurked. Kenny thought back to the tear-up around the Kid Bale fight outside Cardiff. The resistance flourished on connections made.

Kenny pretended he was engrossed in his Palm. Conscious he had no screen, he sat on one of the cruising walls and hunched in close as if sharing a special moment, every so often glancing at the Pearly clock. Four minutes before the lenses were due to be disabled he made his move, using a small olive grove to the right of the entrance as cover. Once under the spread of the trees he was surprised to find a large number of young women sitting on benches drinking coffee. Greasepaint covered their faces and he guessed most were in their late teens and early twenties, though there was one child of seven or eight sitting on the knee of a middle-aged European. He was stroking an exposed leg and Kenny struggled to stop himself battering the man. He'd been told it would be easy to lose his temper here, that he would do more good if he carried out his mission.

Coming out of the grove he was momentarily dazzled by the intense light surrounding the doors to the tower, for a second or two transported to the seaside, back to Bognor and Bournemouth and Selsey Bill as a boy and a youth and a man. These were the best of times and he wished he was strolling to the end of a pier right now, listening to the clank of fairground rides, the thump of rock 'n' roll. But why on earth had he thought of this at such a dangerous moment? He realised that the scales coating the building carried the salty smell of the sea. Close to this terrible skin, which would be illuminated and set in motion shortly, the degree of death involved struck him hard.

Two security guards in leather dungarees watched those entering Pearly Tower. Kenny was behind three Crats as he raised his Palm. No alarm sounded and no lights flashed. Crossing the foyer to the lift furthest to his right as instructed, he realised he was drenched in sweat, but was quickly on the thirtieth floor and on his way to Technocratix, a state-of-the-art relaxation hub with Plaza views and a long advertising terrace. He went to the table at the far end of the glass wall and sat down, took off his black jacket and put it on the seat next to him.

Five minutes here and he would continue. The bar sold cocktails and wine, mineral water and fruit juice, coffee and hot chocolate, but as far as he could see no beer. Lacking Troika he couldn't pay anyway, told the waiter who came over that he was waiting for a friend and would order when she arrived. Left alone, he checked out surroundings that were plush and expensive, but lacked any real character. The place was quiet. Smartly dressed twos and threes sipped coffee as they discussed work-related matters, while several T-shirted bubbleheads nodded to the music in their plugs.

He turned his chair and leaned forward, looking into the Plaza below. The regimented design was clear. Small squares were sectioned by shrubs and groves, portable retail outlets arranged in circles, primers for the larger premises inside the nearby malls. Essential transporters had small lanes to follow, but he only counted four of these machines. The people were insects. He searched the domes for the sparrow, imagined it swooping down and picking them off with a rapid-fire beak. He remembered that there were supposed to be six ravens at the Tower Of London, and hadn't there been six birds loose in the East Side Gates?

He had a book about the original Bethnal Green area back at All Souls, but it was impossible to know where the likes of the Salmon And Ball pub had stood. It was there that the weavers John Doyle and John Valline were executed in the street outside after the Cutters' Riot of 1769. A bit over a century and a half later there were clashes between communists and fascists near the same drinker. Wage protests and political parties were firmly in the past now and this sort of history only survived in hards. Across the road would have been Barmy Park and Bethnal Green Library, one of the greatest of the old book palaces, while the nearby Underground station saw one hundred and seventy-three people die in a crush as they headed down into the tube system in fear of a German air raid in 1943. He doubted there was another soul in this part of the old East End who knew or cared about these things.

When it was time, Kenny reached for his jacket and scooped up the T-wrapped revolver he had covered when arriving. This would do more damage than the package Suzie had lumbered him with last night, and with his jacket on and the gun tucked inside, he left Technocratix, shrugging for the waiter to show he had been stood up. He followed the corridor towards the first of the two lifts he needed to take. Halfway along a trolley was waiting by an unlocked storage-room door. He slipped inside, thirty seconds later continuing in the blazer of a Tenderburger employee as he pushed the trolley, turned a corner and found the elevators. A Cool officer sat nearby, but wasn't stopping people. Kenny got in the first lift to arrive with four Crats. They looked at their Palms, but not at the delivery man.

The journey stopped and started, Kenny the only one left when the doors opened and he entered a small foyer where two Cool stood and stared. They blocked the lift he needed, which was protected by another door and a dead area between. Beady eyes focused. These were specialists, part of Control Division, dedicated to the defence of leaders, and Kenny felt weak in their presence. Even so, he kept his nerve as both he and the trolley were scanned for zap technology, and even here it was the assumption that previous stages were infallible that was giving him a chance. An old, physical gun was not even considered. One of the Cools connected with the penthouse, a female voice confirming the Tenderburger order in detail.

This next lift moved fast. He could see the Gates now, his view widening as he raced to the top floor. Beyond the domes the night had closed in, and lights were coming on. The stars of the USE were above him in the sky and growing in size, and he was able to appreciate the cartoon beauty of the architecture and illuminations, the sheer inventiveness of human beings. They were so clever they could excuse anything, apply justifications where none existed. People wanted to belong. If he had been raised in a Euro-dominated city, his parents Crats or similar, would he have ended up the same way? He wondered if it was possible for someone who had been immersed in the system for their entire life to rebel. It must be. Free will had to exist.

The door opened and he was faced by a guardian. She was small, but hard as nails, her Palm raised ready to zap. He felt his stomach churn. She knew he was an impostor. A light pulsed and he thought he was about to die, but instead of firing she lowered her hand and stepped forward to inspect the trolley, stood aside and motioned for him to continue. A big man was waiting. Although he was grinning and showed a line of brilliant white teeth in a tanned face, the eyes were cruel. This second guardian was about to approach.

– He's clean, the first Cool said. Controller Horace is hungry, Bobby. Follow me, Mr Tenderburger.

Kenny did as he was told, conscious that Bobby was glaring and flexing his fists, found himself in a huge room that reeked of leather. Digitals floated instead of real paintings and photos, but his attention was quickly pulled to a dead dolphin suspended in a glass container. To the left of this horror, the back of a screen hid what he guessed was Horace Starski. Two legs dipped into a pair of Michael Mouse slippers. He had entered a freak show. This was the sort of fantasy world where the doublespeak and babytalk of the USE brewed. He could hardly believe he'd made it this far, that he was in the same room as a Controller.

Kenny felt the gun hard against his body, wedged in his belt under a buttoned blazer, barrel pointing towards cock and balls, and his mind raced back to Hannah's murder via Fred and Suzie Vickers, his library under All Souls, Jan alone at home, Kid Bale and the forger Zacharius Hodd, his trip into London, Mickey Patel deported, Tubby Nowakowski at the wheel as Karen and Steve died on the South Circular, the danger he had dodged. He was ready to kill Starski, but the guardians were close and watching and would zap him before he had a chance to pull his weapon out.

He was a fucking amateur, hiding it in such a stupid place, not thinking ahead.

The sweat was thick on his body and he hoped nobody noticed his growing panic. His chest seemed to be vibrating and he was sure his ribs were ringing, part of a boneyard xylophone, and his heart was banging so loud it had to be echoing through the room. The dictator and his henchmen could hear it and what it meant. He was going to piss himself, puke up, wobble and fall and hit his head, mess up his mission and die a lingering death at the hands of the man who closed his screen and was moving forward in an obscene recliner.

– Hello, my friend, Horace Starski began. Thank you so much for bringing our Tender feast. We have Kangowraps and elephant goulash I believe, but where is Manny, who visited yesterday? I gave him our order and he said he would return.

– His mother died.

– This one has been checked thoroughly, the female said in an assured manner.

– I know, Baby. I am always safe with my buddies. Was it a sudden death?

– He only just heard.

– It is best to turn our backs on Mother and Father, to loosen family ties, which are imposed on us after all. But this is the way of Crats and the Controllers they adore. Freedom of choice. A different approach, but I am sure you appreciate our efforts.

His eyes drilled into Kenny, who was upset by their intensity, and had to stop himself backing away. Then they were on Bobby.

– Bob Terks understands what I am talking about.

Kenny jolted and hoped nobody had noticed. So Bobby was the monster Bob Terks? The man was a torturer and sexual predator, notorious for his execution of anarchist and redneck fighters, his behaviour during the LA clearances. He had never heard of this Baby character, although it could be a term of endearment. Either way, the name was worrying.

– It is hot, is it not, my friend? Horace Starski continued, coming over to inspect the trolley.

Kenny was seen serving the food, arranging dishes on a table as instructed, wondering how he would strike as Baby went to the kitchen and returned with knives, forks, spoons and serviettes. Two places were set.

– Tenderburger is the finest takeaway, Starski remarked. I love Kangowraps best. The hen-flavoured mayo makes my day and the fries are superb. Thank you for your trouble and I am sorry Baby had to check you without a smile, and that Bobby stared and appeared aggressive. He is not, much more of a teddy, like Rupert Bear. But we have to be careful. Not that we have enemies, and if we did they would never stray into a European city, but success is all about the detail.

Starski sat down and looked at Bob Terks.

– Come on now, say sorry, Bobby.

– Sorry, Bobby.

Starski and Terks sniggered. Baby didn't seem to be listening. She was looking at Kenny and he was sure she had worked him out and was about to zap him, but she turned and walked to the kitchen, came back with a silver skewer which she handed to Starski. He placed it on the table.

– Thank you, Baby.

Kenny knew he had to do something fast.

– Seriously, Bobby. We must not make bad impressions. Our chum here will carry a sad notion when he leaves, but please remember Mr Tenderburger, nothing is ever personal. Unknowns can worry those who live at the summit. Controllers and their buddies live narrow lives. It is the price we pay for helping society, and we are a long way from our home. I have come to London from Brussels, but you are a local, are you not?

Kenny stiffened.

– I was born and bred in London.

– A fine city.

The Controller seemed to drift.

– I knew London before you were born. I met the best people here, and I cherish the lessons I learned.

Bob Terks seemed confused.

– I fell in love with a commons and she had different views to mine, but by understanding others we find out about ourselves. That is why the USE works. We listen and reflect the interests of the masses. She was a London girl. I knew the legendary haunts, visited cheap pubs and caffs and markets. Can you believe such a thing? I made sacrifices. We must all make tough choices.

He trailed off and bit into his Kangowrap. Neither Baby nor Bobby had been invited to sit with Starski at the table. Kenny realised there were four meals and only three eaters.

– Please ask Rupert to join us, Bobby.

Whistling as he went, Terks crossed the room and disappeared through a door. Baby stood to the side of Starski, her eyes on the outsider. She did not turn her head when Terks re-emerged. He was carrying someone. Kenny thought it was a mannequin at first, felt sick when he realised it was a man with a hood over his head, the transparent plastic ripped so he could breathe.

– Are you happy, Rupert?

There was no reply. Bobby propped the body on the chair opposite Starski's, began binding him to the back with thick, physical tape. Round and round it went, creaking and yawning, and the American was pulling it as tight as he could, so the one they called Rupert was upright. At best he was unconscious.

– Rupert here is ambitious, Starski said, addressing Kenny. He wants to progress and I have been helping, peeling layers and adding truths, testing loyalty, doing my best to learn if he is willing to make the sacrifices needed to reach the top of the tower. It also helps to pass the time. We become bored, need our games to express the humour that exists at the highest level. He is a willing partner and you must not be concerned. This is consensual behaviour. Adults at play... Liberal politics... New Democracy.

Kenny ran the trolley into Terks, kicking the agent hard in the face when he fell, pulling his revolver out before Starski or Baby could respond, holding it with both hands and aiming at the Controller's chest. He pulled the trigger. There was a faint pop. Starski roared. The gun had jammed.

– Call yourself an assassin? the Controller mocked, turning to Baby for support. Fucking useless.

Kenny grabbed the skewer off the table. It had a padded handle and felt good in his hand. He had only fired shooters in the past, and never at another living being, knew a blade was different, but Starski was a criminal and killing him would send shock waves through the USE. Baby seemed to have frozen. She had still not moved and he pushed her over, rammed the blade into Starski's chest. The skin punctured and he heard a crunch, felt disgusted with himself, but exhilarated as well. The force of the blow carried him forward and he was on the floor, cradling Starski in his arms.

– Move away, Bob Terks screamed, on his feet but swaying. Move away from my Controller.

Kenny felt Starski's weight, instinctively knew that he was dead. Terks had lifted his Palm and was deciding whether to zap. His target rolled away, stood and raised his hands.

Terks checked Starski, his Palm on Kenny.

– You've killed him. Fuck.

He was stunned.

– You've killed a Controller. *My* Controller. Do you know what you've done? I'm going to burn your joints, cut your balls off, then I'll slice you and finally slit your throat, hold you close to me as you bleed to death. No rendition for you. You're all mine. I own you now.

Terks took aim, a section of his head bursting before he could release his first zap. Starski's best American buddy fell to the floor, Baby standing to the side with her Palm raised. She lifted a finger to her lips to stop Kenny speaking, waved him towards the lifts, held up what he recognised as a Fireball. She pointed again, mouthing two words.

– Go home.

– Come with me.

– Go, she shouted.

Baby pressed the ignition and put the Fireball on the table with the Tenderburger meal. Kenny realised it was hopeless, ran to the bigger elevator, but realised he didn't have the code, went to the one he had arrived in, which was wide open. There was an explosion and the room began to fill with a blue mist, flames rising in a fountain. The woman who had saved his life was gone, had chosen suicide over possible arrest. The lift automatically closed and began its descent.

He was alive, but if the explosion had been heard or the aftermath picked up he wouldn't be for much longer. And he was defenceless. No, the skewer was still in his hand. He thought he'd left it in Starski, must have pulled it out of his chest, and he wiped the blood off on the inside of his blazer, found chunks of flesh in the grooves, puked up on the floor.

When the door opened a relaxed worker walked out. Cool glanced and nodded, unaware of what had happened. He wanted to hurry, as it wouldn't be long before the smoke was detected, but had to remain calm. He was another worker on his way back from a routine delivery, waited for the second lift and once it arrived he was soon in and out and jogging down an empty corridor, stopping at the storage room to change back into his Crat jacket. One more ride... There was a chance he might make it out of the tower.

– What are you doing? a voice asked.

A firm hand was placed on his shoulder.

– Turn around.

He faced a Cool with evil on his mind. There was hatred in the expression and before Kenny knew what he was doing the skewer was in the man's head. He was shocked by his own violence and the horrified look on the face opposite, stunned by his quick thinking as he dragged the body to the back of the room and took a tiny back-up taser and two physical gasballs from his victim's belt. He returned to the corridor. When he passed Technocratix a Saviles tune was playing, but the Crats rushing from the bar were not in a musical mood.

Kenny stood with the crowd waiting for the elevator that would take them to the ground floor. A screen played views of the Pearly penthouse, lenses zooming from below and launching flashes across InterZone, shots of smoke flowing from the top of the tower. Reporters spoke of a calamity, rumours that a disaster had been caused by the rogue sparrow, expensive tech destroyed by nature. Flames were visible inside the building and he felt terrible for Baby, remembered the trussed Rupert, still not sure if he was real or a dummy. Hundreds of eyes moved from the screen to the lift doors and back again. Over and over. Back and forwards. Faster and faster.

TWENTY-THREE

THE CONTROLLER'S YOUNGEST buddy was bleeding heavily and going nowhere. Her name was Marie Defossé and she was sick of being called Baby. It was two years since she'd been to visit her family and now she would never see them again. She was dying, but didn't regret her actions. Marie was a proud member of the French Resistance and had been undercover for too long. She was glad Terks was dead, her desire to see an enemy of the French people destroyed matched by a personal hatred for a man who had abused her three times in the last month. She wanted to think about her mother and father and brother and sister, the house in the village of La Gaude where she'd grown up, but instead she pictured Terks standing above her sneering.

He had forced her to kneel and service him while he held a zap to her temple. Once he ejaculated he made her swallow his semen, then stand so he could wrap his arms around her and squeeze until she was gasping for breath. With his lips brushing her right ear he liked to explain that this was New Democracy in action. She should think of the dolphins at Splash! as they bounced in time to a Bob Harley tune. Slow suffocation. A dog at Bark! with a rod pumping electricity into its anus so it bopped along to Robbie Wilhelm. Subhumans had no options – but you do, Baby Blue. She had chosen oral sex to a shattered skull. True, either way he was going to blow her fucking brains out, but that was true freedom of choice. A core value. Bob Terks used similar words each time, waiting until her face was a dark shade of purple before releasing his grip and letting her fall to the floor.

On the third occasion, she had spat the sperm into his face. He didn't speak, appeared amused rather than angry, shifted both hands to her neck and tightened his hold. Realising he had dropped or put away the zapper, but not knowing where, she raised a knee into his groin. Terks gasped and bent forward, but refused to let go. They crashed to the ground and Marie tried to find the zap, thrashing as he got on top of her, and she would never ever forget what it had felt like to be strangled. He was twice her size and heavy with muscle and her ribs were aching along with her neck. Then, as now, she thought about her family as she prepared to die. She had blacked out, yet survived, as Terks knew he wouldn't be able to conceal a murder and Cool would not be amused. He hadn't touched her since, but swore he would be coming back for more.

Marie had thought about telling Horace Starski, but pulled back when her first roundabout attempt failed, knowing that a formal complaint could be seen as a questioning of the State, and a Cool investigation would risk her life and those of her family. If they found out she was a spy she would be shipped to Prinz-Albrecht-Strasse for interrogation, and the Cuddles HQ was infamous for its cruelties. With the London trip approaching she decided to wait until they returned to Brussels before dealing with Terks, as he was sure to leave her alone while they were in unfamiliar territory. Her long-term mission was to move through the ranks and one day reach the President in Berlin, all the time feeding information to the Resistance. While this presented her with a dilemma when it came to her own problem, she hadn't been prepared to stop the assassination, as it would have meant killing one of her own kind.

Before Terks started on her, she'd worried she might have aroused suspicion. She was sickened by the bubblers' treatment of animals and had allowed her disgust to show in the presence of Horace Starski on several occasions. As a teenager, her tutors were at pains to convince her that subhumans had no emotions, that they were stupid and should be despised and, in any case, were the property of the USE and only existed to serve its needs – profit generation, taste-bud pleasure, entertainment, anger management, the creation of menial jobs for lowers. As a young recruit she had tried hard to believe, but found it impossible. Marie was never going to be Crat material, her strengths centring on surveillance, planning and combat.

The attachment to Controller Horace had put her in a great position. In time, she would progress to Buddy Number 1, build years of service, and eventually maybe join a team assigned to the President. This figure was never seen and never heard, but she was driven by the belief that one day she would kill him and bring down the USE. Starski was a high-ranking Controller, with all that involved, and yet on a day-to-day basis he was charismatic and almost likeable. She had to constantly remind herself that this was one of the managers of the dictatorship, someone who had ordered other human beings to be tortured and killed, an exploiter of animals, a thief and a liar. And as she lay dying in his penthouse she guessed he had probably known about Bob Terks and done nothing.

Marie was on a sofa, and while she hated the skin and what it represented, she could not move. She felt as if her arteries had exploded and she was drowning in her own blood. It was filling her mouth. She had set the Fireball at medium, but these were powerful devices and glass fragments had cut her badly. The smoke was thick and the flames were spreading. Her Palm was raised so the zap could be released into her head when she began to suffocate. It would take Cool a little while to mobilise, but they would be charging into the apartment soon. The USE would be badly shaken by this attack, and she was glad.

Ronsberger was screaming. He was conscious and burning to death, and that was horrible, but he was another degenerate with his prostitutes and the animal clubs and all the rest of his behaviour. Marie closed her eyes and felt as if she was sinking into a coffin, imagined the fur of the sofa as a crimson lining and wished she was that last sparrow and able to fly away. But she had to stay alert and listen for the elevator, thinking back to her family and picturing them clearly.

She was determined to make the most of every last second, playing back the best memories, seeing herself as a child without a care, and still she remained sharp and professional, ready to kill herself rather than burn in the flames of her Fireball, and no way was she going to allow herself to be taken alive and interrogated by Cool and passed to Hardcore and sent to Prinz-Albrecht-Strasse. She had wanted to get to Berlin, but not that way. The fire raged. She was ready. Her death would be a liberation.

TWENTY-FOUR

THE GOOD EUROPEANS surged forward. They slapped and scratched each other to get inside the lift. Kenny was carried along in the crush, found himself in the middle of a packed crowd as the doors closed. It was claustrophobic, but he didn't care. These Crats were his shield. People were crying and one man shouted at the top of his voice, and it was strange seeing bubbleheads fall apart so easily, as they didn't really know what had happened. They were responding to newsflashes and a small fire many stories above. These fools were so mollycoddled they cracked up at the first sign of trouble. He wondered if he should let them know there was a Morlock in their ranks, but decided to keep quiet.

The smell of urine was reassuring. The sweet perfumes of the Crats had vanished and their plastic world was melting, yet they would probably revert once they reached the foyer, dismiss their panic and strut about as if nothing had happened. There was a chance everyone would be lined up and questioned, or at least held for later, and the thought of Hardcore taking him away was enough to make up his mind. He had to destroy any sense of relief when the lift reached the ground, and as it slowed he released one of the gassers he'd taken from the dead Cool, chemicals stinging his eyes and throat, and it did the same to every person around him, men and women kicking and spewing and finally charging out into the foyer when the doors opened, hysterical and totally out of control.

Firestoppers were waiting and found themselves pushed aside. Cool and Hardcore stood separately. Knowing he was lost in the stampede he shouted that Controller Horace had been murdered, killed by commons, rebel Englishmen, that there were three GB45s in the penthouse. The Crats continued their mad charge, driven on by this latest information, some falling into and through windows as they tried to leave the building. Cool and Hardcore reacted with fury, another crush forming as the first wave filled the elevator and headed for the stars. The security guards did not join them, seemed happy to usher crying Euros out of Pearly Tower, away towards the marble benches and cruising walls of Bethnal Plaza. First-aiders were outside, ready to assist, but Kenny swerved them and went over to a bed of exotic grasses, knelt down and pretended to be sick.

Three Technos (A-) stood nearby, sipping coffee and nibbling nibbles, nonchalantly watching the spectacle unfold. As one they turned to glare at Kenny, their faces registering disgust at this B+ display. He continued to mimic sickness and they moved. Standing up, he went over to a wall, sat down and ignored the traumatised Crats being shepherded away. He needed a minute to steady himself, even though time was tight, pleased he was already for-gotten. Outwardly calm and confident, he was one more sightseer lounging.

A chopper was about to enter the Gates, hundreds of bubblers pointing at the fizz of electricity as one of the domes relaxed. With the forcefield removed, the AirCav raced in and hovered near the top of Pearly. Small, heavily armed figures rode the sides of the mobile. A murmur went through the onlookers. People peered at each other with concern. Two more choppers arrived. Kenny looked at a nearby screen and saw commandos in balaclavas leaning out as they tried to see what was happening inside the building. He stood and walked away, hand raised and head tilted towards his fake Palm.

Crossing the Plaza, he passed Crats and their dates, the Africans gazing at the top of the tower in awe while their Good Europeans flicked wands and brought up larger pictures on their screens. There was talk of a fire started by a skyline barbie that had gone wrong, one social commentator insisting this was a ridiculous theory, that sparrow-intervention was the most likely cause. Kenny could not resist the temptation.

– They've killed Controller Horace, he called out, disguising his English twang.

Heads turned.

– Horace Starski has been murdered. They used a barbecue skewer.

The Crats were confused.

– Controller Horace has been assassinated. The man responsible is still up there. He is alive and has set fire to the apartment. Horace Starski is burning and so is the USE.

The Crats started to shake. Was it possible?

– Look at your screens. That is Hardcore in the choppers. Why are they wearing masks? Why the heavy arms?

– There is a dirty sparrow that must be polished, someone answered.

– The bird has escaped. Look at the gap in the domes. The Gates have been breached. The sparrow is flying free.

A woman fainted and fell, those around her too slow to respond and too disorientated to see if she was injured. The Crats returned to their screens.

– It was the Wessex Boys responsible.

Really, he should keep quiet, but people needed to know what had happened and who had carried out the mission. This was his chance.

– Three GB45 fighters are moving through the tower. They're killing at will.

If an InterZone clampdown hadn't been imposed yet, the story would be crossing Europe inside the next thirty seconds. That would be a coup in itself. A man collapsed.

– Look, a bubblehead shrieked.

Black smoke was billowing from the penthouse. Flames were clearly visible on the roof terrace. The fire was taking hold and spreading. Kenny carried on towards the Overground, moving as fast as he could without attracting attention, his face down and buried as he left the Plaza and entered one of the avenues that would take him to the station.

– They have killed Controller Horace, someone coming the other way shouted. GB45s. My sister in Lyon has just told me. It must be a mistake. How could this happen?

Kenny kept glancing back, the smoke growing thicker and forming a dense cloud. The dome must have been resealed. It hung in the air, looked as if it was turning solid and becoming increasingly heavy. More people were passing Kenny, hurrying towards the Plaza, and he saw three buggies loaded with Hardcore, wanted to run but didn't, conscious he was moving in the opposite direction to everyone else. He stopped to adjust a shoelace when he saw a column of twenty Cool marching in formation. Gendarmerie followed.

– What's happened? a Bureau asked. Has there been an accident?

– Yes, an accident, a Gendarme replied. Barbie overload.

– Of course, the Bureau said, clearly relieved. People are telling me it is a terrorist attack, but that is impossible.

– No, it was definitely a mishap, said the Gendarme. This is official news. The truth. Some experts believe the last sparrow was being cooked.

The Gendarme was talking to the Crat, but looking at Kenny, who nodded and tried to look upset.

– It is very worrying. I cannot pretend it is not. Controller Horace has been mentioned.

– Yes, the Gendarme mused. Controller Horace.

– He is in London, a Techno said, joining in. He has been staying at Pearly Tower. The penthouse belongs to him, as I am sure you know. I glimpsed him myself. A great man.

The flow of people halted as the Plaza was closed. The AirCav had backed away from the tower. This could mean that an attack was still not confirmed, and he continued walking, reached Spital Station and rode the escalator, reached the platform as a train arrived. 'Sugar Baby Love' played, a heritage song he loved, although this version lacked the sheer emotion of the original. Once it became clear what had taken place, the Gates would be on lockdown, but it was less than ten minutes since he left the foyer and he doubted Cool and Hardcore were in the penthouse yet. It was a stroke of luck that the AirCav had retreated. The Fireball was doing a fine job.

Standing by the glass wall he willed the train on, watched how the smoke was spreading across the roof of the Gates, wondered why a dome hadn't been opened again to allow it out. He could only guess that there had been a malfunction, or someone had lost their nerve.

Kenny stepped back sharply and narrowed his eyes. Pearly Tower was covered in bubbles. He was hallucinating. It was turning into a bubbleheaded monster. It took him a few seconds to realise that the scales that covered it were popping and sliding down the building. The gel that held them in place had failed. It was an incredible sight. A star exploded. More followed. He wanted to dance on the spot.

– Are you okay? a Crat asked.

Kenny turned to the only other person present. The man had been engrossed in *War On Terror*, was sitting with his back to the window as he focused on his screen, oblivious to events outside.

– You are bleeding.

Kenny looked at his hand.

– It looks worse than it is, he replied. I nicked myself and the doc put a healer on. It seems to have fallen off.

– Jagged edges mean danger. Smooth corners are best.

The Crat returned to his game, Kenny leaving at the next stop, finding his way to the Underground and travelling three stops, changing to the suburban service that would carry him out to the car that had been arranged. He chose the quietest seat. Nobody looked his way. He sat down and closed his eyes and pretended to dose, feeling the faint rhythm of the train, doing his best to empty his mind of what he had seen and done, and he focused on his breathing, following it through his nose and into his chest, calming himself as taught by the Buddhist monks of Taunton.

When the Underground came out into the open, the darkness reminded him that it was early evening. He could see the lights of locals housing spreading out on either side and felt less of an outsider, everything that had just happened a surreal sort of daydream. Had he really killed Starski? Had he got out of the East Side alive and was he going to escape? Cool would study the surveillance footage and link his image and it would be circulated, but that was going to take time. He willed the driver on, the stretches of track between stations growing longer as they moved into the outer suburbs.

He left the Underground at Hillingdon, found his car waiting, was quickly on the triple-laner that ran beneath the station, surrounded by vehicles but moving steadily, looking out over Uxbridge to his left and thinking of Tubby and the others, joining the Wall and changing to IR4 one junction later, slowing right down with the rest of the traffic as he passed Slough.

The concrete intensified, another category of non-city commons living here, the masses following the Thames like so many of their ancestors had done in the past, the corporate metropolis sucking them in and spitting them back out when they had nothing more to offer. It was another hour before he was beyond Reading and the estates and factories and depots thinned and the road emptied.

He was moving fast now, hunched over the wheel as he concentrated on the path his headlights cut from the blackness. The further he went, the more his mood shifted. He was going to see Jan again, drink in The Wheatsheaf with Fred, sit at one of Peanut Paul Harrison's tables, tidy the shelves under All Souls, live happily ever after. But his elation was quickly replaced by despair. A Cool roadblock had been set up, the AirCav was on its way, another Bob Terks stood in his house strangling Jan. And he had killed two people. Stabbed them to death. He was a murderer. Except it wasn't murder. He was a killer. It was hard to believe he had done these terrible things.

Soon he would have to turn southwards, should maybe have stayed on the Wall and taken IR3, but the IR4 meant he could get away from London faster, hadn't wanted to risk a jam on the M25 with the number of lenses in operation. It would have been easy for Cool to pick him off, but this route had its dangers as well, and he was a boy again, on the run with his family, not knowing what he was doing or where they were going. He remembered the smell of Zola's fur, felt the dog next to him, compared it to the stink of Starski's dead skins, thought about the cruelty of the bubblers and the way London had been destroyed by greed. He was tired of the lies, couldn't think straight, every dream turning into a nightmare. You only had to scratch the surface. It happened every single time. Zola barked.

The car was veering across the road, Kenny jolting awake and tugging at the wheel, sure he was going to flip over but managing to regain control. He slowed down and stopped on the hard shoulder. Turned off the lights. His heart was thumping. To come so far and die this way... The darkness was total and he felt his eyes closing again, fell forward, fought hard, saw lights in his side mirror and was alert. The beams were rapidly approaching. He was sure Cool had found him, but the car flashed past, leaving shrinking red balls that disappeared in the distance. He had to get off this empty road and sleep. He was a sitting target, waited for his eyes to adjust, could see there was a wood to his left.

Without putting his lights back on he drove along the hard shoulder, searching for an opening where he could enter the fields and cross to the trees. The hedge broke for a gate and he accelerated, crashed through rotting wood, bounced and felt the tyres struggle before they gripped and he shot forward. The surface was hard and pretty smooth, the remains of a forgotten lane or siding maybe, and turning on his beams for a moment he saw a strip of cracked tarmac dotted with grass and weeds, followed it into the wood, low-hanging branches banging on the roof. He entered what he thought was a meadow, but the tarmac was still there under the vegetation, seemed to spread across the whole space. He parked under the trees and turned the engine off.

Kenny opened his window and breathed deep on the fresh country air. Moonlight filtered through a patch of thinning cloud, and he felt safe, would spend the night here, leave the car and walk the rest of the way home in the morning. He knew the way, more or less, and could hitch on one of the old B roads. He would set off as soon as the sun came up. The wind blew and he shivered, felt the cold for the first time, closed the window and made the most of the heat inside, hoped he wasn't going to freeze. His bag was under the passenger seat and he picked it up, looked at his spare shirt and underwear, which wasn't much use, *Fiddle Me Free* and

Suzie's parcel. He opened this and saw John Sommerfield's novel *May Day*. Running a hand over the purple cover he opened it and smelled the paper, thought about Suzie and Jan, finally replaced it in the wrapping and put it inside the bag with his other belongings. He climbed into the back seat.

Despite the falling temperature, he was soon drifting off. His body was stiff, but he was too exhausted to care. The last thing he heard before he fell asleep was the hoot of an owl in the trees, and he imagined the flap of its wings causing the leaves above the car to rustle, thought about the AirCav on the South Circular, Hardcore thugs perched on the boards of their chopper, eager to dismount and get on with their work.

TWENTY-FIVE

EXACTLY A YEAR after the assassination of Controller Horace in a daring GB45 raid, Kenny Jackson raised a pint of Kingdon in the air and silently toasted the anniversary. The location of the attack and the chaos that had engulfed the East Side Gates, along with the rioting that followed in the suburbs and along the M25 barrier, had been a huge blow to the USE. According to undercover source Walter Hope, plans to push into the Free English areas of Wessex had been suspended. Sitting in a corner of The Wheatsheaf's smaller front bar, under beams lined with horse brasses, Kenny was happy enough, but knew he would never be the same person who set off for London.

Crystals were forming on the window behind him, and as the temperature dropped further they would create more complex shapes, mimicking cracks in the glass. The fireplace crackled as it heated the drinkers and a growing collection of tropical plants, and in the warmth and security of the pub, with the Kingdon inside him, the killing of Starski and the Cool officer seemed distant and unreal, as if another person was responsible.

Landlord Tom was in the process of serving Fred his usual, the guv'nor red-faced at the suggestions being made by his tipsy wife Ronnie. Kenny knew that his bookworm friend had something for him, but would wait until he came over. He drank a quarter of his pint and placed the glass on the table, leaned back as he thought about London and everything he had seen and felt and done while he was there. Tubby Nowakowski had been executed after a Cool operation in Uxbridge last May, one of seven patriots shot in the back of the head, their murders blamed on a gangland feud. He raised his face and smiled as Jan came back from the Ladies. She sat down and reached for his hand.

– There's buds on the tree Ronnie planted out back, she said.

Do you think the frost will kill them? Ours will be all right, won't they? They're not budding yet.

– We'll get a good lot of apples, don't worry. It will be fine.

They had taken over an old orchard and were planning to make their own cider. It was agreed on the day Kenny returned home. Jan had been told a tower was burning in London and feared the worst, sure he was dead or in custody. She hadn't been able to sleep that night, at three in the morning leaving the house and walking to All Souls. The doors were unlocked and she went inside and slept on one of the pews, dreaming that she could hear a congregation of spirits singing hymns, prayers being whispered in her ears, but she wasn't scared. Sunlight streamed through stained glass in the morning and woke her. That evening she turned towards the kitchen window as the whispering returned and there was Kenny looking in and waving.

He had started walking before sunrise, using a map left for him in the car, and he took it out of his pocket and dropped it on the kitchen table. This brilliant hard could never be tracked or deleted, and she mustn't throw it away or burn it or anything like that – if she didn't mind – as to do so would be bad luck and maybe even a curse. He was dirty and exhausted and mad, told Jan how he had walked through woods and fields, found overgrown hedges and lost lanes, animals living freely where small farms had died out and the people had moved into towns. It was a forgotten landscape.

There was an orchard out there, not more than ten miles away, and despite his tiredness he'd wanted to know if the trees still fruited, searched in the long grass and found hundreds of rotten apples. He promised himself that if he made it home he would go back one day and get it working properly and make his own cider. It was an unusual vow, he knew that, but was determined to carry it out. Putting a name on the bottles would mean he'd leave his mark on the world, and in a much better way than he had done in London. He would think of a name for their cider. There was no rush.

Jan sat on the arm of the chair in which he had collapsed and listened. It started to snow a few minutes after he came inside, but they didn't notice until later, and by then everything was covered in tiny white flakes. They agreed it was a beautiful sight.

* * *

Flap! was heaving. Bubblers filled the dance floor, their wet bodies packed tight, a selection of dates clinging to their horny lovers, the beat of hearts and wings amplified and blended by Zed. Feathers fell from the heavens, the movement of the crowd creating gusts that drove them back into the air where they swung side to side, twisting and turning before descending once more. Beams of light cut across the scene, producing a snowfall effect. Every so often Zed waved a wand and lightning cracked. The screams of the seagulls were expertly mixed into his rhythm track and the dancers responded by bopping faster, the burnt feathers that reached them sticking to soaked skins. Dead and dying birds crashed to the floor, the clubbers parting to make space, feet kicking and stamping as the music returned to its familiar throb.

Dressed in crocodile shorts, Zed was modelling the T of the moment – *Just Do It* – which expressed his belief that life had to be lived to the max. Flap! was where the real rebels gathered. He was demanding love and equality for his people as he drove an exciting new scene forward. His earnings were soaring and he had invested in a Brixton pad, while the adoration of a line of eager Bureaus and Technos only added to the fun. He was part of the system and had plenty of dates. One of these young cocksuckers was on her knees right now, working on Zed's Z as he rocked the house. Zed was bigging it 10x. He fucking loved Flap! Conjuring an effect, he stuttered the sound.

Noble savages... semi-human fucks... helping the oppressed... a global boho... he loved the black skin of little Afro girls... the brown flesh of Asian boys... his beats were saving the planet... supply and demand... breaking down barriers... fighting racism... and these birds could not fly off whenever they fucking wanted... no no no... freedom had to be earned... they were debeaked for safety... claws removed... and he looked to the screens... floating in the corners of the club... ghosts and retards and throwbacks... the commons were in the darkest nook... along with his dates... ready to service Zed and his team... and he watched the face of the seaside witch... lips silently moving as if she could sing... a skinhead was knocked to the ground by a tough young Crat... a donkey hung under a pier by its back legs... slaughtered... a huge head... nearly severed... and it was all consensual... freedom of choice... freedom of expression... freedom of choice...

Zed would always be grateful to his guru for having the idea and making it happen. He was one Can Do Guy. Flap! was the Crats' fave London night and the brand had already spread to Heartland. Zed had launched in Paris. Soon he would leave London and live in Brussels. That would be a special gig. Everything was fantastic.

Raising his head, he checked his flock. Seagulls dominated, but doves, robins and sparrows had been added for diversity. There were four long perches where they could rest and soon there would be enough settled for a climax, but he had to wait for the right break before he could deliver their dose of love, and here it came, the crescendo reached and electricity released. Small explosions lit up the birds who fell or rose up in their panic, thumping wings and battering at the wire dome, pulled towards a false sky by a fake sun. Salty air was pumped into Flap! and Zed was working their pain into his art, dipping low before pumping up the volume, adding Witch and Geezer effects, picking his moment when enough of these fucks were clinging to the mesh of the dome, thinking they were going to escape. He felt his balls explode. Released an almighty charge. More birds fell and the crowd roared its approval. Feet pounded hard. Arms flapped in a rough sort of time. It was an incredible sight.

***

While Kenny and Jan celebrated in The Wheatsheaf and Zed rocked his flock at Flap!, Rupert Ronsberger was in an equally fine mood as he waited for one of his two best buddies to open a bottle of Champers. The former Crat's bravery during the terrorist attack on Pearly Tower had been rewarded with a promotion to Techno (B-), and in the following months his level kept rising as he was fast-tracked by his superiors. Nine months later he was made a Controller – albeit London-based – then two weeks ago he had been invited to Brussels. It was a shock, but he could not have been happier. This was his first day in the Monnet penthouse and Rupert was in a state of near bliss.

He would be under the care of a mentor for the next two years, but this was normal and he expected nothing less. He had met Michael Baker twice now, and they had become firm friends. He would listen closely and learn from this older and much wiser Controller. He had a profound respect for the man.

The Monnet pad had to be paid for, but credit was not a problem, and the sum was more than covered by expenses. The officers dealing with Controller Starski's affairs assured him that in five or six years he would be able to invest in the tower itself, again with generous assistance. The State wanted the best people in Brussels and was pleased to pay top dollar. The nearer the centre of power, the greater the perks. It made sense. Everyone was satisfied. Rupert was a huge plus.

Tests had been carried out following the terrorist outrage. Under the influence of a secret wonder drug, deep asleep and beyond conscious controls, the ideas of Horace Starski had been touched upon, but Rupert could not be faulted in his responses. Unofficially, the specialist running the probes had found him frightening, but he was one of the new breed and expectations were high. It was only right that he came to live in Controller Horace's apartment. InterZone loved the link.

The story of Rupert's fight for freedom appealed to every Good European. He was a hero. His fellow Crats could be proud of his determination to resist a demented torturer, his rapid promotion filling them with hope for their own futures. The State had spoken openly about the murder of Horace Starski by white-trash baddy Bob Terks. He had been trained outside London by thugs connected to a racist anti-USE cell, subsequently travelling into the city to team up with a notorious cockney firm. Their brutal rampage had been inexcusable. Sixteen other innocents had perished on the day.

Nine terrorists had been taken down by an outnumbered Cool unit, though one of the outlaws had escaped to a Basildon barrio to the east of the M25. Trackers were called in and the authorities were soon concentrating their efforts on two estates known for their pro-English elements. The USE was not going to rest until the last perp had been taken into custody. Cool would treat him with the usual courtesy, that was a given, but justice had to be done. Even so, coffee and muffins *would* be served. There was a popular uprising on InterZone as tougher action was called for, the suspension of nibbles demanded. In the end, Controllers had heeded the will of the people, but insisted that the State would not stray from its democratic, liberal beliefs. Love flowed and Rupert was one of the main beneficiaries.

Instead of being sworn to secrecy or sent on vacation in the aftermath of the attack, he had been invited to take part in a PR campaign that doubled as a tribute to his fallen teacher. Horace Starski could not be allowed to die in vain. It turned out that Rupert was a natural. Found near to death and unable to speak for three days, saved by the first liberators to break into the apartment, the truth had nevertheless been instantly pieced together. It was clear he had fought to protect the older man, ready to sacrifice his life so that his fave Controller could live. Even before he regained consciousness, he had built up a huge InterZone following. This Crat was going places. It had been a roller-coaster ride to the stars.

Heady with emotion, he took a glass of bubbly and walked out to the terrace. He stood by the edge and looked across the Brussels skyline. He loved this city like no other place, hoped that he would stay here for the rest of his days. Mind you, Controller Michael had talked a little of Berlin, but for now Rupert only had eyes for this gorgeous metropolis. London was a slum in comparison. It was terrible what had happened there, showed that they lived in dangerous times.

Controller Rupert raised his Champers and watched the

bubbles rise in small columns, the floating gold stars of the USE visible through his flute, adding colour to the tiny balls of air. Starski had been his role model when he was a youth and had remained an inspiration, and he was dedicating his success to the man. Being invited to Cuddles 1 and then his penthouse had been an honour, but to have his guru strap him in a great artwork to test his intellect was nothing less than sensational.

Controller Horace had turned European history upside down, pushed his imagination towards its limits, corrupting reality in ways that showed the political power of humour. Rupert had not wavered and would never betray the USE, and through these tests the two had become one.

Excitement flushed through his body and, noticing the presence of Hank Malone to his right, he made sure he was composed in front of the square-jawed agent from Boston. Swivelling, he was met by the tray of blueberry muffins the American was holding out. He shook his head politely and Hank turned to scan the city, sharing a special moment with his Controller. Hank was a Number 2 and eager to please. Tonight they could relax, but tomorrow it was back to the hard graft. There was so much work to be done. New Democracy had to be protected *and* expanded. Rupert Ronsberger was thrilled by the challenges that lay ahead. He looked towards the penthouse interior and called for his other chum to come outside and hang with the rest of the gang.

The three pals would have to be vigilant in the years ahead. They could not afford a single error. Controller Rupert was ready to meet the anti-USE brigade and non-PCs head on. It was essential to educate the worst of the locals – the rednecks and crackers and hillbillies, all those commons who lived in a profitless past of public ownership and small-town pride, the veggers slandering the animal industry and the green contraries with their weird love of trees and streams. These were the enemies of progress. It would be done slowly and in gentle fashion, with a smile and a grin and a friendly arm around the shoulders, the wise words of Jean Monnet forever in his mind.

He thought of London again and sneered. Britain was rotten to the core. It was a vile, racist, violent hinterland. He detested the Welsh and Scots and Irish, but not as much as the English. Every last one of them was an ape. Except Controller Michael and his brother Jeremy and their wives and friends. They hated the English plebs more than anyone. Rupert recalled the confusion he had seen on Starski's face as they chatted at Pearly, the games played, Cuddles and the Blackpool vision, the pain that was meant to make him stronger. He had never weakened and the experience made him want to belong more than ever before. Lessons had been learned.

The system was evolving and Horace Starski represented the past. The State was fine-tuning, ridding itself of weaklings and out-dated sympathies, and eventually the restraints would be relaxed. It was time to forget the dead Controller and move on. The silly old cunt had served his purpose. The future belonged to the kids. He moved his fingers and 'Sugar Baby Love' played. Hank handed him his cap and he placed it on his head.

Life was good. His first business venture had been a success and he was zipping Hollywood legend Annie Abattoir over to promote Flap! in Brussels. If things went as he hoped, she would replace that idiot Zed. He thought of the gulls and how they fried in a club environment, the wild flocks flying free across European skies, and for several beats he was angry. Sparrows moved too fast and were not easily killed when they broke into private domes. It was simple for one of the brutes to escape. They pooped on polished stone. Dirty dirters. Robins lurked in country lanes. Seagulls polluted coastlines. But their time would come. And one day he would add an albatross to his collection. Flap! was rocking and nothing could stop him. He was invincible.

Obedience was power. A Controller could do what he wanted as long as he was correct and did not upset other Controllers. He was free to push boundaries. His Number 1 emerged with the Champers, strolled over and started to top up his glass. Controller Rupert never tired of watching the tiny bubbles fizz and pop and sparkle. He thanked Baby for her kindness.

LONDON BOOKS

FLYING THE FLAG FOR
FREE-THINKING LITERATURE

www.london-books.co.uk

PLEASE VISIT OUR WEBSITE FOR

- Current and forthcoming books
  - Author and title profiles
    - Events and news
  - Secure on-line bookshop
- Recommendations and links
- An alternative view of London literature

London Classics

The Angel And The Cuckoo *Gerald Kersh*
Doctor Of The Lost *Simon Blumenfeld*
The Gilt Kid *James Curtis*
It Always Rains On Sunday *Arthur La Bern*
Jew Boy *Simon Blumenfeld*
May Day *John Sommerfield*
Night And The City *Gerald Kersh*
A Start In Life *Alan Sillitoe*
There Ain't No Justice *James Curtis*
They Drive By Night *James Curtis*
Wide Boys Never Work *Robert Westerby*

John King

THE FOOTBALL FACTORY

'The best book I've ever read about football and working-
class culture in Britain in the nineties'
Irvine Welsh

The Football Factory centres on Tom Johnson, a seasoned
'Chelsea hooligan' who represents a disaffected society
operating by brutal rules. We are shown the realities of life -
social degradation, unemployment, racism, casual violence,
excessive drink and bad sex – and, perhaps more importantly, how they fall into a political context of surveillance,
media manipulation and division.

Graphic and disturbing, occasionally very funny, and deeply
affecting throughout, *The Football Factory* is a vertiginous
rush of adrenaline – the most authentic book yet on the so-
called English Disease.

'The most savagely authentic account of football hooligan-
ism ever seen. The book's veins pulse with testosterone and
bellicose rage, effing and blinding throughout the warzone
of macho culture'
Blah Blah Blah

'Bleak, thought-provoking and brutal, *The Football Factory*
has all the hallmarks of a cult novel'
Literary Review

John King

HEADHUNTERS

'King loads his characters up with enough interior life, but it's the raw energy of their interactions – the beano to Blackpool, the punch-ups, the casual fucks, the family skeletons and the unburied fantasies – that make this excellent book run'

Time Out

Following on from his best-selling study of violence, *The Football Factory*, John King considers Britain's other obsession – sex. Formed in the chemical mists of New Year's Eve, The Sex Division sees the once-sacred act of procreation at its most material, as five men devise a points system based on the sexual act. In this lager-soaked league, the most that Woman can offer Man is 4 points – unless, that is, she leaves her handbag unattended.

'*Headhunters* is sexy, dirty, violent, sad, funny: in fact it has just about everything you could want from a book on contemporary working-class life in London...If John King can keep doing this sort of thing, he'll wind up top of the pile'

Big Issue

'The realism and political edge echoes Alan Bleasdale's *Boys From The Blackstuff*'

GQ